Vaughn s Xena

(Dirty Rockhard Series, Book 1)

M.I. Rosegold

VAUGHN'S XENA

First edition. February 11, 2022.

Written by M.I. Rosegold.

To all the writers who fell in love with their own written characters, and to all the readers who got to know why.

Disclaimer

It's a beautiful love story, but…
Mindfuck, toe-curling teases, and filthy sexual activities ahead.
You have been warned.

1 | Fantasy

Xena

"Oh, my god... Vaughn!"

I screamed out his name as I released. Red dots appeared before my tightly closed eyes from the extreme pleasure. The intense release made my entire body shudder violently. My thighs shook, and my chest heaved. The muscles of my core throbbed as I came undone.

With a gentle pull, I took out the vibrating dildo from inside me with my numb, dainty hands.

It felt amazing. Out of the world amazing. Marvelous, fantabulous, toe-curling kind of amazing.

But I could bet on my life that it wasn't as amazing as it would be with Vaughn.

I bet, with Vaughn, it would be something entirely different. Something dark, mysterious, and sinful. I bet the guy could give the word *'amazing'* a completely different meaning. I was sure about it.

I touched the keyboard on my laptop again to lighten up the screen.

There he was.

Looking all hot, smug, intimidating, mysterious, and powerful. There was more, something more about him I couldn't put my fingers on, but whatever it was, I knew I would fall for it as well.

I fell for everything I discovered about him. He was my dark, wild, secret, and forbidden fantasy. My desire. Someone who could make me come again and again just by looking at me through a still picture.

I peeked at the man in the picture once again. God... He had the face of a man. He looked rugged yet sophisticated with his sleek black hair and stubble beards. It gave him a typical Mafia don look, which I hope he wasn't. Well, to be honest, I was so consumed with this man that I didn't care even if he was.

The tanned skin of his toned, muscled body could tempt even an old lady to want to lick on it. His thick brows scrunched attractively in every picture that I've seen, and his full lips looked like something I could kiss all day, any day. Well, all night would do, too—gladly.

The tingle between my legs started notifying me about its presence once again. I felt my core muscles clench and throb once again for him. Goosebumps were once again visible on my sensitive skin.

Oh, Xena! Didn't you just finger-paint your kitty right now?
Oh god, Vaughn, you'll be the death of me...
... And my kitty.
All you have to do is... Nothing. Nothing at all.
And you don't even know about it.

2 | Endangerment

Xena

I was panting in my bed, coming down from my high. My toes were still curled, and my fingers were numb from the vigorous activities. Few strands of hair covered my eyes, but I was too tired to brush it away. Vaughn's picture was still there, messing with my mind, body, and my entire existence.

I had a few boyfriends in the past. Whenever I was with them, their sweet lovemaking, gentle kiss, or their talented tongue couldn't get me off. I tried. I really tried. But I never had the toe-curling, eye-rolling kind of orgasm with any of them. So, I stopped dating soft guys. It had always been a disappointment for me.

But this guy… Just fantasizing about him got me there every effing time.

I was again about to imagine him pumping ruthlessly into my cunt. That was exactly when there was a knock on the door. The sudden tap on the door made my heart jump in surprise.

"Jay... Open the door!"

Danger!

I rushed to pick some clothes to cover my body on my wobbly toes.

"Jay... Are you sleeping? Wake up! I have something to tell you!" She sounded like she was in a pretty cheerful mood.

"Coming, Ron. Wait!" I yelled as I hid my toys, rushing towards the bathroom to clean my hands and then finger-brushed my hair. They looked like a mess, matching with how I was feeling.

The knocking on my door didn't pause. Ron impatiently kept on knocking over the door again and again. By now, she was singing something with her own version of lyrics. It was her trick just to annoy me and make me open the door fast. That was nothing new. She always did that.

"Coming... Coming... You hot, evil woman!" I said, yelling as I hurried to open the door and faced her, finally.

There she stood. The tall, thin, elegant, raven-haired beauty. Veronica Wolf. My best friend and my flatmate.

And Vaughn's little sister.

"What took you so long, bitch?" That was her first question as I opened the door.

"I... I was in the bathroom," I said, stuttering, feeling self-conscious.

Ron finally looked at me, and her eyes widened.

"Or should I call you *horny* bitch? You look so flustered as well. What were you doing?" She looked playful as she smirked at me. Typical, playful—Veronica Wolf.

Before I could say something, she entered the room and looked around with curious, interested eyes, jumping here and there. She opened the closet door, looked behind the curtains, in the bathroom, everywhere with a naughty grin, and said, "Is there anyone in your room, Jay? Are you hiding someone? You know you can tell me," she said, wickedly wiggling her eyebrows.

"What? No! How wicked is your mind, Ron?" I shook my head in amusement. Well, I was not in the hook-up department. She was really something with casual relationships.

Then her eyes dropped on the laptop on my bed, and she squealed, saying, "Well... well... Were you having virtual flings with some hot dude? Let me see!" She went towards the bed with a naughty grin to see what was open on my laptop.

Oh, snuggles! Vaughn!

4

Before she could touch the laptop, I flew to the bed and closed the screen. I could definitely not let her see that I was stalking her brother. More specifically, jilling off from his pictures. I knew how protective she was about him.

Well, jilling off was the female version of jacking off in my dictionary. Like Jack and Jill... you get the jest, right? Right.

"I... I was watching porn." I said as I felt my cheeks getting warm. But I still managed to say the shameless lie.

Ron looked at me in disappointment and said, "Seriously? Girl, you need to get laid. You just can't compare the real thing with these fake acts. It's high time I have to do something for you," she let out a huff.

I released a breath of relief that I didn't know I had been holding.

She bought the lie.

"Yeah, Okay. Now tell me what such an important thing was that you wanted to share?"

"Ah! Yes. I wanted to share that both my parents are in the town finally, and they invited us to stay with them for the coming weekend!"

"Wow! It's great that both of them are back at the same time. I am so happy for you, Ron!" I really was. But did she just say they wanted me to tag along as well?

"But should I tag along with you in your family time, Ron? They aren't usually at home together. This is a precious family time for you," I said, hesitating. I knew how much it meant to Ron.

"What are you saying, boo? You are a family to me, Jay. You are like a sister to both me and Vee! Besides, Mom and dad were very adamant about bringing you with me. They want to thank you for taking care of me when they aren't available."

Hey, who wants to be a sister to your Vee?

But it was okay. You didn't need to know my fantasy about your elder brother, anyway.

5

"In that case, they need to thank me properly. You were a handful, missy," I said as a joke.

Well, she was, to be honest.

"Haha, very funny!" Ron showed me her tongue and squealed again. "Also, you know what? Vee is also back from New Orleans! He would visit too! I can't wait to see him! He has been there for a long time for the new branch of his club, and it has finally settled."

I felt my heart skip a beat.

Vaughn would be there.

My hand started sweating at the thought. I had never met Vaughn in real life. Till then, he was like a man of fantasy who I could only dream about but could never meet. He was like a celebrity for me to think about, see pictures of, and read news about, but never get the chance to meet.

Vaughn was a pretty reserved person, but it was a matter of wonder to me—how come a person like Vaughn kept his profile pictures public on social media. He had always been a mystery to the outer world because of owning a famous nightclub chain. At the same time, his lack of interest in women. Whatever the reason was, I was blessed to have his profile pictures saved safe and hidden in my laptop. Those were my only treasure for both *calming* and *coming* myself.

And that day, I was finally going to meet him... gosh. That was going to be hazardous. What would I do when I see the man in the flesh who made me come over and over in my dreams and fantasies?

You better not come undone just by seeing him, you stupid horny woman! Ron was right. That's what you have become since you got to know the existence of Vaughn.

Ron sat in comfort on the bed and said in a sad tone, "There is no doubt you will enjoy your time at my parent's house. It's just... you just have to watch yourself around Vee. He is not much into female companies. My brother has suffered a lot growing up without parents and taking care of me." Ron looked down in sadness, reminiscing the memories.

6

"They were never home, and Vee is the one who showered me with the three of their love combined. He is more like my dad and mom rather than how much my parents are to me. Nothing in the world can hurt my brother till I'm alive. I can turn the world upside down to make him happy," she said with unbound affection in her eyes for her brother.

"It's not like he will hate you or something. He just doesn't like women around him in general. Girls get too shameless to get into his bed, and he hates how desperate they can get. Just don't anger or upset him if he doesn't want you around, okay? I will be there for you, boo." There was a bright smile on her face as she spoke the last sentence.

"Of course, I understand. You have told me about him already," I said, smiling back.

I knew how Mr. Victor Wolf was a bigshot businessman who was never home, and Mrs. Penelope Wolf was a renowned lawyer who had to visit places for cases most of the time. It had always been Vaughn who loved and protected Ron enough to not miss their parents much since her childhood. He matured early because of the responsibilities, and thus they both were way more protective of each other than any normal siblings were.

This was how Xena knew that Vaughn's reserved personality wasn't the only hindrance to making her unreal fantasy come real.

No matter how much Ron adored Xena when it came to her brother, absolutely no one, not even Xena could cross the line.

3 | Rejection

Xena

A crumpled piece of paper flew and then landed on my desk as I concentrated on my public law professor's lecture, abruptly breaking me out of my trance. I looked around to find none other than my weirdo best friend grinning like a fool in my way. I shook my head, chuckling at her playfulness. Clearly, she was bored as usual.

I didn't understand Ron. She was always adamant about following her mother's footsteps in law, but she never took any subjects with seriousness. It had always been me who helped her with case studies and presentations, not that I complained about it. She was like a sister to me who I adore beyond imagination, and she felt the same way about me. It's the least I could do for my best friend.

I threw a careful glance at the professor to see if he was looking at me or not, then flattened the crumpled paper only to find the neat, cursive handwriting of Ron.

"Club tonight?"

It's not like I didn't enjoy clubbing. I did. But Ron practically *loved* clubbing. I had always been her *wingwoman* to pick up guys. We always relied on each other regarding bad dates and weird guys. Among us, I had always been the good girl and rarely went for one-night stands, but Ron's sex life was pretty active. I could always rely on my girl to save me from uncanny offers, and Ron could always depend on me to keep her from going after weird guys. Together, we were each other's perfect *wingwoman*.

"It's not even the weekend, Ron."

I handed the paper to Jake, the nerdy guy sitting between us. Ron took the paper and chuckled as she read it. The reply came almost immediately.

"So? I'm in the mood. I promise to behave."

That was right. It had always been my untold duty to make sure my weirdo best friend behaved while drunk.

"We are going to talk about it after class. Focus!"

Then I went back to listening to the boring yet important lecture for what my parents were spending grand.

"??? You disappoint me. I need to do something for you. Starting from tonight."

I chuckled as I read the message, but didn't reply anymore. In recent days, Ron was pretty serious about hooking me up. Because according to her, I didn't get laid enough. For some time, she even doubted my sexuality. But when I brought Hugh home one night, she believed in me once again.

But after the night, I didn't respond to any of his calls and messages anymore. He even stopped by one night when I had to decline his offer politely and made him understand it was only a one-night stand for me. Then again, he wasn't the man I was looking for. He wasn't right. No man was right.

How to tell her why I don't get laid enough? It was not like she would understand.

When the bell rang, it was lunchtime already. Ron and I bought some pizza and lemonade from the canteen and then moved to our usual spot.

"So, I call dibs on your makeover tonight," Ron said, sipping on her lemonade and chirping as usual.

"Dibs on my makeover? Is that even a thing? And who told you I'm going?" I raised a brow at her with a smile.

"Of course, you are going to *Aphrodisia* with me tonight." Ron narrowed her eyes at me as if I had been talking nonsense.

"Are you sure you want to go? Isn't your brother in town? Are you sure you want to go tonight?" I raised a brow again. Ron never visited his clubs when her brother was in town to avoid angering him. Apparently, Vaughn was pretty protective of his sister.

"Vee is going to return only today. I know him. He will spend the day sleeping, making up for all his sleepless nights at work. He won't be coming tonight," Ron said in a reply, as if she had Vaughn's daily routine memorized.

Frankly, it disappointed me a little to know he won't be there. It had been more than two years since I had known Ron, but I had never got the chance to meet him. I deeply wanted to know how my only ever fantasy, the sex god I worshipped in secret, looked like in real life. In real life, his hair was as dark as a raven. I knew that from looking at Ron's hair. But... was he really that tall in real life? Did he really have all those muscles and those veiny arms? Were his fingers really that long? Did his face look all rugged and rough? Was his skin really tan? And those lips... were they really pink?

I felt my panties getting wet.

Oh, Vaughn...

"Okay, fine."

Ron was over the moon happy when I agreed. She started planning what I would wear tonight and how she would put makeup on my face. That was when Jack approached our table.

"Hey, Xena... can I talk to you for a moment?" he asked in hesitance.

Jack was a popular kid. He was a pretty handsome soccer player at our college. The guy had been trying to woo me since we started our freshman year. Because of his interest in me, I had become an arch-enemy of several other girls in our college, not that I cared. But to avoid getting into further trouble for a guy, I always tend to decline his offer. Who wanted to get into so much trouble for a guy? Besides, he didn't even drive my hormones crazy like a single picture of Vaughn did.

"You can talk in front of Veronica, Jack." I would not talk to him in private.

Jack looked conflicted but then decided on talking as it was either before Ron or no talk at all. He knew that.

"I know I have been making myself a fool before you, but I can't help it. Just one date is what I'm asking for, Xena. That's all I'm asking for. Please go on one date with me," he pleaded.

I know the guy sounded pathetic and in love. But I always felt like he wanted to take me out just because he couldn't. Probably I was the only girl in the college who wasn't ready to date him, and it made dating me a challenge for him. Even if his feelings were true, still, he wasn't worth the hassle for me.

He was only a guy. Not a man as Vaughn was.

The bell rang, and it saved me from having the conversation with Jack. I just stood up and said, "I'm sorry, Jack. You know, I have told you several times that I don't feel the connection or attraction towards you. You will be wasting your time with me. Keep dating the girls who want you for who you are. I'm not the one for you," I smiled with an understanding yet sorry look and then proceeded to leave the place.

"How do you know without even spending any time with me? Maybe you will feel all that after a date?" he asked from behind, desperate for a date.

"I won't, Jack," I said from my shoulder and then left the place.

Beside me, I heard Ron tsk, loud enough for Jack to hear.

It was soon to feel sorry about Jack yet. When we reached the parking lot at the end of our classes, we found Jack heavily making out with a cheerleader on the hood of his Porche. That was the typical Jack. Never without a girl by his side, yet kept on approaching me all the time he could manage.

Ron was persistent in doing my makeover, and she fulfilled her wish in the end. I had no say in it when she blackmailed me about posting my most ugly pictures on social media. The thought made me shiver in horror as Vaughn was there on her friend list, and I couldn't take the chance. Who wanted the man of her dreams to see her worst pictures?

So, I ended up wearing a navy blue midi bodycon dress with spaghetti straps. I had a pretty blessed body with 5'8" height and curves. As the dress was revealing enough, I went for my strapless 34D bra to make my girls look flattering through my attire. Ron didn't have to spend much time on my blonde, thick hair. Just brushing through them made my hair look luscious enough. She showed her magic in my eyes as she sparkled them with silver glitters and painted my lips with pinkish gloss. According to her, silver made my blue eyes stand out, and pink lip gloss made my lips look pouter.

Ron was looking magnificent as well. She wore a silver, sparkly bodycon mini dress. Her long, smooth legs, straight raven hair, and her smoky eyes stood out, making her look like a dream. She was a true beauty with 5'9" height and lesser curves than me. Sometimes, I envied that she could carry any dress with her lean body, whereas countless beautiful dresses looked too revealing and erotic on me. So, I had no other choice but to avoid wearing them.

The Wolfs indeed had the best genes.

To be honest, I had no interest in showing up at a club, more specifically, his club, without him in it. If it were in my hand, I would love to flaunt my looks to him only. Just the thought of him made me feel my nipples harden.

Gosh... you have got it bad, Xena.

But, as much as I discovered about Vaughn from Ron and the internet—in this life, there was no chance for me to get close to the man of my dreams. Period.

He felt like a heightened orgasm that was impossible for me to reach.

Just as we entered the club, Ron pulled my hand and headed towards the bar.

"Why are you so stiff, boo? Come, have some vodka and let it loose," Ron said, ordering for both of us, and we took the shots together.

After we let loose of ourselves, Ron again pulled me. This time, towards the dance floor. I was already feeling lightheaded enough not to think about a certain someone while dancing in his club. The club had an intimate decoration and lighting that could set the mood just for anyone with no effort. Even I was no exception.

How did the owner maintain his so-called chastity then? It had been a long time since he was seen with women, and it was all some newspapers and magazines could talk about. How come a man like him was single and maintained his chastity was beyond my intelligence.

If it were in my power, I would've licked him all over and then eat him out.

Whole.

Oh, snuggly blankets… and I thought I stopped thinking about him… Even his thoughts brought out the dirtier side of me.

Suddenly, as I was dancing with Ron, I felt an unfamiliar pair of rough, manly hands holding my waist from behind, moving with my body.

I furrowed my brows in confusion, then looked back to find the man with those veiny arms and gasped.

4 | Stranger-Danger

Xena

The man was handsome. I had never seen him around, or I would've remembered him. It looked like he was about 24 or 25 years old. His hair was dirty blond, and the curls looked delicious on him. His eyes were also blue, like mine. I admired his about six-feet height with moderately built muscles. The man had excellent taste in fashion, looking sexy in his blue denim and black shirt with the first two buttons undone. However, what drew me towards him was his sexy face with piercings on his eyebrow and lips. Damn. He looked hot.

But not as hot as Vaughn. He was the epitome of hotness. Every other hot guy seemed cold and stale if compared to him.

Seriously, Xena? A handsome dude was all over you, and you were still thinking of the forbidden fantasy of yours? How more pathetic could you be? He couldn't be yours!

"You don't mind dancing with me, do you? I have been watching you for some time. Can't move my eyes from you, gorgeous," he said, flashing a smile as sexy as his looks.

"Nope, she doesn't mind! She is all yours, enjoy!" Ron said as she pushed me towards the stranger and vanished in the thin air.

Snuggetties…

Let me rephrase again. Earlier, when Ron pushed me towards the sexy stranger, I crashed hard against his hard chest. His arms were fast enough to catch my waist not to let me fall. If he didn't hold me, I would be lying on the floor flat on my butt already. Weirdo. Yup. My best friend was an absolute weirdo.

"Sorry about that, my best friend is… spontaneous. She has been rooting for making me meet someone tonight. This is embarrassing," I said as I hid my face behind my palms and groaned.

"Well, in that case, I can't thank her enough," he chuckled. I had to admit, it was such a beautiful smile. I couldn't help but move my palms from my face to see him.

"If I'm not wrong, we shouldn't stand still on a dance floor. It's not an acceptable manner."

The man pulled me towards him by my waist. He had such a cheerful spirit that put me at ease right away. I placed my hand on his shoulders and started matching my moves with his.

He had his eyes smiling at me as I looked into them, trying to forget a certain someone. *He* was not real to me. But *this* could be.

"So, stranger, do you have a name or something?" I asked, smiling at him.

He chuckled once again with his mesmerizing looks and then replied, "I'm Leo Jackson. What's your name, beautiful?"

"Xena… Xena Myers," just as I said my name, the tempo of the song changed, and it went faster. We danced and grinded against each other throughout the night with no more talking. Once he got the idea that I didn't mind, his hands started brushing on my butt every once in a while. Thanks to the drinks I had earlier.

I might need that to distract myself from a certain someone.

As we had been dancing away the night, our breathing went shorter and heavier with time. It was when my legs were almost giving up, and my lungs were too weak to keep up with dancing anymore, then Leo stopped dancing and pulled my hand towards a corner. It wasn't much secluded, just less crowded enough for him to throw me against the wall and to claim my lips.

Also… oh my… those were some delicious lips.

It had been a long time since I had made out with someone. Leo was definitely a man to make up for all the missing times. His lips felt soft, like a cushion moving against mine. And my, oh my, they were

15

some skilled lips. Even though I wasn't into making out with strangers much, I couldn't push this man away. Instead, I gave in.

I felt his hands digging into my ass cheeks as he pushed his tongue into my mouth. I almost moaned out loud when I sensed him leaving my lips as he was out of breath.

I looked at him and found him smiling, looking at me. It was a gorgeous smile. He was such a charmer. None of us proceeded to continue the kiss, but we didn't feel awkward either.

It wasn't like I was attracted to him, but I really liked the kiss. He was too skillful at kissing. There wasn't a butterfly or spark, but it felt good momentarily.

"Want to grab some drinks?" he asked, flashing me some more of his beautiful smile.

I looked at him and gave it a thought. It wasn't like I was supposed to wait for someone. That someone was nothing but the fragments of my fantasy.

He avoided women, and his sister despised women who chased her brother.

So, he wasn't someone within my reach. There wasn't any point in hanging on to him.

"Actually, I do," I said, smiling back. The amount of alcohol I consumed wasn't much. Besides, I wanted to talk some more with this seemingly fine piece of man. Somehow, I felt at ease with him. So, why not know the man some more?

Leo and I took our seats as we reached the bar, facing each other. He had a playful smile on his lips as he kept looking at me.

"So, Leo, what do you do? Are you in college?"

"Graduated. Last year. I'm a software engineer at an MNC now," he said, shrugging as if it was nothing.

"Wow, that's impressive. And I thought you were still in college," I said with a smile, pointing at his piercings.

16

He laughed, saying, "I don't wear them at work. They are for personal use." He winked and then asked, "So, I assume you are in college?"

"Yes, I'm studying law,"

"Whoa, should I be cautious, Ms. Attorney?"

"Do you have any reason to be, Mr. Engineer?" I said, as I winked back.

He chuckled, throwing his head back.

"Well... I'm at a club on a weekday, having a great time with such a lovely company. I think I would be in trouble if my office knew about it." Leo let out a chuckle again.

"Well... then I think you and I have something in common," I grinned, thinking how I was in the club on a weekday as well.

Time flew by as we talked about our dreams, families, and friends and enjoyed the time together, forgetting everything around us. It was like he was one other person besides Ron, to whom I could open up. I had a problem with trusting people. It had always been hard for me to make friends with my trust issues. Ron always made fun of me, saying how I'd make a brilliant lawyer since I see everyone with doubt. But with Leo, I felt at ease. He felt like a great company, aside from Ron.

At the end of the night, Ron unexpectedly returned to me. Usually, she was long gone with guys she chose for the night. Once again, proving she was serious that night when she talked about setting me up, wasn't she?

"You guuuys... having fun, aren't you?" my drunk best friend purred, wiggling her brows as she put her hands around both of our necks. Her drunk-self acted as she knew him forever when technically Leo was a stranger for both of us.

"I have been having fun, honestly," Leo said with a genuine smile.

"It was nice to meet you, Leo. It felt fresh after a long while."

"Aww, you guys… you should totally go home together tonight!" she exclaimed.

Gosh… Where is the rein of your mouth, Ron?

Did I even say I wanted to go home with him?

Surprisingly, Leo had the same thing in mind. He put his hand on Ron's shoulder and said, "That would be awesome… then three of us could drink some more and have a party throughout the night. What do you say?" This time, Leo wiggled his eyebrows at her.

"B-But… but I meant you and Jay… you know, *to do stuff!*"

Drunk Ron whispered the last three words, but I could still hear her alright, so could Leo.

I slapped my hand on my forehead, and Leo laughed shamelessly at my pathetic situation. Then he winked at me and looked at Ron again.

"But I don't do *stuff* on my first meeting," Leo said in a whisper in her ear exactly the same way she did earlier.

I couldn't contain it in me anymore and burst out laughing, with Leo joining me right away. Ron looked like she was on the verge of tears. She was an emotional drunk. And me? Well, I was more into… Well, no one needed to know that just yet.

"Should we meet again sometime? What do you say?" Leo asked me this time.

"Yeah, I would like that," I said as I smiled.

We exchanged our numbers and promised to meet again. Ron was still distressed about not being successful at making me get laid tonight. But frankly, I was happy to meet Leo. He seemed like a great man. We had so much in common and a lot to talk about. Besides, he seemed genuine. Not the usual horn dogs we come across in the club.

Being like the gentleman he was, Leo walked us towards our car and stayed there until we left.

5 | Little Earlier

A little earlier in the club.

Finn Norman—a tall, handsome, brawny man—was sitting in the VIP lounge. His intense eyes, currently looking down at the bar and dance floor. He had been watching Veronica Wolf and her best friend, Xena Meyers, for a while. They had been enjoying themselves around Aphrodisia for quite some time, and now Finn felt the necessity to inform a certain someone about his sister's presence in the club.

Taking his phone out, he pressed the quick-dial on his contact.

"Mr. Wolf, your sister is here with her usual company. They have hit the bar already, and right now, *quite* enjoying themselves on the dance floor," Finn said.

He felt guilty selling them away. Then again, it was his job as the certain someone's assistant, secretary, bodyguard, and the most trustworthy friend. Finn was sent to look after the club's necessity in his place as usual since the person couldn't come to the club himself tonight.

"I see," the certain someone replied and hung up the call as he got off his bed at once.

Then he walked straight towards the security room of his penthouse in large, impatient strides. To see what was going on through the 24/7 surveillance camera recording everything in the club.

6 | Wolf Meets Sugar

Xena

Last night was torture. One second, I swiped every sexy piece of clothing I owned in my mind, and the next second, I scolded myself not to be so pathetic. Also, *his* thoughts never left my mind. Whatever I thought, I returned to the square, drenching in need for him. After lots of tossing and turning in the bed and pulling the rein of my self-restraints, my fingers had to reach the wetness down there, anyway. I couldn't help it.

Oh, Vaughn...

It had been about three days since I met Leo. He texted me right on the next day with a funny meme. It was so funny that I laughed and texted him back instantly, not thinking much about it. I had always felt at ease with the man ever since I met him.

From then on, we had been texting funny memes to each other every day and then laughing like a fool, regardless of wherever I was. I really liked his company. He felt like a great person to be with. Ron was already attaching our names, dreaming of our future, and counting our kids.

How do I tell her it was her brother's kids that I wanted?

No matter how much I tried to shift my mind to another male, every time my body, mind, heart, and soul screamed of only one name... Vaughn.

The Vaughn who I was going to meet today, finally, for the first time. The thought itself didn't let me sleep all night, and now I looked like a raccoon. I groaned at the thought.

20

When we reached the gigantic mansion, her parents pleasantly welcomed me. I entered inside with my duffle bag containing my two-days' supply of clothes and looked around. The massive, aristocratic mansion screamed of riches and wealth.

I also noticed that... he wasn't here yet.

We were still at the door when I heard a car approaching, and automatically, my heart started thumping. Within a second, a butler flew towards the black, sexy Maybach Exelero that stopped at the front of the entrance.

Holding my breath, I kept staring at the car. I knew what was coming, yet I was scared to the bone—scared of me, my emotion, the reaction of my body.

The front door opened, and slowly, a tall man in a black suit came out. The way his tall frame stretched out from the car and stood in its full form, I *felt* my eyes dilating in desire. I could swear, even coming out of the car oozed power and authority when it came to this man.

I spent countless hours looking at his photos, dreaming of doing nasty things to his body. But never in my life had I imagined it would look far sexier, erotic, and tantalizing in real life. It was a torment, looking at him and not being able to run my fingers and tongue all over his tall, muscular body.

As he hugged his parents and then kissed Ron's head, crushing her to the bone, I kept on reading his body, comparing his actual features with his photos. I never knew I was such a good reader.

Can you catch the sarcasm over here? I am pathetic when it comes to Vaughn.

Simply, shamelessly pathetic!

His hair looked shinier, blacker, and softer; I wanted to touch them, as his head would be buried in between my legs. His shoulder looked broader, muscular, and firmer; I could imagine gripping and biting on them as he ruthlessly thrust into me. His arms looked thicker and veinier; I could imagine them gripping my hair and every part of

21

my body whenever, and however, he wished to. His expensive suit accentuated his firmer and muscular chest; I wanted to hug and bury my face in there, besides having the intense desire to lick and bite on it. His long legs looked thicker and stronger; I could bet he could carry me around and fuck me standing effortlessly. His fingers looked longer; I could already feel them buried deep inside me, gripping my soft skin everywhere, imprinting me.

And his lips… his lips looked softer and sexier; and my, oh my, how I wished to feel them all over me, touch them with my fingers, then suck, bite and kiss them to my heart's desire. How soft would they feel on mine? Even the thought took my breath away…

His eyes? His eyes look more powerful, dominant, intent, and dark; even the thought of them looking at mine as I sucked his cock, or as he thrust in me, jeopardized my existence.

When I was reading his eyes, I realized he was standing before me.

He was standing very close to me with all his magnificent, mouthwatering, and panty-drenching glory. His eyes were looking into my soul as if he could read how I had been sexually exploiting him in my mind.

Oh, snuggles… What if… What if he can do that for real?
It is 'The Vaughn Wolf' in the flesh I'm talking about!
Maybe he can!

I felt my face redden and my body getting weaker, both with extreme desire and mortification.

Did his dark eyes just turn a bit darker than before? Or was it my imagination?

"Vee, she is Jay… oh… I mean Xena. My best friend and my flatmate," Ron said, chirping as she stood beside her brother and then looked at me. "Jay, this is Vee, my most favorite person in the entire world."

I tried to say something when I noticed his silence, but nothing came out of my dry throat. I cleared my throat and tried again, "H-Hi…

22

I'm Xena Meyers," my voice came out raspier and hoarser than usual. I offered him my hand... maybe it was the only chance in my life when I got to touch him. How would his hands feel? Were they hot or cold to touch?

Deep in my heart, I believed that there was no way I would ever get to touch this man ever in my life again, if not today. It felt like he was from a different world, who lived above us, just like a fallen angel.

It was too intimidating to look into his eyes, so I looked down at my hand, greedy, as I waited for him to take it in his strong palms, just for a second. Just a single, innocent touch, if that was all I could get.

But then, to my surprise, he ignored my hand completely, and without any sign of acknowledgment, he walked past me, walking inside the house.

I stilled in my position, my hand still up in the air.

"Hey, don't get upset, Jay. I already warned you about him, remember? He despises unfamiliar, or you can say most female companies. Just don't let his arrogance bother you, okay? Ignore Vee." Ron placed her hand on my shoulder, pressing a little to comfort me.

You said he was not much into female companies, but you didn't say he despised women...

"It's okay. I understand," I said, setting my hand down. Unsure about who I convinced—Ron or me?

How should one feel when the only man she fancied with all her heart completely ignored her? Despised her?

Was it how I was looking at him? Was he angry? To be honest, I *was* looking at him pretty inappropriately.

Or was it my appearance? I looked down at my white off-the-shoulder, ruffled crop, and blue jeans. I thought I looked good in this. It made me look cute, and at the same time, they accentuated my curves, showing off a bit here and there. I even conditioned my hair yesterday to make it look shinier and went for minimal makeup to highlight my natural features.

All my hard work for this attitude?

Oh, Xena, what did you expect, you fool? You knew what he was like? The reality was not your fantasy, girl!

I should have known. A man like him had nothing to care about me. The guy was about ten years older than me. He was not a kid to act like an immature around a woman. He knew what he did.

Well, if he didn't acknowledge me, I didn't need to acknowledge him as well—at least, not in front of him. What came into my imagination, fantasy, and dream didn't count. With whatever self-respect I had, I'll keep my distance from him, now that I first-handed knew his attitude towards me.

I huffed inwardly and looked at Ron with a forceful smile. "Let's go inside?"

Ron understood. She smiled back and pulled my hand inside the house.

I put my bags in the guest room. As I looked at my hands, I found them shaking. There was no way I was again going back downstairs anytime soon. I had been warmly invited, that was true, but I didn't want to intrude on their family time. It had been long.

Also, Vaughn would be there. And I wasn't as much invited there as I was before he arrived. He didn't want me there; I understood that round and clear. I was an unknown, unfamiliar, unwanted female here whom he despised and ignored effortlessly.

When it was lunchtime, I couldn't be in the room anymore and had to give in to Ron. She had been nagging me to go downstairs for some time, and I refused her every time.

When I reached the dining table, I found everyone occupying their seats already. My eyes swept around, and I realized I had to sit either beside or opposite Vaughn. My heart speeded up again. I could turn my world upside down to be close to the man, but not with the cost of sacrificing my self-respect, of course.

I held my chin high and sat opposite him, with Ron sitting by my side. I didn't look at him to see if he noticed me, because this time, I didn't stare at him as I did earlier. I made myself a fool before him already, and there was no way I could afford to do that anymore.

I tried to concentrate on the food that a beautiful young maid served on my plate with a heavy heart. I smiled and thanked her as she smiled back warmly at me.

"So... how is your study going?" Vaughn asked Ron.

"It's going fine, Vee." Her lying came out so effortlessly, I almost choked on my food at how smooth she was at it.

Then I noticed Vaughn raising a brow at her, as if challenging Ron to tell the truth. Ron only flashed an innocent smile at her brother, still maintaining her façade.

"You will not be getting your Lamborghini Aventador if you don't get out of the college with the GPA that you promised me." Vaughn looked unbothered as he took a mouthful of his meal.

How could someone eat in such a seductive way? The way his mouth moved and his throat bobbed had put me in a bizarre position.

I'd rather he ate me.

How was it possible that I could detect his intoxicating scent over all these delicious foods? It felt absurd.

Exactly how deep in shit were you in, Xena?

Where was your self-respect, girl?

I tried to avoid my eyes wandering towards him anymore. But I could feel that his eyes never looked at me, that I was sure about. Despite that, this proximity made my pussy howl in ache.

I was afraid that the wet stain might show through the thick denim fabric of my jeans.

Finishing my food fast, I excused myself and rushed towards the washroom before they could serve the dessert.

That moment, who knew that my decision to go to the washroom intending to fix myself was going to backfire me in just ten minutes?

7 | Marked

Xena

On my way to the washroom, I looked around the place. My eyes caught a few frames hanging on the walls. They were all family pictures—the joyous kind. One could get a false idea about how perfect the family was from the photos alone. Whereas in reality, they only had time for a single-digit number in a year for a regular family dinner. Thanks to Vaughn that Ron had someone from the family by her side. Otherwise, the poor girl would have been lonely.

Not all the void could be filled by friends. No matter how much I tried, there was only a limited emptiness I could fill up for her. This was why I always respected Vaughn. He never let Ron feel lonely. Even after being a busy man, he always made sure to find time for his sister. No matter what. Then again, he never came to visit her in our apartment, and the only reason I could assume was I. Maybe, the idea of another woman around made him feel uncomfortable.

After refreshing, I came out of the washroom and strolled towards the dining area again. The dessert course was left. Everyone was still there, including *him*.

He didn't see me, but I saw him. I'd keep seeing him if it was all I could get. But of course, making sure that I didn't make a fool of myself again. Only the notion of seeing him again made my heart beat faster once again. Gosh, I needed to do something about it. The thought of him messed with my heart and my pussy. Just a flash of his thought in my mind, and in a flick, my heart ran faster, and my pussy went wetter.

Suddenly, I felt a hand grip my wrist, pulling me into a room by the corridor. Before I could react, I was pushed against a wall, facing it. A body was tightly pressed against my back. Also, a large pair of palms covered the back of my hands, flattening on the wall beside me—caging me in. I gasped and tried to look back, but the way the tall, massive, warm, and hard frame pressed against mine didn't allow me to move an inch.

What was happening?

I felt some hot, deep breaths falling on my neck as he inhaled my scent over and over. Yes, it was a *'he.'* It was definitely a man's body. The raw, masculine, spicy fragrance gave me a name as well. But I was too afraid to consider the name to put on this body, which was pressed against mine.

No, it couldn't be him. Why would he?

He pushed his nose into my hair earlier so that I couldn't look back and see him. Bit by bit, the nameless man rubbed his nose from the back of my head towards my neck over and over, as if he wasn't getting enough. His hold on my hands went firmer.

And then he growled in the crook of my neck, pulling the rein over his self-restraints.

He growled like a starved animal. Like the one who had been hungry for a long time and finally found the source of a delicious feast. All for himself.

I took a sharp breath at that thought.

Was it really who I thought he was?

His intoxicating scent said so…

His firm body said so…

His possessive grip said so…

His animalistic growl said so…

Then why was my mind still in denial?

More specifically, why would it be him?

Before I could say anything, I heard him ask, "Why did you look at me that way? As if you wanted to do dirty, naughty things to me? With me? Why, Sugar? Tell me... tell me dammit!"

It is him.

Oh god... it is him! Him!

Someone call an ambulance! This girl here needs to go to the emergency room!

His voice was so deep, so throaty and rough, it vibrated through my skin and hit me directly to my core. The urgency and impatience were evident in his tone. That, in reality, was driving me wild.

Yes, I did. I wanted to do dirty, naughty things to him, with him. So badly...

"S-Sorry." I was so breathless that I wasn't sure if he could hear me or not.

But the way he pushed his nose into the crook of my neck possessively told me he did.

After taking a few deep breaths, his impatient voice snarled again, "Why did you never come looking for me? Why did you make me wait for you?"

He pulled all my hair to the side by one of his hands and then pressed an open mouth, possessive kiss over my shoulder.

I gasped again, shaking visibly under his touch. Unable to form a single word.

He moved his hands and brushed the fingers touching the side of my body as they slid down towards my slim waist. And then, when he reached his juncture, with no warning, his fingers that had been softly brushing against my skin earlier dug their nails into my delicate skin—kneading the soft flesh of my waist.

I moaned in pain.

He hissed as if *he* felt pain on him.

At the same time, the lips that had been resting on my neck parted, and his teeth took the soft skin of my neck into his warm, greedy mouth and then bit on it.

28

Only this time, I moaned out louder.

And he moaned with me.

More. I wanted more of the pain.

"You dance with men, kiss them, touch them and let them touch what's mine, but you never looked for me. Why? Why is it only me who is burning in this flame?" he asked. His nails dug deeper into the soft skin of my waist, as if he was punishing me. Then again, why was it turning me on even more?

Also, what was he talking about?

Then one of his hands went to my underboob and another towards my navel. With his hands, he pulled me closer to him. All the while, one of his fingers pushed into my navel, making the sensation of pleasure and pain rush throughout my body in a jolt. I gasped and moaned together as I felt the air leaving my lungs at the sudden, slightly painful move.

Then I felt it. I felt it between my butt crack.

Raging. Throbbing. Quivering.

"You do this to me." His breath turned heavier. "And you don't even know about it." His nose grazed over my ear.

"Can you feel what you do to me, Sugar? Can you *feel* how much I burn for you?" He breathlessly mumbled into my ear, but the authority, the power in his voice, was still prominent.

I supported my forehead against the wall and then took a deep breath. To make my body stable enough to keep standing. If he left my body, I was sure I would fall on the floor. My body had become jelly under his touch.

"Y-You... You didn't even take my hand when I o-offered. You n-never looked at me throu-throughout the lunch... Then how? Why?" I said. To say the words felt like running across the finish line in a marathon. I had never worked this hard, even in an exam.

His nose that had been resting in my neck moved towards my ears, and then he chuckled throatily, deeply. My body shivered with the vibration.

I felt one of his hands leaving my body to find something from his pocket. Every part of my body was still glued to his. It felt like he was against making any distance between our bodies. And then I felt the hand that left me earlier slide into the back pocket of my jeans. He tucked something in there, and at the same time, took his sweet time, feeling me up.

Then he took my earlobe into his mouth and sucked on it. His warm breath tickled on my skin when in a raspy voice, he said, "There. My personal card with my personal contact number. It's a matter of seconds for me to find yours. But Sugar—" he dropped another kiss on my ear. "—in our case, I want you to reach me. I have burned a lot for you. Now, why don't you burn a little for me?"

Then he pressed a possessive kiss on my neck, in the same place he bit earlier, as if marking his territory.

"I will be waiting for your call, Sugar. I have been patient for a long time. Come to me. Don't test me anymore."

With that being said, he left.

And just as he left my body, my knee gave up, and I collapsed on the floor.

$$-\text{♡♡♡}-$$

It took me quite some time to stabilize my body. Inside and out.

I remember. When I was a child, one fine evening, I was playing outside with my friends in the park. The weather was so beautiful, just a little hot, but no one assumed anything. Without any sign, suddenly it turned black with dark clouds floating all over the sky within moments, and then strong, heavy winds started to blow. I was a little kid; it scared me to the bone. The thunderstorms and pouring rain severely messed with my mind, heart, and body that evening.

The experience rooted deep into me that, till now, I still got scared whenever there was a storm or heavy rain outside. It reminded me of the dark sky and loud thunderstorms. Even thinking about it made my body shiver, and goosebumps appeared on my skin.

Vaughn reminded me of that feeling.

I could feel the goosebumps appear on my skin, my body shivered inside and out... and I got scared. Scared of how much I wanted him. How much I had been burning for him as well.

It was true that it had been me who craved the forbidden, unattainable fruit for a long time. Never in my life had I imagined that he felt the slightest for me, too.

Was he serious? Or was he playing with me?

Also, why did I feel something dark about him? Something close to domineering, controlling, and commanding? What was with that feeling?

I discarded all my thoughts and left them for the time. There was no way I could keep my sanity if I thought about him anymore right now.

With wobbly legs, I stood up and supported myself against the wall, searching for the strength of my legs that gave up on me a long ago.

When I entered the dining room again, everyone was almost done with their dessert. When Ron noticed me, she asked, "Jay, are you alright? I was about to go check on you."

"Y-Yeah... I'm fine... Just..." I trailed off. I had no idea how to excuse myself when I felt a pair of burning eyes staring at me. But I was too scared to look at him. Who knew? Maybe my legs would give up on me again?

"OMG! Jay! What happened to your skin? There are so many red patches on your neck, hands, and waist," Ron yelped, making a shiver run down my spine.

I glanced at my body and found that everywhere he touched me earlier—or I would rather say—manhandled me earlier was bare for everyone to see, since I was wearing a crop top. He wasn't gentle in the least with his touch.

"Allergy… that's why I was late. Something triggered my allergy, and my body is showing a reaction. I think I should go have some medicine and take some rest if you'll kindly excuse me." I wasn't even able to look into their eyes.

The elders immediately agreed, and Ron rushed to take me to my room. They bought the lie. Why would they not? What could they possibly assume?

When I headed upstairs, I could practically *feel* his smirk behind my back.

Oh, Vaughn…

8 | Territorial

Vaughn

A few nights ago...

"Mr. Wolf, your sister is here. With her usual company. They had hit the bar already, and right now, quite enjoying themselves on the dance floor," Finn said, letting me know Ronnie's whereabouts.

"I see," I replied and hung up the call as I got off his bed at once.

Not wasting another second, I walked straight to the security room to see what was going on through the 24/7 surveillance camera recording everything in the club.

My eyes fell on my little sister first. Yup, she was being a brat again and enjoying her usual ways. I quickly called security to inform them about keeping an eye on her, emphasizing their safety.

When I made sure of their protection, finally, my eyes drifted towards her...

She was dancing with my sister. The way her enthralling body moved, she undeniably looked like a nymph coming out of the water, stealing absolutely everyone's breaths... including mine. Just one look at her, and I felt my dick harden at her beauty.

Matching with her moves, I guiltlessly started to move one of my hands on my dick over the sweatpants. Imagining my hand as her soft, captivating, curvy body grinding against my rock-hard hardness.

God. Damn.

She... only she could make me go this crazy... only her.

And she didn't even know about it...

33

My Aphrodite was wearing a navy blue satin dress. Satin... I loved satin. It was my weakness. Did she know that? Over the soft satin fabric, it would be so easy and practical to touch her softness... absolutely everywhere on her body.

Only if I could... She was forbidden territory, and I was on a fence—exactly this close to passing that.

Besides, she was too young for me. She was exactly my little sister's age, about nine years younger than me. Then why did my impudent, shameless dick only feel alive after seeing her? And no other women? Only her thoughts could trigger it to harden. I tried. Nothing else worked. How lowly would she think of me if she knew I jerk off while only thinking about her? Or, if lucky, watching her like I was doing that moment?

Even though she was much younger than me in age, almost nine years younger... but still, I craved her.

I craved her as a caveman craved for his only possession.

It wasn't working. Groaning at my throbbing erection, I took my dick out of my sweatpants and started to pump on it. How would it feel in her gorgeous pouty mouth? Between her heavy tits? Or... inside her. With her hair spread all over my bed. Her nipples hard and darkened for my touch. With her little tight, wet cunt pulsating for my attention.

Mmm... I liked the thought. I kept pumping harder. My eyes never left her bewitching curves, even for a second.

So sexy... as if they were calling for me.

I felt pre-cum dampening my palm at the thought. My rough hands were nowhere near her soft delicacy. Oh, how much I craved her softness. I clasped harder around my dick, imagining her clenching around my hardness, engulfing me inside her scorching cave, as I pumped into her harder... then faster... then again, harder...

Oh, Sugar... the things I want to do to you... do with you...

I bit my lips as I was almost reaching my release, but then something happened...

34

There was a prick who touched my Aphrodite from the back. He laid his finger on what was supposed to be mine. Mine!

And she didn't deny his touch.

Why would she? Did she even know about my existence?

She looked like she had been waiting for him. My bratty sister didn't take another moment to shove my Aphrodite into another man's arms. I had to take out my anger on that brat somehow. She deserved every drop of it.

To my silent agony, she started dancing—or one could say—grinding against the prick. Also, the prick left no chance untouched as he moved his hands on her, on my Aphrodite.

Just a few moments ago, I was on the verge of my awaited release. Now, all my feelings had turned into anger and agony. My body burned in rage, my head throbbing, and my jaw muscles tensed. All I wanted to do was call the securities to throw away the prick from my club right away.

He was in my territory, touching my girl.

But was she truly mine? She wasn't someone I was allowed to have anything with, just how my little sister wasn't allowed to have anything with my friends. It was an untold rule. I couldn't have her.

But I couldn't also *not* have her.

She is mine! Goddammit!

Just looking at a man touching her made my mind go numb with all the burning rage. How could I allow her to belong to someone if the *'someone'* wasn't me?

Nah, I couldn't let her be someone else's.

But I couldn't cross over the line as well.

Fucking shit. I am indeed in fucking deep shit.

Then I found the guy pulling her hands to the corner, making my blood boil. This guy not only stopped my most awaiting release, but also put his hands on my girl. I put my semi-hardened dick inside my pants and then switched to a different camera to see where they were leading.

And then, I saw the prick pushing my girl towards the wall and then claiming her lips...

Fucking hell.

Oh, Sugar... What are you doing?

You had repeated the mistake of letting another man touch you.

I might restrain myself because of the rules and shits, but even a man like me had certain limits.

All I wanted right now was to throw you on my bed, on your stomach, butt-naked, then tie you up against the headrest so that I could spank the shit out of you. You made me see red in anger. And I wanted to paint your ass cheeks just as red as that, while you would cry and moan in both pain and pleasure. I wanted to spank you to the extent where you couldn't even sit anywhere and beg me to put medicine on your skin. Because no one, absolutely no one else, could touch you there.

After everything you have done, you deserve the punishment, Sugar. Don't you?

$$- \text{♪} \heartsuit \heartsuit -$$

I was late already. After going through all the exquisite suits I owned, I felt like not even one was right for me. I wanted to look my best today. Brushing the collar of my black suit, I thought about how I was much older than her. Would she think I was too old for her? Would my well-polished appearance compel her to like me?

Should I go for a white shirt or black underneath? Silk or cotton? What would she like to see me in?

How much should I gel my hair today? Or should I rule it out? Which watch to put on?

Damn. You are so screwed, Wolf!

When I greeted my family, I could swear my inside practically shook in anticipation. What would be her reaction as she saw me?

The moment my eyes fell on her, my heart felt so full, it was impossible to suck in any more air. She looked absolutely breathtaking. And dangerously hot. My eyes fell on her, and I stopped on my track for a moment, looking into her eyes.

I expected a hundred different sorts of reactions from her.

But it was definitely none of them.

It wasn't my suit or my watch that her eyes were on. Her gorgeous eyes raked through my entire body from top to down. She was devouring my body through her gorgeous pair of blue eyes.

She looked like she was eating me up... only through her gaze.

That's my girl.

And gosh... I loved it. So did my dick.

Her eyes compelled me, and I kept moving slowly towards her. My girl's eyes were having a feast on every part of my body, one by one, notwithstanding whoever was watching us. And I was never prouder.

Finally, when her eyes looked into mine, my heart jumped into my throat, and my breathing stopped.

My Aphrodite...

Was she real?

I heard Ronnie introducing us, but I could see nothing other than lust, crave, and desire in her eyes...

... for me.

Aren't I a lucky bastard, or what?

I was standing so close to her that her sweet scent drove my entire soul nuts. If it was in my power, I would've made everyone around us disappear so that it could be only us.

Then it wouldn't have taken me any longer to tear that little tops and those skinny jeans to rip apart from her intoxicating body. Oh, how I wish I could do that right now.

I had a firm belief. I believed she was the one for me. And since my eyes fell on her today, and I saw the raw hunger in her eyes, my belief just became stronger than ever.

I believed she was definitely the one. To match me. In every perspective. The one I needed. The one I wanted. The one I craved. And I would definitely make you mine, my Aphrodite.

For now, just tell me how to cross the door without wanting to rip your clothes off, and then fuck that body of yours?

She offered me her hand to shake.

Was she out of her mind? Did she think I could touch her hand right now? Without fucking her?

Shake your hand, Sugar? I want to shake your world. And I will. Just you see.

Because I know. I know you are it for me.

The entire lunch was torture. I wanted to talk to her, see her. But there were too many people for my liking. What I had in mind was definitely not safe for people around.

Hell. I wanted to crush into her. Body and soul.

On this table? Oh, hell yes. Or anywhere. I didn't care, as long as it was her.

The first chance I got, I clawed at her. I pushed her against the wall with her back facing me. Because I knew if I looked into those eyes right now, I would fuck her right here, right now. The beast in me wouldn't be under control. I could not let that happen. I had waited for her for a long time already. A man had needs. Besides, it was her.

For a minute, I kept inhaling her intoxicating scent and felt her buttery-smooth skin. Thinking of a thousand ways of how I could feel her against me, under me, above me, and whatnot...

When I asked her a simple question like why she looked at me like that, in reply, she said sorry. Oh, Sugar, I already saw the raw hunger in your eyes. I was hungry too. No need to hide from me. Especially me.

My hands traveled over her body on their own accord, and I let them. Her softness was addictive. The things I wanted to do to her body... My grip on her went firmer at the thoughts.

I tasted her skin like a hungry wolf, and she let me. The moment my fingertip found her navel, I took a sharp intake of breath. I swear, I could feel the depth of her navel with a decent-sized grape. That's how deep it was. I couldn't help but push into the button and sighed in satisfaction of her moan.

Her reaction amused me the most. She was more alluring than I imagined her to be. To this day, I thought only I craved her like a maniac. But no, she craved my touch too—if I wasn't wrong, just as much as me. The mere thought thrilled my soul.

I could practically feel her arousal for me as I brushed my nose in her neck and hair. Her supple skin felt surreal against my rogue one. Her breathing was rugged, there were goosebumps on her buttery skin, and she moaned at my touch... gosh... she moaned at my simple touch.

Her reaction to my mere touches was unstoppably arousing for me. I couldn't help but moan with her. Had I ever moaned in my life before? No. I didn't think so.

My dick was happy-dancing for a while.

I grumbled in my mind, "Now is not your time, buddy."

She asked me why I didn't shake her hand and why I didn't look at her.

Still asking me that, Sugar? It looked like you needed some private time with me to be clear of that.

To put my personal card, my hand shifted towards the back pocket of her jeans. Fuck, I really wanted to slap, pinch, grab, and feel up the curvy ass of my girl. As my palm cupped her butt cheek, a different kind of satisfaction waved through me, making me shudder.

The feeling was close to tasting a drop of water after walking miles on a desert. Fuck, it was so worth it.

"Soon, you're going to fuck that ass soon," I thought, restraining myself when I left her panting in there.

When she finally reappeared after I left her there, Ronnie mistook my fingerprints and marks on her skin as allergy, as she referred to them.

I smirked.

Allergy, huh? I promise, Sugar, you are definitely going to get hella allergies in the coming future. I promise you that.

9 | Family Drama

Xena

It was definitely not what I expected when I thought of a family reunion. Mr. and Mrs. Wolf had returned only for two days to be with their children. So, naturally, I assumed it would be a happy two days for Ron. But god, how wrong I was.

It had been over two hours since her parents were fighting. I had no idea what the issue was, but the way they cursed and swore at each other was a lot to take in, even for an outsider like me. When I first heard them screaming in their room, I thought they forgot to shut the door, or maybe the fight would stop. But no, it didn't. It only intensified with every minute.

In the beginning, I was so uncomfortable witnessing such nasty family drama—even embarrassed. But later on, when I looked at Ron, I was mortified. The girl was behaving hysterically. I never saw Ron in such a panic-stricken state as long as I knew her. She had always been a proud, rich, beautiful, confident, and feisty girl. It was nearly impossible to imagine that the girl before me was the same girl I knew.

I tried to reach for her, but Ron shoved me away. She wasn't in her normal state. Her eyes, wide in fear, looked scary to me. I couldn't believe I was looking at my friend Ron, who I had known for years. Her hair looked messy from pulling them erratically over and over. Unstoppable tears kept pouring from her eyes, and her skin kept sweating.

The more I stared at her, the more boundless emotion swirled in my heart for the girl. I tried to touch her again, but she was not in the condition to even recognize me. I was scared.

"Vee... Vee... Where is Vee?"

Ron kept crying as the scream outside amplified, and the diversity of curses and insults enlarged as well.

Vaughn wasn't at the house. About three hours ago, Ron told me he had some emergency at his club.

"Vee! Vee!"

Ron continued wailing and screaming her brother's name as she hugged her knees and kept swaying back and forth, over and over.

How could I stop it? It was too much to see Ron like this! How to help her?

I kept pacing between the door and her. I couldn't stop her parents from shouting at each other, nor could I help my best friend. She didn't want anyone else other than Vaughn.

Where are you, Vaughn?

I had never been in such a situation, and honestly, I was scared out of the wits. Only Vaughn could end this.

Suddenly, I heard a different—a deeper voice screaming louder than Ron's parents.

"Two days! Only two days was what I asked for. You couldn't even do it for your children, could you? I pity you both!"

Then there was a loud thud of a door slamming hard. My heart was racing already. Vaughn. He was here. He probably shut his parents' door, finally.

I heard fast and hurried footsteps towards Ron's door. It seemed like he was coming for his sister. Before I could hide for giving them some privacy, the door was slammed open.

It didn't take Vaughn even a second to find his sister. His eyes completely disregarded me, as if I wasn't there. His sole attention was only for his sister.

The moment his eyes fell on Ron, Vaughn rushed towards her and crouched down on the floor to crush Ron into his safe embrace.

"Vee! You are here. You are here... They are doing it again! Make them stop, Vee! Make it stop!"

Ron kept mumbling, finally calming down as she hugged her brother tightly.

"I am here, Ronnie. Everything is fine now. I took care of it. It's okay. Everything is okay. I am here." Vaughn took time and continued reassuring Ron with his gentle, comforting words.

The moment Ron found her brother, she visibly relaxed. Her hysteria slowed down to the end. I could clearly see how Ron and Vaughn only had each other in the family, even though the outside world saw Victor and Penelope Wolf as successful parents.

That was the moment when I finally felt the wetness on my cheeks. I had no idea since when I had been crying. Seeing the two people in front of me and their genuine love for each other, I couldn't control my emotions anymore.

I noticed how Vaughn hugged and swayed his little sister with the utmost affection, stroking her back in a soothing manner and mumbling comforting words. It was wonderful to see what Ron went through for over an hour. Naturally, I wanted to give the brother-sister duo some privacy.

Careful enough not to make a sound, I tried to leave the room. But this time, Vaughn didn't disregard me as he did moments ago. His intense, piercing gaze found me the moment my stilled body finally moved. As my eyes fell into his penetrating ones, I stumbled for a second. He didn't ask or say anything to me. There was no expression on his face. He just stared at me. That was all it took the floor to tremble under my feet. Those eyes could eat my soul, and I won't even say a word.

I gathered all my energy and broke our stares. Then, slowly, I opened the door and left the room. Until the door closed behind me, I felt those intense eyes on me.

No one went down for dinner that night. Like a good brother, Vaughn brought some food for Ron and fed her patiently. I didn't intrude on their precious moment. The way I had been worrying for

Ron, I couldn't help but check on her every fifteen minutes. That was when I found the sweet brother-sister moment.

Now I knew. I understood why Ron felt so skeptical about her parents and why she was so protective of her brother. Her brother was her only savior.

After a while, I again peeked to see if Ron was alone or not. I thought of sleeping in her room if it helped her. From the ajar door, I noticed Vaughn tucking Ron under the duvet. Then he affectionately stroked her hair as he said good night to his sister.

Before he could see me, I moved away from the door and ran towards my room. But I was late. He saw flashes of me already.

My body kept tingling as I closed the door behind me. I supported my back against the door and panted to calm my nerves. My forehead was sweating. Every time his eyes fell on me, my inside went through havoc. His gaze had this much power over me that only God knew how I would feel if he…

Gosh… Xena… as if he would do that with you…

But then… What was that this afternoon? What did he mean?

My heart went crazy once again when I went through my memory lane. Not that any of the memories of this afternoon left my mind. But after the drama tonight, I was distracted. As soon as Ron and her parents fell asleep, my mind circled back to thinking of him… his touches… and his words.

After taking a shower, I jilled off to calm my frenzied nerves. I had to get off. I was under the same roof as him, and after all these encounters, how could I not? My hormones went crazy, and it was absolutely justified!

When I came out of the bathroom draped in a towel, I went through my luggage to find my nightwear. My eyes fell on the clock, and I noticed how early it was, and still, the house was awfully silent. Everyone went to bed already. The maids once requested me to have something for dinner, but the sudden turn of events and the pressure on my nerves killed my appetite. Worrying about Ron, witnessing the wild fight between her parents… and thinking of Vaughn… They drowned me out.

Oh, Vaughn… my body shuddered.

I picked up my long burgundy nightwear. It had spaghetti straps and a deep, lacy neckline. The silk of the fabric was so soft, it felt like a feather against my skin. Removing the towel from my body, I covered my nakedness with the silk right away. I opted out of wearing a bra. Then again, I never wore a bra in bed.

I lay on the bed for about an hour, but all the experiences from my eventful day were whirling inside my mind, and I couldn't shake them off. At some point, I decided to take a walk.

Everyone was already in their bedroom, so I decided to tiptoe and visit the backyard. The Wolfs had a beautiful garden and pool behind their mansion.

Just how I assumed the entire huge mansion was dead silent. I silently walked out and went towards the beautiful garden. The dewy grasses and earth under my naked feet felt so comfortable that I could practically cuddle the comfort of it. It always provided me with a feeling of calmness when I walked barefooted on soft grasses or earth. It drinks up my tension away every time.

Standing before the rose garden, I inhaled the air. The soothing night breeze was bursting at the seams with the scent of fresh roses. The smell was so seductive that I started feeling my senses and naughty hormones awakening once again. I could feel the hairs on my skin rise and the bottom of my panties wet.

Wrong choice of place. I should've gone to the pool instead.

I crossed my arms under my breasts and exhaled audibly before turning on my heels. The garden wasn't helping my nerves to calm down.

But before I could move, a deep, raspy voice stopped me in my tracks.

"Can't sleep?"

I gasped in shock and turned towards the source of the sexiest male voice I had ever heard.

Vaughn.

Snuggly blankets! I thought I was here to calm my nerves!

I was tongue-tied.

My lips and tongue agreed to move only one way—against his. Other than that, they didn't agree to move at all. I kept trying to force them to say something, but it didn't work.

He slid his hands in his pocket and stepped closer to me. Very close. Too close to make my senses go crazy. Close Enough to make me see flowers blooming, butterflies fluttering around us. Excessively close to making my skin tingle with the warmth radiating from his body.

"You have to say something once in a while, Sugar. I want to hear more from you," he said, whispering seductively.

Gosh… just how sexy can a man sound?

As my lips and tongue betrayed me, I decided not to bother about them anymore. Instead, I checked him out.

He was still wearing the same outfit. The same black shirt he had been wearing today, just the suit jacket was missing. The top three buttons of his shirt were undone, and a trail of chest hair was peeking from underneath. With the eventful day, his shirt looked a little messy. But that only made him look sexier. How was that even possible? Even his chest looked more defined with the suit coat gone. My body started burning then and there, and I gulped down.

He seemed to notice my gaze and smirked. I felt the smirk!

"It's quite cold outside. Why do you have so little clothing on you?" he asked.

Hey, I'm sweating over here!

"I… I like to walk naked—" before I could finish, one of his brows raised in surprise.

Oh, snuggly blanket!

What did I just say?

46

"—feet! Naked feet! Bare feet! Barefoot! I like to walk barefoot on the ground."

I could see the plain amusement in his eyes, and then he laughed, throwing his head back.

He laughed at me!

Vaughn... laughed at me!

How could someone's laughter be so sexy?

Suddenly, his laughter subsided, and he looked at me with his intense, penetrating eyes. They were dark, as dark as the night sky above.

His eyes fell on me once again, and he silently kept staring at me for a long while. After the humiliation, I didn't even dare to make another sound.

Slowly, he brought his face closer to mine. So close that I could feel his warm breath falling over the sensitive skin of my neck. He gently tucked a strand of my hair behind my ears and said, "Now that you've said it, I can't stop imagining you walking naked..." His voice grumbled beside my ear.

My heart, please don't give up on me yet!

"—and I'm not even going to say *feet*," he finished.

God! My heart!

My entire body trembled with overwhelming emotions. I didn't know what to say or do. God, I didn't even dare to move. He was too close! Too close! I couldn't even imagine I was the same girl who had countless dirty fantasies about this exact man, the same girl who could only get off thinking dirty about him, could be this shy before him in real life. Especially when he was this close, talking dirty to me.

Then I felt it. I felt one of his fingertips brushing at the side of my body, burning my skin through the thin silk throughout the way. Beside my breasts, my waist, and then stopped at my hips. His breathing sounded heavier in my ears. At that moment, I felt like nothing could be sexier than his breaths in my ear.

"But I like the nighty on you as well. It gives a lot of possibilities for my imagination to go wild. I can see you through it. And fuck… you are the sexiest little thing I have ever laid my eyes on."

Oh, Vaughn!

10 | Tryst

Xena

Suddenly, the warmth was gone. Cold. I felt cold without Vaughn's warmth around me. The moment his heat left my body, I started craving it again.

"Let's take a stroll? I can't sleep either," Vaughn wordlessly grabbed my hand, pulling me towards another corner of the garden. As if in a stupor, I followed him silently.

I need to say something. Anything. Gosh, why is it so hard?

"Why can't you sleep?" I said in a breathless voice.

Right. Vaughn took my breath away a long time ago. To be exact, right when he said he couldn't stop imagining me naked. Yeah, that's when it happened.

"I had a lot in my mind." his earnest reply came soon.

"I understand. It was a tough day for Ron."

"Yeah. That's a part of it."

"Work pressure? Ron says you work too much." I remember how she always kept on rambling about how he didn't take care of himself and overworked all the time.

He stopped in his tracks, looked at me, and said, "I never let my work pressure get on my nerves. Only thinking of *my* people keeps me awake at night," he said in a firm tone.

"Don't worry, Ron will be fine. With you by her side. I will also do my best to take ca—" before I could finish the line, he tugged the hand he was holding, and I stumbled against his broad chest. My soft breasts pressed against his chiseled, hard abs. I was confident he could feel the softness through both of our thin fabrics.

And I wasn't even wearing a bra! My goodness...

His grip was firm on my shoulder when he looked into my eyes. There were promises, authenticity, and lust in those dark orbs. Then he said in a voice dipped in raw desire, "I was thinking of you."

My eyes widened.

How could he say so? Why did he keep on saying these? What did he want? Didn't Ron and the media say he loathed women?

Looking at my thunder-struck expression, he mumbled, saying, "I can't stop thinking about you. I have been thinking about you for a long... long time."

"B-But... don't you... don't you loath women?" I asked, not being able to stop myself from asking this.

His eyes looked bewildered for a second, and then he sighed and bowed his head down a little. After a moment, he tugged my hand, and we sat on a bench.

"I don't. I don't prefer to be with any woman within three meters around me," he looked at our adjoined hands that lay on his lap. His thumb, brushing on the back of my hand.

"Then? Then why—" I trailed off.

"Why you?" he smiled, looking at me sideways. Under the night sky and dazzling moon, he looked unreal. It felt like a dream sitting here, holding his hands. *Vaughn's hands.*

"Because it's you. It can only be you," Vaughn said, looking deep into my eyes.

I bit my lips. Did my brain stop working? Why couldn't I process his words?

"Didn't I tell you I waited a long time for you?"

The genuineness in his voice caught me off guard. My hand visibly trembled in his hand that was still lying on his lap. He noticed that and covered my hand with his warm, large palms. Then, carefully, he focused on my each and every finger and started playing with them.

Snuggles! I could get off only from this! Only if I wasn't this nervous!

"It's good to see someone caring for Ronnie other than me," he said out of nowhere as he sighed.

I knew what he meant. He was the only one who genuinely cared for Ron. The way his parents behaved today, I could say their roles in their children's lives.

"I do. I deeply care for her," I said, smiling.

He looked at me in astonishment. Then I realized he was astounded to see me smile.

"It was wonderful to see such a genuine sibling bonding."

"She only had me all these years. We only had each other. Until you came," Vaughn replied with a gloomy face. His eyes were still focused on his fingers that played with mine.

"This has been happening for years?" I was shocked.

He laughed dryly. "In such huge mansions that never cease to show off their perfections, behind their closed door, Xena, many nasty things happen. You have no idea."

I couldn't say what made my skin shiver visibly. His words, or him saying my name for the first time?

"But I'm happy Ronnie got you. I have been keeping tabs on her for a long time, and I know how much you have to work to keep my sister on track. Besides, it shows how genuine your affection and care are for Ronnie. She is lucky she found you."

I didn't know how to take his appreciation. My cheeks went warmer, my skin tingled, my heart fluttered, and I felt like smiling like a fool.

You fool, Xena! Don't do that!

"She is all I have here, as well. I am blessed to have her in my life. She is what makes my life better and blissful," I said with a smile, thinking of the craziness of my best friend.

"I'm also happy that *I* got you. I'm lucky that I found you, Xena," he said. His raspy voice vibrated beside me, honesty dripping from his tone.

He said my name once again! Snuggles!

Don't lose track, Xena. He said something more than just your name! Something crazy! Focus on them! Focus!

I bit my lips, with my heart going through havoc inside, worrying for them, aching for them, wondering what was wrong between their parents.

"What did you mean by she is all you have here?" he again asked out of nowhere.

"For studies, I live in New York, almost a seven-hour drive from our vineyard in Virginia. I don't have anyone here. I miss my parents, my sister Aliza, my dog OJ, my friends—" before I could finish, he stopped me.

"Wait… OJ? Did you name your dog OJ for real? Why?" His eyes were full of disbelief. The gloominess that I saw earlier on his face was now gone.

"Because OJ is a beautiful, shiny orange Brittany-bred dog. He even loves to eat oranges!" I grinned, thinking of my beloved dog back home.

Vaughn started laughing again. The same way he laughed at me when he met me earlier. He threw his head back as a burst of deep laughter vibrated through his chest.

"Why are you laughing?" I asked. No matter how sexy he might look, no one laughed at my OJ!

"It's because many people won't be thinking of orange juice when you'll call OJ. Just have some mercy on the dogs and don't name his partner BJ," he said as he burst out in a peal of laughter. The man couldn't stop laughing!

Oh, snuggles!

Why didn't I ever think of that! What had I done? How my mom, dad, and Aliza never stopped me from naming him something so embarrassing! How could I ever call him by his name in front of people anymore? What else could I call him?

"What are you thinking now? Your face looks so interesting," he said in apparent humor.

"I should just call him Doggy from now on..." just when I said it out loud, I realized what I said.

Gosh... could this night *be* any more humiliating? Imagining the line in Chandler's voice, I slapped my forehead with my other hand that wasn't in his grip.

Vaughn again started laughing. No, I didn't blame him this time. I knew what I said. I just learned how bad I was at naming.

"I will never even try to name my kids in the future," I said in a defeated tone.

"Don't worry. I'm here. I'll do that for our kids," he said through his laughter.

I turned my head towards him so fast that I almost cracked my neck.

What did he just say?

He realized how shocked I was and stopped laughing immediately. Then, clearing his throat, he said, "Did you have anything for dinner?"

"No."

"Me neither. Let's go find what we could eat." Vaughn stood up and tugged my hand that he never left.

"It's late already..."

But I was hungry!

"So? I'm here, Sugar. Come with me."

Just then, the night wind wafted, and his shirt fluttered with the blow. My hair also fell on my face because of the breeze. So, I moved them from my face and resumed looking at his sinful sexiness. When my eyes fell on him, I found him gazing right back at me in a daze. A simple gaze, and I felt my heart getting warmer.

I'm so screwed.

When I stood up, he suddenly thought of something and said, "Wait! Sit down and wait for me."

Huh?

Then, after a minute, I saw him coming with a hosepipe in his hand.

"I won't mind you dirtying my house as much as you like. In fact, I would love it if you dirty it in *any way* you want. But I don't think my mother would appreciate it," he said, flashing me a naughty smirk and crouched down before me.

"Oh! Sorry, I didn't think of it earlier." My eyes widened in realization.

How could I not think of it? This isn't our vineyard, Xena!

"I'm here, aren't I?" he asked with a wink as he pushed the hem of my nightie upwards up to my knees.

"Hey! Wh-What are you—" my heart started drumming against my chest as I felt his fingers tracing all the way to my knee when he moved the fabric.

Intentional? Probably. Considering all his words and behavior tonight.

"My girl is dirty. I should do something about it, shouldn't I?" I realized his seductive tone was back again. Well, his voice was always passionate. But he had the superpower to make it sound extra seductive when he wanted.

Lots and lots of snuggly blankets! Have some mercy on me, god! Where are you when I need you most?

Suddenly, I was thirsty. I needed something to drink, to soothe the thirst inside me. Unknowingly, I licked my lower lip to dampen it a little. It became dry out of nowhere. This man had been fussing with my hormones for a while now. For god's sake, this girl here had some limits!

And he was crouching in a position where, if I spread my legs, he would meet my drenched kitty right away! That way, he just had to move forward a little to put his tongue on my—

Xena, stop!

I looked into his eyes and found him looking somewhere on my body intently, as if he was in a trance. I focused on his eyes and then realized he looked at my kitty… *blankets!* Was he thinking the same as me?

Pulling the fabric down, I quickly went to cover my legs. Whereas, in my mind, all I wanted was for Vaughn to rip off the gown and take me right here. No one was around to interrupt us, anyway.

What are you thinking, Xena! Pull a rein on your wild thoughts! Later you'll get plenty of time to fantasize about this man, not now!

"Do you want to sleep in a dampen nighty? Do as I say!" His voice was overpowering, and my inner self went to its subservient mode right away without wasting another word.

He looked at me with wonder and curiosity as I went into my obedient mode. There was a flash of something in his eyes that I couldn't decipher. He either liked it or hated it. I couldn't be sure about it from his intense eyes right now.

A minute later, he looked down and turned on the hosepipe. Taking one of my feet in his hands, he splashed the cold water on my skin. His touches were like fire, and the water felt like ice, but with his scorching touches, soon, all I felt was a fire igniting inside me.

The way he delicately touched my feet felt so sensual. There was a hungry look in his eyes as he cleaned the dirt from my feet.

Probably he was just hungry…

Or did he have foot-fetish?

But soon, the water splash reached higher, dampening my shin. With lust as clear as the clear blue sky in his eyes, Vaughn used the water to clean the shin and calf of my legs one by one. The hunger in his eyes was so apparent. I came to the conclusion that he didn't have only foot-fetish, but an entire leg-fetish.

My legs were already clean. Only my feet were dirty that he had already cleaned a long ago. So, technically, there was nothing more to clean for him. But Vaughn took his sweet time to *'clean'* my legs and then finally turned off the pipe valve.

By then, I was panting at the verge of my much needed, much awaited, and much craved sweet orgasm.

Technically, this was called edging in the kinky world, right?

Hey, stop thinking about kinks when he is touching you! Do you want to die out of edging?

He cleared his throat and stood up, saying, "All done."

By then, I'm sure my face was so red that it went burgundy, and currently, it was matched with my nighty.

"Okay." I somehow managed to mutter, and then before I could step on the ground again, I realized how my feet would be dirty once again if I did that.

Great! I should just sleep here in the garden tonight!

I heard him chuckle above, and then leaning forward, before I could say anything, Vaughn put one of his hands under my knee and another behind my back, carrying me in his arms in bridal style.

He waggled me a little, trying to bring me out of my shock. But what it did was scare me to trip, and I circled my arms around his neck out of impulse.

He grinned at my reaction. Clearly too happy to keep it in.

"Let's take you inside."

11 | Date?

Xena

Finally, when Vaughn dropped me in the kitchen, I was all flustered. My entire body was hot and electrified from his touch. I'm sure my treacherous body was showing all the signs of arousal. While Vaughn held me securely in his arms, I noticed even *his* breathing was short, erratic, and heavy. Did he feel what I felt?

He didn't just drop me anywhere. The man safely dropped me on the chair by the kitchen island.

"I'll see what's in there."

Without waiting for my response, he spun around and walked towards the fridge.

He was fast, but I saw what he wanted to hide.

Yup, he felt it, too.

There was definitely a huge, prominent bulge in his pants.

Oh, blankets!

I felt hot all over. All throughout the time, my head was bursting from the thought of Vaughn getting an erection for me. Was I dreaming? How could it be real? It felt surreal.

I couldn't move my eyes from him. Vaughn's shoulders looked so broad, and his muscle flexes were visible from above the expensive fabric of his shirt. Even his waist was narrowed into a slender curve. Slowly, my eyes drifted towards his tight ass, and I gulped down. Sexy. Definitely a delicious tight butt; round, firm, and muscular. How would it feel to squeeze the buns? Would I ever get to squeeze them?

"I found some rice and salmon dishes. You okay with that?" he asked, looking back, and found me checking him out.

Caught!

I was so shocked that I couldn't make myself move my eyes away from him. His eyes held me captive, and there was a devilish smirk hanging at the corner of his *suckable* lips.

Predatorily, he closed the fridge without giving it another look and sauntered towards me. No more hesitant to exhibit his enormous bulge.

What should I do? Where should I hide?

When he reached me, he put his hands on both sides, caging me in between the kitchen island and his muscular body. His fiery breaths were falling on my face, making a few strands of my hair wave.

Gathering all the courage I had, I looked into his eyes and found them staring straight at my cleavage. Outside, he could see me alright in the garden, but he could see all of me at the highest resolution under the clear, megawatt bulbs. My chest heaved involuntarily, but when I noticed his focused eyes, it ceased my breathing.

I won't die if I can't breathe for a few moments, will I?

"Were you just checking me out?" His voice was full of lust and desire.

For me?

Oh, snuggles!

I gulped down and recollected all my courage once again.

"I was just about to ask you how I could help you."

His eyes moved to my lips.

"You want to help me, Sugar? Think again. Once you *help* me, there is no way out." He challenged me with his signature smirk.

Oh god... did I just say that?

Why do I keep saying all the wrong things before this man?

"Since today is our first date, I'll give you a choice: either you'll help me tonight or not. So, what do you wish for?" His smirk grew, and it looked almost sinful, challenging me to sin with him.

"What date? Who is on a date with you?" My eyes were like saucers.

His eyes now drifted to look into mine.

"Who do you think? Us. You and me." His smirk grew wider.

"We were just strolling in the garden when we bumped into each other. Now we will enjoy food together because we are living under the same roof tonight and because we both missed out on dinner."

"I would rather enjoy you..." he said under his breath, but I caught his words because of the dead silence around us.

"Huh?"

Huh?

"We were on a tryst in the garden, and now we are on our first date. Not only did I ask you to have dinner with me, but also I carried you here." He smiled this time. It was no less devilish than his smirks.

"You didn't mention any date! You asked me to have dinner. Plain, innocent dinner!" I said, almost yelling out to put some sense into this insane man's mind. But then I remember our situation and surroundings.

"Oh, Sugar. I don't need to ask my girl about going on a date with me. I just need to say where and when. Besides, when it comes to you and me, there is nothing 'innocent' between us. Because I know, Sugar, you are innocent just because no one ever found out your naughty sides, have they?" he asked, grinning.

Oh god... where are you?

I need holy water! This guy is already vigorously fucking my mind!

"I will help you set the table. You can warm up the food." With a fluttering heart, I pushed onto his chest, which brought me no luck. I couldn't move him for a thread.

But then he thought of something, and with a deep sigh, he moved from me. He moved enough for me to slip out of the trap. I went to look for the dishes as he moved towards the oven to warm up the food in utter silence.

When Vaughn put the bowl in the oven, he turned around and kept his eyes firmly on me—checking my every nook and curve. If he didn't move his eyes any sooner, I would drop the plates and wake up the entire mansion for sure.

"My plate is the blue one."

"There is no blue plate here." There wasn't.

"It's on the rack above your head."

I looked up. Yup, I could see some blue plates there. But it was too high for my reach. I stood on my toes to reach them, but only my fingertip could touch the plates. There was a chance I would drop it if I tried anymore.

"Help me with the plate." I had to ask.

"Didn't you tell me you wanted me to help with setting the table?" he asked, playfully raising his brow.

"Okay, fine!"

He was playing with me. No need. I would try to reach it myself.

I again tried to reach for the plate. This time, I could touch a little more of it. Maybe I could... Then suddenly, I felt warmth behind me. The tempting, fresh, woody scent again filled my nostrils. My brain again went hazy.

He stepped closer to me. So close that my back was touching his front. Slowly, he reached for the plate and effortlessly brought it down, and kept it on the kitchen island.

But he didn't move.

His fingers touched my shoulder. Then slowly, taking his sweet time, he traced my bare arms and then gradually reached my thin waist. Just when his fingers reached my waist, they paused for a few seconds there, pinching the flesh. Then he moved downwards and brushed his palm over my round, firm, curvy butt.

When I felt the squeeze, I gasped. At that instant, a feeling of soft, warm lips dropped on my bare shoulder.

I was almost panting.

Does it feel the same when someone runs a marathon?

The oven beeps brought me out of the trance, and I moved away from him faster. He didn't stop me. Maybe he was in a stupor as well? He looked so.

I set the table as he brought the food on it. He served the food on both of our plates in silence. His body was tense, and deep eyes never left mine. The look on his face was how it looked when one was forced to restrain himself from something he craved for. What did he crave for?

Me?

But isn't it me who craved him?

How did it happen?

Vaughn went up and brought two wine glasses, along with an expensive wine bottle. He poured the clear drink for the two of us and sat again in his chair. The air was so tense around us as we ate the food silently.

It was the most intense meal I ever had. Under his scrutinizing gaze, I felt my body tremble as I ate. It was true; I had been much more used to being around him than I was first when I met him in the garden tonight. Even so, it wasn't enough.

Especially when he was chewing his food and looking as if he would much rather prefer to eat me.

When we were done with our food and were yet to finish the drink, he asked me a question out of the blue.

"Do you like someone?"

I almost choked on my drink. I coughed as I calmed my nerves, but he didn't even flinch. His eyes were boring on me.

"Yes. I do, actually."

You.

His jaw tensed, and his body stiffened even further.

"Who?" Anger fuming from his tone as he asked that.

"I don't prefer to talk about it," I said, hiding my face behind the wine glass. Why did I have to say yes? I could say no! Maybe I thought it was the furthest confession I could make?

61

"Talk. I need to know who my girl desires," he said. There was a certain authority, power, and arrogance in his voice that I hadn't heard until now.

"I'm not your girl, don't start a confusion!"

"Confusion?" he let out a chuckle, then leaned on towards me with his elbows on the table, and said, "You are my girl, Sugar. Mine only. The sooner you settle this in your mind, the better."

Before I could say something, he again asked, "Who is he?" his eyes searching for an answer on my face.

"It's not someone you should know about. I am done eating. Thanks for the night. I'll go to sleep now. Goodnight." I stood up and turned on my heels at once. To run from him.

Under his eyes, I felt naked. Not just my body, my soul, too.

Just when I was about to leave the kitchen, his firm hands pulled me, gripping my wrists, and pulled me towards him. Just to trap me against the wall and his body.

I couldn't even look into his eyes. He pinched my chin and made me look into his eyes as his other hand gripped my waist protectively, both of our breaths coming in short and heavy.

"Look into my eyes, Xena. Why do I feel it's me who you like?" he asked, testing me.

"I have someone. You… you and me… we can't. You are a Wolf. Also, you are Ron's brother! We can't!"

"Can't or won't? Also, if you have someone in your mind, why would your body react when around me? At my words? At my touch?" he said, with a light brush of his nose at the edges of my ears, breathing hard into my ear. Making my hormones have a party of their own. I realized the sound of him breathing into my ear was an instant turn-on for me.

I tried to push him from me but couldn't manage to move him an inch. My hands could only feel his rapid heartbeats that were drumming inside his chest.

He moved his hands higher and brushed my nipples with his thumbs, cupping my heavy breasts over the flimsy silk.

"If you don't feel anything towards me, tell me why your nipples have been so hard the entire night? Why did you get goosebumps at our proximity?"

His voice was so seductive it sounded like moans to my ear. I bit my lips to control the moans that threatened to come out of my throat as he started dropping soft kisses on my neck that melted me more and more. But when he licked the spot, I could no longer control the moans anymore.

The moment I moaned, his grip on my body tightened.

"Your skin tastes fucking delicious. I bet you taste good everywhere else," he said. The man was practically growling in my ear.

I gripped the fabric of his shirt at his waist... eyes still shut tightly. His exotic scent overwhelmed my senses.

"You say we can't. You say you like someone. Then why is the back of your nighty so wet? You are dripping, Sugar. Are you that hungry for me? How can I let you go without a taste if you crave me so much?" Vaughn shifted his head so that his lips were just a centimeter away from mine.

Just a centimeter, and I could kiss him. I could kiss Vaughn!

Oh, snuggly blankets! Am I really going to kiss the only man I fantasize about?

My mind lost all its rationality when I dipped my head a little to press my lips on his.

But he moved his head just in time.

What just happened?

"I will only let you have my taste when you submit to your feelings for me. Not a second before you accept the fact that you are my girl."

My soul cried. I wanted to taste him so hard!

63

"Will be waiting for your call, Sugar. Come to me soon. I can't wait to have a proper taste of you. I have so much planned for us. Don't torture us anymore." He dropped a kiss on my earlobe.

His fingers were almost going to brush over my cleavage when I pushed his hands and somehow ran from there.

"Xena, wait!" He called me from the back. I stopped in my tracks but didn't dare to look behind.

"Talking about sleeping in dampen clothing. Don't forget to change your panties before you go to bed, Sugar."

12 | Dissonance

Xena

With a slight disruption, I opened my eyes. As I looked around, I found it was still dark outside. Before I could adjust my eyes properly, I felt a weight on me, and a little shriek escaped past my lips as I looked at the body hovering over mine on his all fours.

Vaughn.

He was breathing hard. Evident desire sparkled through the dazzling moonlight reflecting in his eyes. His warm breath brought me out of my trance.

"No. Can't sleep without tasting you. Can't let my girl sleep feeling deprived when I'm right here. Kiss me, Xena. Kiss me, Sugar. Be mine. *Be my girl.*"

My eyes focused on his *suckable*, soft lips, and my mouth watered to have a taste of him.

"Once you taste my lips, I'm going to shove my cock into your mouth, right down into your throat, until you choke on it. Then I'll cream into your mouth, so you taste me. You taste me well and for good. So that you only want to taste me for the rest of your life."

I was dying to taste him. Only God knew how much.

With my index finger, I touched his lips ever so gently. Soft. So soft. I was right. Vaughn kept staring into my eyes, continuing to look into my soul.

Wordlessly, he stayed like that, boring into my soul and offering himself to me—for me to taste him. I moved my hand to dig into his hair and gripped a handful of it. Then slowly brought him close to mine...

A little... just a little more... and then his lips would be on mine...

Suddenly he mumbled, saying, "Jay, kiss me."

Wait. Something was wrong. He didn't call me Jay... only Ron did.

"Jay," Vaughn again called me.

Suddenly I felt like he was pulling away far from me... I tried to have a grip on him, but I couldn't. He was taken far, far away! So far that I couldn't see him anymore. As if he was sucked into a light. I couldn't even taste him, not even a little!

"Jay! What are you dreaming about? Why are you so scared?"

I heard Ron's voice.

I opened my eyes and closed them abruptly because of the heavy, shiny sunlight. Ron was hovering over me, calling me again and again.

I was dreaming. No, it wasn't Vaughn. He didn't come.

"I was just dreaming, Ron. I'm okay," I said, in mumbles with a heavy, gloomy heart.

"Wake up now, boo! I'm hungry." She continued rushing me.

"Give me fifteen minutes."

When I went downstairs, I found Ron waiting for me. She looked all normal once again. No trace of yesterday's panic attack was there. She looked exactly like the Ron I knew. Seeing her, I couldn't help but walk near her and hug her.

"I have been waiting for you. Mom and dad already had their breakfast. Come have some cheese omelets. They are the best!" Ron served a portion of the food on my plate as I sat beside her.

She didn't say anything about Vaughn. I couldn't even see him. Where was he?

"Where is everyone?"

"Mom and dad are in their studies."

And Vaughn?

Also, her parents were home for only two days, and they were locked in their studies? What kind of parents were they?

"Oh…" I was disappointed, not knowing where he was, but decided not to ask anything about it.

"How did you sleep?"

"Great! I didn't wake up until Vee woke me up this morning. He made me promise him I will have a kingly breakfast with you once you wake up."

"He seems like a perfect brother. I'm so happy that you got him by your side, Ron. Anyhow, I didn't see him this morning," I said, trying to sound casual. But inside, I had waves of emotion at his thoughts.

"Vee? I thought he was rude to you, so I decided not to mention him before you. He left. My brother is a busy man. He said he tried, but he had somewhere important to attend. If it weren't important, he wouldn't have left me." Ron sighed with a gloomy face.

Oh… he left. I couldn't see him one last time before he left.

Back in my mind, his business card that I shoved deep inside my duffle bag flashed.

"Will be waiting for your call, Sugar. Come to me soon. I can't wait to have a proper taste of you. I have so much planned for us. Don't torture us anymore."

I couldn't wait too, Vaughn…

It still felt surreal to me. How the only person you crush on felt the same way for you. It felt too easy. So easy that the thought of being with Vaughn scared me.

Mr. and Mrs. Wolf left before lunch. They didn't even bother to spend two full days with their daughter, who was eager to spend her weekend with her parents. Ron looked like she would cry any moment. Her face looked like a little, sad girl. Whose parents were busy elsewhere, giving her less priority. The only difference here was that she was a big girl who still craved her parents' affection.

As they left, I hugged her from the back.

"Boo, let's go home. We have got the day and night. Why not hit the club tonight? What do you say?" I wanted to cheer her up at any cost.

"Let's go home," Ron said in a whisper, and then left. Probably to prepare her luggage.

When we reached our apartment, Ron went for a bath. Both of us loved long aroma baths to relax our nerves. When Ron went to her room, I went to mine. Besides, I needed some time to think of the man. The man who came into the night to stroll in the garden and claimed it to be a tryst. Then later had dinner with me, claiming that to be our first date.

He was also the man who touched almost everywhere on my body and my soul with his possessive hands and mouth, claiming me to be his girl—not even waiting for my approval!

He touched me like he owned me...

He just declared me as his...

... the same man with whom I had all my dirty, bizarre fantasies. *Oh, Vaughn...*

How did I get him so effortlessly? How could he come to me so easily? A man like him... I could only dream. How did it become my reality?

What was the catch?

The dream kept poking me over and over. I wanted him... and I wanted to kiss the hell out of him. He challenged me, right? I wanted to show him what it was to challenge Xena Meyers. My entire body was electrified, burning in extreme need and desire for his touch. Vaughn was definitely passable as an expensive, addictive drug I couldn't go without. I knew I had a crush, but then, after an innocent night with him, ruined me forever.

The night was innocent, right? After all, we didn't hump on each other... even though I wanted to. So bad. Also, I knew how much he wanted to. He did nothing to hide his desire from me.

My thoughts were disrupted when I got a text.

Leo: I'm just sitting around wearing only my underwear. What are you doing, sweetie?

I looked at the text for a long while. By now, I was used to Leo's weird and funny texts. What was wrong with this guy? Did I really kiss him that night? He looked pretty normal while we were dancing. Who the heck was this guy?

Xena: I just casually pulled a huge booger out of my nostrils. Another left.

I laughed as I replied. *Huh! Take it, bish...*

Leo: Eww! Why did you tell me that?!

Xena: Why? I thought we were talking dirty!

Leo: Bye...

Xena: Already going? Okay :(bye.

Leo: We are no more exclusive.

Xena: Why? You don't like a dirty... dirty girl?

Leo: I hate you! Too dirty for my majestic taste!

I laughed out loud, reading his texts. He was a great company to be with. Since that night at the club, we hadn't talked about meeting for another date, but we kept texting, and I loved it. Also, thinking of Vaughn... things definitely changed for me.

For lunch, I quickly made some spaghetti, according to Ron's liking. We both loved it in red sauce with lots of spice. Then checked the fridge to see if we had enough ice cream and beer. I prepared everything to comfort my best friend and then went to look for her.

No matter how many series or movies were out there, we still loved to watch re-runs of '*Sex And The City*.' It never went old for us. I turned on the TV as we devoured the spaghetti. After we finished, I brought the cookie dough ice cream. Then I snuggled close to Ron, so that we were side-hugging like sisters, and silently enjoyed our ice cream as we watched the show.

It was our way of cheering each other up. Just to be there for each other whenever the other was in pain. At some point, Ron ditched the ice cream and hugged me tight as she kept her head on my shoulder and watched the series. I felt a few drops of tears on my t-shirt and clutched her hand that was draped around me.

"I am here for you, Ron," I said in a whisper.

"You didn't need to see that." Ron's voice cracked.

"So what? So what if I have seen? Now I understand my best friend better than before." I said in reassurance.

"Are you sure you are here for me? Will you always be there for me?"

I saw hope in her eyes.

"I will, Ron. Besides, isn't your Vee always there for you? Now you also have me. You always had both of us. Don't you know that?"

Ron's eyes sparkled right away when she heard her brother's name. "Yes, he is the best brother in the world. When I had no one, he was there for me. Since our parents never really paid any attention to us, we were each other's strength, support, and shoulder. He is my father, my mother, and my brother. He is everything to me."

"You know, when any of our parents were angry with me, Vee always used to take the beat for me. He always saved me. When I cried, he gave me his shoulder to cry on. But you know, he never cried before me. He has always snatched the pain and froze inside him... to save me."

"Well... even after everything, Vee still gave me his shoulder, no matter what happened. I always had him. Now I have got you too. What else do I need in life? I don't need my parents. I don't need them."

I didn't say anything, just hugged her tight and let her tears pour, weighing down her heavy heart. Soon Ron calmed down with my tight embrace and light strokes in her hair,

But while I calmed her down, the restlessness in me kept increasing by folds. Ron and Vaughn were so close to each other. Dating my best friend's brother was a big no-no. I couldn't cross the line for my benefit. If somehow Ron disapproved of this, it'd undoubtedly create a fuss in three of our lives. I couldn't do that. I always knew he was my fantasy, so I should let it be how it was to protect the three of us. Nothing started, and I won't let it. I couldn't gamble with three lives. Especially not with theirs, no matter how much pain it'd cause me.

With a heavy, broken heart, I looked at Ron.

"Still up for clubbing?" I asked, smirking at her when she finally relaxed.

Ron sat straight and wiped her eyes using the back of her sleeve. Then, smiling at me, she said, "Yes, bitch!"

My Ron is finally back!

We hit a different club that night, as Ron didn't prefer going to his brother's clubs in his presence. Vaughn was in town, which meant he might have been in any of his clubs that night. So we hit the regular club that we visited whenever Vaughn was in town, Club Empressa.

On my way, I got another text from Leo, so I eventually ended up saying where we were heading to. Leo was free, so he decided to tag along. I didn't mind his presence, since these days, we had become quite friendly with each other. Besides, I needed distraction as well.

Just as we entered the club, Ron hit the bar, as always. But today, she was unusually interested in alcohol. To keep an eye on her, I didn't drink much. I declined all the drinks that the guys offered me and just kept moving with the conversation with Ron.

Soon, a pretty cute blonde guy with light blue, dreamy eyes offered Ron a drink. Ron wasn't interested in anyone's offer earlier, but ended up accepting it from him. Besides, he looked kind of genuine as well.

"Hi, I'm Bryan. I have been watching you for quite a long time. You look upset, and it's not a good look on your pretty face," he asked with a voice full of genuineness.

"How do you know if I'm upset?" Ron asked.

"This is not the first time I have seen you around here. But every time I'm late, and someone snatches you away. Tonight, I got you, finally." He grinned, then said, "As for how I know you are upset, well, I know how you look other nights. So I can compare. There is a certain gloominess in your eyes, and they are slightly swollen. Your friend is also not drinking to take care of you, and you are rejecting every guy... should I go on?"

"No, no, I got you," Ron said, amused at his observation.

"So, will you grant me the honor of dancing with you tonight, Miss—" he asked.

"Veronica Wolf. You can call me Veronica."

"Well, Veronica, care to dance with me tonight?" He offered his hand.

Ron looked at me with a smile, and we had our eye-to-eye conversation. Then she put her hand in his to move towards the dance floor.

Just as she left, Leo entered. As expected, after Leo arrived, we joked around and danced the night away together.

There was no inappropriate touching or kissing this time. We just enjoyed dancing and throwing weird, funny lines at each other.

But in the back of my mind, one person never let me forget his existence. His existence kept roaring at me every time I took a breath.

Vaughn.

13 | Indecisiveness

Xena

"I hate how you always eat a cow but never gain any weight!"

I whined, looking at Ron, who was busy devouring her cheesy pasta. In contrast, I had to workout for an extra hour when I went for such a bowl of cheesy pasta. That didn't mean I didn't like it. I did, but I couldn't eat like her.

"Really, bitch? Are you still talking with those curves of yours? I could die for them." Ron raised a brow at me.

"Ron, you are the hot one, and you know it. Just look around, and you don't even have to work for it!" I rested my chin on my palms as I supported my hands on my elbows, looking at her devouring the pasta.

"Gosh… Jay, a guy could get lost in those boobs and ass, and we won't even find him ever again." Ron was melodramatic, as usual.

"What a drama queen!" I slapped my forehead at her silliness.

"What? Don't you believe me? Why don't you ask him then?" Ron said, smirking almost as devilishly as her brother, reminding me once more about the man who could never be mine.

I shrugged away the thought and scrunched my nose. "Who?"

"Hey, beautiful!" Jack sat beside me with a cheerful grin.

"Hey loser, here to get dumped again?" Ron teased him intentionally.

Jack looked at Ron with venom in his eyes and then looked back at me with gentleness.

"Do you have a minute, Xena? Please? I will even beg if you want."

I looked at his pleading eyes and felt some sort of pity for the guy. If I didn't listen, he would keep pestering me tirelessly, and I knew that.

"Okay, five minutes."

Jack's eyes sparkled at her three words. He stood up at once and said, "Let's go outside where we can have some privacy." He glared at Ron as he said that.

I wordlessly walked over and showed him the way to follow me. Jack followed me like a lost puppy, the grin never faltering from his pretty face. As we reached under a big tree, I stopped there. Most of the students were at the cafeteria for lunch, so we had some privacy there.

"Talk."

"Xena, I have been pinning over you for almost two years. Don't you feel pity for me even once?"

"What do you expect from me? A relationship must be consensual. And here, I don't consent. I'm sorry, Jack. You and I are not compatible."

"How do you know that? You haven't agreed to even one date with me! Maybe after a date, you'll see me differently."

"That's where you are wrong, Jack. I know what I want from my partner. It's not you. My mind won't change. I don't want you to waste your valuable time on me when all these girls are ready to do anything for you."

"I'll forever be hanging on to you, regretting not taking you out on one date. I'll always keep wondering, what if you changed your mind after that? Xena, I don't think I'll ever be able to move on," He said, begging. The guy looked so pitiful I was almost scared he might even drop to his knees.

"So, if after a date, my mind doesn't change, will you stop pursuing me?"

"Does it mean you agree to go on a date with me?" Jack's gloomy face sparkled once again.

"One date. In a public place. I prefer Club Empressa. If I don't change my mind, you will never try to pursue me ever, are we agreed?"

"I will change your mind. Just wait and see!" Jack said with a grin and took a brave step forward to put a kiss on my cheek.

Before I could react, the bell rang, and he said, "Friday, at seven. Be ready, beautiful."

Then he ran away.

I shook my head in cringe and walked towards my class.

After the classes, I waited beside Ron's BMW. None of our classes matched after lunch that day. So just when she found me beside her car, she came running.

"Tell me everything! How did everything with the loser lover boy go?" Ron asked. Her excitement knew no boundaries. She always found peace teasing him.

"Let's get in the car, Weirdo!" I pulled her into the car and placed her in the driver's seat.

"I agreed to go on a date with him this Friday. He needs closure. Or else he'll keep pursuing me, no matter what," I said, after Ron started the engine.

"Are you sure you want to go on a date with such a loser? I'm sure his tongue is in the cheerleader's throat at this moment. You have so many admirers, Jay! Argh! Why him!"

"I just tol—" Ron stopped me before I could finish.

"Yeah, yeah… I know. It's just he is such a loser! He doesn't deserve you!" Ron said, expressing her displeasure.

I just chuckled at her worry and possessiveness. I loved this girl.

I turned on the music to sing for the rest of our way to the apartment. Both of us sang along with Nicki Minaj as we laughed our guts out.

From the corner of my eyes, I noticed Ron's cellphone flash several times, notifying incoming texts. I furrowed my brows in confusion, but didn't say anything. Who could it be?

When we finally reached home, I noticed her running into her room, clutching her cell phone against her chest.

I wondered even more…

Who could it be? Surprisingly, she returned home pretty early last night. I thought she hit it off with the Bryan guy. But then she returned soon, and now holding her phone for dear life. Besides, someone was texting her constantly.

Later that night, when we were busy having dinner, I noticed Ron sitting with her cellphone lying beside her once again. She never kept her phone close all the time. I got a little more confused at her unusual behavior, but didn't pry, anyway.

She was supposed to tell me if it was anything serious, wasn't she?

When she was almost done eating, her phone started ringing.

"I'm done! Today is your day for dishes!" She ran with the phone faster than ever.

When I lay on my bed with a book, all I could think about was the card I shoved deep inside my desk drawer. My heart was aching to call that man. He was my dream, a dream I always thought was way out of my reach. Just when I got a glimpse of it, reality hit me hard and snatched him away from me.

Since the moment I woke up from sleep after spending time with Vaughn, all I was doing was keeping myself distracted from his thoughts. The man had been absorbed deep inside my skin. No matter how hard I rubbed, I couldn't get him off of under my skin.

Once again, I distracted my thoughts from him and called my father.

"Hey, dad! How is everything there?"

"Hey, princess… we are fine here. How about you? Everything alright?"

"Yeah. How about mom? Is she alright now?"

"She is doing fine. Your sister is here. It helped your mom's blood pressure level."

"Aliza is there? Everything okay?"

"Yeah. Samuel is out for a work trip, so your sister came to visit for a few days."

"Oh, that's amazing! It's good for mom. She'll be busy for a few days."

"You know your sister. They are out shopping and kitty-partying mostly," dad chuckled.

"I'm just happy that Aliza can be there when I'm stuck here for such a long time. Don't worry, dad… I'll be there for the whole summer break. I miss you all way too much."

"You won't come for spring break? It's very close."

"I haven't made a plan for spring break yet. I'll tell you, dad," I said.

"Alright. Let us know, okay?"

"I'll call mom tomorrow. You have to take care of both of you, alright?"

"Okay, princess. Don't forget to let me know if any boy bothers you. I'll come right away, okay?"

"Of course, who would even dare when I have a super dad like you?" I smiled.

"Right. Love you, princess."

"Love you, dad."

It always brought a smile to my face while I talked to dad. He was my star, my superhero, my idol… everything. I had never seen such a hardworking, honest, loving father and husband ever in my life. And I didn't think it was just because he was my father. It was because he was genuinely such a wonderful man.

With a smile on my lips, I picked up my nail paint pouch as I walked towards Ron's room. What was going on in her life? I felt the need to have a talk with her.

When I entered her room after a knock, I found her reclining on the bed, hugging a pillow. I walked in with a grin and jumped on her bed.

"Hey, Ron, we haven't painted nails for a long time. Let's do it." I opened the zip bag and held it upside down. All the nail polishes dropped on the bed, making a mess.

"What is it, Jay?" Ron asked me with a guilty face.

It was a tradition between us. Whenever we had anything serious or sensitive to discuss, we painted each other's nails and opened ourselves gradually to each other. We never talked about it, but even then, it had always been like that. So, naturally, Ron knew there was something wrong, and more specifically, she knew what was wrong. That was exactly why she looked guilty.

"Is there anything you want to tell me, Ron?" I chose bright red for me, while she chose hot pink for herself.

"You always know, don't you?" she asked as I snatched the color from her hand and put one of her feet in my lap.

None of us were making any eye contact, as usual.

"Remember Bryan?" she asked hesitantly.

"Hmm. The guy from last night." *What's with him?*

"It was love at first sight for both of us. He has been in love with me for a long time. Besides, last night I liked him right away. I didn't want you to judge me. I know it's a rushed decision…" Ron trailed off.

"Ron… it's okay, boo. I won't judge you. You can tell me," I said, encouraging her to continue, but deep inside, I knew it was rushed. She didn't know anything about him and his background.

"Sure you won't judge me?" She looked at me.

I looked into her eyes.

"Yes. I'm here for you. Tell me everything."

"After we hit it off last night, I brought him here."

It surprised me to see her eyes looking dreamy in reminiscence. I didn't realize there was a guy in our apartment last night. Ron came

78

early. She never came home early if she had a one-night stand. Leo dropped me home when Ron persisted in staying and not touching any more alcohol. I knew when Ron promised me something. She never broke it.

I silently kept on painting her toenails, encouraging her to continue.

"You won't believe it, Jay. We were up all night. But we never went past kissing! Both of us are so suited for each other! We have so many similarities... We talked all night, and then, later on, he kissed me to sleep. For the first time in life, I snuggled and kissed someone!"

My eyes went up. That was *so* not Ron. Bryan must be someone special. No other guy had ever affected Ron like he did last night. That also without sex.

"He expressed his earnest, honest feelings for me last night when we kissed. I thought he would forget me once he left. But no. We have been sending each other texts all day. Jay, it might sound crazy, but I think I'm really, *really* liking this guy..." Ron trailed off, not knowing how to finish.

"If it's really how you feel, then, of course, I'm there for you, boo. If it's how you find your happiness, I'll never judge you. You know that." I hugged Ron.

Ron hugged me tighter.

"I thought you'd lecture me about being rushed and careful and all."

"Of course, I'll lecture you as long as I'm worried about you. But not the way you think I'll. I would just suggest that you know him more before you dive into the deeper feelings," I said, worrying about her.

"Of course, I'll, boo. Do you think Vee will let him go easily if he finds out that I'm serious about him?"

I chuckled and thought about how he said he only passed sleepless nights when he worried about his beloved ones. So I knew the answer, *No, definitely he won't.*

That night, as I went to sleep, I kept thinking about how Ron and I shared everything. We knew about each other so easily. Also, we were so quickly worried about each other. We had never been able to hide anything from one another. There was no way I could ever hide dating Vaughn from her. Besides, one day or another, she would know about us. It would be cheating on her. Everyone knew dating a best friend's brother was forbidden.

Could I afford to cross the line?

No, I can't do that. I can't.

14 | Date Bait

Xena

It had been an entire week since I met Vaughn. Every night before I went to sleep, I took his card out from the back of the drawer and was lost in the thought of him. His card was the only rope binding us together, only possession of Vaughn that belonged to me. Standing to his word, Vaughn didn't call me, and somehow, I knew he had been waiting for my call all this time.

But no, I can't!

Not a single night passed when I didn't think of him ravishing me on the bench in the garden. Or maybe on the kitchen island, wall, or floor... wherever he wished to. There was so much lust, desire, and dominance in his eyes that I could only imagine what an exquisite lover he'd be in bed, or wherever it was.

Every night, when I closed my eyes, I could only think of his tongue on me, his fingers all over my body, and his cock inside me, pounding me hard. I dreamed of his lips on me, the lips that I desired like nothing I'd ever craved before.

The warmth of his large palms, the touch of his soft lips, contrasted his firm grip on my body. Then again, both drove me wild from just replaying them over and over in my mind. Also, when I thought of the sight of his massive bulge... Gosh... Vaughn drove me insane. And he didn't even kiss me yet!

Night after night, I got off from my hands thinking of the man pinning me against the wall, pounding hard inside me, him sucking me dry on the kitchen island, or me riding him on the garden bench... but nothing quenched my need for him. It only left me wanting more and more of the man. I wanted him. I wanted him so bad…

Oh, snuggles! I need help!

After a long agonizing week, finally, it was Friday. After all the ache and pain from my heartbreak throughout the week, when I thought about my date with Jack, I became positive about it gradually.

Jack was a playboy. He had wanted me forever just because he couldn't get me in the first place. He was used to having girls around just by a single look, whereas I never fell into his trap. So, technically, a date or maybe a night with him was all it would take to throw him out of my system? Also, if I got laid, perhaps the thought of Vaughn would be out of my system as well.

Fantasizing about him was okay, but he ruined me with the single card. I was practically this close to forgetting about Ron and calling him, asking him to take me, right then and there. I felt like a horn taco, a bitch with a high, burning libido.

What if I was this crazy for Vaughn just because I needed to get laid? I would never get Vaughn as he was off-limits. So, I would rather take *anything* to help me get him out of my system.

I intentionally picked the club that Vaughn didn't own. Club Empressa was the club Ron and I chose when we wanted to avoid Vaughn. So, there wasn't a chance for me to run into him. God knew what his reaction would be if we ran across each other again. Would he talk to me anymore? Would he look at me? Did he hate me already? The thought of him hating me brought extreme discomfort to my heart.

When the clock hit six pm, I was already busy choosing a proper outfit. Suddenly, Ron barged into my room without knocking, as always, and noticed my piles of dresses everywhere.

"You are this excited to date that loser lover boy?" She furrowed her brows.

"Ron, don't be mean… What's your plan for tonight?" I changed the topic as I chose a black midi dress. It was sleeveless, and the neckline was pretty decent. I opted for a bra, not thinking much about it. That dress didn't need one.

I reminded myself *if it happens tonight, it happens.*

If anything, it could help me get Vaughn out of my system... *perhaps.*

A girl could hope, couldn't she? It was getting awfully torturous to live with such burning desires for a man who was off-limits.

"Bryan is visiting. We decided to take it slow. He is the first guy I love spending time with. Till now, all dating was for me was fucking some random guys. But Jay, Bryan is amazing! I hope sometimes you can spend a day with us. You'll love him once you know him better." Ron's eyes sparkled.

"Ron, if he makes you happy, then he is already my favorite. I'll soon make some time out to interrogate the lover-boy. Don't think I'll let him get with you so easily. He has to go through me." I raised my brow at her in a challenge.

"Okay! Boo! Fine. What I'm scared of most is Vee. You have no idea how protective he can get. He is just like the possessive, protective, dominant alpha we read about nowadays in novels. If he doesn't like Bryan, consider him dead," Ron said, there was clear fear written in her eyes.

My heart flipped inside.

Hiding my arousal and needy eyes from Ron, I sat on the ottoman before my vanity and concentrated on putting moisturizer on my face.

"I'm sure if Bryan is as awesome as you say, your brother will like him. Don't worry about it." I felt my kitty throbbing already.

"You are right. Vee has an expert eye to know people, but you don't know his alpha behaviors. When his alpha mode is on, even I fear standing before him. Thank god he doesn't have a girlfriend yet. I even pity his future wife. Poor girl..." Ron tsked.

Can I be the poor girl, pretty please?

Clearing my throat, I said, "If I don't return tonight, don't panic. Also, be careful. If there is anything fishy, call your brother or me. Don't waste a second. Okay?"

"Okay, boo. Don't worry about me. I wish you get thoroughly fucked tonight. We should get at least something good from the loser lover boy, don't we? Just don't forget to wrap his overused junk." Ron reached me and hugged my neck from the back.

I chuckled at her funny face as she said that.

Exactly at seven, Jack knocked at my door. He was in a light blue shirt and dark blue jeans. To be honest, he looked impressive. His attractive face and player ways were why girls were so crazy about him in college. So, it was expected from him to look extra handsome with any effort he put into looking presentable.

"You look beautiful, Xena." He offered me a bouquet of pink roses, and I smiled at him.

"Thanks, Jack. You cleaned up nice, too." I complimented him back.

He grinned at me as I turned around to put the flowers in a vase. Then, taking my purse and cell phone, I went out with him.

His Mercedes-Benz was waiting in front of my apartment. This was the very first time I was sitting inside his car. Usually, I see jack making out on the hood of this car. My body shuddered at the yucky thought, and I tried not to cringe, thinking any more about it.

Jack wrapped a possessive hand around my waist when we entered the club, as if he was proud to be showing up in the club with me. I didn't think much of it and followed him inside. We went directly to the bar and sat on the stools.

This was the first time I had gone to a club without Ron. Usually, it was Ron, and I who hit the bar together. I was slightly confused about what to drink with him. Should I drink less? Or should I get drunk and live away the night with Jack, forgetting *him*?

I decided to get drunk, but not enough to make any wrong decisions. Decisions such as not wrapping his junk. I chuckled inwardly, recalling what Ron said.

"Two years, and I still can't get over the fact of how beautiful you are, Xena," Jack said, staring at me in a daze.

"What is it in me you like so much?"

"Everything about you drives me crazy. You are the most beautiful girl I have ever seen. Mostly, your smile. You never usually smile at me, but I notice you. You have the prettiest smile, Xena. It drives me crazier for you every time I see."

Wow, the guy is good with words.

One more reason why girls flock around him.

"Jack, it's just... I'm not really looking for a serious relationship now. You can get any girl you want."

"A man can only dream. Only if I could ever have you by my side, you'll be the only one for me, Xena. You are all I want. Tell me, how to be your man?" Jack asked with a solemn expression.

"I... honestly, what I want in my man... I couldn't find it in anyone around me. I'm sorry, Jack. We can still enjoy the night and maybe see where it goes?" I asked in hesitance.

I couldn't just let my secret slip. Just thinking about what I needed brought unimaginable hunger into me. Probably, the drinks started to kick in, and I was hungry.

Hungry for what? Right. My brain was still working.

In response, my pussy throbbed, letting my brain know exactly about what it was hungry for.

Just as I was having an intimate conversation with my body parts, he noticed something in my eyes. Did he detect my hunger? His eyes flashed with something, and he asked, "What do you want in a man, beautiful? Are you sure I can't give you that?"

As he asked, I felt his hand on my upper thigh. He was bringing it closer and closer to my kitty. Not that I didn't like it, but I wanted to feel more. More of everything.

I looked around and found that no one could see us. It was in public, but behind the public eyes. Only those who are upstairs could see us if they really looked. The sneaky thought hardened my nipples instantly in anticipation. Jack's eyes went to my nipples at once and darkened. I was such a slut for the night for not wearing a bra at a club and doing the nasty in public, wasn't I?

He was almost there. Almost. I bit my lips with burning anticipation and shut my eyes.

Could he make me come? Could he make me feel bliss?

But catching both of us off the guard, we got interrupted by someone behind me, poking my shoulder.

"Ms. Meyers, sorry to interrupt your conversation. Boss demands to see you. Upstairs, at the VVIP lounge. Please make it quick. He doesn't appreciate waiting." I looked back to find a tall, brawny, handsome man in a formal suit standing behind me. At a glance, he looked like a very charming bodyguard of some wealthy businessman.

I was beyond annoyed at being interrupted. The tingle in between my legs needed to be cared for. Snapping at the handsome stranger, I asked, "Who is your boss? And what is his business with me?"

"He just said that you want to see him, and you'll be delighted once you go see him. Please make it faster. You don't want him to be pissed off. He really despises waiting."

I scrunched my brows in confusion. Who was this boss? And why would I be happy to see the guy? What did he want from me? Besides, he was making me high and dry. Obviously, I wouldn't be thrilled to see him.

"Who is this guy? Do you even know him? Let me come with you," Jack asked, furrowing his brows, clearly equally irritated.

"Let me go and check it out fast. Okay?"

His eyes were hazy with lust, and he wasn't ready to let me go. Besides, it wasn't long we'd arrived in the club.

86

"I'll come looking for you if you are late, okay?"

"Yeah," I agreed. He didn't know I knew self-defense, and I could save myself pretty effortlessly.

Then I followed the guy towards the VVIP room to meet this anonymous, intriguing, tardy boss.

There were securities at the door. Once they saw me, they opened the door for me right away. Was it my illusion, or did they bow to me to show respect?

As I entered the room, an irresistible, manly scent hit my nostrils, and the tingles between my legs started letting me know of its presence once again. To my surprise, I found the room totally empty until my eyes found their way towards the glass wall that granted the full view of the club's ground floor.

He stood there. I could only see his back, but it already made me feel hot in awkward places. The silhouette looked familiar to me, and it was kind of drawing me towards him. He had sleek black hair, broad shoulders with bulging muscles, which showed through his expensive suit. His hands were tucked inside his pockets, making his rear look tighter and more defined.

I felt my mouth water at the striking sight. So tall, so sexy, so manly... So hot.

"You are late."

I swore I could come from that deep, sexy voice of his alone. Who was this man? Wait, why did it sound familiar? I shrugged away the absurd thought peeking in my mind and furrowed my brows.

"Who are you? Why did you force me to come to see you?"

"Because *you* want to."

"What the fuck are you talking about? I don't even know you! Why would I want to see you in the middle of a date? I was very much enjoying my date!"

"Is that so?" he asked. Then he slowly, he turned around with a very prominent smirk on his face.

Vaughn.

15 | Claiming

Xena

I kept staring at the man standing before me. The man, who I had been avoiding since I met him... since he declared me as his... since he challenged me to come to him willingly. I hadn't, but God knew how much I wanted to. How much I struggled every day thinking of running to him, dropping to my knees, and then sucking him good to compensate for my tardiness.

The man was currently standing before me with all his glory.

There was no gentleness, no playfulness in his eyes like the night we spent knowing each other. This time, his eyes held raw dominance, possessiveness, and fume.

I suddenly remembered what Ron told me about his alpha traits.

Snuggly blankets! You are dead, Xena... he has probably seen what you were about to do downstairs...

I felt my breathing speed up just by his sight. In the shadowy black suit, the man looked illegal. He looked like something dark that would destroy me with a single touch, but I was dying to have a taste of him even when I knew that. I started having the urge of being destroyed if it meant that I could touch him, even if it were for once.

"Is that so, Xena? You enjoy having men touch and play with your pretty little pussy in public?" He slowly moved towards the couch in the middle of the room as he said that. Then undoing his suit button carelessly, he sat there with his leg spread and with his hands stretched out on the back of the couch. He sat there looking at me as if he was getting bored with my presence.

He saw me!

He blatantly said I was his, waited for my call the entire week, and then saw me dating some other guy just now. *Oh, blankets!* He didn't just see me on a date; he saw me almost getting fingered by some guy in public!

I gulped down the lump in my throat. I could support myself against the door and play with my pussy right here, right now, just by looking at this man before me, coming multiple times for sure. He looked that tempting.

"You... You were watching me..."

"Yes. I was. What I just saw, if it's really what you are into, then I can guarantee you, Sugar, that I can do it better."

My eyes widened, and my kitty clenched. I clasped my hands in a tight grip—only to control the tornado going on inside me. The man was the walking definition of sex. I was almost on the edge of my sweet release, that also, without even playing with my pussy.

"Wh-Why are you here? Club Empressa isn't yours..."

How did I walk right into the wolf's den? Just how unlucky was I?

He tilted his head a little with a mocking smirk hanging by his lips and said, "It is now."

Yup... my bad luck was even the worse of the worse...

"Come here."

There was some authority in his voice that I couldn't ignore. It pulled me towards him even before I could process his words, and before I realized what I was doing, I was already standing in front of him, looking down. My dreams started replaying in my mind.

"Sit on my lap."

That brought me out of my dream. *What did he just say?*

"Huh?"

"I said, sit on my lap, Sugar."

"I... I..." Before I could think of some meaningful words to say to him, he pulled me by my wrist and made me sit on his lap. That way, I was practically straddling him.

He pulled me closer by my hips and whispered in my ear. "Better..." Then his hand found its way to my hair, and gripping a handful, he pulled my ear closer to his suckable mouth and said. "You look better here. Right on my lap. Where you belong."

I moaned.

"Moaning already, Sugar? Not that I mind. Now I want to know more than before how you'll moan and scream when I tie you to my bed stands and then ruthlessly pound in your tight little cunt with my cock over and over again, till you pass out." His grip on my hair tightened as he murmured the words in my ear, brushing his nose against my neck, inhaling me deeply... as if I was his drug.

"I can't stop picturing that night. You bent over the kitchen island as I drank every last drop of cum coming out of your pussy. I can't stop picturing you lying before me, with all your golden locks spread over my pillow. Your legs on my shoulder as I pounce into your wet little cunt with my raging hard cock until you can't take anymore."

He paused to breathe... with every breath in my ear, taking my soul away.

"Even if you cry when it's too much for you, I won't slow down, Sugar. I'll not hold myself back. That will only make me thrust harder, faster, and rougher into you. I'll slap your ass, I'll pull your hair, and I'll choke your throat until your entire body turns red—deep red. I want you to scream. I want you to scream my name. I want you to gasp for air. I want you to scream so loud that everyone knows who you belong to. Even that pitiful excuse of a cunt who was about to touch what's mine."

"V-Vaughn..." I moaned once again. *Someone, please stop him!*

"Yes, Sugar? Anything else you want to add? Tell me. I'm all yours." Then he bit on my neck, with one of his hands still tightly gripping my waist and another fisting my hair.

I just clutched his shoulder tightly so that my body didn't limp entirely on him.

"Let me check what we have in here, hmm…"

He didn't ask. He just said that, and then bringing the hand from around my waist, he entered his hand under my dress. My dress had already bunched on my upper thigh due to straddling him. His hand seemed to get lost under my dress, and then I felt him cupping my core.

"Hmm... Hot. Scorching... sizzling hot. I like it."

I threw back my head and bit my lips at the close contact and scorching heat blazing from his large, possessive palm.

His grip on my hair tightened, and he brought my face back to him so that we could look eye to eye and then said in his dominant voice again. "Keep looking into my eyes when I touch you. You like men touching you there, right? Today, I'll ruin you for every man, Sugar. Then you'll crave for my touch only. No one else touches what's mine. You need to learn that the pussy belongs to me. The faster you learn, the better. You got that?"

I gasped and panted at his words and the anticipation.

I kept looking into his eyes, panting heavily, when I felt him entering his long, callous fingers inside my lacy lingerie.

I clutched his shoulder tighter.

"Wet... Soaking wet. Is it for that douche out there? Or for me, Sugar? Answer honestly. Tell me, dammit!" He sounded angry.

"You... You, Vaughn... You..." I truthfully admitted in a breathless, panting voice.

"Good girl." His mood changed at once.

Then he started stroking everywhere in my pussy, as if printing the picture in his head just by touching it. Just how painters do before they paint a wall. Yes, he painted my pussy with his possessive touch, painting me as his.

"Hmm... Plump pussy, ample clit, tight little whole, sensitive, responsive, and creamy. Just exactly what I dreamed of. You are hiding every man's wet dream in between your thighs, Sugar. But unfortunately, no one else is going to find it out anymore. The treasure belongs to me. It's exclusively mine from now on."

I couldn't. I couldn't anymore. My body went limp at Vaughn's words, and my head dropped on his chest, my body shaking.

"Not yet. I've not even started with you. Look at me."

Again with the alpha tone.

I used all my energy to look into his eyes. Hard. It was so hard.

I felt his finger rubbing rhythmically on my nub, then enter two of his fingers in me to stroke. Then he again brought it out to graze, then again entered to stroke. It went on a few times, building my impatience and frustration. At some point, I groaned against his forehead out of exasperation. He chuckled darkly, and at the same time, pinched my nub in a certain way that both pain and pleasure rushed throughout my entire body, making me scream and release right on his hands.

He paused and released my hair finally. Holding me tight by one of his strong arms as my swollen breasts heaved against his rock-hard chest heavily.

Slowly bringing out his fingers that were in my underwear, he showed me and asked, "See what a dirty girl you are. You've dirtied all over my fingers. Can you see how naughty and dirty you are, Sugar? You need to be tamed."

Then he keenly sniffed and licked all of it, making a delicious, contented sound.

"Delicious, and mine."

Like a maniac, I kept looking at his mouth that just licked every drop of my dirty juice from his fingers.

I wanted to lick that mouth. That filthy mouth that just licked all my nasty juice.

"Want to taste yourself?" He tilted his head and asked with a raised brow.

I wanted to taste anything that belonged to his body. Anything.

He chuckled darkly and brought his fingers to my lips just to part it. Then he started leaning towards me so that I could taste myself from his tongue.

Was he finally going to let me kiss him? Was I finally going to kiss him? In a trance, I was about to touch his lips with mine when there was a knock on the door, and someone barged in.

I was still sitting on his lap, straddling him.

Clothed, but still!

I just got finger-fucked by this man, for God's sake!

"Boss, Miss. Xena Meyers's date, Mr. Jack Perez, is looking for her. We asked him to go. But he is adamant about meeting her."

I gasped. *Oh, snuggles! Jack!*

I totally forgot about him!

"Hmm... That's an unwanted interruption. What do you want to do about it, Sugar? *Carry on* and let him go? Or *carry on* and let him come? I'm fine with both."

"N-No. I want to say goodbye to him. Let him come. But before that, let me down. I-I can't be sitting on your lap when he enters."

"No," Vaughn said, finalizing as he frowned.

"Please. It won't look good. I just left him in the middle of our date! And now if he—"

He thought for a second and then agreed with a devilish smirk. "Fine. I hate the part where you call the douche your date." He sneered. "But as you wish, Sugar." There was a mischievous twinkle in his eyes.

What? He agreed? There must be some hidden agenda behind it. What could it be? He must have something going on in his filthy mind.

Thinking about what it could be in his mind, I slipped down from his lap and sat on the couch beside him, straightening my clothes—trying to look like I didn't just have an orgasm from the fingers and filthy talks of the man sitting carelessly beside me. He casually flicked his finger to the guard to let Jack enter. The fingers that were in my kitty about a minute ago. The finger which had my juices on it, he licked with his tongue.

Jack entered and looked baffled when he found me sitting cozily beside Vaughn on the couch.

Before he could mutter a word, Vaughn put his hand around my shoulder and tightly brought me closer to him. Our bodies crushed against each other side by side.

"What's going on here? Who are you sitting with, Xena? Who is this guy?"

"Jack... Uh... I'm... I'm sorry we have to end our date early tonight..." Guilt coating my words as I muttered hesitantly.

"End our date? What the fuck are you talking about? Who the hell is this guy? Come over. You are with me." The chap looked agitated.

I felt Vaughn look down and smirk beside me as he took his whisky glass from the table and took a mouthful of it.

Then he gripped the back of my neck tightly and pulled me towards him, fast. I couldn't help but gasp at the suddenness of the situation. My lips parted as his other hand grabbed my jaw in a tight grip. And then he poured the whisky from his mouth directly into mine—all of it.

I gulped it down heartily. As if I was out of breath and it was my only source of oxygen.

He ended with a lick on my lips.

Oh! Heavens...

Then the filthy man looked at the now stunned Jack and said with Jack and said with mockery evident in his stern tone.

"Who is she with, again?"

94

16 | Licked

Xena

His broad arms and large palms seethed their warm comfort into my skin as he possessively held my bare arms. Even though there was a slight scent of my arousal on both of us—Vaughn's intoxicating scent overpowered my sense of smell. My head felt so light every time I took a breath in, as if I was floating on a soft, plushy cloud. His scent... only his scent made me feel that...

Is this how addiction felt like? Gosh, Xena, just how screwed are you?

Focus, Xena, focus. Focus on Jack.

But *snuggles*... he smelled so good!

Involuntarily and subconsciously, I leaned towards him a little more and then sniffed his captivating fragrance once again, giving my lungs a fill of their own feast.

"Xena! Did you agree to come here on a date with me, just to ridicule me in front of people?" I heard someone yelling, seething in anger.

Who is that?

Oh... Jack!

How did I keep forgetting him every time? That also at a time like this! Just how addicted was I to Vaughn?

Jack was fuming. That was justified...

"I'm sorry, Jack..." I murmured. I wasn't truly sorry.

Which was also justified...

"I'll not let you end this. You are with me, and I'll make sure of it. Watch it!" Jack was fuming in anger as he threatened and then left the room.

Vaughn was about to command his people, but I held his hand. "Let it go. His reaction is justified."

"No one threatens you." The man was practically growling like a wolf he was.

"I'm not a weakling to be scared of such threats, Vaughn."

Vaughn gazed at me for about a minute, peeping into my soul to take a glimpse of it. Then, slowly, his expression changed before my eyes. He evolved from an angry wolf into the cunning wolf—who had his fingers inside my kitty just a few minutes ago.

"Really? Then who was that limp woman, moaning on my lap a little back?" Vaughn wickedly smiled as he asked, raising a brow at me. The playful Vaughn was back. One of his hands was still around my shoulder.

"That was different," I said in a whisper and felt my cheeks turning hot as I hid my eyes from him.

"Really? How so?"

I felt him brushing the index finger of his other hand as he slowly traced my cheeks, gradually moving down. His eyes took in every inch of me with unbroken focus.

I was once again breathless, trembling, going limp under his touch and all his uninterrupted attention.

"It's... It's just..." I trailed off.

His fingers reached my upper chest and brushed over my deep cleavage. Then slowly went down towards my nipples, circling them with his fingers from above the fabric.

"Your nipples are as hard as my cock, Sugar."

I moaned.

What the hell is wrong with me? He is just talking... And tracing my nipples over my clothes. There is no need to moan, Xena!

96

"Mmm... and? It's just what? Sugar?" He pinched my nipple hard, sending a painful yet delicious shiver throughout my body.

"You! You... It's just you..." I confessed.

"Good girl," He murmured in my neck, "Good girls deserve rewards... wait... Where is your bra?" He asked while cupping one of my large breasts, his brows furrowed in displeasure.

"Didn't wear any..." I heaved.

"Bad girl... Very, *very* bad girl. Bad girls deserve punishment," he said, nibbling on my shoulder. Then slapped my breast—hard.

What?

"Now tell me. Which one do you want first? Your reward or your punishment?" he asked as he licked my neck.

"I-I'm sorry…" I didn't know how to calm the wolf in him.

"Wrong answer." He slapped my breast again. Harder.

"P-Punishment first..."

Whoa! Who said that? It certainly wasn't me. But why did it sound like my own voice?

He smirked at my neck.

"Excellent choice, Sugar," he said as he threw me flat on the couch.

My hair spread erratically all over my face. With a trembling finger, I moved a few strands and looked at the Adonis before me, looking magnetizing, pulling me towards him with immeasurable force. He looked sinfully, illegally, unfathomably sexy. He maintained eye contact with me, pulling off his suit coat and loosening his tie— just to throw them away somewhere behind.

My eyes went wide, and my mouth started drooling. How sexy was it to look at some suited sex god undressing before your eyes with uninterrupted eye contact?

Especially the very one you couldn't stop fantasizing about?

He smirked wickedly as he loosened the top few buttons of his shirt and left it there, just like that.

Whatever peeked through the shirt was illegal to be true.

I wanted to lick there.

Argh...

"Now, where were we?" Vaughn leaned towards my body, and then after two seconds, he said, "Right... tasting the delicious cunt of yours." The man smiled like a devil and pulled off my underwear at once.

I whimpered out of surprise and hid my face behind my palms. *Gosh...*

Vaughn lowered himself to focus on my pussy and took a closer look at it. He looked at it as if he was studying something extremely valuable in the store before purchasing it.

He brushed his palm on my hairless core and cupped it, feeling how it feels skin to skin. Then narrowed his eyes as if he was focusing on something and parted my pussy lips to look at what was hiding behind my plump flesh. His eyes widened a little, just for a second, when he took a close, clear look at it.

Vaughn ran his index finger around my clit and felt the softness of it. I continued to look at his focused, concentrated face with amusement. He was truly observing every nook and corner of my kitty. *Oh, blankets!* I could look at him as he noted my body all day, any day.

"Beautiful. You are majestic." Vaughn whispered.

No. He wasn't talking to me.

He was talking to my kitty. Literally.

"More beautiful than I imagined you to be. And you are mine. Mine only." Then suddenly, he ran his thumb over my drenched clit, and I screamed.

My scream finally brought him out of his trance, and he smirked, looking at me.

Keeping eye contact, he lowered down, and then flaring his nostrils he sniffed my core. His eyes looked like those dominant wolves, looking above to see their prey. His forehead had heaps of sexy, delicious folds.

Oh, blankets...

Wolf... he looked like a cunning wolf!

Then, as if he was worshipping it, he pressed his lips lightly over my nub.

Electrocuted. That was exactly what I felt, and my body jerked.

He licked my nub and inserted a finger in me. Electricity rushed through my body as I squirmed under his caress. His touch was different. Different from any other touch I had ever felt before. His simple strokes made my sanity go poof.

Oh, Vaughn...

His finger curled inside me, hitting somewhere that made me jolt. Vaughn immediately held my thighs and put me still in my place.

All of a sudden, he covered my core with his mouth and started sucking the life out of it. His tongue became more and more disobedient, and was gradually rebelling against my nub.

I felt my core throb and clench. With all Vaughn's teasing, his filthy words, and building anticipation, I was already sensitive. It wasn't long when I was almost on the verge of releasing.

"Stop. You can't cum. Not yet."

What?

Suddenly, he stopped touching me all the way and started kissing my inner thighs and my belly, going nowhere close to where I wanted him the most.

"Vaughn... Please!" I begged.

"No, Sugar. You have been a bad girl coming to a club without a bra where you have such gorgeous and heavy tits, and your hard-rock nipples were constantly begging for attention. You need to be punished. And you will be."

Then he put another kiss and a lick on my nub before abandoning it once again. It was aching for a release, and tears were pouring out of my eyes.

"Vaughn... Please... I beg you!" I whimpered.

He went further away from my core to kiss and lick my legs.

The sexy, obnoxious, hot piece of a specimen...

He kissed my feet, and then, pressing butterfly kisses, he moved near my pussy once again to stroke it with a lick and dropped a single kiss.

I screamed in frustration and clawed on the couch as tears of exasperation overflowed my eyes.

"Vaughn, let me go! I can't... I can't anymore!" I said, kicking him and stood up on my wobbly legs to leave the place, to leave him behind.

But he had other plans. He pulled my hand and made me fall on his lap once again, this time with my back facing his hard chest. With his left hand, he groped my right boob, and his right hand went directly inside my cunt.

Heaven!

"Time for your reward, Sugar." His hoarse whisper in my ear brought goosebumps on my skin.

Under the rapid, speedy, and skilled fingers of his, I released fast, throwing my head back. As I was cumming, I felt him slapping over my cunt over and over again, making me shudder in pain and pleasure throughout my release.

He found access to my shoulder and started dropping pepper kisses while I came down from my high, and my breathing became normal.

"Clean the dirt you have made all over my fingers."

He offered me the fingers that were inside of me moments ago.

And I willingly took his fingers in my mouth, licking it clean. The moment his fingers entered the warmth of my mouth, he bit on my shoulder—hard. As if to control over his restraints.

When I finished sucking them clean, he still kept his fingers in my mouth, and I carried on sucking them gladly, keenly, eagerly. At some point, I felt him fucking my mouth with four of his fingers altogether. I accepted the strokes gladly. After a long while, he asked from my neck, "Did you like your reward, Sugar?"

100

The question made me come out of my trance.

What?

"Excuse me, Mr. Wolf, what was that? You frustrated me! You rejected me from my release over and over! You... you obnoxious jerk!" I released myself from his hold and moved to sit further... somehow. My legs weren't still awake to let me run away.

"Didn't you ask for your punishment first?"

"I was begging... and crying... and you..." I didn't know how to finish the sentence.

"And that's why later on, I showed you a little piece of heaven. Didn't I?"

"Ugh... You are frustrating, you bastard! I hate you!" I stood up, feeling my legs somewhat stable, and grabbed my clutch as I walked towards the door.

"For this one time, I'm letting this attitude of yours slide. Be careful next time. Also, you definitely don't hate me, Sugar." I heard his playful yelling behind me.

"Yeah, I do!" I snapped at him, looking back.

I looked back and realized my mistake. The huge mistake.

He was clutching the huge, supposedly painful bulge over his pants and said, "My dirty, naughty Sugar. You definitely didn't sound like you hated me when you were moaning under my mouth."

"I-I'm not yours!" I managed to say, surprising myself with my energy and courage to talk to the man of my dreams whom I couldn't be with.

"Don't you know the phrase? When you *like* it, you *lick* it. I licked it, so it's mine," he said, maintaining a careless expression. His hand never leaving his bulge... his eyes never leaving my body.

But how on earth did he not look like a creep but a damn hot sexy, fucking Adonis?

Then he playfully bit his lower lips, as if controlling his laughter. A naughty gleam was prominent on his handsome face. He knew about my inner struggle. He knew it.

My heart started drumming, and I ran away from the room faster than ever… before treacherous heart could betray me, and I turned around to kneel and beg him to give me a taste of the enormous, throbbing bulge that remained hidden *'not too subtly'* inside his pants.

17 | Well-Wisher

Xena

My legs trembled violently as I closed the door behind me, with a smug Vaughn still sitting on the other side of it. Whatever confidence I had left with wafted in the thin air as I closed the door. With wobbly legs, I started walking towards the stairs. I wasn't even sure how I would reach downstairs, stepping down calmly or rolling over— depending on my shaky legs.

I breathed in relief when I finally made it to the ground floor. The club was still bursting at the seams, and people were having a blast. Whereas my inside was in chaos. In my mind, I switched off the incident that happened upstairs for the time being. It was more important for me to reach home fast. The realization hit me when I thought that my date had long gone. So was my ride home.

When I stepped outside the club, I stilled in shock. I left my underwear in Vaughn's room.

Oh, snuggles…!

How could I forget such a vital thing?

Standing by the road, I felt chills at places that caused shivers down my spine. Gosh…

Should I go back to Vaughn?

Oh god! No! I can't… he is Ron's brother… off-limits, Xena! Off-limits!

Well, you weren't such a good friend a while ago… My subconscious mind reminded me. I'd messed up, hadn't I?

I was in the middle of calling an Uber when a black Cadillac stopped before me. Suddenly, my legs started shaking for an entirely different reason. Was I going to get kidnapped tonight?

Why did I come on a date with Jack? And why the hell did I stay and give into Vaughn? Why couldn't I control myself when it came to that man? It was all my fault.

I tried to walk past the car, but the car door opened right away, and someone came out. Thinking of hundreds of worst scenarios, I tried to walk faster.

"Ms. Meyers, wait, please." A familiar voice shouted from behind me.

I looked behind and found the same tall, intimidating man who asked me to meet Vaughn earlier, interrupting my date. I furrowed my brows at seeing him. What did he want now? Did Vaughn want me again? Or was he here to return my panties? Gosh… I could feel my cheeks getting warmer, even in the cold weather.

"Mr. Wolf told me to drive you home."

I looked at the man in bewilderment. I didn't even know him. How could he expect me to sit in a car with him?

"I don't even know you."

"Pardon me for not introducing myself earlier. I'm Finn Norman, Mr. Vaughn Wolf's assistant, bodyguard, and most trusted person," he replied with a slight hint of a genuine smile through his rigid composure. According to my assumption, this man didn't smile much.

"Thank you for your offer, Finn, but I don't intend to bother you much. I was calling for an Uber anyway," I tried to avoid getting in a car with him. I didn't even know the guy. How could I trust him? Was he really Vaughn's most trusted person? He looked genuine, but I couldn't be sure.

"When Mr. Wolf asks for something, it has to be done, Ms. Meyers. The sooner you accept it, the better for you," he said with a solemn expression. "Here, talk to him. He already assumed you won't agree."

I took the cell phone from his hand and pressed it against my ear. "Hello."

I felt my voice shaking. Why?

"You should listen to what Finn says, Sugar. If there is one other person you can trust beside me, it's him. Get in the car." Vaughn's deep voice flipped through my heart.

I could feel his voice ringing in my ear, shooting right through my entire body and stopping at my toes, making them curl in desire. I shut my eyes, and then, taking a deep breath, I opened them again.

"Trust you? Why should I?"

"Do you want me to come and carry on with what we were doing? If not, listen to what I say. Get in the car. Go back home, fast. I can't sit worriless knowing my girl is out there without a trace of innerwear under the thin, black silk. I need you to be safe, Xena."

"I-I don't know him." I wasn't sure what to ask. Why did he keep claiming me as his?

"I'm being generous tonight. So, you have two options, Sugar. First, get in the car and let Finn drive you home. Or I come. Then again, remember, before I drop you home, I'll claim that little cunt of yours completely and fuck you senseless in *my* car. I'm warning you, Sugar, I'm clinging onto my self-restraint by a thread, and this is the sole reason it's not me but Finn out there with you right now."

My heart was drumming inside.

"So, which one do you choose?" he asked, growling like a beast—no doubt aroused.

"I-I'll get in the car. You trust him, right? So, I-I'm giving you some face here," I stuttered like a fool. Both aroused and scared by his words. And that voice... gosh... his voice on the phone was like a rabbit vibrator, stimulating me both from inside and out. My heart was thudding inside, my pussy pulsating vigorously, and my skin had goosebumps.

"Good. Reach safely. When you reach home, will you call me?" His voice dropped the wild sensuality and sounded rather sad.

I wasn't ready to call him yet. The friendship between Ron and I was too important to me to betray. I couldn't date her brother.

When I didn't respond, he sighed and said, "Just turn on the lights of your bedroom. Finn will come back only after you do that. I need to know you reached safely."

"Okay." I sighed in defeat. He was persistent, and I was tired of saying no to him. He didn't listen to any of those, anyway.

"You'll call me soon, won't you?" The desire in his voice was so high I almost said yes to him.

"Ah... I..." I trailed off, not knowing what to say in response.

"I'll be waiting for your call, Xena. You are already mine, but I need you to submit it to me. I want to hear from you that you are mine. I can't rest until you come to me." He sighed and then added, "Give the phone to Finn."

I wordlessly handed over the phone to Finn while I tried to calm my heart. Every time he talked, he set my heart on fire. Vaughn said something to Finn, which I failed to catch. Whereas Finn just replied in monosyllables. I waited no more, and opening the backdoor of the car, I hopped in carefully without flashing anyone any inappropriate view. Within a few seconds, Finn hung up and sat in the driver's seat to start the car.

"So, you are Vaughn's most trusted person, huh?"

"Yes. I am."

"That means you know everything about him."

"Yes, I do, Ms. Meyers. As an assistant, bodyguard, and friend, I have to know and understand everything about him. That's both my job and my concern."

"So, what do you think of him?" I asked in a casual tone.

He narrowed his eyes as he kept them firm on the road, frowning. "I'm sorry, Ms. Meyers. I'm not interested in him. We are superior and subordinates... Well, you can also say—friends. Nothing more than that."

Is he serious or joking?

Even the men in his close surroundings were as perplexed, obnoxious, and intimidating as him!

"Okay, calm your tits. I was just asking."

"He is the best man anyone could ever look for as a partner. He places a high priority on his friends and family. Responsible, well-settled, caring, and honest. Any woman will be happy to be his partner. Being his bodyguard, you have no idea what I have to deal with every day, but as you know, he only has his eyes for a single woman."

I frowned. *Does Vaughn have eyes for someone?*

I hated the thought.

"Who?" I irritably asked before I could stop myself.

He looked at me through the rearview mirror and smirked. "I think you have an idea, Ms. Meyers."

Oh, snuggly blankets!

Even Finn knew about us!

Did that mean whatever Vaughn said or did to me was genuine? But a man like Vaughn... how could he have feelings for a girl like me? Also, of his little sister's age?

I cleared my throat to grasp on my dignity, brushing off the fact that I was sitting in the car with no underwear. "What do you know, Finn?"

Finn chuckled faintly, then said, "That's his tale to say. As I am always with him, following his orders day and night, I tend to know a lot about you, Ms. Meyers. Rest you should know from him. I know more or less what he knows."

Oh god. That meant Vaughn not only maintained tabs on Ron, but me as well. Also, this Finn guy knew things about me as much as Vaughn knew.

Snuggles! Vaughn knows a lot about me, doesn't he?

When I was deep in thought, Finn said again, "I just want to add one thing, if you don't mind, Ms. Meyers. It has been long enough. You won't regret opening up to Mr. Wolf. He deserves a chance after all these years."

My head felt dizzy. What was the guy saying? He had been waiting for me for years? How could that happen? Now that I think, he did say something about not making him wait any longer. He said he had waited so long for me… which meant he had been telling the truth?

Had Vaughn been really waiting for me?

Vaughn? The Vaughn? The Vaughn from my fantasy?

When I was silent for a long time, Finn was concerned for me. Looking at me through the rearview mirror, he asked, "Are you okay, Ms. Meyers? Should I give a call to Mr. Wolf?"

"No! No, god… no! I'm okay."

I had reached my limit of *the dose of Vaughn* tonight. I couldn't take it anymore. So, I decided to change the topic to distract myself.

"So, Finn… Do you have someone you like? Or love?"

Finn's eyes went a little more rigid. "All I care about is the safety, well-being, and orders of Mr. Wolf. There is no space for any other attachments."

"Are you sure that is life? There is no life without love and care, Finn. As your well-wisher, I suggest you go and find your love fast! I'm so sad for your partner! Gosh… you are already so old! You are making her wait for a long time! Or is it *he*?"

Finn intensely glared at me through the mirror, and then after a few long seconds, he said, "Such a wonderful well-wisher you are, Ms. Meyers. However, for your information, I'm only 30 years old."

I snorted and said, "30? Wow! You are already so old, and you look even older! I think it's the effect of the men around you."

"I only stay around Mr. Wolf. So, you think he is old too?"

Oh, blankets…! No, he isn't! He is anything but old! Even when he gets old, the man would definitely look as exotic as fine wine.

But I can't admit that. Can I?

So I used the same ambiguous method as him to reply, "You should know that by now, shouldn't you?" Then I flashed him a toothy grin to rile him up some more. Such a trusted and loyal person he was! He deserved it.

I chuckled as I saw his scrunched brows and then said, "You know, your Mr. Wolf doesn't like you very much. Otherwise, why would he want you to keep working and not find the love of your life? You shouldn't be so loyal to him anymore. He doesn't care about you for real."

Finn just gritted his teeth and said nothing. What would he say, anyway? I looked at him and laughed in my hand.

18 | Little After

When Xena left, Finn grabbed the cell phone he threw earlier on the passenger seat and pressed it to his ear. "Mr. Wolf, I have followed your order. Her room's light has turned on."

Vaughn, who was on the line the entire time, listening to Xena and Finn's conversation, said, "I'll double your salary this month. Now, come back."

"Yes, Mr. Wolf," Finn smiled. He knew why Vaughn doubled his salary for the month. It was because Finn attempted to convince Xena to date his boss. Vaughn didn't have anyone else to help him get the girl he wanted. Finn was the only wingman he had.

It was not like whatever he said was to butter Vaughn up. He meant every word. For Finn, Vaughn was like his master, friend, and brother. And there was nothing he wanted more than Vaughn to claim the love of his life finally. He deserved it.

"And Finn, you have my order to look for the love of your life." Vaughn hung up the call right after saying that.

Finn brought the phone before his eyes and kept staring at the cell phone screen with a puzzled look.

19 | The Call

Xena

I tip-toed into the house, not letting Ron know about my arrival. I wasn't brave enough to face her just yet. For god's sake, her brother just fingered and sucked me out. I didn't have the eye to look into hers. My guilty conscience already started kicking in.

But I had no such luck.

"Did I just see Finn's car downstairs?" she looked baffled.

I gulped down the lump in my throat and said, "Yeah. Finn dropped me home."

"How do you know him? Weren't you on a date with Jack? How come Jack changed into Finn? By the way, he is Vee's second hand. How did you even find him?" It truly puzzled her.

"I-I found Vaughn there. My date went wrong, and Vaughn ordered Finn to send me home."

"Really? What did the son of a bitch do? Thank god Vaughn was there to send you home safely, and by the way, Vee wasn't rude to you, was he?" Ron asked, rushing forward to hug me.

I tried my best to avoid her hug since I had just had a heavy make-out session with her beloved brother. I couldn't let her touch me right now. My guilt intensified and gloved me as I avoided her eyes.

"I need to take a shower, Ron, then we'll talk, okay?" Reaching my room, I closed the door behind and turned on the lights. I need more courage to face my best friend. Also, Finn wouldn't leave unless he watched my bedroom's lights on.

When I entered the bathroom, I looked at myself in the mirror. Gosh... I glowed. I didn't even go all the way with him, and here, I was already glowing like this. He practically had me in his palms.

How would I avoid an amorous relationship with the man? Just a word of command from him tonight, and I gave in. I had no self-restraint before him. Tonight, he could fuck me any way he wanted, and I would've let him. But he didn't. He wanted me to give in first.

He didn't even kiss me, keeping up with his promise!

Was it so hard for him to let it slip for the night and drop a single kiss on the lips? Just from where did the man find such iron-clad self-restraints? Could I have some of those? Pretty please? I was dying over here... wanting him, needing him, desiring him.

As I showered, I touched every place I felt his hands on. My touches weren't even the tiniest part of how his traces felt. I tried to replay his touches in my mind as I touched my nipples, my thighs, my kitty... but no... no avail. Only Vaughn could make me feel what he made me feel. No one else could do that. Not even me. The man ruined me for me! Even masturbating had lost its perks.

Gosh... I'm doomed, aren't I?

After a few tries, I huffed and stopped trying. Taking a quick shower, I returned to my room and changed into my silk mini Victoria's Secret pajama set. By the time I was blow-drying my hair, Ron had entered my room with two plates of sandwiches. I joined her at the window seat, placing a few cushions behind my back.

"Bryan made a few sandwiches earlier. I saved some for us. Quickly, have some. They are delicious!" Ron pushed a plate in my hand. To be honest, I was hungry.

"He left?" I asked as I bit on the sandwich. Damn, it was good, actually.

"Yeah. He will come again tomorrow," I found Ron blushing.

Huh, this is new.

"Oh, by the way. Earlier, it confused me when I heard you met Vee at Club Empressa. Then I remember him telling me he had been planning to acquire a few more clubs in New York. That must be it. So here goes our substitute club now. Club Empressa also belongs to my dear brother from now on. We have to look for another option." Ron continued explaining.

So that was what happened. That was how Vaughn became the owner of the club where we used to go when we wanted to avoid him… *great.*

I was deep in thought, forgetting about the delicious sandwich in my hand.

"I called Vee. He was there to sign the papers tonight. Thank god he was there. What did the jerk Jack do to you, Jay?"

I bit the inside of my mouth. What should I say to her?

"Jack… Well, we didn't match, just how I thought we wouldn't. He isn't for me, Ron—in any way."

"Yeah. I knew that. I just thought he might help you relieve some tension, you know—Date with benefits? But it's okay if you don't feel anything for him. I want the best for you." Ron held my hand in reassurance as she said that.

Can the 'best' be your brother?

I wish I could just ask her that. But what if it ruined our friendship? No, I couldn't take the risk.

After Ron left, I opened the desk drawer again and picked up Vaughn's card. It felt hot in my hand, making my fingers and palm tingle, and the blood rushed to my core. My pussy pulsated once again, remembering his fingers and mouth devouring it at his heart's content.

I supported my other hand on the desk, stopping my wavering body from falling. Even his thoughts made my knees go as weak as jelly. *Oh, Vaughn…*

It had been about an hour since I kept looking at the calendar on my desk. After returning home from college, I didn't even change. Those handsome features of the only guy I desired consumed all my thoughts. Three days had passed since Vaughn devoured my body, turning my world upside down. Three days of constant desire, three days of trying to jill myself off, three days of failing to get off, three days of wet-dreaming about him… three days of my torment and agony.

No, I couldn't go one more day like this. The fire of my need for him was already there. He just ignited the flame with the spark of his touch. I need him to burn me with the sparks, engulf me with his form, and swallow me whole.

But what about Ron? Could I betray her?

With tremendously trembling fingers, I picked up the card and pressed the numbers on my dial pad. Then, sucking in a deep breath, my finger reached for the green button. It wasn't me—I was so damn sure it wasn't me who pressed the dial button. I wasn't in myself. I was summoned by some other spirits, and I was sure about it.

My heart was drumming against my chest, and I could hear it. It wouldn't be long when the poor heart would burst out, and I'd die right here out of excessive anxiousness and expectancy. I bit my lower lip so hard that it almost bled. Sitting at the desk chair, I looked outside—if truth be told—nowhere in particular. I couldn't, even if I wanted to. Because the tension was so high, I only saw blur before my eyes. *Snuggly blankets!* I was calling Vaughn. The man of my dreams—Man of my fantasy, who sucked me dry three nights ago and ruined me for everyone else. Even for me. Only Vaughn made me feel like that.

By the time I could hear the first ring on the other side of the call, I was sweating all over. My fingers were white as they clasped the phone, convulsing. So did my lips. I bit them again to stop them from trembling.

When it rang the second time, I was almost on the verge of canceling the call. No, I couldn't do it… what would I say to him? That I wanted him but also didn't want him?

Before it rang for the third time, I moved the phone to hang up.

But then I heard something on the other side.

"Heavens… Xena… you finally called."

I pressed the phone again against my ear, hearing his deep sigh of relief. I could tell from his deep breath alone exactly how tranquil my call made him feel. My heart flipped in my chest once more time, making my inside go all mushy.

"Xena? Sugar, you are there, aren't you?" he asked in a concerned voice on the other side of the call, and I melted.

"H-How do you know it's m-me?" I asked, already panting. How to talk to him when I was heaving like a dog in heat?

"I always know when it's you."

The gentleness of his voice caught me off-guard once again. It was just like the night in the garden. Until now, I had seen two sides of Vaughn. The gentle Vaughn from the garden. Then came the dominant Vaughn in the kitchen, or more specifically, at the club.

"I-I need to see you."

"You do, don't you?" There was a slight playfulness in his voice. And gosh, I loved it. I could feel the pool between my legs. Before I could muster my courage to say something, I heard his deep, sexy voice once again.

"I'm coming over to get you."

"What? No! Don't come here!" he couldn't just come here. Ron was here. What if she saw? God, I was such a pathetic friend, wasn't I?

Vaughn went silent for a few long seconds and then said, "I'll send Finn to bring you to me. He'll park the car a block away. Receive his call when he goes, and… come to me, Sugar. Fast. I can't wait to see you," he said with a raw growl, and my phone vibrated against my ear. Just by his voice. It sounded much more intimate on the phone.

I could feel the chair staining from my wetness. *Oh, snuggles… his voice!*

"I want to see you in a public place…"

I had to make it clear beforehand.

"Public place?" he asked, sounding astonished.

115

"Yes, somewhere people can see us but can't hear us." I shut my eyes tightly and bit my lip in shyness and anticipation.

"Are you afraid I'll suck your sweet, tight little cunt once again, Xena? Because you bet, I'll, Sugar," his voice trembled in need. Raw need. For me.

I squirmed in the chair, almost crying in need. I rubbed my thighs together to lessen the throb, but it only intensified the pulsation and ache.

"Public... Public place..." I said in a whisper as I heaved.

After a second of pause, he said, "Public place it is. Now come to me." There was such urgency in his voice, which couldn't be forlorn.

I hung up the call without another word and limped into the chair. Only talking to him through the phone sucked all the energy out of me. Just how much power he had over me?

After rummaging through the closet, I decided to wear some jeans and an off-the-shoulder loose boho top. They were more towards the modest side. Even though I wanted to feel sexy before him, I didn't dare. He already went beastly over me every time we met. I didn't want to lure the wolf hidden in him anymore.

It wasn't long before an unknown number flashed on my phone screen, and proving me right, Finn greeted me from the other side. I told Ron I wanted to see a random friend and went out. Oh, the guilt I felt lying to her.

I'm sorry, Ron...

When I reached the car, Finn came out from the driver's seat and opened the backseat door for me with a slight hint of a smile. The guy should smile more.

I greeted back with a smile and hopped in the car. Finn genuinely felt like a good guy. And for some reason, I felt at ease around him. Even though I was reluctant to trust him at first sight, I liked him just as much as I liked Leo.

116

Leo had been worried about me, as I was pretty tense for the past few days. I hadn't shared anything with him yet. It felt so hard to go through something so huge, but not being able to share it with anyone. Maybe I should share with Leo someday? He seemed like a thoughtful guy.

"We meet again," I said casually to Finn.

"If I'm not wrong, we will be meeting many more times in the future, Ms. Meyers. Also, I deeply hope we do."

I rolled my eyes at his intuitive words.

"How is your love searching going on, Finn? Found anyone yet? Should I set you up?" I teased the giant, handsome, intimidating guy who had his steady focus on the road.

"Or do you like me but can't do anything about it because of your rough and tough boss?" I asked with a smirk, teasing the big guy some more.

That brought some unexpected expressions out of Finn. He frighteningly looked at the cell phone that lay on the passenger seat, as if it wasn't the phone but Vaughn himself. Then said, "Don't just say anything, Ms. Meyers. You already know who you belong to. You shouldn't joke about everything."

The fear didn't dissolve in his eyes as he looked at the cell phone again. His throat bobbed in worry.

What happened? Was I so scary? That even a little joke about Finn liking me scared the shit out of him?

When we reached the luxurious hotel—Finn—who had been silent for the rest of the journey, finally talked.

"Mr. Wolf is waiting for you at the rooftop restaurant."

I tried to thank him, but he didn't wait and entered the car immediately. As I looked at his disappearing figure, I grew more confused than before.

Then, with a shrug, I turned on my heels as I entered the hotel.

20 | On the Other Hand

On the other hand, Finn pressed the phone against his ear and almost cried, "Mr. Wolf, I'm so sorry. You know I carry no such feelings regarding Ms. Meyers. She is all yours! She was just joking. I harbor no such feelings!"

"Finn!" Vaughn's angry voice rang on the other side, and Finn went silent.

"The doubled salary I promised you are canceled."

With the words being said, Vaughn hung up on the call.

21 | Second Date?

Xena

The walk towards the elevator drained all the energy out of me. Within minutes, Vaughn would stand before me with all his shining glory, and with just the thought of it, my heart went through a whirlwind.

Before pressing the button, I sucked in a deep breath and summoned all the energy I could muster, then walked inside the elevator.

As I entered the rooftop restaurant, I was welcomed with a magnificent view of the entire New York City. It was evening, just before twilight, and the sunlight dimmed beautifully. People seemed to have their snacks and drinks, minding their own business. Vaughn was true to his words. It was a beautiful public place indeed.

My eyes went to look for the man in question. It wasn't long before I found him. How could I not? No matter how glorious the evening view was, he was the most wonderful one out there.

My steps haltered, and my breath hitched as I looked at his backview. He looked just how he looked in the club that night—standing with his hands in his pockets. He donned his usual black suit, appearing cold, aloof, and powerful. I didn't know about others, but I… I loved black on him. There was a powerful aura around him that made him appear out of reach for anyone but me. I could reach him. He was waiting for me.

Just the thought melted my heart.

As if he sensed my presence, he slowly looked behind. Just when his eyes fell on me, I could see thousands of night stars sparking in the dark abyss in the sky of his eyes. Then, little by little, his lips turned upward.

Oh... my heart!

With a few long steps, he lessened the gap between us. And before I knew it, he was right in front of me. The first waft of his intoxicating scent whipped my nostrils, and my, oh my, I was a goner, right then and there.

I was still unmoved.

"You came to me. Gosh... you are finally here..." Vaughn said in a trance. But his passionate and deep voice made it sound like some raw, animalistic growls.

Is it wrong that I want to tug him towards me by his collar and kiss the shit out of him?

Controlling my libido and wild emotions, I played with the hem of my tops and said, "I think we should talk."

The corner of his mouth tugged in a playful smirk, and he said, "We should do a lot more than just talk, Sugar. Come with me."

He tugged my hands towards a two-seater couch facing the city. There was a table in front of it with a bottle of champagne and two flutes half-filled with the sparkling crystal clear liquid. The setup was entirely different from the other seats—the other tables had chairs, not a couch. But here, for us, Vaughn arranged a place to sit closely, side by side. What else could I expect from him?

He agreed upon a meeting at a public place but arranged everything accordingly so that he could keep touching me.

He pulled my hand to settle on the couch as he took the seat beside me. My hand that was sheltered in his was already tingling fiercely. Now, sitting side to side made our hips and thigh rub together. *Oh, snuggly blankets!* Too much. It was too much for my already frail nerves to handle! My body was no different from melting ice cream.

I tried to loosen my hand from his, but it only made his grip on my hand tighter. Shamelessly, the man sat sideways to face me while sitting beside me and then yanked my body to sit in the same way as him.

Now we were sitting side to side, facing each other, and still holding hands. Not just that. Even our thighs and knees nuzzled against each other.

My goodness. The intimate sitting arrangement caught me off guard. How could I talk to him sitting like that?

I avoided his eyes and bit my lips as he continued staring at me. My body trembled under his passionate gaze as usual, but he never left my hands. Our bodies kept pressing against each other, and he had no problem with that, whereas I almost had a hysteria.

"Thank you for calling me."

My heart started drumming faster. I just nodded, not daring to utter a word.

"Is it because you missed me? Or did you just miss my fingers, my tongue, or…" Vaughn sucked in his lower lip. "Or is it my mouth?" There was a confident smirk tagging on his kissable lips.

I took a sharp breath and looked at him in shock. No control. The man had absolutely no control over his filthy mouth, just like his sister.

Don't think about Ron now, Xena. I reminded myself.

"Sugar, you need to stop shaking and calm down. I will not eat you up unless you are willing to…" he said as his smirk went playful.

"It's just… It's you…" I breathlessly said, not knowing from where to start and what exactly to say.

"Yes, it's me, Xena. What about that?" He looked genuinely confused.

"I… I always had a…" I trailed off, unable to finish the sentence, blushing furiously, as I hid my face, sheltering it with the curtain of my hair.

"You always had a what?" His voice sounded firmer than before, while his clasp on my hand went tighter. The shrewd man knew how that sentence ended. He was smarter, much more intelligent than that.

"Ever since I knew you… from Ron, even though I never met you, but… but I developed a… a crush on you."

I wasn't as brave as to look into his eyes as I exhibited my deepest secrets before him. If I looked up, I could've seen how dark his eyes went from wanting me.

"You have a crush on me?" He was the one breathless this time.

I nodded and continued. "You are Ron's brother. Off-limits for me. Even after knowing that, you were still the only one who I truly ever… wanted." I paused to beckon some more courage, then said, "I couldn't date anyone. I couldn't like anyone… because no one matched you. No one was… *you.*"

I stole a look at him and found his eyes widened and his lips parted in shock. It even looked like he wasn't breathing. His looks alone made thousands of butterflies tickle fiercely inside my belly.

"You never came to me…" he said in a whisper in a breathless tone, but since we were sitting so close to each other, I heard him loud and clear.

"Why would I? I was wrong to want you in the first place. The furthest I could go was looking at your pictures in secret."

"My pictures? From Facebook?" he asked, tilting his head a little.

"Yes." Guilt was clear in my tone. Then again, it had to be done. I had to confess and have closure with my feelings over him.

He stayed silent for a long time. The uncanny man was no fool. I could even see the wheels of his brain turning as he deeply thought about something.

I took a few glances at him, but his eyes never moved from our intertwined hands that were lying on our snuggling legs.

After a long pause, finally, I heard him talking.

"Did you ever wonder why my pictures were public on social platforms?"

I scrunched my nose and pouted my lips, something I did when I went deep in thought. Actually, I always wondered about it. Vaughn was clearly not much a public person.

"Yes. You maintain a private life, but your profile pictures were always public."

He let out a dark chuckle. "That's because I wanted you to see them."

This time, my eyes widened in shock. I could swear I was melting right then and there. *Snuggly blankets!*

What is the man of my dreams saying, again?

Out of the blue, he chuckled again, and then his chuckle gradually turned into a laugh. His laughter intensified, and he threw his head back as he laughed in a totally carefree way.

"What happened?" I couldn't help but ask.

He subsided his laughter and looked into my eyes intently. "You happened, Xena. I wanted you to see me, notice me, come to me... and you did see me. You have no idea how happy that makes me, Sugar."

The genuineness and intensity in his eyes didn't lie. His pupils were so dark that I couldn't separate from the end of it. Was he happy because I stole his pictures and rubbed myself off? Not that he knew about the latter. But something in the back of my mind told me he would be the happiest man in the world if he got to know about it.

"You... You keep saying you wanted me to come to you. What does it mean?" This question kept whirling in my mind constantly since the first time I met him, about two weeks ago.

In response, he took both my dainty hands in his and held them firmly in his huge ones, covering them entirely. Even though the man looked cold, his hands felt unusually warm. In seconds, the warmth absorbed in my skin and hit my heart right away, melting it.

"I have been waiting for you for years, Xena. You are all I want. There is no one else for me. You are the only girl I want to keep, I want to care for, and I want to fuck... Gosh... Xena. After everything that happened between us, there is no point hiding my desire and longings from you. I want to fuck you so bad. Especially after knowing you wanted me too…" Vaughn trailed off.

"I-I just had a crush, okay? There is nothing like what you are insinuating." I blushed profusely.

Suddenly, he left my hands, and taking the champagne flute, he took a sip from it. But all the while, his eyes never left mine. The way he sipped the drink and his throat bobbed as he gulped it down, I felt my throat drying. I gulped down to make my throat less dry, but it didn't work. His intense eyes went more penetrating, as if looking into my soul.

He picked up the other flute and offered me the drink.

Just when I accepted the drink and took a mouthful, he said, "I don't want my girl to be high and dry." Then he spread one of his hands behind me on the backrest of the couch, and his other hand on my thighs, as if he owned me and then said, "I prefer her to be wet and well-fucked."

I spitted out my drink at his words, drenching my lap and his shirt. His filthy mouth knew no boundaries, did it?

He patted my back with the hand he had behind my back and took the flute from my hand right away.

"You okay?" he asked with concern in his eyes.

"Next time, please warn before you talk."

I kept coughing, trying to calm myself. But that felt absolutely impossible with his hand behind my back.

"You must always be well prepared with me."

Previously, his hand was patting my back for genuine reasons, but later on, when he knew I was alright, it turned into a not-so-innocent touch. Previously, to pat on my back, he leaned towards me. He chose to stay like that, close, very close to me as he sensually caressed my back. His eyes bored into every feature of my face, and his breath fanned into my face, making my skin tingle everywhere he gazed or touched.

I could feel my nipples harden and panties pool with wetness.

"Xena, you said you had a crush on me. Why did you use the past tense? What about now?"

My throat dried again… This man would be the death of me. I could swear…

"You still like me, don't you? Because I do. Tell me you do, too."

I felt my body shudder again. I wanted him. God knew how much I wanted him. But we weren't meant to be together… we couldn't. If he was any other man, then maybe? Unfortunately, he wasn't just any other man but Ron's brother.

"Ron will flip out if she ever knows…" Before I could finish, I felt his thumb on my lips to silence me.

I could feel the hand on my back slowly reaching towards my neck. As I was wearing an off-the-shoulder top, my shoulders and neck were open for him to play with. Did he forget we were in a public place?

Touching your female companion's neck in a public place wasn't a crime, right? I was sure he would definitely take full advantage. I was a fool to go for an off-the-shoulder top today.

The brush of the tip of his finger was delicate on my neck as he said, "Shh… I'd rather want you to tell me when you stalked me, what did you do with the photos? Except for just looking at them?"

Oh, blanketty blankets!

22 | Negotiation

Xena

"Shh... I rather want you to tell me when you stalked me what did you do with the photos? Except for just looking at them?"

"I... I didn't do anything! I just looked at them. What else will I do? They are just photos!" I was too fast, proving how bad of a liar I was.

He chuckled—low and full of mockery. But even then, the vibration hit me everywhere in my body. I was sure my skin was beet-red by now, reddening my neck and upper chest for the feast of his eyes. I came here to have closure. How did I end up like this?

Oh, Vaughn...

He brushed my earlobes lightly, and I almost whimpered in ecstasy. Then out of nowhere, he pinched my earlobe. Hard. An irrepressible moan of pleasure escaped my throat...

Wait... Shouldn't I feel pain? Why did I feel the pure bliss of pleasure?

"Liar. Don't tell me you didn't fantasize about anything. Because I know I did. Every time I stalked you—physically, on Ron's profile, or the security camera of my club, I always ended up touching myself. I couldn't keep my hands off of my dick whenever you were before my eyes, no matter in what form. And you want me to believe you did nothing?" he asked, challenging me.

The smarty-pants knew I jilled myself off to his photos. Who was I kidding? Who wouldn't, when it came to an Adonis as him?

"Tell me. Did you imagine me drilling deep in your tight little cunt ruthlessly, or did you imagine me to be gentle in your fantasy? Which one, Sugar?" His mouth was so close to my ear that the sensitive skin felt warm and tingly from his heavy, hot breathing.

I was almost hyperventilating.

"Shhh… calm down and tell me." He brushed his lips lightly on my earlobe.

"D-Don't… people… around us!" I wasn't lying when I said I was hyperventilating.

"I know…" he said in a seductive whisper, breathing into my ear. "Now, if you don't want to give them a free show, answer truthfully. I will know if you lie."

His fingers were busy doing things on the skin of my neck. Also, there was such authority in his tone I couldn't dare to lie.

"Rough… ruthless… merciless." I couldn't keep it in me anymore and blabbered out my deepest secret.

His body went rigid. His fingers stopped on my neck and my thighs. Even his breathing stopped for a while.

Then suddenly, he left my body and moved away from me, taking away all his warmth and leaving me with ugly coldness. He straightened himself as if we were just discussing the weather just now. Only the dark abyss of his dilated eyes gave away his inner thoughts.

"Let's order our dinner. What do you want to eat?" Vaughn asked in his usual casual way.

You.

I gulped down and somehow muttered. "Nothing. Thanks, anyway."

Vaughn narrowed his eyes at me and said, "It's our second date, Xena. Of course, we will have dinner together. I'll go for salmon steak, you?" He called the waiter right after he asked me.

I was stunned at his sudden change in attitude.

"Second what?" I couldn't keep my surprise anymore.

He gave me a puzzled look and said, "Date… you know, a meeting between a man and his woman who have feelings for each o—"

I stopped him.

"I know what date is! We don't have feelings for each other!"

The waiter came, and he ordered the same salmon dish for both of us. Then looked at me with a raised brow as if challenging me.

"Except that we do."

I was gritting my teeth at his sudden change of demeanor, but the man in question looked so unbothered about it. I looked at him only to find him sipping champagne carelessly. As if nothing in the world bothered him anymore.

"We can't, Vaughn…" Before I could finish, he sprinted his head at me in a jolt.

Looking at my confusion, he said, "I like my name on your lips. Gosh, Xena, I want to fuck you so bad right now. Especially this fuckable mouth of yours." He brushed his thumb on my lips.

I bit my lips to stop the sensation his thumb caused me. I heard about mood swings before. But what kind of swings was this that Vaughn had? Hormonal swings?

"W-We can't. Ron will flip out… she won't like it, I know that. I can't risk our friendship and your sibling bonding."

"And you are ready to risk me? Ready to risk us? We are meant to be together. Both of us have been wanting each other for years. Don't you want me, Xena? Am I so easy to forget?" For the first time, he looked hurt.

"You are not even in it! There is no us!" I exclaimed without thinking, and his face darkened. Only then did I realize how hurtful my words were.

He kept telling me how much he wanted me. On the other hand, I said something so harsh.

"I'm sorry, I didn't mean it. It's just… Vaughn, you know what I mean."

How to make him understand when he wasn't ready to accept the reality?

"You are worrying about Ronnie, but what if she likes the idea of us together? What if you are scared for no reason at all?"

His mentioning us together set my heart on fire. I wanted that… God knew how much I craved that…

"I know how much you mean to Ron. I can't risk coming between you two."

"You'll never come between us, Xena. She is my precious little sister, the only existing blood relation that matters to me. And you, Xena, you are my girl. To care and to fuck. You both have your own place in my life. And none weighs any lesser than the other," he said every word with utmost earnestness.

It left me speechless. I really wanted to fall on my knee and beg Vaughn to take me, but what if Ron wouldn't accept us? They only had each other, and I never wanted to be a thorn in their beautiful sibling bond.

"Xena…" Vaughn held my face with both his palms. The warmth radiated from his skin and sank into mine.

"I know how brave you are. You are no weakling, no push-over, and I know that. So what are you scared for? You want me. I want you… God, I'm this close to dragging you into a room downstairs and fucking you till you can't take it anymore. Then I want to take care of you until you regain your energy. So I could fuck you once again. I want you, Xena. I terribly, unfathomably, earnestly want you."

"Is that all you want from me, Vaughn?" I wondered. Because I want that from him as well. But I also want more than that.

"Why don't you find it out yourself, Sugar?" he asked, flashing me a beautiful smile. His fingers brushed against my cheeks.

As he noticed my mystified expression, he thought of something. "How about you give me a week? An unrestricted week to gain your affection? If you give in, we become exclusive at that instant. And if not… who am I kidding? I'll keep chasing you," he said as he

129

chuckled and one of his hands went to find mine just to intertwine together.

Oh, my heart!

I thought about it. The man would not give up, anyway. So what was wrong in trying to find if we could be something or not? It was true. We both wanted each other. I would rather like the idea. Besides, where would he find me in these seven days? At most, we would talk on the phone. I didn't mind that.

"Okay. But I have one condition. I'll only come to an agreement if you agree to my condition."

He brushed my chin and lips with his thumb in a daze, as if he was in an inner struggle.

"Ron knows nothing about us. If it doesn't work between us, then nothing happens, and I don't want her to bother her with this matter in such a case."

Suddenly, he was very close to me. Very, very close. Just a little, and his lips would brush mine. Then he breathlessly said, "I really, really want to kiss you right now. Why don't you submit your feelings to me, Xena?"

The intimacy was so intense among us that my body started shivering again. The sun was setting as it glowed with its majestic shades of tint, dyeing everything with its own beautiful rays of colors. I thought he looked handsome under the daylight, but proving me wrong, he appeared even more attractive, mysterious, intimidating, and passionate in the dim light. I kept looking at him as the twilight drifted into the dusk. Even under the dusky sky, he appeared as enigmatic and striking as ever. If I had to choose one, I didn't think I would be able to.

His palm, which had been resting on my cheek, moved behind my neck, bringing me closer to his lips. Shocking me to the bone, he lightly brushed his soft lips against mine, and I jerked in response. The electricity generated from the gentle touch of our lips felt so real—it couldn't be untrue.

Vaughn sighed softly and backed away from me as soon as our lips touched. The pull between us was so strong it couldn't be avoided by any means. I was left as a trembling, wet mess, whereas Vaughn's knuckles were white as he fisted his hands. I could see his nails digging into his palm.

I almost held his hands to calm him down, but then the waiter arrived with our dinner. After the food came, Vaughn looked a lot calmer than before. I sighed in relief and accepted my plate when he offered me.

I failed miserably as I tried to cut the fish or pick the fried rice with my spoon. My hands were shaking terribly, and it felt impossible to eat in such a condition. The entire day since I called Vaughn had been such a nerve-racking experience for me—it drained me out. Besides, eating while sitting beside this man was no such joke.

Vaughn noticed my failed attempts. Then, wordlessly, the man took my plate and cutleries from my hand. I tried to be reluctant, but when he wanted something, he would do it. No matter what.

"Let me."

He pushed his plate away and started cutting my fish into pieces, then taking some on the fork he offered to feed me.

"Y-You don't have to. I can do it. Your food will turn cold."

I can't believe Vaughn was trying to feed me! Am I dreaming or what?

The corner of his mouth curved in a smirk as he said, "It doesn't matter, Sugar. You do."

Blankets!

With quivering lips, I took the mouthful of the food he offered. His eyes lingered on my lips intensely as they darkened to an abyss. Affectionately, he stroked away a few strands of hair from my face with his other hand.

"Ronnie won't know. And it will work between us. You are mine. My girl. No matter what, I'm not letting you go, Xena. Try for us, fight for us. Don't give up without trying. Alright?"

I gulped down the food and nodded softly, agreeing, giving my consent to him consciously.

Then he flashed me the most genuine, most elated smile I had ever seen on Vaughn. Not even in any of the photos had I seen of him had this smile on his handsome face. Unknowingly, it brought a smile to my face as well.

After we finished with our dinner, or according to him, our second date, he dropped me home while Finn drove the car.

When the car reached a block before the one I lived in, he stopped the car. The moment the car stopped, Finn immediately climbed down, leaving only Vaughn and me in the small space.

Vaughn didn't waste a second and pulled me into his arms. His hands were both at the nape of my neck and another on my hip. Subconsciously, he was crushing me into himself with all the strength he had. His mouth was hot against my neck. For a second, he went wild. It was like he couldn't decide what to do with me, kiss or bite on the skin of my neck and shoulders.

He went wild, and I didn't even dare to stop him. He pulled me onto his lap, kissing and licking the skin exposed before him to devour. His hands, rough on my body—feeling, gripping, pinching my body, and then pulling my hair.

When I was almost passing out from the excess oversupply of estrogen and progesterone hormone, he finally stopped. Vaughn took my face into his palms, bringing me even closer to him, penetrating his gaze into my eyes, as he asked in a thick, hoarse voice, "You won't forget about our deal, will you?"

I shook my head to diminish his insecurity. "No, Vaughn. I won't."

How could it be possible? Vaughn Wolf, feeling insecure about me?

After pressing a kiss on my forehead, he smacked my ass and said, "Good girl, don't forget to call me."

I somehow loosened myself from his secure hold. It was extremely difficult, given the resilient pull between us.

When I finally left his car, I didn't dare to look back, or I'd have been back to square one, right on his lap, which I was sure about.

Right when I entered our apartment, Ron came running towards me.

"Jay! You won't believe what happened! Vee just called! He wants us to enjoy our spring vacation at his vacay house with him. Can you believe it? Four days with Vee! I can't wait!"

I cursed the man and his shrewd trick under the breath and then mumbled to myself,

I can't wait either.

23 | Gataway

Xena

In a blink and loads of sexual frustration later, the day for our Hudson Valley vacation had arrived. I opened my eyes and jumped out of bed earlier than usual. I packed my suitcase with the clothing Vaughn requested I wear for his eye candy. On the other hand, Ron was also super excited about the vacation. She behaved just like little kids did when they vacation with their parents. Vaughn was indeed everything for her.

By then, a few things had changed in me. First of all, I was genuinely looking forward to this retreat. The luxurious thought of spending a few days with Vaughn formed all sorts of somersaults in my heart. The hesitation had decreased by folds, and I blame the man in question for that. His constant texts about how he was looking forward to the trip got me excited, too.

Moreover, I couldn't stop thinking about him. In the past, when I thought he was the man of my dreams, now I could say that I firmly believed that he was the man of my heart. Little by little, my reluctance to him was wearing off, and I had no grip on it. I wanted him shamelessly. For this as well, I blame him. Vaughn's constant dirty innuendos and messages held me by a thread to go down on my knee and take him in my mouth.

Finally, I was mentally prepared to give myself to him if he could erase the last bits of my hesitation by the end of the given week. One day had passed, and I was already more than halfway towards him. So it was safe to say that I knew about the aftermath of challenging Vaughn. I knew how things would end up for us.

But what would happen when I tell him why I didn't have a proper boyfriend, ever? Would he cringe when I knew about my deepest secret aside from him? What if he wouldn't want anything to do with me then?

Don't fuck it up, Xena. Be positive.

Ron was already chanting my name at the top of her lungs by the time I finished my morning rituals. I rushed out, only to be shocked at the beautiful sight of the brother-sister duo sitting in the kitchen with breakfast takeaways lying on the kitchen island before them.

I could swear I felt all the blood rush towards my face as I realized the lack of clothing on my body. I was still barely covered in my silk mini nightwear, not to mention with no underwear underneath. My morning bed hair was scattered in a wild mess. Also, for freak's sake, I was in my favorite pair of fuzzy panda slippers!

Whereas, he? He was still embellished in his usual dark, expensive suits that threatened to bring me to my knees at just one glance.

"Jay, come fast! Look, Vee brought breakfast for us! I'm sorry I started without you already! Come, join us!" Ron was grinning from ear to ear.

From the corner of my eyes, I stole a luxurious look at Vaughn. I noticed his tight fists as his already dark eyes raked me from top to bottom repeatedly, then sunk his hungry teeth into his kissable lips. I wanted to do that, god!

Ron sensed some tension between Vaughn and me and then said, "Don't worry, Jay. Vee looks a little intimidating, but my brother is a good person. Come, sit with us."

The moment Ron said it, I took it as an alarm of precaution and recollected my wits. Slowly, I walked towards the kitchen island and sat beside Ron. Ron offered me the waffles Vaughn brought, and I tried my best to cut them into pieces and swallow them down.

But it was hard, given the fact that the sexiest specimen in the world couldn't keep his eyes off of me. My heart pumped so much that I felt like it would burst any moment. I glanced at Vaughn, opening the gate of my agony a little so that he could detect what I was going through under his intense stares. But the guy had no mercy. He continued watching me as he would much prefer eating *me* instead of the delicious breakfast lying before him.

Ron noticed his intense stare at me and gave it a completely different meaning. Both Vaughn and I were close to her, so she took the bold initiative to make peace among us that *she* thought we needed. She put down the coffee cup and looked at her brother with certainty in her eyes.

"Vee, I know you don't like women around you. But Jay is my special friend. Behave for these three days and don't bully my best friend! Otherwise, no matter what, I'll beat your ass—" Vaughn raised a brow at her, which changed her demeanor to one-eighty degrees within a second. She ended up looking like a puppy with a tail between its legs and then finished with, "—or whatever."

"Hey, Jay, I'm done with my breakfast. You can continue, okay? I'll just—Um—go get ready fast!" Then she really ran towards her room like a scared little puppy.

"Ron!" I couldn't stop and called her. Did she just leave me alone with her brother, just after that one glare from him?

I turned my neck around again, only to find Vaughn smirking, looking right at me.

The infuriating man!

"Finish your food." The authority of his tone overpowered the simple three-word sentence.

"Why are you so early?"

"If I weren't early, how could I savor the pleasure of seeing your tight little ass in these tiny little shorts? Your bed hair that delivered me the idea of how your beautiful blondes would look once I'm done with thoroughly fucking that ass of yours? Don't you enjoy my eyes on your body, Sugar?" Vaughn said all those dirty words in his seductive husky voice as he squirted some chocolate syrup on my waffles with utmost focus.

"Now, take them in this pretty little mouth and swallow." He pointed at the waffle but with a different, filthier meaning.

Vaughn was truly one filthy man.

"You caught me off guard, Wolf," I said, looking into his eyes, summoning up my courage.

He grinned and said, "That's one of my favorite things to do. And I plan to do many more of that." He paused to sink his teeth on his lips again and then asked, "You have packed some of these night wears with you, right?"

I darted my tongue out to lick some of the chocolate syrup from my lips and then nodded in response.

Vaughn took in a sharp breath and then poured some coffee for me. I really, really liked him showing these little forms of affection for me. After all, it was Vaughn. My Vaughn. Vaughn of my dreams.

When he offered me the coffee mug, his thumb deliberately brushed my hand as I jerked at the electrocuting sensation.

"Had a hard time sleeping last night?" he asked playfully.

He intentionally asked me the question to redden my cheeks to his heart's desire. He was the one who was firm on the '*no orgasm*' rule. Even though I tried to convince him last night, he was fixed on his verdict.

"Don't you want to know, Wolf?" I asked, raising a brow at his playful self.

"Don't worry, Sugar. You will get plenty of orgasms. Soon. I'll make sure they are extraordinary, compassionate, and mind-shattering for you to make it up. That's my job from now on."

His voice dropped to a husky tone that *already* had me on the verge of those mind-shattering orgasms.

I stood on my wobbly feet to leave this man with all his dirty mouth, smugness, and sexiness and then said, "That's what *you* think! Well, I have to get ready now."

"That's what the cunt of mine between your legs thinks as well, Xena. Otherwise, why are your shorts already soaking?"

Oh, snuggles! Because of the lack of panties, my treacherous kitty drenched all over my shorts. That was also before his eyes!

Suddenly I was so nervous and embarrassed that I ran into my room, not looking back even once. I had no courage to face that smug, sexy man right at that moment. I was relieved only when I was sheltered by the protection of the door behind me.

That was so embarrassing. Could it get any worse?

I chose a bottle-green polka spaghetti strap dress. It had a square neckline with bow tie spaghetti straps. If anything, it only made my curvaceous body look enticing enough to untie the straps, and there was only one person who was invited to do so.

After brushing over my thick waves of blondes, I decorated my eyes with two symmetrical strokes of winged eyeliner. When I was about to put on some brownish nude lipstick, Ron entered the room.

"Jay, I heard running earlier. Did Vee bully you so much to run away?" Guilt was apparent in her beautiful facial features.

"As far as I remember, I wasn't the only one running away." I raised a brow at her.

"Sorry, Jay. It's just... even though Vee is my brother, he is so intimidating when he wants to be. I'll talk to him again." She looked so guilty by then.

"Hey, Ron, it's okay. I can manage myself around your brother. You don't have to worry about me, boo." I said, taking the initiative to reassure her.

"Are you sure?"

"Yes. Besides, what can he do to me?" *Other than delivering plenty of orgasms*, as he claimed earlier, I thought.

"Okay, Jay! Thank you for understanding Vee! Now I can rest assured! I will now go call Bryan, and then we can start! If I don't call him now, I won't be able to, in front of Vee."

I shook my head at her retreating figure in silent laughter. Then, after tying my hair with elastic, I took hold of my luggage, and I went out to put my shoes on.

I was crouching down on the floor to put my white sneakers on. That was when Vaughn entered the room while he was occupied with talking on the phone. As expected, he took a few more steps to stand in front of me as he continued talking, looking down at me.

Let me rephrase our current position. Me—crouching in front of him. As he stood like a mountain, and my face squarely at the level of his high-quality jewels. I gulped down the lump of my nervousness and carefully looked up, only to find a pair of dark abyss looking down at me. Those dark, aroused eyes held such hunger for me that suddenly I couldn't move.

Was he the only one aroused? I felt a warm pressure of arousal in my pussy as I flickered out my tongue to wet my lips. The action somehow intensified his desire by a few more degrees, and so he brushed the back of my head with his spare hand. As if I was his little pet. Then, slowly, his hand moved to the back of my neck and pulled the hair tie to let my hair loose. Caressing my hair a little, he pulled me closer to his bulge a little by little.

I couldn't deny his touch...

Suddenly we heard footsteps coming towards where we were, and Vaughn shifted away, still talking on his phone. I was too engulfed in the unexpected addition of sexual tension; it took me longer than usual to tie my laces.

When we went downstairs, I was awestruck at the car parked in front of us. With all its black beauty, a very real Marcedes-Maybach Pullman was waiting for us. As I silently admired the car, I felt Vaughn's deep eyes on me.

As I entered the car, I was even afraid to put my feet in it. It was so luxurious that I didn't even dare breathe in it. Even though Vaughn usually uses his Maybach Exelero, this one was no less than that. The most exciting fact was that the four seats in the back faced each other. Suddenly, I had an idea why he chose the car for today.

I really wanted to sit opposite him so that our legs could nuzzle once again as they did on our second date. Well, at least that was what he claimed it to be. But with Ron's presence, it wasn't possible. Ron and Vaughn sat opposite each other, and I sat beside Ron.

Suddenly, I heard the text tone on my phone. As I looked at the screen, my eyes widened, and my eyes bounced at him. He wasn't even looking at me, busy talking about their parents with Ron.

I read again.

Filthy Wolf: What are you thinking so hard?

Xena: I wish you could sit opposite me.

I was honest. From the corner of my eyes, I could see the slight hint of a genuine smile on his lips. Then he carelessly tapped something on his phone, and my cell phone screen flashed. I had already put it in silent mode.

Filthy Wolf: I would rather have you on my lap, Sugar.

I bit my lips at the sudden rush of blood to my face.

Xena: That could work, too.

It was so hard for me to maintain an expressionless face when he talked dirty to me. But no, I couldn't take a chance to let anything out yet.

Filthy Wolf: That could more than just work*, Xena. Want to know how?*

I bit my lips again and looked at him. Our eyes met, and he understood from my expression that I *did* want to know.

Filthy Wolf: We could discuss the first thing that popped up in our mind or *our body ;)*

Xena: I have heard it somewhere before... on the internet, probably? ;)

140

Filthy Wolf: Okay, let me rephrase. I would rub that ass of yours to calm your uncertainty first, then finger that little cunt to release all the stress from that gorgeous face of yours. After that, I'll shove my dick right inside the heat of your pussy and cover your goddamn body with my shoulders and arms, so we are no longer two separate people but one. Sounds right?

After reading the message, I turned off the screen of my phone and squeezed my eyes to calm down the rocking nerves of my body.

And then, when I opened them again, I was determined.

Two can play a game, Wolf.

24 | Green

Xena

I tapped on my phone screen with a smugness that mirrored Vaughn's. I could see how curious he was, waiting to know what I was typing.

My mind was still in a daze as my fingers tapped. I was so much in a trance that when Ron said something, I wasn't really listening to her at all. Then finally, when I was satisfied with my words, I sent Vaughn the ultimate outcome.

Xena: I can imagine that. While you'll be buried in me, I'll ride until you can't help but explode inside me. As we do that, I'll trace those warrior-looking hard cheekbones of yours with my fingertips, leaving a rain of kisses in the process. After that, should I route towards the wide, muscled neck of yours? Or those mysterious-looking lips? Tough choice.

The moment Vaughn read the text, I noticed him reading it again and then again. The more he read, the darker his eyes went. His sharp-as-knife jaws squeezed shut while he was gathering his self-restraints. I could see that. As I observed him, the coat of self-satisfaction covered me in its warm comfort.

"Are you okay? Vee? Do you need to visit the loo? Should I ask Finn to stop?" Ron cautiously asked.

I almost let out a giggle.

Vaughn noticed that. And he didn't look happy. *Oh, snuggly blankets!*

"Yes," Vaughn said. His deep voice rumbled in the luxurious car. "Let's stop for a while."

Vaughn grumbled some orders to Finn, and soon we stopped at a hotel. The lovesick Ron didn't waste the opportunity, and vanished into thin air when we entered the place. Suddenly, I became acutely aware of the fact that I was standing alone in the presence of the wolf himself.

So this is how it feels when a sheep is mortgaged to a wolf?

And the betrayer was none other than my best friend!

Slowly, I tried to sneak out from under Vaughn's protective yet dangerous side. Standing next to this man sapped all of my energy. That was how intimidating he was.

He didn't stop me. Shocking me to the bone, the wolf didn't stop me, but he followed behind me to wherever I was heading at a terrifyingly slow pace. There was a particular look on his face that gave me a fair warning—about how it was impossible for me to sneak out of his hands. My heart thumped against my ribcage, warmth pooling in between my legs as I truly felt like a sheep—a prey to the wolf, *my Wolf*.

He kept the distance among us, never trying to eat up the few steps of space that were so easy for him to get rid of. As if challenging me to run away from him. So that he could prove to me that no matter how far I'd go, he'd catch me.

He and I both knew I could never run away from him. We had already gone way deeper to move past each other, even though I hadn't submitted to my feelings for him yet.

I didn't know where I was heading to, but somehow, I ended up with Vaughn cornering me right where he wanted. We were at the corner of a corridor where no one could see us. Vaughn finally closed the distance among us in the blink of an eye and then slammed my back against the wall with a thud, pressing the front part of his striking body against mine, crushing the softness of my tits with his chiseled hard chest, poking the apex of my thigh with his rock-hard boner.

I tried to push him away from my body when my treacherous soul was already busy pulling him close to claim his lips. My push did absolutely nothing to the tall, gigantic mountain of muscles. All he did was hold both of my wrists in one hand and push them above my head against the wall, trapping me in his cage.

In no time, he trapped me in between a wall and a sexually worked-up hungry wolf.

His other hand found my throat, and soon he throttled me with his five strong, large fingers. I looked up at him in the most vulnerable state I'd ever been in, while my heart already missed several beats, and once again, my pussy, drenching my panties all the way. The glint on his dark arctic stare brimmed with power, authority, and ownership. Ownership of me.

"What did you say, again?" he asked. His eyes sparkled as he grumbled out the question as his hot breath fanned my face.

"Nothing. I said nothing." I was breathless. Gosh... I was so aroused I could even agree to hump him if he wanted to.

"Did you say you wanted to kiss me, Xena?" His face was so close that our noses were nuzzling against each other as our parted lips brushed. The warm breath of Vaughn was a naughty, hot caress on my mouth.

I didn't know from where I found the courage and energy to say the next few words, but I surprised myself by saying, "Not yet, Wolf. We were just talking about *what-ifs*. I need to see how hard you want me to disregard the rules and forget the fact that you are an off-limit for me."

A feral growl of frustration found its way out of his throat as he buried his face in the crook of my neck. He let my hands loose and hauled my body closer to him by the waist as his nose was lost to inhale my fragrance at the garden of my neck. Deliberately, my hands found their way around his muscled neck, and I held him tight against my body.

"Fucking hell, Xena. You got me right on my knee. For you. Only for you." His cry was full of pain. The pain from his frustration.

The pain from all the self-restraints, the pain of not being able to make me submit to him yet.

His words melted a little more of that reluctance in my heart, and it opened for him a bit more than before. I know, slowly, he was opening my heart for him, and I didn't care anymore. I wanted him, too, and I wanted him so badly.

Suddenly, he shifted his face from my neck and looked into my eyes. Inexplicable desire was evident in the dark arctic stare. Not only for my body, for my soul as well. His eyes were half-lidded as he tried to hold on to my soul, boring deeply into mine.

Dammit, I want to kiss him.

I slid my hands along with the corners of his suit jacket and gripped both the lapels. His lips were gentle as they brushed the corner of my mine, and I shuddered at the luxurious feeling of Vaughn's skin. It felt excessively unnerving, yet so right.

"Take off your panties."

I was surprised at the ridiculous proposition of the man whose body was absolutely covering me like a blanket right now.

"Do you have some kind of fetish for my panties, Wolf? I already forgot one in your club that night."

"Maybe. That pair of panties is what helps me get off and then finally sleep every night, Sugar. But I want the one you are wearing right now. I know how soaked it is, and I *need* it." He growled when he uttered the word '*need*,' revealing his raw, animalistic, and unrestrained desire for me.

There was a certainty in his voice, and I knew he wasn't going anywhere without it. So, I decided to pull my dress from the corner and tucked my finger inside the elastic. Then slowly, I pulled the thong off of me as he held me captive under his hungry stares.

When I was done, Vaughn snatched the thong from my hand right away and then pressed it against his nose to inhale my wet scent of arousal, as if he was starving. His eyelids were squeezed shut as though he were in a state of euphoria.

Then his eyes opened, and they found mine. With one hand, he gripped my wet panties hard, and another found my throat once again. It wasn't firm enough to stop me from breathing, just enough to make my arousal drip down my thighs.

I was dripping down my thighs, for freak's sake.

"Gosh… Xena, I'm desperate to push between your legs and claim you to be mine forever." He pressed his face against mine, tickling my skin with his subtle, scratchy beards—something that I loved about him.

"What I am today is all my blood and sweat. But you, Xena, you made me face the most difficult circumstance I've ever encountered. Goddammit, Xena! Submit your soul to me! I fucking need it. I need you."

The vibration his lips created against my skin twisted my soul in an equally painful yet pleasurable state. I moaned into the intense feelings and said, "No decision until the seven days finish."

After taking a long moment to comprehend my words, the man let out a dark chuckle and then looked into my eyes. "You are one stubborn girl."

I grinned at him and said, "Then, maybe I'm just like you. You said I'm the one for you, didn't you?"

A slow grin appeared on his face. Sparkles twinkled in his eyes as his thumb stroked a possessive brush on my lips and said, "Damn right. You are mine. Mine!"

To freshen up, or precisely, to wipe up my dripping wetness, I went to the washroom. Ron was still there, busy talking to her boyfriend. The girl was head over heels for the man already. I had never imagined seeing a head-high girl like Ron behaving like a teenager in love. As her eyes fell on me, I smiled and walked into a booth to freshen myself.

When we walked back to the front door, we noticed Vaughn, waiting, leaning against the door. Just from the sight of him, I felt the wetness pooling between my legs once again.

146

My eyes went towards his coat pocket, where he securely hid our deepest, filthiest secret from the world like it was nothing to be ashamed of.

When we settled in the car once again, I was in a dilemma whether I should text him again or not. That was exactly when something happened, putting me in the most terrible situation I could have envisioned myself.

"Who have you been texting since the morning, Jay? I bet it's Leo, isn't it?" Ron asked with a smug hanging at the corner of her lips.

My heart skipped several beats, and my back started sweating. Oh god! Not in front of the wolf! *Oh, blanketties!*

My eyes widened when I looked at Ron. "Don't say just anything, Ron!"

From the corner of my eyes, I noticed him. His eyes were shooting fire of questions towards me. I swear I could feel the heat flaring up from it. He looked furious. I had never seen such a fierce look on his face. It turned my hands, and my feet turned cold.

"Don't feel shy. I know about him, and other than me, Vee here won't judge if you have a boyfriend. It's cool."

Gosh… Ron, where is the reign of your mouth, girl!

I decided to stay silent. I could see Vaughn's posture going rigid in an instant. He was fuming. One of his hands gripped my panties inside his pocket, most probably to calm himself. With another, he held his cellphone, supporting his chin to look outside. One more word from Ron would make him snap, regardless of whether our secret would reveal that way or not. I couldn't risk that.

The drive to Hudson Valley from New York was just two hours, but the rest of the journey felt like a long twelve hours-journey with Vaughn fuming like a volcano about to erupt fiery molten lava.

The villa Vaughn owned was, in a word—magnificent. The exterior was so dreamy that it gave an illusion of a painting that could take your breath away in a good way. It had both a natural and modern vibe, and honestly, I couldn't wait to check out the interior.

Ron pulled my hand despite Finn's reluctance, rushing inside the villa as Vaughn helped Finn with the luggage. The inside of the villa was just as beautiful as the natural scenery we viewed outside. There was a slight lofty feeling with every modern daily facility I could think of. I could imagine myself spending months here with the company of some good reads.

Also, with Vaughn. Not that I could dare to think so far.

First, we checked out the ground floor, comprising a guest room, living room, kitchen, dining room. But the part that I loved most was the patio outside with a decent-sized Jacuzzi and lounge chairs.

Then we moved towards the top floor to see two beautifully decorated bedrooms. They were probably where Vaughn and Ron would be occupying. Ron didn't dare to show me inside Vaughn's room. Although I knew she did it because Vaughn was usually a private man. The slight tinge of disappointment hit my heart, anyway. Oh, how I wished to peek into the bedroom to see the bed where Vaughn had slept, even for a night in his life. Gosh, I was so pathetic.

While Ron was giving me a tour of her room, I received a text.

Filthy Wolf: I will show you my room later.

My treacherous heart jumped in thrill from reading the text. A satisfied smile sneaked its way out on my lips, as I couldn't help it. God, this man!

Vaughn already carried Ron's luggage as we went upstairs, leaving her to settle in comfort.

"You take some rest and come downstairs in an hour. I'll help her settle in," Vaughn said to Ron and walked out of the room.

I hugged Ron and then followed Vaughn downstairs in silence.

My room had an extraordinary view, I was sure. But I couldn't say because I was in no condition to tell now. When Vaughn and I carried my luggage into the room, it took no time for Vaughn to throw them aside and pin me against the wall, leaving me gasping and vulnerable.

Oh, snuggly blankets! The fuming, frustrated, angry wolf, delicate, apologetic me, a locked room, and about an hour of uninterrupted time.

The first thought that came into my mind was—*what is he going to do?*

25 | Envious

Xena

Vaughn's nose flared as he pressed into my body, resembling exactly what happened in the hotel on our way here. His breathing was short, heavy, and hot. Dark eyes restlessly wandered over my face, searching for a way to go deeper into my soul, to grasp every bit of it. He heaved like a wild, starving, and angry beast, and nothing turned me on as a vexed-up Vaughn clung onto my body as he owned it.

Is there something wrong with me?

Before he could practically blow fire from his elegantly sharp, straight nose, I decided to pacify the worked-up man. I surrounded his sharp-as-knife jaws and warrior-cheekbones with my dainty palms and looked deep into his eyes.

"He is not my boyfriend. Just a friend—a good friend."

Vaughn covered my hands in his big ones and pressed them against the wall over my head, turning me even more vulnerable before him. Then he pushed his face into my neck, breathing hard.

"Even though you didn't say his name, even though you just mentioned *he*—fucking hell, Xena! I can't even take it. A good friend? *Fuck…* You are mine!" he said, sounding like a wounded beast.

I loosened my hands from his possessive hold and found my way towards his charcoal, soft curls that had been tempting me forever to touch. The moment I pushed my finger through his hair, Vaughn groaned in contentment, and I breathed a sigh of relief. None of my imagination matched what I felt. It felt better. Gosh, it felt better to touch him, inhale him, and even see him when compared to my fantasies.

And whenever he pushed his nose into my neck, touched my sensitive skin with his lips, or held me possessively, it felt like I was dreaming of something surreal. Like I was dreaming with my eyes open. How could Vaughn want me like that? How did it happen?

I buried my fingers into his hair, running them in slow, comforting strokes that noticeably calmed him down. His hands rested around my waist, close to my hips. My lips found his ear, whispering into it.

"When I promised you an unrestricted week, I meant it, Vaughn. Right now, you have got me. There is no one else. Even if you weren't here, still, there would be no one else for me. You have me right here. Now show me how much you want me. One week isn't much time, Wolf. Your clock is ticking."

Vaughn lifted his head from my neck in slow motion and looked at me. The moment the man looked into my eyes, my heart started thumping at its highest pace once again. The hungry, challenging look in him matched not a wolf but a starving lion.

"You are already mine, little girl. You are just in denial. And I'm going to strip that denial from your sexy little face before the week ends. That—I promise you."

I brought one of my hands out of his hair and slowly stroked his heaped forehead, the straight bridge of his nose, then leaving his lips untouched, and my finger shifted towards his high cheekbones and chiseled jawlines. His lips parted a little with the escalating anticipation as he leaned into my subtle touch.

Before my eyes, I saw a growling lion turning into a lovesick puppy.

The moment I felt him weaken before me, I grabbed the opportunity and shoved onto his chest to release my body from his tempting trap.

"There is no denial! In your dreams may be, Wolf?" I ran from him, grinning like a naughty kid.

As expected, it didn't take long for the wolf in him to catch me. But what put me off-guard was he threw me flat on the bed with him on top of me. His knees supported his glorious body on my sides while he pushed my hands onto the mattress—trapping me in.

"Are you sure you are talking about *my* dream? Or is it *your* dream? Don't dare to say you don't dream about me, Xena. Your reaction to our proximity gives away your inner thoughts more than you know. Deny as much as you want, Sugar. You are right there, where I am," he said. His warm breath deliciously tickled over my sensitive face.

Who said I would deny that?

But there was no way I would tell him about him being the only one arousing me, awakening my insatiable hunger. Hunger—that existed only for him.

For a moment, I just wanted to lie like that and feel his warm breaths on my skin. It was like a dream, a beautiful dream for me.

"Who is Leo?"

Blanketty blankets! He wasn't over that!

"He is just a guy I met at Aphrodisia half a month ago."

"The man whose hands were all over your body on the dance floor and then fucking *kissed* you?" his voice went stiff once again. What a testy man!

"How do you know?" *Really, how?*

"I always know when it's related to you."

"Were you there? We thought you weren't there that night."

"I have my ways, sweetheart."

"Were you stalking me, Wolf?"

"Always. Now tell me, is he the guy?"

Did he stalk me? For real? I know I shouldn't like what he said, but *snuggles*! I did. His body hovering above me when I was lying on a bed didn't help. The slut in me was crying for his attention, and right now, it was finally beaming with joy as I became the center of Vaughn's endless devotion.

152

"Yes, but nothing happened after that night. We became good friends. That's it, Vaughn." Even though I tried to sound casual, deep inside, his anger was scaring the shit out of me.

But I loved it. Yes, I was a pathetic piece of excuse when it was about Vaughn.

"He kissed my girl! Even *I* haven't kissed you yet!" he said, growling above me like a possessive yet helpless beast.

"It was a onetime thing, Vaughn."

"Then care to say from where Ronnie got that absurd thought?"

"We text each other, share some memes or something funny we come across, that's it! He is a good friend, Vaughn. Don't get jealous of him."

"*Don't* get jealous when my girl is texting some prick out there? What do you take me for? A saint? Let me burst your bubble, Sugar. I am no fucking saint when it comes to you."

That's right. He is Vaughn Wolf, and he is no saint. He is filthy. He is possessive and protective of who he loves.

Am I also one of them?

Suddenly, he sat on the corner of the mattress with his feet reaching the floor. Then, yanking me up, he placed me on his knee with my face down.

"Wh-What are you doing?" I asked. My voice was shaking. Somehow, I knew what he was going to do.

"You need to be punished, Sugar. I need to tame you, you naughty little bratty girl. You need to remember who owns you—body and soul."

He raised the hem of my dress around my waist with no hesitation, as if he really owned me. The suddenness of the cold air hitting my heated, sensitive skin took me off-guard. Only then did I remember my bottom was naked under the dress.

I was out of words when I felt Vaughn brush his callous palm over the subtle, smooth skin of my ass. As if he was testing his own possession.

153

"Your ass is a piece of art, Sugar. Then again, I'd like it better when it's red. That's the color that suits best for a bratty girl like you."

The first slap fell on my ass, making it bounce and the sharp pain generating from his palm shot right towards my pussy. Making it go crazy with the painful yet pleasurable sensation. He didn't hold back when he hit my ass, and I couldn't hold back when a whine struggled out of my mouth.

"Don't even dare to fucking enjoy this! I'm fucking punishing you here. Goddammit, Xena! You have no fucking idea how mad you made me."

His next slap was harder, making me squirm on his lap in both pain and pleasure. I felt drool sliding from the side of my face as I felt his hands hitting the intimate part of my body as the cold air hit places that were meant to be kept covered.

My pussy was on fire after a few more spanks. I didn't want to enjoy them, but I knew I did. Who was I kidding? I could feel my wetness making a mess, wanting more of those.

"Look at you... soaking all over my pants. You have some nerves, Sugar. Don't you have any shame? You kiss other men, play text games with them, defend them before me, and then when I punish you, you dare to enjoy it?"

I pushed my ass higher in the air, a silent invitation for him to spank me some more. I was on the verge of my sweet release after days, and I *needed* it.

"You dared to get aroused by my punishment, huh? Fine."

He shoved two of his large, long fingers roughly into my pussy, stretching me painfully, making me squirm.

But I liked that, too.

Vaughn manhandling me aroused me like anything I could ever imagine.

As if noticing my heightened arousal, Vaughn started to push his fingers in and out my pussy. His other hand firmly, possessively

154

placed on my burning ass cheeks. I had no doubt they looked beet-red by then.

My core muscles clenched, anticipating a strong orgasm building inside me. I gripped the bedsheet, trying to control the feral sound coming out of my throat.

Just before my release, he pulled his fingers out of my scorching cave. My body protested his action, and I whined throatily as he denied my highly awaiting orgasm.

"Yeah, that serves you right. Remember this when you think about any other guy who isn't me. Because if you do, this is exactly what will wait for you." He covered my ass and carefully placed me on the bed.

When he noticed the tear stains, he said, "I promise, Xena. I'll make you come really soon. Just not now. What you said deeply troubled me. Bear with the punishment for now."

Then, dropping a kiss on my forehead, he wiped my tears with his thumb and said, "We have twenty minutes left. Get ready and come out soon. It's okay if you need some extra time."

And then he left.

Lying there still, I recalled what had just happened. The thought wasn't new. He did the same thing many more times in my dreams, but it never felt so real because it was indeed real this time—with him... with Vaughn.

It took me an additional fifteen minutes to get ready and come out. No, I didn't defy his command. I didn't jill off. But I had to take a cold shower to calm down my simmering body. I wore a cherry red summer flowy short dress with a sweetheart neckline, which proudly showcased a decent amount of my deep cleavage. That would put a certain someone right in his place.

When I came out, the siblings were already seated. Vaughn wore a black windbreaker over a black vest. Since he was sitting, I couldn't see what else he wore, but I assumed it to be a pair of black jeans. The sight of him in casual for the first time was delicious, but I didn't

155

allow myself to swoon over his handsomeness. At the round table, there was only one seat left. Nevertheless, it was between Vaughn and Ron. There was no other way to sit among three people.

I could feel his penetrating, intense eyes on me. Giving him no glance at all, I walked towards the chair. When I sat down on the hard surface, I hissed out loud as my ass cheeks stung in pain. It was an unfamiliar experience for me since no one had ever spanked me before me.

"Hey, Jay, you okay? You took time, and now you look in pain. What's up with you, boo?"

I could feel his penetrating stare at me. The proximity coated the situation with its intenseness.

"I'm alright, Ron. Just tired."

Ron bought my lie and said, "It's okay. You can take a rest if you want."

"No, no. It's okay. I'll hate it if I ruin our plans. I'll just sleep earlier today. What's our plan today?"

His eyes never left me. I felt it. When I noticed Ron busy serving the takeaways, I looked at Vaughn and met his eyes. His eyes were full of concern, and it didn't seem fake. But I glared at him, anyway.

His punishment was brutal after days *with* Vaughn and *without* orgasm.

It's a deadly combination, I'm telling you!

"We are going to visit some outdoor arts and gardens today," Ron said, squeaking.

I smiled at her as I dug into the food.

"Are you sure you can walk that much?" Vaughn asked.

Ron started coughing at his question. The food probably went to her wrong pipe. This was the first time Vaughn talked to me in front of her. That also, with his usual arctic eyes warm with full of concern.

I maintained my expression, calm and controlled. "Yes, thank you for your concern, Mr. Wolf."

He narrowed his eyes at how I said his name.

The day went eventful, with Ron and I taking lots of pictures of each other. Ron even forced Vaughn to take a few pictures of us together. Vaughn, on the other hand, never seemed tired from glancing at me. The warmth of his concern for me still coated his dark eyes. However, I was way too pissed at the fact that he took me to the edge and left me hanging in there.

At night, I returned to my room earlier than usual. No matter how much time I spent with Vaughn, his intense looks and touches drained me out. Maybe sleep could help if it came at all.

I adorned my dark purple slip nighty and went to bed with slightly wet hair. Even after an hour of tossing and turning, sleep didn't come. My ass cheeks slightly stung, but what bothered me most was my need to release *and* the fact that Vaughn was sleeping right in the room above me. How could I sleep this way?

Another half an hour later, I heard a faint knock at my door. I thought I was wrong, but when I heard it again, I went to open it.

Is it Vaughn?

With anticipation simmering inside my body, turning everything into a puddle, my shaky hands opened the door carefully, expecting his arrival. No matter how pissed I wanted to be, I couldn't be pissed at Vaughn. It was Vaughn. My Vaughn.

And when I opened the door finally, my heart jumped inside.

It was him.

26 | Taken Care-of

Xena

Vaughn leaned against the door frame, looking as smug as ever as he checked me out from head to toe. Even though I busted a gut to fake being pissed at him, there was no doubt I was miserably failing.

"Sleeping?" he asked.

Ah, that deep voice again.

"Yes," I said. My face carried an angry façade as I crossed my arms under my breasts.

Bad move. Because his eyes immediately moved downwards and hovered over the deep cleavage and swells of my tits.

Beyond the shadow of a doubt, his eyes turned dark and hooded in desire. The man straightened himself, taking his sweet time. His tall frame made me look and feel defenseless to his sexy, domineering charms.

With a playful smirk, he snarled. "Liar!"

"Is Ron asleep?" I asked, attempting to change the topic.

"Yes. It's only you and me now, Sugar." Then tilting his face a little, he said, "I'm playing by your rules, Xena. You can't hide from me anymore." Excitement glinted in his dark orbs. Too hard to miss.

His way of stating every word was overly sexual. It startled every single end of my nerves, turning me into a puddle.

"It's time for my beauty sleep. Uh—See you tomorrow. Good night!" I hurried and was about to close the door as his strong, veiny hand stopped me in the middle.

"Don't worry. I'm here to make sure you sleep well," Vaughn said with a devilish smile. Then the man brushed past me into the room.

I turned around to follow his unhesitant-self walking around the room, and then he laid onto my bed as if he owned it. Well, technically, he owned it, but right now, I was staying in. So, it wasn't normal behavior, was it?

He grabbed the pillow I was lying on and lifted it to his nose. His chest puffed as he deeply inhaled my scent on it.

Oh, snuggly snuggles!

"What do you think you are doing?" I asked. My eyes narrowed on him, but inside, I was breakdancing in anticipation. Hell, I loved every moment, every damn unnerving moment with him, no matter how much I denied it.

"Lock the door and come here."

Gosh, the dominance in his voice! If I could, I would've slept with just the voice itself.

I went goo under his domineering voice. Wordlessly, my hand reached for the door and locked it. I took small steps towards the man of my dreams, who had been lying on my bed with one hand curled under his head and another still holding the pillow against his chest. His eyes, raking over my long legs that were bare under the hem of my short slip nighty.

Vaughn moved a little and reclined on the bed. When I stood by his side, he yanked my hand, and once again, I was lying on his lap with my butt facing him.

Within no time, my heart started racing fast, and heat pooled in between my legs. As though the man had a switch to my kitty that he could flip whenever he pleased.

Was he going to spank me again?

"Vaughn… I-I can't take anymore today. It still stings."

Without a single word, he pulled the hem of the nighty to my waist and dragged down my panties with no hesitancy, like he owned my body. All happened within a matter of a second.

"Vaughn…" I whined breathlessly with my uprising needs. What did I want again? Him to not spank me? Or him to push his fingers into my pussy? I couldn't even say.

In utter silence, he traced the marks that were left as an aftermath of his spanks.

I couldn't help shivering from his careful, intimate touches over my injured, tender skin. Then, to my surprise, I felt something cool smeared onto my sore skin, Vaughn rubbing it all over my butt with his rough yet gentle fingers.

"Wh-What is this?"

I heard his heavy breathing before he replied. "Ointment. It'll make you feel better."

"You could give it to me."

"Not a chance. I come with the ointment. Give it or take it. Tell me your call." His fingers went closer to my aching pussy when he said so.

Goodness, I could take him in any form. How could I deny it?

"T-Take it…"

"Thought so."

His smug voice drenched my core even more.

I laid on my cheek and closed my eyes, giving in to the blissful feeling. The man kept on rubbing the ointment all over my aching butt until the cool greasy thing completely absorbed into my skin. Only then did he let me go, but not allow me to put my panties on.

I gathered my mushy self and reclined on the bed. Vaughn tucked me in the blanket and stroked my hair. "Too tired for a movie?"

With Vaughn? Never!

I just shook my head. Vaughn smiled and went towards the TV. After he set everything up, *Pretty Woman* started playing on the screen.

"*Pretty Woman*, huh?" I asked as he scooted under the duvet, making a place for his large frame beside me.

"Don't you like it?" he asked. The man looked like he was in a daze, lifting my body so that my back laid against his hard chest. His chin rested on my shoulder and his arms wrapped around me in a tight embrace under my tits. Even the soft skin of my tits rubbed against his muscular, veiny arms through the thin fabric.

So intimate...

His embrace was a blanket of pure bliss and comfort, burying me in its divinity. I had never felt anything so wonderful before. *Is this how heaven feels like?*

My hands found their way to his upper arm as I felt his nose brushing over the sensitive skin of my neck.

"So you want to watch a movie, Wolf?" I asked, mumbling in breathlessness. Vaughn was already busy raining soft kisses on my neck and shoulder.

"Hmm."

That was his reply. Just that.

Nope, I couldn't keep a calm and controlled composure under such pleasant torture. I turned my head towards him a little and looked into his dark, hazy, hooded abyss. Immediately, his eyes dropped to my lips, and I sucked in a breath. He was so close there was only about an inch of unwanted space between our lips that I so wanted to get rid of. I was pretty positive he felt the same way, too.

Abruptly, I turned away from my head and looked forward to continuing to watch the movie. Not that any of us had any intention of watching it at all. His hot and heavy breathing in my ears gave me an idea about how aroused he was. And me? Even the thought of his name turned me on. All the freaking *blanketty* times!

The nighty had a pretty huge neckline, and from his position, Vaughn could enjoy the deepest part of my cleavage just as clearly as I could. Besides, I knew his eyes were on them rather than on the movie.

I was sure about the fact the moment I felt his hand coming close to my erected bud little by little.

I was so turned on that there was no room for reluctance anymore. Besides, the heat radiating from Vaughn's body, sinking in me, didn't help. I'd rather take what I could get from him. My constant orgasm denials had me in a pretty vulnerable position. Especially when I was scooted right in his arms, in a bed, under the same quilt.

Slowly, his finger reached the destination, and ever so gently, Vaughn brushed his fingertip around my tightened nipple, but not on it. Even though his fingertip totally disregarded my aching nub, I gasped from his soft caress on my areola. Gosh, I had never felt this ever.

"Shh. Close your eyes and give in. I'm going to make you feel good, Xena. Trust me." He said in a whisper. His voice was hoarse in my ear.

Damn, yes. You already do!

His fingers brushed around my nipple, never making even a faint attempt to touch it. His large palm cupped and felt my heavy tits. He touched the outsides of my swollen tits, the underside of them, and the anticipation in me kept heightening at the fastest pace.

It felt like hours when his fingers finally reached my nipple. By then, I was a quivering, horny, wet mess. The constant denial of orgasm already had me right on my edge. The moment when his fingertip touched my aching, tightened, awaiting nipples, my back arched, and I let out a needy moan. His lips kissed my neck once more before slowly drifting towards the route to my ears.

Because I was wearing silk, the friction of his strokes on my nipples felt extra sensitive. Every stroke pushed me a little more towards the orgasm building inside me for days. I was panting, trembling, writhing in his arms. At some point, my twisting was so uncontrollable it became difficult for him to focus on his desired area. Then, with one of his firm hands, he wrapped me around to press my shoulders against his chest and carried on with his sweet torture.

162

Downright at his mercy.

I cried out his name in unimaginable pleasure and frustration. "Vaughn…"

"I know, baby. I know." He breathed into my ear. I clutched his other hand that wrapped around my upper chest, holding my shoulder to keep me in place.

All he did was tease my nipple with the soft, delicate strokes of his fingertips, but it was taking my soul away. I threw my head back, squeezed my eyes shut, and sank my teeth into my lips. One moment I breathed hard, and then on another, I held my breath. The throb in my pussy was so violent I kept rubbing my thighs against each other again and again. I didn't care anymore how I looked before him. My body needed the release. I could do anything for it. Gosh… I was dying for it.

Just the moment his fingers pinched my nipple and squeezed it, my overly sensitive nipple could take no more, and I came for the first time in my life, only from nipple stimulation.

I ruffled my carnal growl and the loud moan of the primal release with my palm. My pelvis arched, pussy creamed, God knew how much, under the blanket. Behind my eyes, all I saw were white flashing lights. It felt just how it felt with the clitoral release, if not more, and I loved every second.

Right after my release, my body went limp. I let it lie weightless on Vaughn's body. Even though it was I who had a mind-shattering orgasm, Vaughn was panting with me as well. It was intense for him, too.

Never in my life had I ever thought about coming just from nipple stimulation. But Vaughn's touches, along with the fact that it was *he* who was touching me, got me undone.

"You okay?" he asked. His breathless voice buzzed into my hair.

"Mmm." That was all I could manage to mumble.

He chuckled in a throaty voice and loosened his hold from me. Then he walked to the bathroom to bring a washcloth, probably to clean me up.

"No, please no! I can't take any more of you tonight! My daily dose of Vaughn has already exceeded! Give it to me."

He chuckled again, looking amused. Then he muttered something under his breath that kind of sounded like, *"Too adorable,"* but I wasn't sure. My mind still buzzed from the fantabulous orgasm I just had.

He handed me the towel and kissed my forehead. "I hope now my girl will finally be able to fall asleep, no?"

I was suddenly so shy when I realized he knew why I couldn't sleep. Until now, he somehow managed to know everything so effortlessly when it came to my body. I hid my face with my palm like a pathetic loser. How come I was shy after getting a nipple orgasm from this man?

He lightly chuckled this time and then pressed a soft kiss on the back of my palm that hid my face from him. Then left with a faint good night and a playful *'dream of me'* remarks.

The following day was another adventure with the siblings. We went to visit an antique shop, a sky ride, and a beautiful waterfall. Among us, Ron was over-the-moon excited. Vaughn, on the other hand, was too careful about us not getting hurt. He seized every opportunity to hold my hand to protect me when I didn't even need any protection. It was my luck that Ron was busy taking selfies and didn't notice much. Vaughn was tricky enough to take an opportunity to click a selfie of us. In the photo, I looked at him in surprise, and he gazed at me with a smug expression. But somehow, it came out to be so beautiful.

After coming back that day, both Ron and I had our entire bodies aching. Vaughn set the Jacuzzi at a comfortably warm temperature for us. We adorned in our bikinis and hopped in. Vaughn was nowhere to be seen when I got rid of my cover-up and then rested in the Jacuzzi in a relaxed mood.

"Hey, what's up with Leo?" Ron asked after a while of talking nonsense.

"Good. We text."

"Aren't you guys going on a date when we return? I'll be at Bryan's when we go back to the city. What are you going to do, Jay? Don't tell me you will be alone!"

Suddenly, I had an idea.

"Yeah, I guess I'll call Leo to see if he is free."

"I'm sure he will be, even if he wasn't in the first place." Ron flashed me a devious smile and wiggled her brows.

I felt both guilty and excited. To hide my eyes from Ron, I looked around, and then I saw him. He was standing by the window of his room, eyes fixed on me. Suddenly, an intense desire to be close to him overwhelmed my senses.

"Ron, I want to go to my room now. Is that okay?"

"Of course, Jay. I'm not getting out of this heaven for at least an hour. It's so soothing!" She closed her eyes, leaning her head on her back.

"Okay, take your time." I smiled at her, feeling a little guilty inside.

"Okay, boo. Just hand me over my phone."

I handed her over her cellphone, and then, summoning all my courage, slowly, I headed towards Vaughn's room. As I reached closer to his door, my breathing went heavy in anticipation.

His door was a little ajar.

I never claimed myself as a nun. I was nowhere near so innocent that I wouldn't be tempted enough to peek inside his room... *Vaughn's room.*

And when I did...

Oh, blanketty snuggles!

27 | In Flagrante Delicto

Xena

There were moments in my life when I felt unbelievably horny. Exceptionally, unimaginably, incredibly horny. When I felt the ground under my feet turn into a surfing board, making it way too difficult for me to stay put. My heart rate and pulse rate rose so high that I thought I would die. My tits and clit, swelling and aching so much, it grew unbearable to stay calm.

But none of them could compare what I felt at that moment.

My insides turned so hot. At the same time, my skin turned so cold. The collision between them caused cold sweats to break through my skin.

Should I stay? Or should I run away?

But...

Snuggles!

I couldn't. Even if I wanted to, I couldn't move from there. My feet stayed rooted, and my eyes stayed glued.

Long. Thick. Massive.

Hard as a rock.

Raging. Fuming. Twitching.

And Vaughn's large, sexy hand wrapped around it.

Vaughn still had both his black shirt and sweatpants on. Just his enormous cock was out on display, proudly in a standing ovation as he stroked it with one of his large palms.

I want to do that!

I cursed the voice that came from the back of my irrational head.

166

It was the veiniest cock I had ever seen, even on porn. The tip of the cock was curved in a way I could swear it could hit places I was dying to be felt on. Even from afar, I could see how purplish it looked from all the blood rush and extreme points of desire.

Bloody engorged purple monster!

His strokes were slow but hard. I could see how hard he squeezed his pulsing cock as he pleasured himself. The throbbing between my legs became even more acute as I watched his hand slide up and down his enormous length.

I really wanted to touch myself. My nipples, heavy and aching, my clit yearning for a touch, but every time my hand approached there, I couldn't make it to pleasure myself. Every freaking time I recalled Vaughn claiming all my orgasms as *his*.

I couldn't disobey him. I couldn't.

Thick white liquid appeared on the slit of his crown, and I was a goner.

I licked my dried lips, almost feeling his pre-cum on my lips. I was that deep into the scene where Vaughn, *the* Vaughn, pulled out his monster cock from his pants and pleasured himself.

Snuggles! I want a lick!

Previously, I was so into staring at his enormous, veiny precision that I didn't look at the man's face. But my, oh my. When I did, a gasp almost sneaked out from the back of my throat. Only god up there knew how I ruffled the sound under my sweaty palm.

His other hand had my thong pressed against his nose, sniffing it as his hand sped up on his monster. He looked so dangerously fascinating. The sight both sent chills to my spine and took me to the point of almost having an orgasm just from peeking into him while he was busy jacking off to my panties.

I was in a heated discussion with my mind about where to look. At his hand, which was right now pumping hard on the monster cock? Or his face that was half-covered with sweat and a half behind my panties?

Almost... I was almost touching myself, watching him, wondering how his balls would look. I couldn't see them since his sweatpants curtained them behind.

Right at that very moment, I heard him scream my name hard enough for me to hear.

"Xena..."

"Gosh! Fuck... dammit, Xena. Fuck... Xena... Xena..."

I focused on him to see if he saw me, but no. He ejaculated with his back arching, his hip pushing higher into his hand. His growl came from the back of his throat... and gosh... I had never heard anything as raw, as primal, as alluring as *the* Vaughn coming.

And he said my name!

Oh, snuggles!

Vaughn? My Vaughn came groaning out my name?

Was I dreaming?

But the ache in my pussy and my tightened nipples disagreed with the idea. Real. He was very much real.

And yes, it was my name on his incredibly kissable lips that he had been biting at this moment.

Gosh, I want to bite on that!

The moment Vaughn came, his chest heaved in heavy panting, and his eyes remained closed. His palm still had a tight grip around his pulsing rock-hard length that was stubborn to show signs to limp down anytime soon. It was a beautiful sight that I could look at all my life and never get bored. Nothing could compare to Vaughn's face as he came. His handsome face looked sinfully beautiful, and all I wanted to do was lick that dripping cum off of his enormous monster cock.

Suddenly, I was aware of the situation. I couldn't even imagine what would happen if Vaughn knew I watched him at his most intimate, private moment. This was wrong. So wrong from every angle. Slowly, I turned on my heels to leave the door to heaven as quietly as I could muster.

Yes. Heaven. It's exactly what it felt like to leave the place.

I hadn't even taken a step when a voice from behind stopped me in my tracks, and my heart dropped to my stomach, leaving me to taste how it felt like to drop from a drop tower.

"Where do you think you are going, Sugar?" His deep, throaty, sexy voice questioned me.

I stood still on my legs. Could I turn around? Or just run away from there? Or make a hole in the ground and bury my sneaky loser self in there?

"Answer, Xena. Do you really think you can just run away after what you just did?"

There. Once again, his dominant voice.

I turned around and slowly looked at him from the ajar door. His cock was still raging in its full form, with his large palm shamelessly wrapped around it. Oh, and my thong was in a tight grip in his other hand as well.

"H-How do you know?" I asked in a breathless whisper.

"Didn't I tell you? I always know when it comes to you."

I just kept staring at him with my mouth open in surprise.

"Lock the door and come here."

Somehow, I couldn't say no to this specific voice. It made me do all sorts of crazy things with just a single command.

With wobbly steps, I entered the room and closed the door behind us, separating the two of us from the world.

He reclined on his chair and said, "Go, lie on the bed."

My eyes widened.

"I-I want to lick you."

Wait, what?

Is it my voice? Really? Am I asking that? What?

Vaughn chuckled darkly, and his deep, sexy voice buzzed in the locked room.

"You are not getting a taste of me, Sugar. Not yet."

"But you get to do it..."

169

Seriously, is it me? What possessed me? Am I bargaining for licking a man?

Well, then again, the man is Vaughn. So it's understandable. Woo! Way to go, Xena!

"Of course I do it. But you can't. Not before you give in to me, Xena. That's your punishment. I can do anything I want because I'm head over heels for you here. The moment when you give in to me, you'll also own me completely, Xena. Every part of me. Like how I own you."

Desire and many other emotions that I couldn't put my finger on clogged my throat, and I tried to gulp down the lump. Was it wrong that I really, really wanted to give in to him right that very moment? I wanted him. I wanted Vaughn, all of him.

"Don't you want to come, Xena? Have I not deprived you enough from doing so? Don't you want to touch yourself to the point you cream all over that pink, gorgeous pussy of yours? So... do what I say."

I couldn't disregard his authoritative tone. It could make me do anything and everything as he wished.

Slowly, I crawled up to his bed and reclined against the headboard.

"Take off your bikini bottom."

I did what he said. His eyes scrutinized my every movement.

"Now touch yourself how *you* want to, Sugar. Show me what you do to that gorgeous piece of cunt when you think of me, fantasize me."

I went with his command and opened my legs, spreading them only for him to have a clear look at what lay in between my thighs. He was clearly obsessed with it, and I was obsessed with his obsession. Then, slowly, my fingers reached the apex of my thighs, and I touched the scorching, swollen, wet pussy lips. A breathy moan struggled out of my throat before I could stop it, and I heard Vaughn sucking in a sharp breath.

"How does it feel?" Vaughn couldn't keep it in anymore.

I looked at him and found him stroking his monster cock once again. The look in his eyes made me feel powerful. Powerful enough to hold his eyes captive this time and play with my pussy—legs spread on his bed as he stroked his cock before me.

"Hot and needy," I said. My natural husky voice lowered into a whisper.

"Fucking hell, Xena." He said, cursing in a painstaking tone, squirming in his chair.

One of my hands gradually moved towards my tits, and I picked a hold on to one of them. Squeezing it over my bikini top and then reaching to the nipple to give it a sweet pinch for the love of Go—no, Vaughn.

I rubbed my hand slowly over my clit, making a few throaty, wild moans come out from the back of my throat. My other hand was on my mouth to ruffle the sound. Ron was right below the window.

Then, slowly, I put two of my fingers inside me as Vaughn's pumping grew faster. The most intimate part of all this was his eyes never leaving mine.

"One more finger." His raspy voice caused a wave to shudder in my body.

"I can't," I said, crying out loud.

"You can and you will." After a second of pause, he again said, "How do you expect to fit my cock in that little hole if you can't even put three fingers in? Do. It."

But as I went closer to my orgasm, I couldn't keep up with the eye contact anymore. I went wild, crazy, a moaning mess at the need for my sweet release. It had been long, *really* long, since he allowed me to touch myself.

One moment my free hand was up into my hair, fingers pushing deep into it, and another moment, it was gripping the bedsheet hard.

The moment I let myself go, I could hear the groan from Vaughn as well. He had released with me.

Oh, snuggles. If this wasn't hot, I didn't know what was.

I knew I should've felt shy and awkward after jilling myself off before Vaughn. But it surprised me how right it felt. I felt more confident, more powerful, and more tempting before him.

Vaughn gradually stood up from the chair and stepped towards me, just like the wolf he was. As he reached the end of the bed, he took hold of my ankles and yanked me towards him. I was still on my high, and my soul still didn't return to my body. So, I just silently watched him doing what he wanted to do to my body.

The man dipped his head down in between my legs. He licked my cum that smeared all over my pussy. He devoured every last drop of it like he was starving for it for years. After my orgasm, my swollen clit was extremely sensitive, to the point of being slightly painful. So, whenever his tongue touched my clit, it electrocuted, and I jumped involuntarily.

"Done. Licked and cleaned."

Now let me clean you too.

Accept he wouldn't.

Taking his sweet time, Vaughn hovered over my limp body with his hands and knees. His usual Amber woody fragrance was now mixed with the smell of Vaughn. He came twice before me, once smelling my thong and another watching me jilling off. No doubt he smelled male, but his perfume left a hint of vanilla smell over his body, which made me giggle like a little girl. His perfume suited him perfectly. Usually, he smelled like something like a mixture of amber and wood. But when he was like this, it smelled like vanilla.

Isn't Vaughn exactly like that? When he was with me, his usual demeanor changed into a softie every single time, no matter how domineering he was, as a person or a partner. At the end of the day, he finished by begging, *"Be mine."*

"What makes you smile, Sugar?" he asked. His eyes looked playful.

I took another lungful of the scent *'Pure Vaughn with a hint of vanilla Eau de Parfum'* and smiled, saying, "You."

"Me? After what just happened, giggling is the last thing I expected from you." He said, grinning. His hand, stroking a few strands of hair from my face—something he loved to do.

"I want to know which perfume you use." I bit my lower lip after saying that.

"You like it?" He asked, murmuring as he dropped affectionate kisses over my forehead and temples.

"Hmm. A lot."

"It's Noir Extreme. From Tom Ford. I thought I was the only one crazy enough to know what my girl wears." he said. A throaty chuckle released from him as he kissed my cheeks, drifting towards my nose and then my chin, leaving my lips all lonely and miserable.

"Mine isn't as exotic and expensive as yours. But it's my favorite. Rebelle by Rihanna."

"So warm and as sweet as sugar. It drives me insanely crazy." Vaughn's dark, throaty voice vibrated in my ears as he proceeded to kiss on my neck and ears. "It's my most favorite smell in the whole fucking world, Xena."

I moaned as he kissed my sensitive skin and said, "How come our conversation turned into discussing perfumes?"

"Because smelling each other's scent drives us crazy and worked up. And here I thought it's only me," he said. Then moaned as his face dropped on the swells of my breasts, and his tongue made small strokes over them in a daze.

Dropping a soft longing kiss on my cleavage, he looked up with dark eyes that shined like white stars and asked, "What else do you want to talk about?"

Like a pathetic loser, that was the moment I decided to feel shy before him.

I *am* a pathetic loser, aren't I?

"Do you want to talk about how fucking gorgeous you look when you play with your cunt that belongs to me? You want to tell me what exactly you fantasized as you fingered this pussy that I own?" He asked as his hand reached there, cupping my core.

"I-I imagined licking you a-and then making you come again," I said. My voice trembled like a loser.

His eyes darkened again, and before he could react, I shoved the very much entranced Vaughn aside. Then, putting on my panties, I ran to the door, saying, "Ron will be here any moment." I fled like the loser I was.

I thought this was the dirtiest he could get on our little vacation.

No reasonable part of me could've ever imagined that he had such a dirty trick in his pocket for the next day…

Only if I knew…

28 | Play

Xena

The villa had a magnificent view. Among the beauty of several shades of green, there was a lake flowing on its own accord and grace. The greens from the trees and the blues from the clear sky—together, they ornate a beautiful painting on the canvas of the water, making it look like an artistic piece of a watercolor effect.

Even though the scene was surreal, another dreamlike scene was right in front of me in the pool, currently swimming with his sister piggyback riding him.

Ron laughed in a carefree manner as she hopped onto Vaughn's back once again after he shoved her in the water. They looked like a couple of naughty little kids playing in the water. I couldn't help my lips from stretching into a happy grin as I watched them laughing and messing with each other.

After swimming and goofing around, the siblings started playing pool basketball together, where Ron kept losing to Vaughn again and again. When Ron could take no more defeat, finally, she looked at me with sad, pleading eyes.

"Jay! Come join us! It's our last day here! Don't be a joy kill! Come on!"

"I'm enjoying the view here," I said with a smile.

"Oh, come on, Jay. See, I'm miserably losing here. Come, give me a hand to win! This smug guy here is getting too confident in himself. Humph!"

Looking at her miserable face, I didn't want to say no. But as my eyes fell on her filthy brother's smirking lips and challenging eyes, I whole-heartedly wanted to say no. But at the same time, I wanted to take on the challenge.

I chuckled at her misery and said, "Fine. You'll owe me!"

I was wearing a black set of triangle O-ring bikini sets. The moment I took off my cover-up, I could feel Vaughn's deep eyes burning all over my body. I smiled inwardly. He had been swimming in the water in his black boxer with a confident look on his sexy face. Whereas, here I was having a problem controlling my crazy hormones, looking at the man with sex on the legs.

Payback time, Wolf.

Ron laughed at Vaughn and grinned devilishly. "Jay is really good with balls when it comes to games. You are going to lose!"

"Really? Let's see how *good* she can be with *balls.*" With the smirk and those eyes, the man reeked of sex as he said so.

That sexy piece of a... of a caveman!

Totally disregarding his nasty, filthy comment, I strolled towards the pool. I leisurely walked towards the pool handrail and got down in the water in slow motion. Even though I appeared unconcerned and carelessly took every step for the sake of the show, havoc was raging inside me as I remembered those penetrating, sexy pairs of eyes watching me.

Is he as hard looking at me as wet I am looking at him?

Right when I was down in the water, Ron wasted no time splashing water at me, breaking the intense moment between Vaughn and me. Though I wasn't looking at him, I knew how his eyes never left me.

The moment we started playing, I knew how good Vaughn was. There was no way I could win against him. But a girl could try.

Every time I got a chance with the ball, Vaughn swam towards me with those distracting flexes of muscles and secretly touched my body inappropriately to unnerve me. I felt his palm brush against my

176

belly one second, and then he brushed against my butt cheeks the next. And, for freak's sake, his filthy techniques worked every *effing* time!

Sometimes his firm hand squeezed my butt, and then in the next moment, he accidentally brushed his fingers on my nipples, which were already painfully erected. Thanks to the black bikini top, Ron didn't notice them.

He even whispered into my ear once. Reminding me what I said to Ron earlier. "Enjoying the view, huh?"

This. Guy!

"See, Jay! Vee is really good. Even both of us altogether can't score against him. He could at least give us some chance, but no! He had to play like a professional here!"

I glared at Vaughn angrily. If he didn't try his dirty techniques, I would've scored one or two points against this filthy beast of a man.

"Okay, fine! Ronnie, I'll let you win this round. Don't be upset. Let's try once again." Vaughn moved towards his sister to cajole her. But Ron was too pissed at him to be coaxed at all.

"Don't be upset, Jay! Let's go back to our room. I'm hungry. Besides, I don't want to play anymore!" Ron already dove to the corner before Vaughn could say anything else. Sibling fights. I had no space in between them.

So I just looked at Vaughn and shook my head in disappointment. Then wordlessly, leaving the dumbfounded Vaughn back at the pool, I also left.

Within a few minutes, Ron was alright again. We were still in the living room when she chuckled, repeating something Bryan said to her last night. I guessed that was how the siblings behaved around each other. They hit each other's nerves, forget in no time, and then love each other with all their hearts.

I went to my room and took a warm bath immediately, taking time. With a towel around my body and another wrapping around the hair, I walked out of the bathroom. Just the moment I stepped into the room, I found Vaughn in his signature suit, sitting at the edge of my bed with a mauve square box in his hands.

When his eyes fell on me, placing the box on the bed, he stood up immediately. I could clearly see his eyes widen and dilate before my eyes. Watching a man you want getting aroused only for you, before your eyes, was a wonderful sight—especially if the man was Vaughn.

When he crossed the space between us, I raised a brow and said, "You play dirty, Wolf."

I waited for his reply. I thought he would say something like, "I could play dirtier," but he didn't. He didn't say a word.

What he did was circle one of his hands around my waist to pull me closer to his warmth. The sudden force caused me to clutch on his chest to balance my body from falling down. Under my hand, his heartbeat with the profanity of jumping out at any moment.

His other hand slowly reached my cheeks, and then he traced his fingers downwards to my lips, my chin, and then gradually moved it to my throat. My breathing hastened when I felt his fingers tracing the swells of my breasts and my deep cleavage popping from under the towel.

"What are you thinking?" I asked. I couldn't help it since he was never this silent.

"If I tell you even a fragment of what's going on in my mind, you'll be having a hard and strong orgasm standing right here."

I gasped and sank my teeth into my lower lip.

"I brought something for you, Xena."

"What?" I asked in a daze, playing with the lapel of his suit jacket.

"A dress and a set of lingerie."

"Bu-But why?" My brows furrowed at his words. His sudden gesture surprised me.

"I have my purpose. But I want to ask for something in return. Will you give me?" His voice dropped to a nasal, husky tone.

"What?" My voice matched his.

"Don't be mad, okay?" Then, sighing, he said, "I want to dress you up."

My eyes widened as I looked at him, cheeks flaming in embarrassment at the mere thought.

"Will you?" he asked expectantly.

"N-No… it's too embarrassing."

"Xena, I want to dress you up."

There it is. The tone. The dominant one, which I can't say no to. Has he already found that out?

I just slightly nodded and stood at a hand gap.

Vaughn's next move, however, caught me off guard.

The man had seen me butt-naked; he had licked and sucked my cunt on more than one occasion, but when he brought the white set of lingerie and put on the panties on me, he didn't even look under the towel.

When he crouched down before me, I put one leg into one loop and then another, holding his shoulder as a support, as his eyes held mine captive, not wandering anywhere else. Just in my eyes.

Then he picked up the bra and stepped behind me. I sucked in a breath, knowing it was time for the towel to go. What surprised me most was Vaughn dropped the towel as I assumed and then offered me the bra to put my hands into the loop. But the entire time, he buried his face in my hair.

He hadn't looked at my bare tits yet. Despite that, he didn't take a peek and carefully clasped the hook from behind.

I was feeling heavy in my chest and couldn't form a word. Momentarily, I lost my ability to talk or make a single sound. I leaned back onto his chest, and he wrapped his hand around my upper belly. Then, with audible, hard breathing, he dipped his head to kiss and nibble on my neck.

His palm brushed on my abdomen area, making it shudder to the tingles his callous palm created on my sensitive skin.

179

Suddenly, I lost his warmth, and I abruptly looked behind to hold on to him. I didn't know what had happened to me for a second. But I didn't want to let him go. He had me as vulnerable as I ever could be.

Vaughn held one of my hands, and then, stretching the other hand, he picked up the dress. As if he knew what I was feeling inside.

His eyes raked me from top to bottom with raw hunger clearly written on them. Under his eyes, I couldn't help but feel sexy, beautiful, and confident. He made me feel beautiful, just from his stares.

Slowly, he put the dress on me with eyes full of fondness. When he finished dressing me up, Vaughn finger-combed my wavy waist-length blonde and turned me around to look into the mirror.

For a second, the dress completely distracted me. It was a beautiful yet simple white dress. The top part consisted of a white knitted triangle design covering the breasts. There was a cotton flowy fabric from under the breasts till about two inches above my knee, making it look serene, ethereal, and beautiful.

"Gosh, Xena, you look like a goddess. A beautiful, tempting goddess. And *so* mine. *Mine.*" With the last word, he clasped my waist hard, making me feel the intensity of his feelings towards me.

I turned around and looked into his eyes, leaning forward. I didn't know what I would do if I couldn't kiss the man right at that moment.

"Are you giving your heart and soul to me, Xena? Do you submit your feelings to me?" he asked desperately. "The moment you do, I'll do the same. And I will not kiss you until you say you are mine."

The need, despair, and desire in his eyes were so fascinating that the mischievous girl in me couldn't resist making him suffer for a little more.

When he noticed my silence, his eyes were full of anguish. Disregarding his blues, Vaughn kissed the top of my forehead and said, "You look beautiful, Xena."

Then he left me feeling cold. I stood there with coldness surrounding me as I watched Vaughn leave.

"Come down when you are done."

And he left.

When he was out of my line of sight, I faintly murmured to myself. *"Just a little more, Wolf. Then your wait will finish."*

When we were ready to leave, we found Finn already waiting for us beside the car. I greeted him with an amiable smile and took my seat.

Vaughn mostly remained silent after the car started. Inside, I felt a little guilty towards him. The moment was so perfect, and I absolutely wanted to shower him with the gift of my kisses. And I knew, I knew just how desperate he was for my lips.

Just before I lit up the screen of my phone, a sudden shock rushed throughout my body, making me jump in surprise, and a scary gasp came out of my mouth.

Vibration. Yes, that's precisely what I felt—*right in there!*

Did Vaughn… Did Vaughn… make me wear some vibrating panties?

"Jay! Are you okay? What happened?" Ron asked, looking at me from her phone.

I thought of something quick.

How to cover up the situation?

"Ah… Leo sent me some cockroach GIFs. You know how much of a cockroach-phobia I have."

"Oh! I thought you were feeling sick or something." Ron said, losing interest, and again looked into her phone.

I stared at Vaughn and found him glaring at me. I knew saying Leo's name would anger him. That's exactly why I did that.

But oh, my, my… it was a mistake.

181

The filthy man was operating the vibrating toy in my panties from his cellphone. And to punish me, he increased the speed and then looked at me.

With a devilish grin…

Oh boy.

29 | Car Rush

Xena

A silent car, a devil whom I wanted so badly, a best friend I was keeping secrets from, and panties on vibration—not the perfect combination, I could assure you.

My shaky hands reached my thighs to clutch onto them, but it didn't help. One second I squeezed the car door, then the next moment on the car seat, squirming all the way to keep my composure straight. But nothing seemed to work. To avoid moving too much to escape from Ron's eyes was the peak of my problem here.

I looked at the man in question and found him typing something on his phone. Somehow, I knew he was writing to me. I just knew.

Proving my earlier assumption correct, the screen of my phone lit up. I picked the phone from my side to read what the filthy devil had to say to me.

Filthy Wolf: Trust me, Xena. I'll make sure we both enjoy it.

My widened eyes drifted towards him in astonishment. He sat with calm and collected composure, but the time we spent together had done a great job of teaching me to read him better.

His jaw clenched, breathing came in short, and his shoulder tensed. I knew those dark, familiar eyes. I could comprehend how stirred he was, and it wasn't any less than me. To watch Vaughn being so affected by me aroused me even more than I already was. I couldn't help it. This man had me in his palm, *one hundred percent.*

One look at the man, and I was a goner. His being affected by me was such a turn-on that the daring part in me agreed to give in to this absurd idea he had in his wicked mind. With excessively shaky fingers, I picked up my phone and typed back in the shortest way to flash him an idea about what was going on with my body.

Xena: Can't keep calm.

When Vaughn read the text, I noticed him sinking his teeth into his soft-looking, kissable lower lip, taking in a sharp breath.

"Finn, turn on some music," he said, ordering Finn without even looking back.

"Yeah, I would love some Weeknd and Ariana Grande, please, Finn." Being a big fan of Weeknd, Ron didn't let the opportunity slip. All the swimming and playing in the water tired her more than she realized. She closed her eyes and settled in for a nap.

Thank god. Because the constant tingles in my clit made it unbearable for me to keep my whimpers in. The moment I heard Ariana's voice overpowering the silence in the car, finally, I felt at ease.

Filthy Wolf: Solved. Still want me to stop?

I bit my lips.

Do I want him to stop? I guess no, not anymore.

I began to love the feeling between my legs, right against my most intimate bundle of nerves. Besides, the thought of Vaughn controlling the rhythm and speed of the sneaky little thing in my panties upraised my need and desire for him to the point that I didn't want to back down. If I couldn't have his tongue or fingers in me right at that moment, then I wanted the next best thing, which was what he was already doing to me.

Xena: Continue

My text brought a heavenly smile on Vaughn's face that inevitably flipped something in my heart, making me go all gooey, wanting him once again.

Filthy Wolf: That's my girl

This time it was me who was smiling like an idiot reading the text. I knew my body showed every sign of being turned on, and none escaped Vaughn's scrutinizing eyes. But the moment I smiled, it happened to strike him the most. He looked like he was hypnotized, looking at me like I was some sort of ethereal beauty, spellbinding him with my smile.

Looking at Ron's closed eyes, I drifted my eyes to look outside. Just within a few seconds, I felt the vibration going on a pulse mode in there, making me jerk slightly.

Easing my body, I crossed my hands under my boobs, deliberately making them look bigger and fuller. From the corner of my eyes, I watched Vaughn drawing sharp breaths at that sight. I felt a different sort of pleasure building inside me as I pleased him. I had no idea how, but pleasing him pleased me just as much as arousing him aroused me.

The man knew exactly how the vibrator was playing inside. I was sure he checked every mode before putting the damn thing on me today. Every few minutes, he changed either the rhythm or the speed, and I went little by little to the verge of my release.

God, I had never felt anything like this.

The things I had been experiencing with this man, even before I gave into him—they were all new for me. *And snuggles, do I love every moment of it!*

He knew, god, he knew what he was doing. When I felt the pressure building in my lower region, I knew it was coming. I knew I was going to come. Writhing in my seat, I turned a little and pressed my face into the neck pillow, biting on it. It wasn't precisely what I wanted to bite right at that moment. But the one I craved to bite on was so far, and there was a high wall between us—the wall, who was currently enjoying the music with closed eyes, taking an innocent nap.

The moment I let go, the sound of The Weeknd playing faded to the point of nothing, nada, zero. There was no one for me other than the man who was very much aroused and stared at me with his hypnotized, spellbound eyes. Eyes—only for me.

The moment I recovered, I realized how sweaty I was. Even the luxurious air condition of this abnormally luxurious car couldn't help me with the heat of *Vaughn syndrome*.

Just when my heart was coming back to its usual pace, I felt the vibrator making me aware of its presence once again. My clit was so swollen and sensitive that I thought my heart skipped a few beats at the sudden act.

My phone screen lit up, and I checked it, only to find a text from the devil sitting before me.

Filthy Wolf: Want me to stop?

My body was still shuddering, every nerve of my body awakened, and the goosebumps mixed with the cold sweats of my skin were visible. My engorged nipples ached inside my bra, wailing to come out and hang free and then to be inside the hot, filthy mouth of this filthier man.

So, I typed what I wanted, and with no hesitance, I pressed send.

Xena: Continue

And *holy, snuggetty blanketty blankets.* He did.

By the time we reached our apartment, it was dark outside. After coming thrice from Vaughn's teasing, I was taking my few minutes of rest. He was nowhere near bored. In fact, it looked like he enjoyed it even more than me. His face was calm, just like it had been the day we were both released in front of each other. He looked happy and satisfied.

Finn helped us with our luggage as we were about to part with him. Ron hugged her brother as if he were the most precious person in her life. As if she was nowhere ready to be apart from him.

I didn't want to be apart from him, either.

Can't I hide him in my room and keep him for myself?

In front of Ron, I couldn't talk to him like I wanted to. God, I wanted to hug him, inhale his expensive perfume, feel the warmth of the skin of his pulsing neck, and—

—and kiss him.

I wanted to kiss him as much as I wanted the last freaking cheesecake from my favorite cake shop.

And I loved my cheesecakes.

But before Ron, we could only stare at each other longingly and over and above that, secretly.

When Vaughn bade goodbye and left our apartment, I couldn't bear to break apart. I wanted to feel him, inhale him, and touch him so badly that it was unbearable.

"Ron, I think I left my charger in his car. I'll go bring it."

Not waiting for her reply, I ran. I had to catch him. There was no way I would allow him to go without a hug, with all that caused havoc inside me with all my pent-up emotions.

I closed the door behind me hastily, ready to run down, but unexpectedly, my steps haltered, and I stopped in my tracks.

He was standing right there as if he was waiting for me… expecting me.

Just as my eyes found its lost sparks back, I pulled his hands towards the corner of the stairways, where it was unattended by the security camera… where no one could see us.

When we stopped, I looked into his eyes, only to find them smiling at my act in astonishment. Those arctic orbs looked thrilled, surprised, and proud as they penetrated deep into my eyes.

"Forgot something, Sugar?" he asked in his signature panty-dropping voice.

"Yeah," I said in a breathless tone as I shoved my arms inside his suit jacket and hugged his waist. My ears, pressing against his chest. The moment my ears touched his chiseled, hard chest, I could hear the thumping of his heart increasing by folds.

Yes, I affected him just as much as he affected me.

"You didn't say goodbye to me." I rubbed my cheek on his chest like a rabbit and accused like a coddled child.

"Did you want me to? Because I still want to claim you as mine before the world, Xena, not hide at the corner of the stairs. I don't care how Ron takes it. At some point, she has to accept it, anyway."

"No. Not yet. I need to figure out how to say this to her. She is protective of you, Vaughn, and you know it. Even I'm not allowed to cross the line when it comes to you."

Vaughn hugged me tightly in his arms and said, "Xena, I know you are mine, but have you accepted the fact yet? In your heart, are you mine yet?"

I smiled in his chest and said, "Don't you still have two more days to persuade me, Wolf?"

Vaughn groaned like a shackled beast in my neck. "Argh, I can't, Xena. I want to feel those entrancing lips of yours on mine. I fucking want them to wrap around my cock, taking me in completely. I want your hair all over my pillows, your butt cheeks imprinting my bedsheets, as your legs remain wide open for me as your cunt glistens—swollen, throbbing, and wet. I can't stop thinking, Xena. I can't stop thinking about you on all your fours, as your knees turned purple and bruised, but we will be nowhere near done with each other."

"Even when my knees turn purple and bruised, you won't stop?" I asked in disbelief as I felt my eyes closing in the comfort of his embrace and dirty talks.

"As much as I know you, my sweet little Sugar, it's not only me who won't want to stop. You'll want it as much as me."

Finally, I opened my eyes a little and shifted my head to look at him with hazy eyes.

"Why don't we find it out tomorrow?" I couldn't believe it was me saying those words to him. But gosh, I knew I meant what I said. I meant it very much.

He looked dumbfounded. Flabbergasted. Tongue-tied.

"Text me where we'll meet for our date tomorrow," I said as I lightly dropped a kiss on his cheek. "I, too, can't wait to kiss your lips, Wolf. Not even for two more days."

Then, leaving a stunned, astounded Vaughn back at the corner of the stairs, I ran into my apartment. What I said was true. I couldn't wait for the entire seven days to say yes to him. I wanted him, and I knew it, my body knew it, my soul knew it.

Before I entered my room, Ron appeared. She looked confused. "Hey, did you find your charger? I looked down there, but you weren't at the car."

"I found Vaughn at the stairs. He asked Finn to look. When he confirmed he found nothing, I came back. Maybe it's in my luggage." I felt guilt rising inside me already.

"Oh, you can use mine if you don't find it, boo."

She left as she said that, buying my lie. I couldn't help but think how wonderful it would be if Vaughn wasn't Ron's brother and I could talk to her about him. But there was no way I could do it. The situation bound me—hands and legs, and then left me utterly helpless about this issue.

After taking a shower, we ordered pizza and enjoyed the cheesy deliciousness, swooning over *Lucifer* running on Netflix. That was when Ron informed me about her staying over at Bryan's for the next two days before the college opened.

At night, I waited for his call. But he didn't. A tinge of unsettled feeling unnerved my senses, expecting the unexpected. Was he backing out? Didn't he want me anymore? Was he really my dream? Was he wanting me, was truly the fragment of my imagination?

Before I could think any further, cold sweat broke over my skin, and I sat on the bed, hugging my knees. I panicked out of nowhere and swung back and forth on the mattress, hugging myself.

I knew my reaction was too much. Then again, the man already over-consumed my emotion so much I couldn't think of my life without him or his filthy mouth anymore. Being with him gave me the

189

same rush I got when I first rode a motorcycle—frightening, exciting, freedom, and carefree. My heart pumped like crazy, yet I felt weightless. I wanted it. Over and over.

Right that instant, the screen of my phone lit up, making my soul find its spirit back once again.

Filthy Wolf: Same place, same time.

A slow smile appeared on my lips.

30 | Third Date

Xena

I gazed into the mirror, trying to see myself in the eyes of the man. I wore my hair down, watching the waves cascade down my back to my waist like a waterfall. Vaughn enjoyed touching and stroking my hair. This way, he'd get easy access. When his hands were in my hair, contrasting with my blonde, his firm, muscular, and large palms looked so out of place, yet it felt so right. I smiled, imagining his hands playing with my hair already.

God had blessed me to have a clear face with a bit of freckle around my nose. I decided to only moisturize it to look plump and healthy. Eyes adorned with winged eyeliner, a bit of mascara, and a bit of pearl sparkly highlighter in the inner corner of my eyes. Then I put my clear gloss on my lips to beautify my original cherry lips. There was no way I'd stop us from claiming each other's lips today. And I didn't want to ruin his face with lipstick marks. Not today.

Then I looked down to glance at my white dress. The same dress that he put on me yesterday in Hudson's Valley. I washed and dried it today, only to wear it on our first actual date, or one could say the third date if they decide to follow Vaughn's method of counting.

Ron was already gone for her romantic getaway with her boyfriend Bryan. It made leaving the house for my date with Vaughn easy for me. I put on my white heels that had crisscrossed lace up until my mid-shin. It was a bit of work, but damn, they looked sexy and went perfectly with my little white dress. Vaughn would like these on me, I knew.

I was so excited today when Finn arrived to pick me up that I didn't even poke him how I usually did. Just after greeting him, I sat in the back silently, wondering about what was going to happen in the next few hours. My heart palpitated more and more at the thought. Waves of excitement washed over my senses over and over again.

When I stepped out of the lift, this time, my eyes wandered nowhere but to where I knew I would find him. There he was, looking as handsome as Adonis. Just like the last time, my steps haltered, and I kept staring at his beauty. I knew, no one, absolutely no one present there was as handsome as this man in black.

Is it just me, or does he look more handsome than ever?

Vaughn strode with quick steps, eating up the space separating us from each other in utmost impatience that showed on his handsome face. When he was right before me, only mere inches apart, he held my face securely in his large palms as if I was the most mesmerizing, valuable, priceless treasure for him.

"You are here," he said. His voice, trembling in breathlessness, dropped to a whisper.

With a light touch, I cupped his palm that was still around my face. His eyes, desperately searching for something on my face— anxious to read my expression, to know what was going on in my mind.

"Are we repeating our second date, Wolf?"

Looking at my pretty obvious sparkle in my eyes, he went a bit deeper into his daze, and in a trance, he said, "We can do anything. Any. God. Damn. Thing… that you want, Xena. Just say it, and I'll be right on my knee for you."

I felt my heart jumping into my throat, his words catching me off the guards and rushing my blood faster than ever in my veins.

"Then why don't we go and take our seats?" I asked, smiling at him. Then, taking his hand in mine, I pulled him towards our usual seat.

The tall, broad, handsome man followed me without a word. As if he was ready to follow me just anywhere, even if it was the end of the earth.

As we took our seats, his entranced eyes were still fixated on me.

"You look otherworldly beautiful, Xena. Ethereal beauty. Like a goddess."

I felt my cheeks flaming at his unusual words of compliments. And *snuggly blankets!* The way he said those words, it was as if he was under a spell.

"You also look extra handsome today." I hid my face behind the curtain of my hair as I heard him laugh.

He scooted closer and placed his arms around my waist to pull me closer to his warm and firm body. I didn't protest and let him pull me into his warm, secure embrace. With one hand around my waist and another holding on my hand, he shifted closer to my ears and said, "You wore the dress again."

The position was exceptionally intimate. His possessive, territorial, and protective hold told everyone present about who I belonged to without even saying it.

"I thought you would like it."

"I do. I really, *really* do. Do you?"

His face was very close to mine as he intimately asked, not caring about a single soul around us.

Suddenly, I couldn't form a word and just nodded. Vaughn took a sharp breath and pushed his nose into my hair, pressing a possessive kiss at the side of my head as I leaned more towards him.

Vaughn and I had never really disregarded our touch and intimacy from the beginning. I had always been a little insecure about this relationship between us, thinking of Ron. But Vaughn, claiming his stake over me, never bothered me. If anything, I always ended up wanting more in my heart.

"What was that last night? You naughty brat. You didn't let me sleep all night. My dick has been hard for you since the moment you kissed me. I can't keep it down."

His grumble made me giggle like a true naughty brat.

"Maybe you deserved it after your little play in the car."

"You say it like you didn't enjoy that, Sugar. You'll be punished for your little stunt, you know?"

I turned my head a little towards him. Then, looking deep into his eyes, I feigned a sad puppy face and said, "But I just wanted to confess my feelings to you. Was I wrong to do that?"

His grip around my waist went firmer, his fingers digging into my delicate skin over my thin cotton, turning more and more possessive.

I took his other hand in mine, tracing over his rough yet soft skin.

"How are you going to work it out?" I asked.

"However you want to. As long as you are exclusively mine."

That was his answer? It didn't help a bit.

But then why do I find it so damn hot?

Oh, snuggles…

His movement stopped me before I could say anything.

"About that—" Vaughn brought out something from his pocket. When I saw what it was, my eyes widened in surprise.

Carefully, Vaughn put the bracelet around my wrist. And my, oh my, it was beautiful!

The fragile-looking gold chain hung from my wrist elegantly as the single solitaire diamond shined even under the drowning sun. I had never seen anything as simple yet so elegantly gorgeous. It looked so perfect on me; I felt nothing was ever going to look as good as this on my wrist.

"Vaughn… it's… it's beautiful… but… but isn't it so expens—" he pressed his thumb over my lips to shut me up.

194

"I have to shackle down a naughty brat like you. Even though I know very well that you liked me already, you took so long to give in." His thumb stroked my lips with a rough, possessive caress. "Publicly, I can't put handcuffs on you, so this little thing has to do the job. Although the bedroom is a completely different subject."

I didn't know what to say.

"I—Uh... About handcuffs... I have to confess something to you."

He brushed his thumb on the shining diamond, then moved his fingers into my hair, stroking with utmost fondness, warming up his usual arctic eyes.

"Mmm..." He was staring at me in a daze.

I took my lower lip in my mouth, thinking of ways to confess. I had never shared this part of the secret with anyone in my life. Until today, I had carried it in myself, always. But with Vaughn, I knew it was my time to open up.

In fact, he was the only man with him I could open up.

"It's about something... something private."

"It's okay, Xena. It's me. You can tell me anything," he said, encouraging me to continue talking.

"Ever since I was introduced to the world of sexual pleasure, I knew I wasn't the same as everyone else. As you know, I never had a serious relationship, nor do I go for usual hook-ups. There is a reason, Vaughn."

Now I got his absolute attention. His eyes were clear from the daze he was in earlier. His breathing almost stopped in the anticipation and possibilities of my next words. His hand slowly dropped onto my lap.

I took his hand in mine once again and said, "The guys I have been with, they weren't bad. In fact, any girl would've loved to be with them. But for me, I needed *more*. More of everything. But none of them were capable of understanding what I needed. So, at the end of the day, we ended up parting. Always. This is the reason I don't hook up as well."

Taking a few seconds of pause, he asked, "What is it that you need, Xena?" His voice was careful yet gentle, lacing with fondness and affection.

Oh boy, I didn't know what to say. But what I knew was that it needed to be said.

So I took a deep breath and continued spilling all my secrets to the man.

31 | Secrets

Xena

Every second passed, my grip on his hand went tighter and tighter.

Almost as if I loosened my grip on him, the man would puff in the air. He still felt like a dream to me, and I was too lucky to know he was real. What if he left after learning about the truth?

I hid my eyes from the man and started to talk.

I could feel my voice tremble a little. "With none of them, I felt any connection. I-I want to be told what to do in bed. I want to be dominated in the bedroom. I don't come with gentle vanilla sex or with wannabe dominating partners. When I need to come, I need it raw, ruthless, exciting, edging… I like to play, not just lovemaking. This is one reason why I could never come with any of them."

"You always come for me."

The rasp in his voice pooled between my legs. This man.

"Yes, I do." Once again, I pressed my hands on his large one, assuring him. "You are an exception, Vaughn. Only because it's *you*. When I didn't see you, meet you, even then, you still drew me towards you. I knew things with you would be different. And it was. Every time I came for you, you told me to come… you permitted me. You are what I wanted, what I needed. There is a reason."

"What?" his voice, out of breath.

"I didn't know when or how, but without my least bit of awareness, I built a demisexual relationship with you a long ago. Demisexual means that I developed a strong emotional connection with you, even though I didn't know you. Only you felt right, only you fitted, no one else. No matter how bad men tried to bed me, I didn't have any emotional connection with them, but you—only you. Which means I get aroused, only for you."

Vaughn kept staring at our intertwined hands for a long time. His breath got caught, and his cold, aloof face had at least a hundred emotions in them at that moment. I waited for a word from him, but he looked deep in thought. The more seconds passed, the more worried I became.

Would he leave me? After knowing how desperate I was for him? Would he lose his interest in me now? Knowing I was so easy?

For the love of God, why wasn't he saying anything?

When finally I heard a light chuckle from him, I felt alive once again. My soul returned to my body. The sudden coldness of my body once again wrapped with warmth from just that chuckle from the man.

"I always knew. I don't know if you'll believe me or not, but I always knew you had it in you. The kink in you is one of the charms that drew *me* towards you. But demisexual—that I never could've imagined. You never cease to surprise me, Sugar."

"Y-You do not mind?"

"Why would I? Jesus Christ… Xena. My girl is opening up to me about her sexual interest. If anything, I'm glad and proud of you. You have a demisexual interest in me, where the only person who arouses you is me—*fucking hell*, Xena, I'm in heaven. Besides, if you don't know already, I would love to dominate you in bed or wherever we fuck, too. But I would love to cherish some vanilla moments with you as well."

"Vaughn… I… I get turned on when I… when I imagine you d-degrading me."

Vaughn's grip on me tightened.

"You want me to call you names?" His eyes darkened further with apparent shock and surprise.

I bit my lips, not knowing what to say.

198

"You want me to call you my slut? You want me to call you my whore? My rag doll?" His voice trembled as it went harsher.

"I-I know it's so shameful. I… I shouldn't have told y—"

"As long as you are only *my* slut and *my* whore, I will cherish you like *my* queen, Xena."

The man sounded so confident, yet tender, with a certain sexiness coating his raspy voice. My heart started pounding, and I felt blood rushing to my ears. But then again, I heaved a sigh of relief.

"I-I have never talked about it before, not even with Ron. I didn't know how anyone would ever take it. The feeling of insecurity, self-esteem, and self-consciousness was too strong. Because, Vaughn… I… I can't come for anyone else. Never. I can only let go if I imagine you going ruthless over me."

Vaughn affectionately took my head into his chest, and I laid against his hard, chiseled frame. "You have no idea how happy that makes me. No fucking idea. Now I *am* in your life, Xena. Now we both have time to find out what we both want. Because I know for sure that one thing we both have in common. We want each other, and we believe that only we can fulfill each other's needs and desires. There can never be anyone else for us. If anything, I'm demisexual for you, too, and just like you, there can be no one else for me as well."

I wrapped my hands around his waist, rubbed my cheek against his chest while I murmured. "Really?"

He patted my head. "Really, my sweet little Sugar. You are the world to me. Thank you for trusting in me." Then he dropped a kiss on my forehead.

"You know, I had always been wondering why my girl was such a goody-two-shoes, even though she is best friends with my sister, who lives a colorful life. Now I know you've always been a slut, but since you're only my slut, you had to pretend to be a good girl. In reality, you are no good, my naughty little trouble."

"Yes. Yes, I'm. You weren't there," I said, sighing a whimper against his chest. The man was so much older than me, yet he was the only perfect one.

"Yeah? And all these days, you have been tormenting me for nothing? You naughty little brat. You are demisexual for me, and even then, you tortured me for days and nights, even for weeks."

I looked at him from under my lashes and smiled. "I'm sorry?"

"Now you are sorry, huh? So naughty. You need to be tamed, my little brat."

"Uh-huh. I agree." I rubbed my face against his chest even more.

"I can assure you, I am quite a ruthless, dominating fucker."

"Gosh... you are so proud and filthy, Wolf!" I slapped his chest, and laughter vibrated under my palm.

"About that... If you are such a rough lover, how come you are chastising for so long?"

"You really want to know, don't you?"

"Yeah, I just shared my deepest, darkest part with you, and here you are, stalling."

"What if I say I was waiting for you?"

I rolled my eyes and said, "That doesn't make any sense! You probably know me for over two years, but nobody saw you with any women for much longer than that." My eyes narrowed at him.

Peals of laughter burst from deep within his chest. "Promise I'll tell you, but not now. Some other time. I promise. All you need to know for now is, you, Xena, you are on my mind for a long time."

I scrunched my brows at his vague answer.

his hands went even tighter around me. "Besides, all I want to do right now is... think about how, when, and how many times I'm going to fuck you, Sugar. And how many times you are going to come to my cock. Every time I want you to, every time I tell you to, you will come for me."

"I know I will," I said, looking into his eyes.

Right that moment, the waiter arrived with our food. This time we properly had our dinner. Even though the surrounding air was clouded with sexual tension, it felt good. Around him, I felt like I could breathe, I could live, I could be myself.

And most importantly... *he will understand.*

When the dinner was over, and we were sipping our last bits of wine, the live music started on the rooftop, making the ambiance livelier than before.

Some sort of oriental song was going on, and a beautiful lady was belly dancing to it. The hosts asked people to take part with the lady in dancing, and my eyes lit up.

"I want to do it!" I said to Vaughn as I jumped up a little in his arms.

"Not a chance! There are so many men around here. Do you want to give them a hard-on as well?" Vaughn looked grumpy.

I rolled my eyes and said, "Jeez... You are allowed to tell me what to do in only the bedroom, not outside of it. Gotta keep that in mind, Wolf."

I joined the lady, trying out belly dancing with her. I was nowhere near her because she was professionally trained, whereas I took self-lessons from YouTube. But I could say I enjoyed it, and the lady appreciated me. After I joined, the ambiance went even livelier than it was earlier. People were cheering, and many other ladies joined as well.

My eyes went to Vaughn. His eyes held a surprise, humor, fondness, and something else I couldn't point my finger at. But whatever it was, it looked dangerous.

The lady offered me the mike and asked me to sing a song. I I chuckled in slight embarrassment, but went along, anyway. I sang the song that was on top of my mind. That fitted us, our surroundings, and our situation.

I started singing '*I see the light*' from tangled. It was so appropriate for us, our feelings. The entire time, my eyes fixed on Vaughn—my man.

Just as the song had mentioned, I was truly where I was meant to be. Yes, after my confession, the fog had truly lifted, and the sky looked as bright as new in my heart. The world truly shifted for me, now that he was in front of me, with bottomless affection lingering in his eyes, now that I could finally see him.

I noticed him cast a glance at a little girl, who was singing along to my song and calling out to her mother. The cute little button thought I was the real Rapunzel with long blonde hair. Vaughn turned his head again. Once again, his dark, stormy, hazy eyes fell on me. Only this time, it held even more emotion in them.

As I continued with the song, I noticed Vaughn walking closer to me in small steps. As if he was in a dream. For a second, I thought he would join me.

But then I remembered. He wasn't a regular guy; he was Vaughn.

Without one word, he picked me up. He hauled me over his shoulder and headed towards the elevator, leaving everyone behind us with their jaws dropped.

32 | At Wolf's Den

Vaughn

The ride to my place was silent.

A deafening silence overpowered the ambiance of the car, pushing both of our adrenaline higher than before. Anticipation, excitement, desire shot higher and higher for both of us. In the entire ride to my penthouse, we kept our eyes and body detached from each other with the most sincerity. I could take the luxury of assuming her pent-up frustration was too much to burst out at any moment, and I... I was having a hard time keeping my hands off of her.

When we arrived in Aphrodisia, I didn't carry her to the elevator as I had in the hotel. Instead, I took her hand securely in mine, pulling her inside the elevator, and pressed the topmost floor—the penthouse that I lived in.

In the elevator, we stood at a hand gap, looking into each other in the mirror. My Xena looked like a freaking angel in her white dress and shoes, and last but not least, her blonde hair. The way her eyes moved over my body, I felt pouncing on her right then and there. It was hard not to when her eyes fucked me with no curtain of shame this time. I gripped the bar of the elevator tightly to keep my composure.

A few more seconds, fucker, keep it cool.

"It feels like I'm in the set of Lucifer, you know? Nightclub, penthouse, you in devilishly delicious black suits, me in an angelic white dress... The only difference is, you are not a womanizer."

No, I'm not.

I grunted out my following words, panting in breathlessness. "Because there is only one girl I want, Xena, and I have it so bad for you."

That was it. I was so done with keeping myself off of her and reaching for my girl, I pressed her against the elevator wall. I pulled her upwards against my body with my hands under her soft, squishy thighs so that she wrapped her toned, smooth, beautiful legs around me.

Damn it... Control loser! Don't kiss her just yet. Not in the elevator, you fucker!

I attacked the next best thing—the sensitive skin of her neck. My lips drop open-mouthed kisses with passion and hunger all over her neck and shoulder, driving out strings of sweet little moans from her throat. I could bet she didn't even realize she was already a moaning mess under me. Her sweet voice filled my ear, swelling my chest with affection, driving me insane.

"So much with being dominated, huh? You have got me, Sugar. If anyone could satisfy you, it's me."

"Yes, Vaughn. Yes… only you," she said, pressing my head more into the crook of her neck, panting already.

The door opened with ting as I stepped into my place with Xena wrapped around my waist, and then I pinned her against the wall beside the elevator.

"I always wanted to carry you in here for the first time," I said, licking and nibbling on her neck, driving her senses crazy.

"Is it the proper way, though? Don't men carry their women for the first time in bridal style?" She was as breathless as me. Goddamn. I loved her reaction to my touch.

"It's our way." My wet kisses reached the swells of her tits. Gosh, I wanted to see them… desperately.

"It's a beautiful way, Vaughn." She moaned after that and then said, "Put me down first. I need to get out of my shoes."

"The shoes stay. The way the laces are wrapped around your skin, *Goddammit*, Xena! They make your already toned and beautiful legs look so irresistible. And then the way they perked up your ass. I…" I nibbled onto the soft swells of her tits. "I fucking love it."

"Ah… Vaughn… I'm going to dirty your place."

Fucking hell…

I looked into her eyes. "And I can't wait, Sugar."

Slowly, I dropped her down, taking her delicate face in my palm. I was over and done with all my iron-clad restraints. Now, I need to claim these lips, *my lips*. Right. Fucking. Now.

She knew what was coming. We had been waiting for a long time for this moment. Our little play of chasing each other had both excited and tortured us beyond imagination. I burned in need of her—I burned like hell. And I knew I wouldn't be done with kissing these lips anytime soon, or it was safe to say—ever.

Just before my lips touched her, being the naughty brat she was, Xena fled under my arms and ran inside the penthouse, away from my touch, burning me more and more for her in the process.

What the… fucking hell!

"Sugar, you know I'm going to kiss you, don't you?"

"But you have to catch me first, Wolf."

"You are so going to be punished, Xena," I said before striding after her.

She reached the kitchen first, circling around the kitchen island as I tried to catch her. Every moment I thought I got her, somehow, she escaped successfully every fucking time.

We ran around the living room, giving her enough space to run from me. She circled around the couch, laughing freely. The sound of her laughter was like a melody to my ears. Subconsciously, I had no idea when I started laughing with her as well. If anyone told me a few minutes ago in the elevator that I'd be chasing and laughing after this girl instead of claiming every hole of her body, I would have laughed at the joke!

205

What surprised me most was she deviously avoided the bedroom, knowing there was nothing in this world I would want right now other than pinning her against my mattress, under me.

Damn, she was right.

Fuck, this sneaky girl had been making it hard for me.

So naughty, aren't you, baby?

When she decided to take the spiral stairs to reach the rooftop, I was right behind her. I could easily reach for her ankle, but I didn't. I didn't want my sweet girl to trip and hurt, did I? After all, I had a night-long plan with her.

The moment she reached the rooftop, she halted in her escape, standing there like a statue, evidently awestruck by the scenery laid before her.

I knew she'd love it. Nevertheless, I did all of these only for her, didn't I?

"Vaughn…" my name was breathless in her voice. Her hands clasped in a tight grip on her chest. A clear sign of shock.

Slowly reaching behind her, I wrapped my hands around her waist and supported my chin on her slender shoulder.

"You like it?"

"This… this is magnificent… I d-didn't even know it was possible!"

"The first day we met, you said you liked to walk on grass barefoot. Do you remember I was out for an emergency the next day? I hired designers to turn my boring rooftop into something you'd like."

"Like? Vaughn, I love it! Did you really do it for me?"

Did she still have a doubt?

"Yes. For you, Xena. Who else would I make changes in my life for?"

"H-How much did you change?"

"I only had this sofa set before and that center table." I pointed to the earthy-colored sofa sets at the corner. "The grass ground, the plants all around the rooftop, and the tatami bed in the middle—they are my recent additions."

"Bed for?" She turned her head and looked at me with playful eyes.

"Let's just say—I'm hopeful," I said, as I grinned at her with a wink.

"Come, I want to lie down on the bed with you," she said.

Holy fuck. My girl was so excited about the rooftop. It somehow gave me a feeling of accomplishment. I felt fortunate enough to give her something to be this happy about.

Grinning like a fool, I followed her. Walking on the grass, she hopped on the wooden frame and then laid down on the mattress. I stood by the wooden frame in a daze, looking at her lying on the bed before me. Under the night sky, on the rooftop with dimmed lights on, she truly looked like an angel fallen from the sky—*for me.*

She looked so excited, overjoyed about everything around her. "Come! The sky looks so beautiful from here!"

You bet I will!

I laid beside her, staring at her with my head turned towards her side. To look at the goddamn sky was nowhere near my mind. All I wanted to see was—her. It felt like I wouldn't stop feeling like that for a long, long time.

I turned off all the lights except a few white translucent lights with my phone so that I could see her every move and expression. Those lights only enhanced the moonlight to see my surroundings clearly. To see how her eyes sparkled like fireworks, the way her lips stretched unceasingly in a content smile, her smooth skin reflecting under the blanket of the soft moonlight, and the rapid ups and downs of her gorgeous set of tits as she breathed in excitement.

Slowly, I hovered over her, breaking her unbroken stare at the night sky with the mountain of my body.

"Xena, I want to kiss you." My fingers slowly, deliberately, reached her lips, feeling the softness.

She didn't shy out. She didn't waver. Fuck, she didn't even look hesitant at all.

The smile stretched a little more on her lips.

"Then kiss me, Wolf," she said in a low, husky, seductive voice, and I was a goner.

Aren't you a natural seductress, my Sugar?

Just when my lips touched hers, sparks burst into explosion from the simple touch. I could swear I almost came in my pants just from the first proper touch of her lips. I could hear moans of satisfaction, but had no idea they were coming from within me or from her. And I didn't care, as long as we kissed each other.

I entwined my fingers into her hair. With the other hand, I clenched her jaws and kept her in place. But Jesus Christ, she clearly had no intention of going anywhere. My naughty little brat wrapped her arms around my neck, bringing me more towards her lips. The moment our mouths opened for each other, our tongues collided with a wild dance under the night sky. I heard moans again. Whose? I still had no fucking idea.

After waiting for years for this moment, when I finally got a taste of her lips, I couldn't let her go. No matter how breathless we went, no matter how in dire need of oxygen we were, I couldn't leave her lips.

Tonight, if I die here kissing her, I die.

But my girl needs to breathe…

Even after I ceased kissing her for a while, I didn't move my lips. I couldn't make it myself. To move my lips away from hers felt as impossible at the time as starting a family on Mars.

My lips brushed over hers as we panted for breath. Her fingers trailed in my hair as my hand that was previously gripping her jaw was now tracing her cheek, cupping it to take a proper look into her eyes.

My thumb brushed onto her cheek as I finally inched away a little to see her properly, as hard as it may sound. Slowly, she untangled one of her hands from my hair and brought that between us to trace her fingers on my face. With light strokes and brushes, she traced my eyes, brows, nose, cheeks, chin, forehead… everywhere. Like she was stunned to see me.

"I can't believe *you* kissed me."

Oh, that?

"I can't believe I'm *not* kissing you right now."

Just after the words fell from my mouth, I claimed her mouth once again. Time seemed to halt for us for a while as we slowly, passionately explored each other's mouths. Like we owned them. We did, didn't we? Officially, after tonight.

Our tongues were like desperate lovers—dueling, battling, thrashing, and mating with each other, for each other.

I honestly had no idea how long our lips battled against each other, but I could say we were nowhere near done. Nowhere near done in terms of both kissing and with the night. The way her delicate curves squirmed beneath me screamed of her need and desire for me. And I was sure it wasn't any less than me. Me and my girl—we were on the same boat.

I didn't know what made me feel this light-headed—if it was the romantic night sky above or this goddamn lovey-dovey ambiance. Or was it the intoxicating spicy, warm smell of vanilla, cinnamon, patchouli, gingery fragrance, or my tender heart, full of emotion? But fucking hell, I had to confess.

I cupped her face again, securely. Searching for her eyes to check if she was in a state to comprehend the depth of what I was about to say next.

"Xena, I know it might be soon for you, but it's not really... at least not for me," I said, looking into her half-hooded, hazy eyes as clearly as I could, under such hypnotizing spell I was in.

"I love you."

33 | Staking the Claim

Vaughn

Her eyes kept staring at me in obvious shock. The previous haziness was long gone, and her half-hooded eyes, currently widened in clear surprise. Her breathing hitched to the point that it concerned me if she was still breathing or not.

I shocked my girl to the core, didn't I?

I gave her a few seconds to process the three simplest yet heaviest words I had ever spoken in my 30 years of life. Even after a minute passed by, she was still as shocked as before. I had an assuring smile on my face. But inside, I was freaking out like hell. *Goddammit.* Why wasn't she showing any response?

I showered her face with rains of kisses to bring her life and wits back to her body. I didn't plan on pushing her any more than I did, but there was no way I was going to let her stay in such a shocking state any longer.

When I was kissing all over her face, leaving not a centimeter of space *un-kissed*, gradually, I felt her coming back to her senses. She lightly cupped my face in her palm and looked at me, *really* looked at me.

"You… you… you…?" She couldn't put words to her question, but I understood her.

"Yes. I love you, Xena. I love you so fucking much. And no, I'm not out of my mind. I'm also not unsure about my feelings. I have loved you for a long… long time."

Slowly, a breathtaking smile appeared on her face. I looked at her stretched lips and sparkly eyes and wondered if I was watching it for real? Or was my impish mind playing tricks on me based on how much I craved for this smile?

Then, unexpectedly, I noticed her eyes turning red. Unshed tears glistened in her sparkly orbs. Suddenly, I was anxious about if I had done something wrong.

Dammit, you fucker, what have you done? Couldn't you wait a little longer?

"Did I do something wrong? I… I—" She pressed her lips on me for a peck to shut me up. Then said, "Everything felt so dreamlike, I went overly emotional for a moment. You did nothing wrong, Wolf. You are perfect. Everything is perfect. But—"

I felt my heart speeding up, thrashing against the rib cage out of nervousness.

"But we have some unfinished business left." She smiled like a naughty little brat she was, sucking in her lower lip.

"We do?" I grinned. Her smile gave me hope, and finally, feeling my soul coming back into its life.

"We do."

"And what could it be?" I narrowed my eyes at her playfully.

"Don't you want to find out?" The naughty girl in her had taken over her entire personality and then challenged me with my own words.

I was slightly off the guard, and she grabbed the opportunity to push me on my back and then straddled over my waist. Goddamn. She was hot—scorching hot—down there, sinking the heat onto my dick through the thin layers of fabric. She looked so fucking gorgeous straddling me. How gorgeous would she look when she would ride me with her tits bouncing before my eyes, inviting me to play with them?

Hard. I'm so fucking hard it hurts.

211

She leaned over me, with her arms on both my sides, giving me an exquisite view of her deep cleavage. Her hair spread like a curtain all around her face, hiding both of us from the entire world. Fuck...

"You shackled me, tied me with you as you claimed me as yours forever. Don't you think I should do the same?"

Fucking hell... "I'm yours, Xena."

"Nope, not until I fulfill the condition you gave me. What did you say?" She had a wicked smile on her face, and I loved every bit of it.

And maybe I had an idea where this was leading to.

Xena started kissing my neck. Her hot lips brushed against my inflamed skin. In the process, undoing a few of my shirt buttons, kissing and licking the sharp curves of my chest. I could hear the slight whimpers that escaped past her throat, and I groaned at the sound. Damn.

Then, proving my assumption right, she moved between my legs and turned to unshackle my belt that separated the huntress from her prey. At least, the look on her face said so. Where did my usual shy little girl go?

Not that I don't love this tigress who was currently unzipping me.

I love her. All of her.

My naughty girl had a hard time unzipping me since I was painfully hard under her touch, and it didn't allow her to unzip me smoothly. But when someone had as much dedication as hers, they didn't stop before they could complete the task. Neither did she.

Just when she unzipped me, finally with relief, my rock-hard hardness sprang out and stood in a salutation before her sparkly, awaiting eyes. I heaved as I kept staring at her with eyes dilated and mouth open. My girl carefully wrapped her fingers around the base of my shaft and looked at me with eyes full of playful, naughty humor. My balls were tight, aching, twitching, howling to erupt like a volcano.

212

"I have been reciting in my head since the day you told me—"
She pressed a soft kiss on the tip of the crown of my dick, and as I
shuddered, she continued saying, "The moment I lick you, all your
pleasures will be mine as well, forever."

Time stopped with a bam when she darted out her tongue and
slid it from the base of my shaft towards the tip of the head of my dick.
My hands reached for her hair, and I moved it from her face, gripping
it in my hold with uncontrollable force. The grip was so tight that she
hissed and then moaned as her eyes closed in pleasure. Then she
opened her eyes and looked at me with a seductive stare and said, "It's
time, Wolf. It's time all your pleasure becomes mine."

A raw growl came out of the back of my throat at her words. Her
every fucking word—staking me, claiming me as her. *Gosh... I.*
Fucking. Can't. Wait.

My pre-cum was already dripping, dick hard as ever, quivering
in the embrace of her warm palm. I had never seen her so confident, so
determined and powerful, and that only turned me on more than
before. As she took me in the warm glove of her mouth, I took a sharp
audible breath in and threw my head backward. Fuck.

For years, I had played and replayed this very moment in my
mind. It had been one of my favorite fantasies to entertain in my lonely
hours. But, hot damn... it was nowhere near what I felt right that
moment. If her mouth was way out of my imagination, then how was
the rest of her body going to be? Just thinking about how I would feel
inside her gave me goosebumps all over my skin.

For a moment, I pulled my hands and ran them over my face and
into my hair. Looking for a way—any way to hold onto my wits to
control myself. To save me from the humiliation of coming into her
mouth already. *God help me.*

She closed her mouth over my shaft, wrapping it with her soft,
full lips, and sucked on it once, deeply. With just once suck, she was
heaving my cum out already. My hands reached her hair once again,
gripping tightly.

"*Goddammit...* Xena!" I arched my waist and growled under her sweet torture.

She swirled her tongue over the crown of my dick, and I cursed once again. "Fucking hell..."

This girl—this girl and her mouth—only she could ever do this to me. If I didn't hold onto every last bit of my self-control, I would've come into her mouth already, embarrassing myself. And she had just started. My girl was not even trying yet.

When she took me deep into her mouth, her head began to bob as she started to suck my dick like a fucking lollipop, her hands working at the base. I placed my hand behind her neck, and the other kept a firm fist on her hair. I could push my shaft into her throat, I could fuck her mouth, I could claim and mark that mouth as mine forever... but not tonight. Tonight was about all she was going to give me. Besides, I didn't think I could keep it in anymore if she deep-throated me right now.

"Holy hell... Xena... you got me right on my edge." God, she wasn't even trying...

She raised her eyes at me, looking at my helplessness under her mouth. For a second, my breathing stopped. Gosh, I thought she couldn't look any more beautiful.

But there she is.

My Xena

My sweet little Sugar.

The one I had been waiting for, craving for, obsessing over.

Her eyes held me captive, and I drowned in them. Momentarily, forgetting how to swim, how to survive. I was drowning, drowning deep in her. And there was nothing... nothing in the world I wanted more than dying right in her eyes.

Holding my eyes just like that, I felt her smiling at my state, and then she gave a final suck that heaved my load out even before I was ready to give in. My cum filled and overflowed her mouth as she greedily sucked and licked all of it, leaving not a single spot over me.

In the end, she finally let my dick go with a pop and smiled at me with a triumph of joy in her eyes.

Hot damn…

Slowly, she crawled on me and again straddled on my waist, her hot cave rubbing against my still rock-hard hardness. Then coming closer to me, she said, "Licked. You are mine now, Wolf."

She had me tongue-tied.

I just stared at her. Not knowing how to talk to this girl anymore after she made me come with so much ease.

"Goddamn… Xena… I—" she pressed her index finger on my lips to shut me up.

"Now that you are finally mine—" She pressed a soft kiss on my lips and then said, "I love you, too, Wolf."

In an instant, she was again underneath me, and my lips crashed against her. The mouth that just confessed her love for me—I wanted to savor it, devour it, and conquer it. Gosh… I wanted to worship it.

After god knew how long, I pressed my forehead against hers and chuckled. My hands were placed under her waist and into her hair. Whereas, she held my shoulder with one and my hair with another. Even in such intimate proximity, I couldn't help but chuckle.

"Are you sure you like to be dominated in the bed, Sugar? You seemed more like a naughty little dominatrix to me."

She sure did.

"Are you sure you like to dominate in bed, Wolf? Looked like you quite enjoyed it on your back." She came back with a savage reply.

I laughed into her hair, feeling the happiest I had ever been in my life.

I dropped pepper kisses on her neck as I moved towards her ear, inhaling her bewitching scent, filling my lungs with only her smell. She pulled my body tight against hers as I rested my head on her shoulder, my lips still nibbling on her tender flesh.

"I still can't believe you gave into me, Xena. I still can't believe you said you love me."

"And where do you hear about a girl who can only jill off with someone's picture and at the end of the day gets to know he loves her as well?" Her voice was full of humor.

"Jill off?" *What the fuck is that?*

"You know the rhymes—Jack and Jill went up the hill, right? Only you jack off with your junk, and I jill off with my cunt."

Laughter vibrated within my body as I let it out. Xena laughed with me, too. Her laughter was like a melody to my ears, and I couldn't stop listening to it.

"Aren't you my sweet, little Sugar?" I kissed her temple.

"Yeah, I am," she said, grinning.

"Okay, enough of these lovey-dovey moments. I need to take you somewhere else now," I said as I slapped her ass and unwrapped her leg around my waist.

"Where?" she asked with curious eyes.

I stood up, zipping my slacks, but left the button undone. Then I took her in my arms, carrying my girl downstairs.

"On my bed."

34 | Exploring Her

Vaughn

I threw her in the middle of the bed as soon as I entered the bedroom. Her body bounced on the mattress, and then she sat up with her eyes full of clear desire, lust, and invitation... all for me.

"Dammit, Xena. You look so fucking good on my bed." I sunk my teeth into my lower lip, sucking it in.

"Before I am out of my clothes, I want you out of yours. Now." I could swear her eyes sparkled at my command. She loved my commanding tone that could only belong to her.

"Yes, master." She nodded with a grin and started to get rid of her dress.

I think I just came in my slacks. My little Sugar calling me master felt right. My pre-cum gushing against my black pants, soaking it, threatening a moan to come out.

I panted as I watched her. My eyes, hazy in need, cock throbbing, pulsating in my slack and heart thrashing against my chest. But holy hell... I couldn't move my eyes from this angel.

"What did you just call me?"

She halted in her movements, looking into my eyes. Pink tints spread across her cheeks and neck adorably.

"I-It came naturally. It feels so right to submit to you."

"The hell you will submit to me. From now on, you are calling me that. Now continue."

Before I even finished with my shirt, my girl was lying before me in her underwear. On. My. Fucking. Bed.

For a moment, I forgot what I was doing and continued staring, standing in my position. My little Sugar looked so fucking gorgeous in the white lacy lingerie I bought for her. Her tits looked huge, almost spilling out of the cups, and the curves of her hips looked delicious enough to devour in that thong.

She took my breath in every way. *God... am I ever going to get tired looking at her?*

Wait. The same lingerie that I bought for her... Did that mean?

"You have been wearing that lingerie." My eyes darted towards her crotch, right on the wet spot where I knew the vibrator could be.

"Yes, it's a shame you didn't realize it earlier, Wolf." She grinned once again, like a vixen.

"You. Hot. Damn. Thing." I said, growling, specifying every word.

The command rolled off my tongue. "Out of it. Now!"

I was faster this time. There was no way I could wait any longer to be close to that body—her body. I need her body, her soul, her heart—every goddamn part of her like I needed my next breath.

When I got rid of my pants, she got rid of her soaking panties, showing me a glimpse of those swollen, wet pink lips. Then finally, as I got rid of my boxer, she unhooked her bra, making her heavy, perky tits bounce out of prison.

I sucked in a breath as I stared down at those pink, swollen, clearly aching nipples. This was the first time I saw them, but holy hell... those tits looked sinful. And I couldn't wait to commit the sin.

"Lie down for your master. Hands above your head. Hold the headboard bars." My voice had downed to a raspy, controlling level.

She did just that.

I stood at the edge of the bed, staring at her. Still processing the fact that it was Xena lying naked on my bed. It was Xena, my Xena, and she said she loved me.

"Won't you come to me, master?" she asked, whining in a husky voice that I loved. God, I loved everything about the girl.

"Later. I need to see you first. Open your legs." My dominance, clear in my tone.

She wordlessly sighed in need, and her tits heaved. Slowly, her legs parted, displaying her hidden treasures I could die for. But it was not enough.

"Wider."

She spread her legs even wider than before. *Aha.* Now, this was what I wanted to see. Sleek, wet, swollen pussy. Dripping already, staining my bedsheet with her soaking wetness.

I crawled onto the bed, hovering over her body, pressing my lips on hers. I kissed her as I dominated her. Body and soul. Like a good little girl, she kept her hands tight and firm on the headboard bars when I knew how much she wanted to run her fingers into my hair. By now, I had an idea how she liked to touch them. But she wasn't allowed to for the moment. I wanted to see just how submissive my girl liked to be and just how much dominance she preferred from her master.

I moved a little down, caressing her breasts with my lips. Brushing the tip of her nipple, I took it into my mouth and moaned in satisfaction—so perfect in my mouth. Swirling my tongue around it, I nibbled and then sucked a little, all the while teasing it with the sweet torture of my tongue. At the same time, my other hand was busy, teasing and squeezing her other mound that craved my attention.

My girl was already moaning under me. I switched between sucking the tits and giving them both my full attention.

"So beautiful, Xena. Your tits are so fucking beautiful. I can suck on them all night."

"Please." My girl whined under me.

"Please what, Sugar? What do you want?"

"More… I want more!"

"You want me to suck you anywhere else?" I said as my teeth kept nibbling on one of her nipples, and my hand restlessly pinched and tugged on the other one.

219

"Yes... oh, god. Yes!" My sweet baby cried out in frustration.

"Where, Sugar?"

"On my pussy," she said, whimpering in both pleasure and frustration.

"Yours? Aren't we clear about who this pussy belongs to? It's my property. Mine!" I said. Growling, biting on her nipple, hard.

"Oh god! Yes, yes, yes. Yours. Vaughn, yours. My pussy belongs to you. Only you. Please!"

I hummed in satisfaction and said, "Not so fast, Sugar."

I dipped down to her navel. God knew how attracted I was to this sweet little hole. Goddammit. I was attracted to every little part of her body. I was crazy about it. Did she have any idea?

My heart was like a factory machine. Pumping and stamping. This sweet little girl, she was my aphrodisiac, my drug.

I inserted my tongue into her navel and moaned in content. Gosh, for how long had I wanted to do that? I swirled my tongue inside the little hole and sucked it as she squirmed beneath me.

Then slowly, I reached down, where she was a wet, swollen mess, which I knew was aching badly.

"So wet, so beautiful... so mine. You are mine. My pussy. Only for my mouth, my fingers, and my cock. You can only please me whereas I will only pleasure you... mine." I brushed my thumb inside her swollen lips and then lightly touched her clit.

"Oh, god... Vaughn!"

"Keep your hand on the bar as I devour my pussy." I used my naturally dominant voice, which only belonged to her. Just as the command rolled off my tongue, she obliged willingly. Or should I say eagerly?

Brushing my thumb and index finger over the swollen clit, I sweet-talked to my pussy that I missed for days. Then, not wasting another moment, I hauled her legs above my shoulder and pounced on my prey.

The moment my nose went closer to her hot cave, I felt the familiarity of home. The feel of security and comfort gusted throughout my body, and I sucked the little clit in my mouth. My girl was so fucking wet that it looked like she was already coming but damn, she wasn't yet. I smiled against her pussy, and a sense of pride swelled my chest, realizing just how much I affected her.

She felt my smile. I knew it when I heard her moaning out my name. God, I loved her moaning my name. I loved my name on her beautiful lips that I couldn't wait to fuck. Upstairs, on the rooftop, I came so fast, like a lunatic. With this girl, I needed to learn about controlling my emotions to last longer. She had me right in her palm.

I licked every ounce of her dripping cum, slurping against her folds. My tongue teased the opening of her cave with long licks in circles, zig-zags, and then sucking it out whole. Her thighs started trembling around me, and I looked up to see her.

The moment I looked up, I found her eyes fixed on me with evident lust and the desire of touching me yet not being able to do so. It was a maddening feeling, I knew, but I had to know just how much dominance she craved.

My hands rested on her soft, smooth stomach, holding her in place from writhing so much. My tongue weaved on her clit and then teased with quick flicking licks. Holy hell, it drove her crazy. I slurped her dripping wetness and then repeated the process. After three repeats, my girl couldn't take it anymore, and her body started to shake under me, releasing right over my mouth. I covered her whole cunt with my mouth as she released on my tongue, her thighs pressing me tight between them.

Right when she finished with her orgasm, she expected me to leave her cunt alone.

Huh, dreaming, aren't we?

Even while she was coming, even after she finished coming, I didn't let my cunt go. Spreading my tongue, I covered as much as I could and warmed my pussy even more with slow, broad licks.

"Gosh... Vaughn... a-aren't... aren't you done?"

"I'm nowhere done with this pussy, my little Sugar. This is. My. Fucking. Pussy." I growled and hummed against her, and she jumped at the vibration my humming produced on her sensitive skin.

"I want to touch you. At least let me touch you... Please," she said. My baby sobbed as I kept with my slow, broad strokes.

"Not yet. You haven't earned it yet." I growled, then hummed once again.

Just when she let out another sob, I flicked right on her clit with the tip of my tongue. The precision stimulation drove her crazy, and her moan turned into screams. Instantly, I inserted two fingers inside her, and she was done for.

After her second release, her body shook non-stoppable. Slowly, I sat up on my knees and left the bed. My eyes, still reluctant to leave her flushed, panting, and erotic face.

I left her to bring back something, and when I entered the room again, my girl was still in the same position, with her hands still clutching the bars of the headboard. Pride swelled in my chest, and I was awestruck once again at her beauty. She looked so fucking gorgeous on my bed after coming twice to my mouth.

Xena...

My Xena...

My girl looked up from her daze, sensing my presence. Her unfathomable desire, still prominent on her beautiful face, matching mine.

"Where did you go?" Her voice was hoarse and seductive from desire.

"To bring back my phone."

"Now?" The question was evident in her beautiful doe eyes.

I stepped closer to the bed and stared into her eyes, flashing her a smirk that buzzed with nothing but a warning bell. "Yes. Now."

Then, moving closer towards her thighs, I parted them once again, settling myself in between them.

"Do you really think I am done with this pussy, Sugar?"

I tapped on my cell phone screen and turned on a particular device that started vibrating on my bed, startling my girl.

"V-Vaughn…"

"Shh… no matter how much you deny, I know you can, and I won't stop. Besides, you brought it upon yourself." I said in an announcement. Then I grabbed the vibrating panties and then moved towards my desired destination.

I ran the vibrator on her inner thighs, teasing her. My eyes fixed on her tired face. But besides being tired after coming twice, her face still held desire, anticipation, and fear under my touch. Her eyes wandered between my misbehaving naughty hand and my dick. Only the look on her face alone made my dick twitch, standing high in an ovation.

I teased the apex of her thighs for a few more minutes before pressing the vibrator right on her clit, making her jump. This time, her hands left the bars and grabbed the bedsheet, crumpling it in fists. I didn't blame her, though.

She was already screaming my name when I inserted two fingers inside her cunt as my other hand controlled the vibrator, pressing against her little bundle of joy. Her body tossed and turned under the overflowing of pleasure from both the vibrator and my fingers. To keep her in place, I used my knee to imprison her legs. She couldn't move her lower body anymore under my weight.

My baby squirmed on the bed, screamed my name, whined, and cried under the sweet torment.

And my eyes never left her.

It wasn't long before she released once more under the vibrating bullet and my ruthless fingers. But I didn't let her go even while she was released. My fingers continued moving in her with no mercy, along with the bullet pressed against her clit as she came the fourth time that night.

When I finally finished with her, hovering over my girl, I kissed her lips. She stayed unmoved under me. After a minute, when she started responding to the kiss, it was only then I felt relieved because she hadn't passed out. I put one hand under her waist and another under her neck to devour the sweet little mouth.

My sweet little girl couldn't respond like she did before. I didn't expect her to, especially after the fourth round of orgasms like that. I laid sideways, and curling her into my arms, I rained light kisses on her soft, subtle face.

"You look beautiful when you come for me. I can't wait to fuck you, Xena."

Her half-hooded, tired doe-eyes looked at me. "I thought tonight... w-we—" she said, trailing off.

"After how much you made me suffer last night, you still expect me to fuck you tonight, Sugar?" I asked, smacking her naked butt cheek. "Not tonight."

"You are cruel. You know, Wolf?" she asked.

"After coming four times, do you think you can take me, Sugar? You are silly and delusional, my love," I said with a chuckle, kissing her forehead, stroking her hair that stuck to her drenched forehead from sweat.

She bit her lips as her eyes sparkled.

I chuckled at the eagerness of my girl and pressed her head against my chest. Our bodies overlapped each other as our hands circled one another in a tight embrace.

"You did good tonight, Sugar. Now sleep. We have a long day tomorrow." I said as I kept stroking her hair.

"Long day? What will happen tomorrow?" she asked, her voice already drifting off. Her tired yet satisfied body, giving up.

"Don't you want to know?" I smirked in her hair as my hands kept caressing her hair and smooth back.

Then I whispered in a low yet rugged voice.

"Tomorrow, Xena, I'm going to fuck you."

224

35 | Sweet Dawn

Xena

When I woke up the following day, I found my naked body tightly wrapped in a rock-hard embrace. It wasn't just any embrace. My entire body was encased in a way I never imagined possible with another hard, chiseled body. The light from the rising sun illuminated the room dimly, allowing me to see my surroundings. With careful movement, I looked up to gaze at a face I never imagined waking up to ever in my life. But what could I say? Life had been pretty blessed for a while, and I couldn't be more thankful to God up there.

I loved him. I loved this man, and there was not a tinge of doubt about it.

And the man said he loved me.

What an irony!

A smile appeared on my face as I stared at the most gorgeous features with fondness blooming in my eyes. My lips turned up, and my eyes sparkled as they wrinkled in delight.

His face wasn't too white. With a sharp jawline and deliciously scratchy beard, Vaughn exuded manliness. Even those thick, long eyelashes couldn't cease his reeking masculinity. There were faint wrinkles on his forehead since he frequently used them to express his emotions, which aroused me every time.

This man… he was all mine. He belonged to me.

Oh, blankets!

My smile turned into a grin as my eyes drifted to the man's beautifully curved lips. Those who say men looked sexy with thin lips didn't see a man like Vaughn. He had pretty pouty lips that drove my sex hormones crazy every time I looked at them. That was exactly how I felt at the moment.

Summoning my courage, I inched a little closer to those beautiful, soft-looking, kissable lips and planted a soft peck. A surge of electricity rushed through my body, causing every hair on my body to stand up in a wave of pleasure.

Just from a peck.

And he was doing nothing but sleeping!

You need help, Xena!

After scolding myself for being overly hormonal, I carefully untangled my body from Vaughn's tight yet secured embrace. He was a pretty deep sleeper. Even though the man was reluctant to let me leave his embrace, he was still deep in his slumber.

I wouldn't leave the safe and comforting embrace of the most handsome man on earth if I didn't have a pressing need to use the washroom. As I rolled out of bed, I looked around for something to cover my nakedness, and my gaze was drawn to Vaughn's black shirt. My lips stretched a little, thinking about how I always wanted to wear a man's shirt. Grabbing the shirt, I inhaled the smell of the sexiest fragrance blending with his exotic perfume and natural, manly scent. I squealed like a little girl and grinned against the shirt. Finally, putting it on before spinning around in it in joy.

I was wearing a man's shirt for the first time, and my, oh my, it belonged to Vaughn. The only man I ever really wanted.

My soul danced as I spun a few times, and only then did I recall my need to use the washroom. I bit my lower lip in delight and returned my gaze to the man, who was still sleeping with his compelling muscled upper body peeking out from under the quilt. The man didn't appear as content as when I was entangled in his body. His brow furrowed a little as if irritated by something.

I kept staring at him with a smile for a few more seconds before rushing into the bathroom. Surprisingly, I found everything I needed to complete my morning rituals. There was an extra toothbrush, towels, and a bathrobe. I used his face wash to clean my face, too. It smelt rich—like Vaughn. I giggled at my reflection when I found my well-satiated face in the mirror.

We hadn't gone all the way, yet I looked satiated. Nobody had ever made me come with penetration, whereas this man made me come last night even without using his cock. Gosh... I was craving for that monstrous cock more than anything I had ever craved in life.

My lips looked as red as a cherry. Pink shades and tints were naturally visible on my cheeks. My eyes sparkled like this only when I used to cut my birthday cake. I was the type of person who got the most excited about her birthdays, and it appeared that Vaughn had been added to the list as well.

My wavy, long blondes were a mess. I tamed them using my fingers, but not much. From how much I knew Vaughn, I was sure he would love it just how it was.

I smiled a little at my flushed reflection and walked out to see a still sleepy Vaughn on the bed. I stared at him for a few more moments before a sudden desire to see the rooftop in daylight overcame me.

As I climbed up the stairs, the feeling of nakedness troubled me a little. But the way Vaughn used the panties on me last night left it no more usable until or unless I washed them. The thought alone made my cheeks warm up as I smiled at the memories playing in my mind.

God... he is one filthy man. My filthy man.

Last night, I didn't get to walk on the grass barefoot. I wasted no more seconds and stepped on the cold, dewy grass. Even though it gave me a feeling of more nakedness, it felt amazing. The thought that Vaughn had done everything for me made my heart jump and then happy-dance all over again.

I sat on the wooden edge of the bed—my feet, lying on the grass, not getting enough of the serene feelings. Even though my body was there, my mind was busy replaying everything that happened last night. The moment we entered the elevator until we fell asleep in each

227

other's arms. Everything felt so magical that my heart kept jumping every time I realized it was real—all real.

A sparkle caught my eye, and I looked at the single solitaire diamond on my wrist. The smile spread even further, remembering him telling me how he wanted to shackle me down with this bracelet. Gosh... didn't he know he already shackled me with his charms? My finger brushed over the shining diamond, and I dazed off.

I couldn't recall for how long I sat on the middle of the most fascinating rooftop my eyes ever perceived. My gaze was still fixated on the diamond shining under the ray of sunlight. It was only when my sense of smell was overwhelmed by the familiar intoxicating scent of my man. The hair of my body stood instantly in acknowledgment of his presence. Everything about the man felt so erotic—even his mere presence.

I was suddenly so nervous that I didn't dare to look back. Only when I felt Vaughn sitting close enough for me to feel the warmth of his body that I look at him. But yet, I couldn't look directly at his piercing eyes. My gaze moved little by little upwards... as if I was looking at something illegal.

He was only wearing a pair of gray sweatpants and nothing else. His abs looked too delicious to run my tongue all over it, but like a good girl, I tamed my wild thought for a moment. His nipples were dark, in contrast to my pink ones. They reminded me of chocolates, and I found myself drooling in an instant. Wild thoughts once again consume my naughty, dirty mind.

"Coffee?"

That voice!

Can I make love to it?

That was when I realized he had two mugs of coffee in his hand. His smell overpowered my senses so much that I didn't realize he had brought coffee for us. With a smile, and took the mug from his grip. I could feel my cheeks were warming up once again by full force.

"You look too tempting in my shirt, Xena. Women wearing their men's shirt isn't overrated after all."

I smiled at his words and said, "I always wanted to wear one. I'm happy that it's yours."

I could feel his smirk as he wrapped one of his hands around my waist and buried his face into my neck.

"You are the first one to wear mine, too. Besides, it looks much, *much* better on my girl than me." Boring his nose deeper into my neck, he pressed kisses on my tingly skin.

Snuggles! My cheeks were on fire! And my heart went crazy, knocking violently against my chest.

Oh, Vaughn...

"Wh-When did you wake up?" I asked, breathing hard.

"Not long ago. Why weren't you in my bed when I woke up?" Vaughn tried to complain that sounded more like doting in his slightly nasal tone.

"You are a heavy sleeper. You know that, Wolf?"

"Nope. How would I? You are the first person I spent sleeping the entire night with," he said, mumbling in my neck, inhaling my scent.

I was confused. "How? You obviously had partners before."

He shifted his head to look at my scrunched nose and then smiled.

"Partners? What do you take me for, huh?" There was a mischievous smile on his defined, handsome face that glowed like honey under the daylight.

I tilted my head to look at his spellbinding handsomeness and asked, "Then?"

"Partner. Only one."

I felt my nose wrinkle even further. "That sounds serious. Want to talk about it?"

"Not really. It was long... long ago. It's all in the past, Xena. You are my present and my future. It can only be you." He dropped a

229

kiss on my lips, and suddenly, everything became alright again. I hugged his strong, warm body with my free hand and rested my head on his shoulder, making myself comfortable.

Vaughn's playful hands started exploring the area around my waist as we sipped our coffee in silence. Then suddenly, his wandering hand halted, and his body stiffened as he looked at me with surprise written all over his face.

"You are naked down there," he said. His voice was hoarse, full of disbelief, along with deep lust.

"Yeah, don't you remember what you did to mine last night?" I asked, grumbling in the complaint.

A slow yet naughty smile appeared on his face as he sucked in his lower lip and thought of something.

Gosh… how could a man look so damn delicious when sucking his lips in? How was that even possible?

"Let's go. I need to feed your cute little belly fast."

"Can we go after five minutes?"

It felt good to be there, hugging him leisurely, sipping coffee. I didn't want to burst the bubble of this comfort so fast.

"No. Now. The faster, the better."

"Why so hurry?" I asked, scrunching my brows as she picked me up in bridal style.

"I need my girl well eaten before I fuck her."

"…" I was speechless.

Vaughn approached the kitchen with me in his arms.

"Hey, I need to borrow something to wear. Lend me a pair of your boxer or something."

"You are already overdressed."

"…" He silenced me once again.

When he dropped me finally, Vaughn went to the refrigerator to check what he got in there. I peeked from behind his shoulder and asked, "Can I make some sandwiches for us? I can see the ingredients."

"You want to?"

I enthusiastically nodded.

"Okay, I'll help," Vaughn said as he moved, so I got access to the refrigerator.

I handed him the lettuce and tomatoes to wash and cut. Then taking some bread, I used roasted garlic mayo sauce, eggs, grilled cheese, and roasted beef to complete making the lunch for both of us. Like a good, obedient person, he *wasn't* for real... Vaughn didn't try to annoy me in the entire process, which surprised me.

I put the food over the kitchen island as Vaughn leisurely sat on a stool. Before I put my naked ass on one, I scolded him with my hands on my waist as I glared at his sexy face.

"How can I sit here when I'm literally butt-naked?"

Vaughn threw his head back and laughed. My frustration climbed higher at his expression. I pouted, narrowing my eyes at the irritating, filthy, sexy man.

"You have got your own personal special seat over here, Sugar. Where you can sit butt-naked or not, anytime."

I looked at him in doubt. "And where is it?"

With a filthy smile on his lips, he yanked my hand. In a matter of seconds, I was sitting on his lap with my arms around his neck.

"Here. On my lap."

36 | Honeyed Morning

Xena

"You are so filthy, Wolf."

He smiled at me with mischievous eyes. The corners of his eyes had a slight crease, telling me how genuinely happy he was. The mature appearance of the man caused a tickle in between my thighs.

"I'm filthy only for my naughty little Sugar," he said, pressing a doting kiss on my temple as his hands around me tightened. "Now eat fast. We have got plans."

"Plans? I don't remember any," I said, teasing him. My eyes glinted as I stared at his handsomeness.

"Do you need a reminder, then? Mmm... Alright." His mouth is already nibbling the skin of my neck. His hand found its way to one of my tits through the unbuttoned gap of the shirt, squeezing it.

Snuggles!

I moaned out loud before I screamed.

"Remember! I remember! Let's eat! Aren't you hungry?" I asked. There was no way I would want to rile the lion with an empty stomach.

"Very. For you."

Oh, snuggly blankets!

Neither his mouth nor his hand left my body. In addition, another hand started squeezing my bare butt cheek, raising the shirt to gain proper access. Even with the shirt on, I felt naked. His misbehaving hands were everywhere on me.

"V-Vaughn… food… food first," I said, moaning under his attack, panting.

"Mmm? Hmm…" He reluctantly pulled out his hand from under my shirt and picked up a sandwich gracefully. I bit my lips at the manly sight. I always had a thing for strong, veiny arms. Who knew the sexiest pair of hands would belong to me someday?

He offered the sandwich to me as if I was his little pet. My stomach grumbled, and without any protest, I took a bite of it. The hot grilled cheese, along with the roasted garlic mayo sauce, dripped from it, coating the side of my lips.

Vaughn inched his lips closer to mine, licked the sauce, and then sucked my lips clean.

"Mmm. Tasty. You have done a great job, baby."

The words of appreciation sent a jolt of adrenaline through my body. My cheeks flamed, and redness appeared on my face and neck, lips stretching a little unknowingly. I had no idea I was a sucker for praises until today. Or was it also a part of my Vaughn syndrome?

His scrutinizing eyes followed my every reaction, and his eyes darkened. His cock twitched under my butt. Throbbing and pulsating.

"Eat. Fast."

I used both my hands to eat the sandwich like a pig. Whereas Vaughn sat there, eating as gracefully as a king with one hand.

As I ate, my eyes never left his stunning face. I couldn't have enough of the sight of him eating the sandwich I made. A sense of pride swelled in my chest. At the same time, my kitty drenched as I looked at the sexiest man alive. Vaughn didn't spare me a look anymore. The man ate like he didn't have any idea about me staring at him. But I was sure he knew… he knew very well.

Oh, Vaughn…

Since my eyes were so busy staring at him, I was slow to finish my food. When Vaughn finished his sandwich, he finally looked at me and smiled.

Gosh… my heart! How in the world can a man be this handsome?

I smiled back and offered my half-eaten sandwich to him. Keeping his eyes locked with mine, the man took a large bite on it and chewed the food as if it was me he was eating.

"Finish it, Sugar. I want this little tummy well fed before I fuck it." Vaughn's large palm was spread across my belly, almost covering all of it.

I forgot to eat for a moment. There was a tightness in my throat at that promise, and my kitty went wild once again. Slowly, I swallowed the lump in my heavy throat, which naturally didn't escape his intense stare.

With a devilish smirk in his eyes, Vaughn took a bite of the sandwich and moved towards my lips—offering me to eat from his mouth. My heart started drumming against my chest at the change of event, making me have a second thought about our sanity. Gosh, why did I find it hot rather than gross? What the heck was wrong with me?

My lips trembled slightly as I bowed down my head a little to meet his offering mouth. Slowly, Vaughn slid the food into my mouth with a thrust of his tongue, and I received it wholeheartedly. I chewed the food with a pounding heart when he went to take another bite for me.

It took four bites to finish the remaining sandwich. By the time we finished with the food, both of our mouths were bathed in dripping cheese and sauce. Also, my body went as wobbly as jelly, and I could bet I would fall on the ground if he placed me on my legs. But thankfully, he didn't.

Carrying me in his arms, he took me to the sink and washed my hands first, then his. Then, Vaughn hurled me on his shoulder like a sack of potato, as if I weighed nothing, and headed towards his bedroom. His shirt that was previously hiding my naked bottom earlier raised, and my butt was all bare for him. The air felt chilly as it brushed against my drenched, soaked, wet pussy.

234

I tried to pull the shirt to hide some of my naked ass from his eyes, but all he did was give a tight slap on my ass and rub his hands all over my tender skin. His legs never halted in the steps.

"You dare to hide this ass from me? It's fucking mine!" His finger brushed from top to bottom in my butt crack until it touched the entrance of my soaked cunt.

"Ah." I moaned out loud at the suddenness of his invasion.

"Just wait for me to fuck it." His wet finger from my pussy juice poked in my asshole, teasing it a little. "I can't wait to take this ass. Hell... I want to fuck this so bad, Xena... so bad." Then he bit at the side of my ass cheek.

Before I could come up with a word, he already threw my body on the bed with him on top of me. With the sudden rush of movement, breath gusted out of my lungs, and I looked at Vaughn with widened eyes.

He propped on his elbow that rested on both my sides and looked into my eyes. One of his hands came up, gently brushing my hair away from my face.

"Xena..." A single mumble of my name, yet it weighed as heavy as a mountain.

"Vaughn..." I took his face in both my palms.

There were one thousand emotions in his eyes that sparkled like a starry sky at me. Something pulled inside me, and suddenly, I felt like crying with overwhelming feelings for this man.

With a blink of an eye, Vaughn's face was covered with seriousness, and he said, "Xena. You know that once I take you, there is no way back, right? No matter what. I have lifelong plans to cling to you forever. Eating lunches and dinners and breakfasts with you sitting on my lap—butt-naked or not. Feeding you from my mouth and taking care of you. Being territorial and ruining every single man laying eyes on you. Loving you till the end of our time and even after that. And then fucking you until you can't take anymore... until you know to whom you belong. I don't share, Sugar. Once I take you, you are mine forever. Mine!"

The tug in my heart amplified, and I ached for this man. My eyes glistened with tears, and his face blurred a little. My hands that were still placed on his face went firmer, as did the resolution in my eyes.

"Wolf. I have been yours for a long time, regardless you've taken me or not. It's me who wants to be clingy for your affection and love. It's me who finds your each and every filthy action unusually arousing. It's me who is a sucker for your love and dying here to reciprocate the same, if not more. I love when you get territorial and remind me who I belong to. Because I want to remind myself over and over again that I belong to you, to *my* Vaughn."

He heard every word I said in a daze, not even making a single sound, not even breathing. For a moment, I was confused if the man picked up my words. But then, I noticed a slow smile gradually appear on his exquisite face. Vaughn brushed over my cheek with his thumb to wipe away the tears I didn't know I shed.

Why was I crying?

With undivided attention, Vaughn stared at my tear-soaked face. Right before my eyes, I noticed his expression change dramatically.

Oh, boy. I think I knew what was about to come.

And I couldn't wait.

37 | Hot Noon

Xena

From my face, his hand traced down my neck, then my shoulder, and then finally my throat. Just when his long fingers reached my throat, they tightened around me. His grasp was tight enough to take in all the control but still allowed me to breathe somewhat.

"You love it when I remind you who you belong to, huh?" He asked breathlessly as his forehead and nose pressed against mine. His other hand went between my legs, and as two of his long manly fingers entered my cunt. "Then let me remind you once again, Sugar."

"Yes... take me, Vaughn. I want you," I said, equally breathless.

"You want me? What is it you want? Tell me," he asked. The command in his voice was unshakeable.

"You... all of you. Mouth, lips, tongue, fingers... and... and cock. Your cock. Fuck me, Vaughn," I said. Crying out under the torture of his fingers that went in and out of me.

His wicked fingers curled inside me, making a whimper come out of my throat."See how soaked you are. Aren't you a slut for me, Sugar? Wanting my cock so shamelessly? Wanting me to fuck you so brazenly? Have you got no shame wanting to be fucked so badly, Sugar?"

"No. I am your whore, Vaughn. Fuck me. Fuck me as you like. Fuck me like a whore, your whore."

My sanity was overpowered by the man and my desire for him. I was no longer thinking as I moved my pussy to meet the thrusts of his fingers. His wrist rubbed against my clit, sending electric current throughout my body.

"See, how needy my whore is. How shameless she gets for her cock. No worries, I'm here. I'll fuck you enough to shut that mouth from being so shameless again."

Within a second, his shirt was ripped off from my body, and his sweatpants were off. While he got rid of his sweatpants, he showed me the wet patch on it.

"See, how shamelessly aroused you are. You want my cock so much that you even drenched my pants when sitting on it. You are such a slut for me. Such a shameless slut."

I wordlessly kept staring at the monstrous cock. Anticipation whirling inside me, causing a tsunami in my body. Greed for him and his body amplifying by folds. And the muscles of his legs, God, I craved to fuck his thighs.

Then, hovering over me, he positioned his cock at my entrance. With one hand, he held his cock, and the other one above my head so that he could balance his face an inch over mine. His cock was rubbing my wetness all over my pussy, and then the tip pushed a little against the entrance of my cunt repeatedly—teasing me.

"Are you ready for me, Sugar? Are you ready for this dick? Are you ready to be mine?" he asked as if he was angry with me. His expression pained in need.

I held his face once again and said, "Make me yours in every way, Wolf. Fuck me."

His nose flared, and a primal, animalistic grunt vibrated from his throat as he pushed his cock inside my cunt. The entire process reminded me of nothing but a worked up beast. My beast. My wolf.

"Ah... it hurts, Vaughn... Too... too big... it-it won't go in." Suddenly, I started to panic. *Oh, Snuggety blankets!* Just how big was his cock?

"It will. My cock is yours. How can your cock not fit you? The tip is already in, baby."

"It... it won't go any further... it's impossible."

"Loosen up, baby... don't squeeze me already," he said in a strangled, wounded tone. As if he was in agonizing pain.

I could feel myself stretching as his monster cock teased my opening. Even his tip inside me felt like heaven. It was painful, yes, but it also felt so fucking good, nothing I had ever felt before. It was a blissful feeling of euphoria, and I was ready to dive into the sensation any day.

"Do I need to prepare you more, Sugar?" His hand went to my clit to tease it, rubbing it, pinching it. "Hell... so wet. Mmm... so fucking wet," he said the last few words in a breathless, nasal, and strangled tone, making me pool even further, drenching all over his fingers and the monstrous cock.

The man kept pushing his hot rod inside me, invading my tight hole more and more. I felt like a virgin once again.

"I-I think I'm going to split." I was horrified as I tried to accommodate his girthy length inside me.

"Weren't you a slut, begging for my cock earlier? Now take it, my pretty little whore. Take my cock. It's halfway in your slutty tiny cunt already."

I moaned at my sick pleasure from the degradation.

Suddenly, his full-length slammed inside my cunt. Even though I was ready, even though I knew what was coming, his sudden invasion caused me to gasp in shock.

Was it my lack of sexual activity? Or was it the size of his monstrous cock? I didn't know what brought tears to my eyes as I accommodated his length and girth inside me. My soaking cunt clasped and clenched around his cock as I tried to adjust my body for him. Both of his hands clenched on the sides of my pillow as Vaughn squeezed his eyes shut. His unmoving body was stiff on top of me.

"Fucking hell. Goddammit! Your cunt... it's too little for my cock. So tight... I love it, Xena. I love my cunt."

I pulled him by his neck and pressed my lips against his soft ones. Maybe he wanted to or to find control over himself, so he kissed my lips domineeringly, taking each and every ounce of control over the kiss. His cock still buried deep in me—unmoving.

"So good... My cunt is so good... I feel like exploding this very second. My goddamn cock is so feeble inside you, Xena. How? Oh, damn... I want you."

He kept mumbling against my lips, and I stopped him, saying, "And I want you." Tears rolled out of my eyes.

"Pain?"

There was certainly a concern in his tone, even though he clenched his jaw to hold onto the last string of his self-control.

I shook my head.

The moment I flashed him a green signal, he buried his face in my neck and pulled out his cock until only the tip of his cock was inside me. Before I could recover from the movement of his meaty girth, he slammed his entire length inside me once again.

And then again... and again... and again.

My hand moved from his neck to his broad, hard, muscular back, holding him for life. It wasn't long when his relentless strokes brought me to my edge, and I let it go, digging my nails into the skin of his back. My scream echoed around the room, but the man had no intention to pause. If anything, from the deep, long strokes, he switched into short, faster strokes, taking my soul away. My body was too sensitive and responsive to him.

"Gosh... Vaughn..."

"Yes, baby... I know," Vaughn said. He buried his finger in my hair, fisting them around his wrist, and pulled them. Whereas his other hand pressed down one of my hands tightly, showing me who was in control here.

"Goddamn... I can't have enough of you, Xena... I can't have enough of you. I want you... I want you more... more... more." Vaughn kept on panting as his pace went wild.

His mouth attacked the skin of my neck, sucking it so hard that I knew it would leave marks. But to be honest, I didn't even care. I wanted him too. All of him. All of Vaughn.

My Vaughn…

My pussy clenched around him once again, riling him wilder than he previously was. Soon, I couldn't hold it in anymore, and I let it go one more time.

Sweat prickled over both of our skin. Drops of sweat ran over his body and dripped over me, absorbing in my skin… blending in with mine, just like our intertwined body.

Right after I released for the second time, I felt the man's body tremble over mine, and suddenly it went stiff. I felt the warmth of his seed shooting inside me with a few jerks. I thought this was when he would drop over my body, but no, he didn't. He reached for my lips and kissed me intently. This kiss wasn't the dominating type of kiss that we shared earlier. It was full of love, affection, and gentleness.

My hands ran on his abs and then buried inside his hair as I drew him close, responding to the kiss as devotedly as him.

"I love you, Wolf," I said.

He chuckled against my lips. "I love you, Sugar."

Then, pressing another kiss of promise on my lips, he mumbled again.

"And I love to fuck you."

38 | Peppery Afternoon

Xena

Right after we had the wild taste of each other for the first time, Vaughn kissed my lips and then laid on the bed. His eyes, staring blankly at the ceiling. Eyebrows scrunched slightly, showing signs of anger and irritation.

I propped over his chest with my arms and then put my chin on them. My eyes scrutinized his expression, trying to decipher his thoughts.

"What's wrong? I wasn't good for you?" I asked, teasing him.

He glared at me, looking at me with anger and shock.

"You are my girl. How can you not be good for me? You are my dream come true and the only one for me." His palm stroked on my head.

"Then? What's bothering my man?"

"It's just… I'm irritated with myself." His eyes flashed in frustration.

"Why are you suddenly irritated with yourself?" I asked, stunned, to be honest. My brows scrunched as I kept thinking.

After going through havoc in my mind, the only plausible reason I could come up with was—no, it could not be! Could it?

"Are you pissed at your… performance?" I asked, suppressing a chuckle.

His brows scrunched some more.

What? This man!

He can't be serious, can he?

I was already aching between my legs and came twice with him inside me!

"Are you even serious, Wolf? Or are you fishing for compliments from me?" I couldn't control my high pitch tone of surprise.

He didn't say a word and just glared at me some more.

I chuckled a little. "There is no reason for you to think so," I said, pressing a kiss on his pouty lips. "I was too responsive to you as well. I have never come with any guy before. You are the first. That also more than once."

"Was it important for you to mention other guys fucking you right after *I* fucked you?" His mood grew terrible.

I bit back a smile. "Hey... I just want to say that this is the first time of many for us. This is the first time we gave each other our body and soul. It's okay to be responsive. Besides, when was the last time you had sex?"

This drew a different reaction out of him.

"About five years ago."

My jaw dropped at his honest, straightforward answer. He was too hot to remain chaste for that long.

Isn't it too long for a man?

How?

And why is his celibacy... his abstinence from sex arousing me so fast?

"Wh-How? Aren't you 30? So, you haven't been intimate with someone since you were 25? *What?*"

"Not just intimate. I haven't been with anyone since then," Vaughn said, keeping a straight face.

"So, you are saying you just had sex for the first time in five years?" My eyes kept widening more and more in shock.

"Why is it so hard to believe?" Vaughn looked confused.

"And you are pissed at your performance?" I couldn't help but ask.

243

He didn't answer and kept stroking my hair. Then, wordlessly, I hauled on top of his body, holding his hands on both sides. A wicked twinkle appeared on my lips.

"What do you think you are doing?" He asked, raising a brow.

"Proving you," I said. Then I leaned down with an inch gap between our lips, and my voice dropped to a husky whisper. "Action talks better than words, Wolf."

I kissed his lips gently, with him lying stiffly under me, shocked at my bold initiative. I inched away from him a little before I looked into his unfathomable abyss. His expression changed from anger to shock. My hands traced on his bare, chiseled abs as I sat straight. My body, naked before his feasting eyes.

With one hand on his hard chest, taking his cock in my other hand, I slowly slid it into my pussy. Gosh… his size… My pussy ached as it adjusted with the dimensions of his cock. But the ache to get fucked once again by this man overpowered the pain in my pussy. Slowly, I started riding my man. It hurt, but the tingle was so delicious and addictive, and I couldn't pause or stop.

Vaughn was still in shock when he squeezed his eyes shut. But the next moment, when his eyes opened, I only found raw lust in them. The anger, frustration, shock—all gone. Only the promise to fuck me senseless was apparent in his dark abyss.

His hands moved to my bouncing tits and squeezed them together, pinching the nipples. Then his wandering hands moved to my shoulders, and within a second, he rolled our body together, and suddenly, he was on top of me again. His cock was still buried in me, throbbing in need.

"Want to ride me, Sugar? Not so fast. I'm nowhere done with you." His raspy, needy voice vibrated against my ear as his fingers curled around my throat, choking me once again.

Mmm… I like it.

He started pumping inside me with powerful thrusts as his mouth found my neck and ears—my most sensitive parts. As he rammed into me, one of his hands wrapped around my waist, making my body curve a little for him to hit better. The fiercer his hit grew, the louder I screamed out his name, floating in the pleasure with a man's cock for the second time in my entire life. Before Vaughn, I never knew sex with a man could feel so good when this was the first day we had each other for the first time.

"Hard… I'm so hard for you." He grunted from above me, taking me to a different level of heaven.

"This pussy is so good, Sugar… so good that I lose all my control… so… so good that I lose myself. I can't get enough of this pussy. I can't get enough of you."

I moaned out louder.

His filthy, needy mouth, along with his hard pounding, was so hot that it made me go limp with strings of orgasms. But as I expected, this time, he didn't stop.

I had no idea how long he lasted this time, but I could swear it was nowhere less than an hour. My mind and body weren't cooperating, and there was no way I couldn't tell. I heard my cell phone ringing a few times, but none of us was interested in paying any heed to that.

This time around, the man fucked me. Railed me. Before he released for the first time, he made sure I came thrice from his cock. To be honest, I wasn't surprised. If a man could last twenty minutes for the first having sex after five years, it's expected from him to last for an hour every time after that.

After we finished, he took me in his embrace, and I laid, tangling my legs on his body, my head against his chest. One of his hands, brushing on my back and my butt. Another rested on my cheek as his fingers twirled a strand of my hair.

"Have I proved my point?" My voice was harsh and dry.

Vaughn chuckled and kissed on top of my head. His laughter vibrated from within his chest, and my heart filled with immense love and affection for this man.

245

"Yes. You did."

There was a sharp pain aching in between my leg, reminding me of what he had just done to me.

"You are a monster, Wolf," I whined as I blushed.

"And you are too tight, Sugar."

"Any girl would be tight for you."

"And I don't give a fuck to any other girl's pussy. The only pussy that matters to me is what lays in between your legs. Soon, very soon, I'll mold it into my size."

"And what about yours, Wolf? How do I mold it only for me?"

"You don't have to. Because it only reacts to you, to start with. You have no reason to worry."

I hugged him tighter.

"Now, take a nap. My girl is tired."

With a satisfied smile blooming on my lips, I embraced the man of my dreams and drifted into a peaceful sleep.

With the faint sound of my phone ringing, I opened my eyes once again. Vaughn was still sleeping with me wrapped around his body. But this time, when I unwrapped my body from him, he woke up. His eyes were half-open and reluctant to let me go. With a quick peck on his soft lips, I parted from his and picked up my phone from the bedside.

"Finally, you picked up the phone!" Ron's high-pitched voice rang from the opposite side. I looked at Vaughn, and with a finger on my lips, I signaled him to stay silent. As expected, Vaughn didn't like that and furrowed his eyebrows to express his displeasure.

"Sorry, Ron. I—"

"You stupid woman! I was so worried I left you alone at home. I thought something happened to you and was about to start my car to check on you!"

"No! No! Don't! I'm not at home—"

"Not at home? Where are you?" Ron asked. Her voice exuded her apparent confusion.

246

"I... I-I'm at Leo's." I squeezed my eyes as I lied. Beside me, I felt the mattress move, and when I looked, I noticed Vaughn sitting straight, glaring at me. He looked mad.

"Oooo... that's great. It's finally happening! You are finally getting some dick, huh?"

I knew Vaughn couldn't hear what Ron said, but the blush reddening my face gave away the dirty talk his sister was blabbering to me.

Suddenly, Vaughn picked me up and settled my naked body on his lap. One of his hands was squeezing my breast, and another, squeezing my waist. His beautiful dark orbs challenged me as he silently mouthed, "Leo?"

I helplessly looked at him.

"Wait... is he beside you? Am I interrupting your devil's dance?"

"Yeah, he is." I almost moaned as Vaughn pulled my breast to his mouth and flicked on my nipple with his tongue. All the while, his eyes were on me.

"He is... with me."

Vaughn's reached between my legs and entered two of his fingers inside my drenched pussy. He started thrusting them in and out, his thumb stroking my clit.

I helplessly put my free hand against my mouth to ruffle the moans. My entire body was at his mercy, as he punished me.

"Whoa... seems like I'm really interrupting your devil's dance. Carry on. You have been depriving yourself of the delight of some good dicks for a long time. I'm so happy for you, Jay. I'll hang up then, bye. Happy fucking!"

I canceled the call and threw the phone away somewhere, not really looking. Vaughn's mouth and fingers went rough and wild on my body, clearly punishing me, and my entire body was trembling at his mercy.

Vaughn placed me between his legs with me leaning against his chest, and then one of his hands again went to squeeze my breast. The other continued fucking my pussy. His mouth went to my neck and earlobes to add to the torture. The man attacked me three ways as I felt his rigid member reminding me of its royal presence as it poked on my back.

Revenge. That was what he was doing.

I clutched both of his hands, and I bit my lips.

"Don't dare to hold it back. Scream. Scream my name. Scream out loud and remind your little slutty-self who is doing all this to you. Scream!" He growled out loud.

"Vaughn…" I screamed out his name.

"Again… keep screaming my name. If you pause even for a second, I'll edge you so bad."

I didn't pause. Even if I wanted, I couldn't. Vaughn was merciless.

It wasn't long when I came all over his hand, sullying his bedsheet even more with my creamy cum. His light grey bedsheet had white patches of both of our love juices all over.

I panted, throwing my entire weight on his chest as his hands continued caressing my sore body with intense affection. My eyes started drooping once again when I heard his voice.

"Tell me who is fucking you," he asked possessively.

"You Vaughn… It can only be you."

"Tell me who you belong to… to whom this body and your soul belong."

"You Vaughn… I only said his name because I can't tell Ron about us yet… you know that."

"Tell me who you love."

"I love you, only you. You have no reason to be jealous about."

"The hell, I'll be jealous! *My* girl is talking about another man fucking her! On my fucking bed!" He was still mad.

I turned my head and, holding his face carefully in my palm, I pressed my lips on his soft ones. Within seconds, he pulled me closer to his body with me straddling him and deepened the kiss. His tongue invaded my mouth and slurred as he sucked my soul out of my body.

And I gladly gave in.

After a long while, he parted an inch from my mouth and said, "You must be sore. I'll prepare a warm bath for you."

My heart went warm, with butterflies fluttering in my stomach. How could a man be so tender, gentle, and considerate after fucking like a primal animal? Gosh, I loved both his personalities.

After placing me carefully on the bed, he got off the bed with all his naked glory and went towards the bathroom. His confidence in his naked-self was so damn sexy. Whereas I looked at the bed and the mess we created starting from last night and shied out.

After a while, he came out and carried me to the bathroom. Then, with a soft peck on my forehead, he settled me inside the bathtub, filled with warm, soothing water with the perfect temperature.

"Do you need my help?" He asked.

I shook my head in sudden shyness overwhelming me.

"Take your time," Vaughn said. He smiled with a knowing look and kissed my lips again as he left the bathroom, leaving me alone with all our wild memories.

39 | Spicy Evening

Xena

I stepped out of the bathroom wrapped in an oversized bathrobe that belonged to Vaughn—engulfing my entire body. The moment my eyes took in the surroundings, it looked slightly different. I found the room cleaner than before.

The bedsheet was changed, there were no clothes scattered on the floor, and our cell phones were placed neatly on the nightstand. My heart started racing with the thought of a mighty man like Vaughn doing all the household chores so effortlessly and neatly.

I took another step inside the room, looking around for a glimpse of the man. Earlier, I thought he would come inside and interrupt my bath—which I wouldn't have minded—and now that I knew he was busy tidying up the room, I missed him even more.

A soft peck fell on my cheek, bringing me out of my thoughts with a jerk. I looked around and found Vaughn, still in his confident, naked glory. When did he come? The man walked like a cat.

"Looking for me?" His hand stroked on the side of my face and brushed away a few strands of my wet hair. His thumb stayed longer on my blushing cheek.

I gulped down, looking deep into his eyes, and nodded.

"Come, lie down on the bed." He took hold of my wrist and brought me to the neat surface, settling me on it.

Only then did I notice a glass of watermelon juice in his other hand.

"Drink it. You haven't had enough water today."

I stared at him in awe.

Is he real?

Vaughn put the quilt over my body, and after dropping another kiss on my forehead, he attempted to leave. I held one glass in one hand, and I clasped on his arm with the other. His pure male scent aroused my sleeping senses.

"Don't go."

I felt a sudden rush of emotion and attachment to this man.

He smiled and held my face in affection, pressing rain of kisses trailing from my forehead to my lips. Then he said, "I'll take a quick shower and then join you. Wait for me and drink it up like a good little girl. Alright?"

I nodded in reluctance and loosened my hold on his arm with a pout.

Vaughn patted on my head like I was a pet and said, "Be good."

Then he parted, and his gorgeous body lost behind the bathroom door.

I felt like a pampered little girl and obediently drank the juice from the glass upside down. My mind dozed off, eyes already missing his handsome face and tempting body. After finishing the drink, I put the empty glass on the nightstand. I thought of washing the glass myself, but the sharp pain and soreness between my legs didn't allow me to get up.

I curled up and hugged my body, tightening the bathrobe around me. A shameless smile appeared on my face, and I bit my lips from letting them stretch any further. Heart and mind, getting impatient waiting for him.

Vaughn kept his words and took a quick shower, indeed. When he emerged, he was dressed in a bathrobe similar to mine. The robe somehow looked manly on him, making him look even sexier, along with his fresh skin and wet hair. He was drying his hair with another towel as he came out, then threw it on a chair as he stepped closer to the bed… to me.

After getting into the bed, he wrapped his strong arms around me and took me in his embrace. I covered both of our bodies under the quilt and put my head on his chest. His heart thumped under my ear. I tightened my possessive grip on him, wrapping my arms and legs around his hard, warm body.

He lightly chuckled at my act of possessiveness, and his chest vibrated deliciously under my ear, causing a tingly shiver to flow throughout my body. Vaughn, too, wrapped his hands around me and started stroking my head like I was his pet.

"Comfortable?"

"Uh-huh," I said in accord as I rubbed my cheek against his chest like a rabbit.

"It feels like a dream," I said to myself. My voice was low as I murmured the words.

"Mmm?"

"You, me, and… everything. Everything feels too good to be real."

"I'm right there with you, baby. I feel the same way." He pressed a kiss on my head and said, "Even though you are right here, in between in my arms, I still can't get enough of you. You are the strongest drug I've ever tasted, and I'm addicted to you, Xena."

Such gentle, romantic words in his deep, sexy voice brought me to my edge. I couldn't help myself as I snuggled even closer to him, feeling the heat emitting from his body. Then holding his face, I locked my lips with his.

The kiss started slow, but with both of us losing control over our bodies, it turned into a heated make-out session. I awoke from my trance only when I felt Vaughn's rock-hard cock poke against my lower abdomen.

"Vaughn… stop." But he was nowhere ready to stop as he sucked the skin on my neck, putting a mark of his name—stamping me as his.

"Vaughn." I pushed his head away from my neck and looked into his eyes. "We need to stop, Wolf. Behave."

Vaughn squeezed his eyes and took a few sharp breaths in, collecting his composure. He was hovering over my body, supporting his entire weight on his hands, trembling in need. His eyes opened slowly and his dilated, penetrating gaze bored into mine… like a wolf.

"And why do I need to behave around my girl, huh?" he asked in a husky, nasal tone.

With tenderness, I placed my hand on his face and said, "Since the morning, all we are doing is… you know, doing the deeds. Don't you think we should have some heart-to-heart talk and know each other better in a rational mind?"

He didn't reply and just stared at my face for a long time. Then, gradually, a sly smirk appeared on his face. He stroked my hair in affection and caressed my face.

"Xena… My Xena… My beautiful, naïve little girl…"

He licked on my lips in degrade. Then said, "Dumb. So dumb."

I looked at him in a puzzle—excitement building in my sore region.

"You think I need to have a heart-to-heart talk to know you?" I felt a rough bite on my lower lip as if he punished me for saying that.

Then, in abrupt, he left the bed, without giving me a chance to speak. He entered through a different door, which I assumed was his closet. When he emerged, Vaughn had black jeans and a casual black shirt on.

Mmm. Yummy.

"Where are you going?"

"You'll know." With a few long strides, Vaughn picked up his cellphone and wallet and put them in his pocket. Just before he left the room, he looked behind and said, "I'll be quick. Be good and wait for me."

Then he left.

I was dumbfounded.

253

What just happened?

I was pulling my hair, wondering what was going on in his mind. The man was a mystery to me. I was still unaccustomed to his mischievous ways, and he never missed an opportunity to surprise me with his unusual gestures. But *snuggly blankets*, I loved him.

I dragged myself out of bed and took slow steps around his apartment. Though I wanted to go to the roof, his living room also had a spectacular view of New York City. I stood there, looking outside for a while. Then I wandered around the room, looking at the photos and paintings on the walls. I could see mainly Ron's picture on his wall. Other than that, there was an old photo of Vaughn and Finn from years ago. Finn really was his good friend. The poor guy wasn't exaggerating. There wasn't a single photo of his parents.

I was deep in thought when the lift doors opened, and Vaughn took slow, confident steps. I looked behind, and my eyes began to suck in his handsome appearance once again, like how plants suck in light to survive.

He rolled his sleeves up to his elbow, and in one of his veiny, sexy hands, he held some takeout boxes, and with the other, he carried a beautiful bouquet of blue dendrobium orchids.

Wait, what?

Is it coincident?

It has to be!

I looked at the bouquet of the fierce blue-purple shades of the orchids as my eyes widened.

"*Your* most favorite flowers, for *my* most favorite girl." Vaughn offered me the bunch of orchids, and my heart started thumping more violently.

"Wh-How do you know it's my most favorite?"

Vaughn chuckled and said, "Not red roses, not lilies, not peonies... my girl loves orchids—blue dendrobium orchids. If *I* don't know it, who will? Who would dare enough to gift my girl flowers other than me?"

254

"But I never told you about this… how do you know?" I was shocked.

"Let's have dinner first. Aren't you starving?" Vaughn mischievously handed me the bouquet and then opened the takeout boxes, avoiding my question smoothly.

When he opened aluminum boxes, my jaws dropped once again. *Baked ziti pasta.*

I stared at him as if I was looking at a ghost.

Vaughn looked at me with a hint of a smirk at the corner of his lips.

"Come on, dig in, baby. It's spicy, just the way you like it. Besides, it's from your favorite restaurant," he said with a playful wink.

I took a fork wordlessly and pulled the box closer, still in a trance.

Vaughn took a mouthful of the same pasta he brought for himself as well. Then, getting up from his seat, he went to the liquor cabinet and pulled out a bottle of chardonnay, shocking me yet again on the same night. It was from my father's farm.

He poured for both of us and handed me a glass. Silently, I took it from him, still floating in the dream.

"Your food is getting cold, Sugar. Do you want me to feed you?"

"N-No… I can." I abruptly took a mouthful of the food.

We ate in silence for a few minutes, occasionally glancing at each other. My mind was still jutted in the shocks I experienced in the span of the last half an hour. My heart still raced as if it was in a competition, and there was no other option other than winning.

As usual, my clumsiness caused the pasta sauce to smear at the corner of my lips. Vaughn leaned towards me and then used his thumb to wipe the sauce tenderly. Then, with a smirk, he sucked his thumb clean. My heart was about to explode with every action of this man.

After finishing with our food, we sipped the wine in silence. Hundreds of questions whirling in my mind.

"You like watermelon and orange juice. Even though you look absolutely angelic in white, your favorite color is black, but you mostly wear blue and green. Silk is your most favorite fabric, and I love to see you in silk too. You are not into clubbing much for apparent reasons, yet you go, just for Ron. You've got an immense ambition to become a successful lawyer, and I absolutely support you. Aside from all that, you are careful about your weight, but you are a foodie with a special craving for Italian dishes. Also, the spicier, the better."

He took a deep breath before continuing. "For coffee, you prefer white mocha with cream, especially from Northend Café. Your favorite flavor of ice cream is cookies and cream, and your favorite chocolate is Reese's. You rarely buy dresses from luxury brands; instead, you shop at Shein, Boohoo, and Zara. You've countless admirers, even more than *you* know since many have them couldn't pass through the shield I had created around you. You mostly have one good friend—Ronnie. But recently, a prick is hovering around you from time to time, which I must include that I *absolutely* detest."

"You are pretty much in control of your emotions all the time. Make no rash decisions. Family means a lot to you. If I'm not wrong, you are close to and love Ron more than you love your own sister, Aliza. Also, you absolutely love when I dominate you or degrade you while fucking. But when I'm gentle to you, you blush close to the shade of crimson. You show more emotion to me than you do to most other people. You, Xena, have fallen head over heels for me as well, and I couldn't be any happier."

"The only thing I regret not knowing earlier is your sexual fantasies, also your secret about fancying me for years. But then again, even if I wished to know earlier, I would never stalk your IP address because I would never hamper your absolute privacy. So, you can say,

256

I'm pretty much harmless as a stalker." He finished with a wink. A playful smirk lingered at the corner of his lips.

It was like someone pushed me from the edge of a hill, and now I was skydiving—floating in the middle of the air.

I remained seated in total silence. My brain crashed, and I had no idea about how to react or what to say.

After a long time, warmth returned to my cold body, reacting.

"You… me… you—" I continued to stutter, entirely out of my wits. My eyes felt blurry because of the unshed tears.

"Xena." Vaughn pulled me on his lap. My eyes gazed at him, still as big as saucers. As if I had seen ghosts.

Vaughn wrapped one arm around my waist. And with another hand, he brushed into my hair, his thumb tracing on my cheek. Leaning towards me a little, he supported his forehead against mine… then quietly, our nose touched, and we stayed like that for a long time. The sensation in my heart was so overwhelming and tingly it brought tears to my eyes.

"And about you knowing me… I've been in love with you for a long time, baby. I'm way past this heart-to-heart phase. All I want to do is dote on you, keep you around, love you, and fuck you until you can think of no other man—*only me*." His warm lips pressed against mine, taking my soul away with every movement of his soft lips and skillful tongue. Our breath went heavy, and our chests started heaving. At some point, my bathrobe loosened, and one of my breasts peeked through the gap. His eyes traveled there and darkened visibly.

Then, taking me in his arms, Vaughn stood up and headed towards his bedroom.

"So, my sweet Sugar, don't ever tell me I should slow down fucking my girl just to know her. I know her alright. In some cases, more than she knows herself. I've waited enough for this moment." He pressed a soft, gentle kiss on my head before dropping me onto my bed. Then, pulling out the sash of my bathrobe, he tied my hands with it to the headboard.

257

"Now, don't dare to stop me from fucking my girl when and however I want to."

40 | Raunchy Night

Xena

I panted as I looked at the man leaning above me, tying my dainty hands against the headboard. I was still reeling from his confession, and my mind was preoccupied with processing everything he said. Even then, I couldn't control my rising arousal for him.

Oh, snuggles... I wanted him so bad.

With one hand gripping the headboard above my hand, he wrapped his other hand behind my neck. With the rising anticipation, I squeezed my eyes shut, and then I felt his warm breath tingling on my lips. Slowly, he touched his forehead and nose against mine. My toes curled, listening to his heavy, short, needy breath so close to me.

Every time I heard the man breathing like that, it felt like they tickled right at my g-spot. And every *blanketty* time, my toes curled on their own accord.

"Goddamn... Xena... you have no idea how many sleepless nights I've spent longing for you. How many nights I passed imagining how it'd feel hearing you say my name, hearing you say you love me, claiming you as mine... about how it'd feel kissing you, touching you, to be inside you... fucking you. Some nights, it was so torturous that I felt my dick will break with all the frictions of my hand." A throaty chuckle escaped his lips. "Hell... baby, I can't wait to spend the rest of my life living out all of my fantasies."

"Vaughn..." I said. His name came out as a moan, with my emotions overflowing all over the place.

Vaughn Drifted towards the edge of my ear, sucking my earlobe and biting on it playfully.

"Xena Meyers... I can still remember your first day at college. You were wearing a beautiful mint-orange floral dress that made your waist look narrow, accentuating your tits and your fine ass. Despite that, you looked like a young, lively spirit. I remember those greedy stares of those boys for the curves that belong to me. Yet, I couldn't claim my territory. I had to endure those little boys eyeing and fantasizing about *my* girl. Do you have any idea how I felt?"

"You... you were there?" I was breathless.

His mouth rained open-mouthed sloppy kisses on my neck and shoulders, moving down to my upper chest.

"I was so mad... so angry that I wanted to hurl your ass over my shoulder, bring you to my bed, and then rip off that dress from your body that made you look so irresistible to those guys. Then I wanted to spank this sorry ass until it turned all red and purple," he said, groping and squeezing my butt cheek.

"On your first day at my club, you were wearing a dress with a deep neckline. Your heavy tits overflowed over the neckline, grabbing attention from every *goddamned* guy," Vaughn said. His growl was primal, reminiscing about the moment as if he was still seething over that.

Moving the bathrobe away from my chest with his teeth, he grabbed both of my tits and pressed them together, squeezing them hard, as if punishing me.

"These tits... *my* tits... all the fucking guys had eyes over what's *mine*! When you danced, carefree of the world around you, and they jiggled and bounced for every eye around you. Do you know how that made me feel? You were in my territory, and still, I couldn't claim these tits as mine!"

His mouth attacked my nipples in turn. As if, with a bottomless hungry appetite, he sucked both my nipples successively... licked them, nibbled on them. As if he was hungry for them all these years.

There was nothing gentle about how he sucked and bit my nipples, pinched on them. With my tied-up hands, I helplessly squirmed and moaned under him. My tongue darted out to wet my dried lips. Clearly, the man held grudges all these years.

Slowly, he moved downwards, and my limbs trembled under him. His large palm cupped my pussy as he leisurely unbuttoned a few top buttons of his shirt. I laid naked under him with the robe hanging on my arms while he was fully clothed, touching all over my nakedness however he wanted with apparent ownership.

"The nights you went home with guys, my heart twisted in pain thinking how some pricks were touching *my* girl's pussy. This fucking pussy. Whereas, *I* maintained celibacy for you." He slapped over my pussy and then entered two fingers inside me, emphasizing. "The thought alone killed me thousand times over the years. Do you think you can get away, after all, Xena?"

"Vaughn…" I trailed off. Did I moan or cry? Even I couldn't even say.

"No. you'll not get away with all the sleepless nights, heartaches, and longings I suffered craving you, loving you from afar." His eyes emitted anger and frustration that he carried in his heart all these years as his fingers increased pacing inside my pussy, fucking me.

Tonight, Vaughn opened up his gate of emotion for me he kept locked for all these years. His eyes held bottomless love, affection, anger, and frustration, and I felt scared yet excited looking at him. Once he opened up with his overwhelming emotion, he couldn't keep it in any longer.

And I? I wanted to see the end of his emotion for me. I wanted to know him, his extent of love for me. Gosh, I loved him.

"Vaughn… I love you," I said. There was so much I wanted to tell him, but all I could muster to say was, I love this man.

"And I love you… I've been in love with you for a long time, Xena." His fingers didn't slow down, torturing me, as his other hand

261

went to wrap around my throat, choking me. "From now on, there is no way back for us. I'm going to mark every inch of you. Then I'm going to fuck you so hard for all those missing years. I'm going to make sure you know to whom your soul and this body belong. I'll mark not only your body, but also your soul. I'll love you so hard, Xena… I'll keep reminding you about my love for you every single day for the rest of my life."

Without giving me any time to react, he pressed his mouth over my cunt, sucking it in, taking my soul out of my body from the very second his tongue touched my clit.

I cried out loud with my overflowing emotion. Vaughn hurled my thighs over his shoulder and sat straight on his knee, his mouth still attached to my pussy. Because of the position, my body arched like a bow, making heaps of folds appear on my abdomen. His monstrous cock poked at my back through his jeans.

He inched a little, staring in a daze at my cunt shamelessly— hanging in the air in his hold, all exposed to his thirsty eyes.

"Look at you. All dripping and exposed for me. Can you see yourself right now? You are here under me, on my bed… at my mercy. Finally, you are mine. You are *my* slut, *my* whore, *mine* to fuck. *Mine* to love, *mine* to dote on, *mine* to get territorial for. *All mine*." Vaughn said, emphasizing every time he claimed me as his, flaring through his nose in possessiveness. His mouth once again attacked my cunt in aggression.

He looked so hot I wanted to hug him and say that I was his, only his. But my throat felt clogged, and I couldn't mutter a single word other than being nothing but a moaning mess.

His tongue went deep as tongue-fucked me. The man's long-term celibacy didn't show from his skillful touches at all. After a while, he started slurping on my clit again as two of his fingers went back inside me. It wasn't long before I came hard all over his filthy mouth and his long, skillful fingers.

With triumph in his eyes, he moved closer to me.

"Kiss me. Taste yourself. See what I do to you. See how hard you come for me... how shameless my little whore gets under my mouth."

I leaned forward to meet his lips, licking them all over, sucking them in. Soon he took over his dominance and kissed me as if it was a punishment. With one hand around my head, he reached his other hand to my cunt again.

"Mmm... pain..." I said, somehow mumbling through the punishing kiss. We had sex multiple times today, and after getting hit by his monster cock, I was yet to recover.

"Like that's going to stop me, Sugar." He inserted two fingers, curling them inside me. "Take my fingers, my little slut. I know you *can*, and you *will*. For me."

His kiss intensified as his fingers increased the pace, fucking me roughly, hitting my sensitive corners. His aggressive, wild kisses moved to my neck, then to my tits as he squeezed them with his other hand. Under all his bestial tortures, I writhed and twisted, but he never slowed down, at least not until I came for the second time that night.

Covered in sweat, I was yet to come down from my high when Vaughn settled on his knees again. When I heard him unbuckling his belt and unzipping, I went concerned.

"I can't... not tonight. I-I'm sore..."

"I can still fuck my whore..."

I moaned again, helplessly. Vaughn spat on his palm and then stroked his cock, dampening it, making it ready. Then, surprising me, the man pressed my thighs together and pushed his cock between them as it slid over my pussy lips. My eyes widened in surprise, but soon I cried out loud when his cock went back and forth, sliding against my clit. My clit was over-sensitive, and every time his cock stroked it, I couldn't help but cry out loud. Even though he didn't penetrate his cock in my cunt, the feeling was nowhere less exciting. I was dripping with my cum, creating enough lubricant for him to push between my pressed thighs.

"How does it feel like pressing against your cunt, hmm?"

I was a moaning mess, calling out his name again. My wits were nowhere in my body to form an answer. His hot rod felt so hard, and it twitched and throbbed against my thighs as he thigh-fucked me.

"So wet… you are dripping for me, baby. So wet for me." His voice trembled.

His frictions brought tears to my eyes as my clit was too sensitive after an entire day on the bed with Vaughn. Finally, when his cum flowed all over my stomach and tits, he leaned over me, again kissing my lips.

But this time, he was gentle.

"Gosh… Mine… so mine… I love you, Xena. I so fucking love you."

I had no more energy to answer as I retired for the night.

41 | Guilty Conscience

Xena

"OMG, boo. Leo did a total number on you!"

My best friend exclaimed with bright eyes when she found me in the corridor towards our class.

Without any reply, I hid my eyes from her. How could I even face her with calm and composure? After a weekend of getting fucked by her brother—her Vee? After sucking her dear brother's cock and feeding him my pussy?

Guilt coated my eyes, and Ron took it as my shyness.

"I need every little detail, Jay. Don't even think about hiding a thread of details. Finally, you are getting some dick, and I'm so happy for you!"

Her wiggling eyes caused my heart to drop to my stomach.

Not saying a single word in reply, I pulled her hand instead. "Walk faster. We are getting late for the class."

I yanked her hand, dragging my annoying best friend to our classroom, but she never shut her mouth all the way. Well, knowing her characteristics, I didn't expect her to.

But when the class finally started, I wasn't as attentive as I always was. Today, I left all my attention to the black-eyes, black-haired rock-hard magnificence I left this morning.

Without my awareness, all my thoughts dozed off to the memories of this morning. It had just been a few hours since I woke up to Vaughn's rain of kisses, and honestly, waking up had never been so wonderful before in my life.

The man never ceased to make everything sparkle for me.

I still felt my soul swoon thinking of how he woke me up with kisses, how the sexy specimen of a man cooked omelet and sausages for me for breakfast and then fed me with his own hands like I was his queen and he was there to serve me.

The man knew me as well as his palm. Perhaps he knew me better than I knew myself. With him by my side, I felt treasured, protected. With Vaughn by my side, I felt genuinely happy after—well—since I could even remember.

The man awakened my soul.

With the man's slightest touch, my body reacted just how a trivial touch shrinks the leaves of a shameplant. The only difference was that my obstinate body only responded to him and him alone. No one else but him.

Even before I could worry about what to wear for college, he had prepared everything for me. By the time we finished with our morning coffee, Finn was there with bags from boohoo and Victoria's Secret in his hands.

I felt slightly shy because Finn had to go shop for my clothes, but if a possessive alpha, like Vaughn, was okay with it, I had nothing to worry about. So, brushing off the thoughts, I checked out the outfit. It was a stunning pastel pink floral dress that covered me well but beautifully. Mentally, I thanked Finn for choosing something so beautiful.

Finn brought one more thing, and I couldn't contain my surprise when I saw that. He did not know I was already on the pill because I was aware of what was about to happen between Vaughn and me. So, the man arranged morning-after pills and regular pills for me.

When I asked him about it, he said, "I can't wait to start a family with you, Xena. I'm already 30, and I'm not getting any younger. But, baby, I know you need to finish your study and achieve that dream of yours first. We can have our little team later." Then he kissed my forehead with unbound fondness.

My heart trembled at his thoughtful words.

How can it not tremble? Especially when your man gives importance to your dreams as much as you do?

He looked at me like he worshipped me. His restless, possessive, affectionate eyes never left me, at least not until I left his line of sight. When I got ready, he was by my side. When I left his home, he held my hand by my side. Even when Finn dropped me to a block before my college, he was there, by my side. The entire ride, the man held me in his tight embrace, on his laps. By no means had he allowed me to sit in the car seat as if his lap was absolutely exclusive for me to sit on, just how he said a day before.

As if it was my throne.

He was reluctant to let me go. Those hands felt tight around me, and they only went tighter when my time to part from him ran closer. At some point, it was hard for me to breathe but never had I ever felt any more relaxed.

What he said before I left still buzzed in my ears—making my heart go frenzied all over again.

"I can't wait for the weekend to come soon."

"You will call me, won't you?"

"Miss me, okay?"

"Stay away from boys."

And especially when he said...

"I love you to the point of insanity, Xena... love me back, okay?"

Only the thoughts of him brought sparkles of joy to my eyes. Without my awareness, a bright smile appeared on my face. Even though I didn't realize it, nothing escaped my best friend's eyes.

It wasn't long when a crumpled paper landed on my desk as usual. I flattened it just to find Ron taunting me.

"Each and every fucking detail. Can't leave even a thread of detail about the red marks on your neck and also, what brings that creepy smile on your face, bitch."

267

My heart dropped once again, restless, thinking about what to tell her when the time came. How could I tell her it was her brother who had done all these unspeakable things to me over the weekend?

When the lunch bell rang, Ron didn't waste a second to yank my hand towards the canteen. I knew how restless she was to know about my weekend. Even so, my heart was thudding, and I felt nauseous with guilt.

"Girl, your skin is glowing. I have never seen your eyes sparkle so much. This is the first time I could tell a man truly, genuinely, utterly satisfied you. Just tell me already!" she said, devouring her donut.

"Uh... Um—Ron, I... I think I want to be with him."

The pain of not being able to share it all with your best friend was indeed heart-wrenching.

"Atta girl! Momma is proud of you! Today, you really make me proud!"

Her reaction was so genuine. Her eyes sparkled with joy and pride as she hugged me, leaning over the table.

But what about me? My guilty conscience was eating me from inside. There was no control over my perturbed emotion as my fingers tapped on the table, long forgotten about the food before me.

Ron noticed my turbulence and narrowed her eyes. "He wants to be with you too, right?"

"Yes. Yes, he does."

"Then why do you look so upset, boo? What's wrong? I swear if Leo dares to hurt my babe, I'm going to beat his ass up!"

"No, no! He is alright. It's... it's just... What if being with him affects my relationship with you? Can I afford that? That's a high price I would have to pay if anything happens between us."

"Jay, why are you so worried about our relationship? I'm not going anywhere. If the man keeps you happy, nothing in the world could shake our relationship. You are my soul sister, and you are not getting rid of me in this life."

I stared into Ron's eyes. The genuine feelings and love for me sparkled in her eyes. For a moment, all I wanted to do was spill out my guts about her brother and me.

Gosh... Vaughn and I even confessed our love for each other. It was big news. But yet, I couldn't share it with Ron. I felt trapped within my feelings.

I smiled at her, returning the same looks with a gentle smile, appreciating all she just said. I was about to say something in return when someone interrupted us.

"Look who it is, pretending not to date but showing off hickeys so blatantly. Where is the proud woman who tosses men like rugs and never sleeps with anyone? At the end of the day, aren't you the same as well?"

Ron looked enraged, but I somehow still managed to keep my nerves cool.

As I moved my eyes upwards, I found Bianca—the infamous bitch, standing arm in arm with Jack.

"Jack, didn't you say that this lackluster hoe wasted your time on your date, and then you had no option other than ditching her? Then right next moment she left to suck another rich dude with no shame at all?" Bianca tsked and asked, "Poor you. Feeling sorry for yourself for pursuing this so-called pathetic beauty?"

"This is new. A renowned slut is slut-shaming others. Wow!" Ron couldn't keep her cool anymore.

"Hey, isn't this the partner of the hoe? Haven't you taught your partner how to hide hickeys? Or do you plan to show this off to get more dicks, now that you are in the field?"

"You—" Ron was furious when she darted towards her. I held my head-high best friend from reacting rashly.

I slowly stood up, leaving my barely eaten lunch behind. Looking at them disgusted me, especially at Jack. I stared right into his eyes, finally opening my mouth to speak.

"Jack, I know what I did was not the right thing to do in the middle of a date, and I'm sorry for that. But I really wished you would handle it with maturity. Today, you disappointed me."

I saw a flash of regret passing through Jack's eyes, but he remained silent.

Then I finally peered at the barely covered, fake beauty with a dark soul—suppressing my disgust at even having to look at her.

"Bianca. First of all, I want to say that I don't live to please any of you. So, whose dick I suck shouldn't matter to you. And secondly, whatever you say or think about me isn't nearly as bad as what I know about you. So, it's a wise decision to keep your opinion to yourself."

Bianca's eyes went as wide as saucers as she didn't expect me to reply in such an icy tone.

I took hold of Ron's wrist and yanked her towards our next class, not wishing to stay there for even another second. But before I left, I looked back at them and said, "I hope you get to clean your soul and grow up."

From the corner of my eyes, I saw a glint of triumph in Ron's eyes and smiled.

After I arrived home and lay down on my bed, I finally had time to reflect on what was going on in my life. I was in dire need of talking to someone about the turmoil in my heart. But there wasn't anyone who could be trustworthy enough for me to spill out my secrets. I didn't want to hurt Ron, I swear, but there was no way I could think of a life without Vaughn in it, not anymore.

How on earth could I keep the two most important people in my life?

Ting!

I glanced at my cellphone to find an incoming text message.

Leo: Why do women rub their eyes when they wake up in the morning?

Xena: Isn't it natural?

Leo: It's because they don't have balls to rub.

I laughed out loud as I read the text but then worried about the mental health of my friend.

I was about to type something back, then a thought came to my mind, and instead, I called Leo.

"Hey beautiful, miss me?"

"Hey Zippy, can you meet me?"

"Whoa! The beauty not only misses me but also wants to see this handsome, loyal, devoted servant. Am I dreaming?"

"Okay, drama queen, enough. Now hurry up and meet me at Northend café after your office hours."

"Okay. See you. Should I be prepared?"

"Prepared as in?" I asked.

"I mean, should I book a hotel room or something?"

"Just come, you Zippy! I'm going to kick your ass first, and then we'll see where to go. Hotel or hospital, you Buster!"

"Whoa, feisty! Yummy!"

I hung up the call with no more words and huffed out loud. Talking to this guy was a tiresome load of work.

As decided, when the clock hit five, I left to meet Leo with a dense heart.

42 | Friendly Deal

Xena

"You've got to be kidding me!" Leo was stunned to the core.

"No. I'm pretty much sure I'm serious," I said with a straight face.

"So, I have to act like your boyfriend, yet I won't be having the cream of the milk? That's so unreasonable."

Such a drama queen!

"Not act, buster! Only Ron will *think* of you as my boyfriend. Otherwise, it will be difficult for me to meet Vaughn or spend any time with him." My frustration flowed uncontrollably in my tone. Then I lowered my voice and took a deep intake of breath. "I just need an alibi. Aren't you my best friend?" I asked, flashing him my puppy eyes.

"Huh! Who is your best friend? Who are you calling your best friend?" Leo narrowed his eyes at me in a dramatic interrogating tone.

"Of course you! You are my only handsome best friend, whereas Ron is my only beautiful best friend." I grinned at him with an innocent face that had nothing to do with innocence at all.

"No way. There has to be something in return. Otherwise, this handsome isn't swayed to take the trumped-up relationship status," he said. His arms crossed against his chest to show his child-like stubbornness.

"I promise I'll give you something in return that will more than make up for it. Right now, I don't know what it is, but you have to trust me, buddy."

After staring at me for a long minute, Leo looked at me with inspecting eyes and asked, "You promise?"

"Gentlewoman's promise." A soft smile of triumph appeared on my face as I offered him my pinky finger.

Leo pretended to think with his finger on his chin, and then, after a long pause, he accepted my pinky finger as an agreement to the deal.

I huffed in relief. It was a lot harder than I assumed. When he agreed, instead of making me feel better, a different kind of sadness overcame me. "Leo, I'm doing the right thing, right?"

Leo detected a shift in my demeanor and became serious as well. "About what? Pretending?"

"Yes—No... I mean... Ron is my best friend, and to her, Vaughn—her elder brother means the world... I feel so guilty about it, Leo. I feel like I'm cheating with my best friend."

"Do you think it's wrong for you to be with Vaughn when you're with him?" Leo asked after taking a moment of pause.

"No. Of course not. I love him. It can only be him, Leo. And he loves me for longer than that. We can only be for each other."

"Then? Don't you have your own answer?"

"But what if Ron doesn't support our relationship? She is extremely protective of her Vee."

"In that case, what if she is happy that it's you and not any other skanks? Well, not being disrespectful to skanks or anything."

"When I'm with Ron, I feel extremely guilty." My teeth sunk on my lower lip in nervousness.

"Hey, Xen Xen. Listen to me... You and Ron are two important people to Vaughn, of course. But two of you hold completely different positions in his life. One can't make up for the other. So, if you think that there is anything wrong with your being with Ron's brother, shake that thought off, alright?" He peered into my eyes.

"Being consenting adults, you can be with whoever you want. When genuine feelings are involved, you can't consider such trivial issues as an obstacle to your path to heaven."

My gaze was fixed in awe on my Zippy. I had never expected to hear such thoughtful words from his mouth.

"This is your first experience of falling in love and being loved back. It's such a beautiful feeling—in fact, it's a blessing, Xena. I don't think you should hide it from anyone." Leo placed his hand on mine in assurance.

Leo's eyes bored into mine, soothing my soul from the inside out with his words. "Even so, if you want to take some time to be prepared to have a face-to-face talk with your best friend, I understand, and I'm ready to help you. But never give a second thought to whether or not you did the right thing. When two people who feel deeply for each other confess and dive into the sacred ocean of love together— there is nothing wrong about it."

When I returned home after meeting Leo, I felt much better. I knew I should tell my secret to Ron, but I couldn't make myself tell her yet. When she asked, I just said I went to buy coffee, and she believed me. It wasn't unusual for me to buy coffee every now and then from that cafe.

I received a text message as soon as I walked into my room.

Filthy Wolf: Where were you?

Oh, snuggles. I forgot how the man kept a tab on my whereabouts.

Xena: You know, don't you? Don't you trust me?

Vaughn called me right back.

I tapped the green button with a racing heart.

"You know I trust you." There was no *hi* or *hello*. The man was right on point.

That voice…

Gosh… I miss him.

"Then why are you upset?" I asked. My pussy tingled, and I was already breathing in short and heavy.

"I don't trust men. You know, it pisses me off when some guy gets to be close to my girl. The prick is around you way too much than my liking."

Jealous Vaughn… lovely.

"Wolf. You know it can *only* be Vaughn for Xena. *Behave*," I said. My tone had a tinge of scolding to it.

"Are you threatening me?" There was a slight hint of smirk coating his voice this time.

"So what if I am?"

"Do you want me to answer literally or figuratively?"

Great. The jealous Vaughn had blended with the playful Vaughn now. Just great.

"Both." I bit my lower lip to control the grin from spreading any further. I lay on my bed, cuddling my soft bolster pillow.

"Figuratively, I would press you against wherever you are right now and choke you until you say that you are *my* dirty little slut, and you deserve the punishment after talking back to your master. After you are done repeating all that, I would fuck that disobedient, misbehaving mouth of yours, and then I would fuck that little throat as deep as I could go."

I clasped my bolster tighter in between my legs, squeezing with my thighs against my throbbing clit. My heart, thudding against my rib cage at an uncontrollable pace.

"A-And… literally?" I was breathless already, feeling the surrounding air heat up along with me.

I heard Vaughn's sharp intake of breath, listening to my shaky, husky voice.

"Literally? Right now I'm fantasizing about doing so."

A treacherous little moan escaped my mouth before I could muffle it in.

"Please…" I begged him.

"Please what, Sugar."

He knew. He had to know. How could he not know?

"You know."

"Yes, I do. But you have to ask." I could detect the smirk in his voice.

"Let me…" A whine slipped my lips this time.

275

"Let you what?"

Damn you!

"Let me do it." I squeezed my eyes shut as the words left my mouth.

"Do it how exactly?"

Is this man even serious?

"Let me…" I lowered my tone even more that it was almost impossible to pick up my words. "Hump my pillow." There was no point in secrecy when I was aching this much in need.

"You can hump your goddammned pillow as much as you wish. But my precious, little Sugar, you can't come without me. Remember? All your orgasms belong to me."

"But you are not here right now…" I cried out in need. Already grinding slowly against the pillow without my awareness.

"Then you will wait until I'm there for you." He showed no sympathy for me. Nada.

"Wolf, you are heartless. Are you made of rock?"

"Yes, baby, I'm. I'm rock-hard for you. Be good, alright?"

"Damn you, Wolf!"

The man chuckled and then hung up the call for real.

I looked at the cellphone screen in shock. Did he hang up?

Growling in frustration, I buried my head in the pillow.

Damn you, Wolf! Damn you! Damn you! Damn you!

Before I could reach the point of insanity, Ron knocked on my door called me for dinner. I splashed cold water on my face to control my unruly hormones. After dinner with Ron's constant questions, finally, I managed to hit the books for a while when I was free.

Studying had never been a tough job for me, but the scenario was completely different tonight. The deep-set, dark-eyed, black-haired magnificence kept appearing before my eyes no matter how focused I was. If I thought I was pinning for Vaughn before, then *snuggeties*… I was wrong. Falling in love with someone was absolutely a different kind of feeling.

276

Leo was right.

43 | Midnight Rendezvous

Xena

After a thousand tries, I managed to hit the books for two hours. It was already eleven, but my brain couldn't concentrate anymore. Again and again, my mind drifted to the thoughts of Vaughn.

God... I missed that man... my man.

The moment I closed my books, I heard my cellphone ringing. It was so unexpected that my heart thumped at the suddenness. When I moved my books aside and looked at the screen, my heart started knocking even faster than before.

I answered the phone without wasting another second.

"Wolf..."

"Still missing me?" Vaughn chuckled when he heard my out-of-breath response to the phone call.

"A weekend wasn't enough with you, Wolf. I'm craving you."

Who said I should contain my desire for my man? Who said only a man could speak of his desire? Damn you—decency.

"We have got our lifetime ahead, Xena. I'm not here to leave."

"I wish I could see you right now."

He let out a big shaky breath of longing and then said, "Then come downstairs. I'm waiting for you."

My eyes sparkled like thousand watts of bulbs and stood on my legs resembling a bouncy spring.

He is here...

He misses me too... he is here!

"Wait for me..."

"Careful. Don't hurt yourself. I'm not going anywhere." The concern in his tone melted my heart like a puddle.

Gosh, my heart. Could I run any faster? That also silently? I couldn't afford to wake Ron up.

I was already downstairs when I received another text saying he was at the back of the apartment. It relieved me to know this because, that way, Ron wouldn't be able to see us through her window. I noticed his car as I ran to where he said he would be.

The moment my eyes fell on Vaughn, my steps halted, and I stopped in my tracks. The illegally handsome, tall, muscular man leaned against his car door, waiting for me.

The man stayed put as a strong gust of wind swayed his shirt. His hair was unruly—reminding me how he looked in the morning. His skin glowed like a fallen angel under the soft light of the moon. The hint of a smile on his face challenged me to move closer to him. His lips didn't stretch—it was his eyes that told me how glad he was to see me.

Suddenly, my feet had their own accord as they hurried towards the man and jumped into his open arms. The minute the familiar scent hit my nose for the first time in the entire day, I felt like I could breathe. My arms tightened around his waist as I rested my head against his chest, inhaling his intoxicating scent deeply.

To remind me, it wasn't a dream. We exist. Our love exists.

"Wolf…" my voice was no more than a soft, contented whisper.

If I thought my hands were tight around him, then his were even tighter. His grip was firm and secure as his arms wrapped around me as if his life depended on it. Face burying in my neck, Fingers digging deep into the soft flesh of my skin. His longing and desire to see me were all placed on the table.

"Xena… baby…" Vaughn sounded like he was deep in a stupor. His voice carried a soft whisper of need, but the dominance in his voice was what made it sound sinful. His hands stroked me with affection, love, and, of course, lust.

After we stayed like that for a minute or so, he finally regained bits of his composure.

"Let me see my girl." His deep, panty-melting voice was back as he tried to inch away from me to see my face.

I shook my head and buried my face more into his chest, tightening my grip on him, nowhere ready to let loose of this man. I missed him all day long, and if anything, he had already become my oxygen—the major component of my survival.

"At least come inside. It's windy, and you're wearing so little."

That was the moment I recalled what I was wearing. I was wrapped in my light pink midi sleeping robe, and under the robe, I just had a flimsy light pink tank top and matching loose shorts with no underwear.

I knew Vaughn already had an idea about it when I felt his fingers digging into my hips with a light growl. "Come inside."

I obliged.

"You drove?" I asked. My surprise couldn't be restrained as I glanced at Vaughn, watching him enter the backseat of the car after me.

"Hmm." He yanked my body as if it weighed nothing and pulled me on his lap sideways. Impatience was written all over his face and demeanor.

I wrapped my hands around his neck, pulling him closer. Vaughn buried his face in my neck once again, inhaling me as if I was a drug he was addicted to.

"Missed you, baby," he said. I felt the softness of his lips, leaving scorching traces everywhere they touched, burning me in the fire of Vaughn syndrome.

"I missed you too," I said. No wonder my voice was hoarse in need once again.

"I hate it when some guy looks at you. You are too beautiful, Xena. How to keep you only for my eyes? I can't and won't share you with anyone. Never."

Here comes my possessive alpha.

"You don't have to. It was just Leo, and trust me, he is just my goofy friend," I said as a matter-of-fact.

"Did you have to meet him alone?"

"I decided him to be my alibi in case I need to meet you, and he agreed." My fingers brushed in his hair—a mere try to soothe the raging lion. "If you trust me, drop the topic, Wolf." I cried out his name when he sank his teeth into the supple skin of my neck. Like he wanted to imprint his mark on my body.

"Why are you wearing so little? It's windy out there." Once again, his concern hit the deepest corner of my heart.

"I like the weather. It's okay."

Vaughn narrowed his eyes. "*Like* the weather, huh?"

"Are you jealous of the weather too, Wolf? Feel like punching it?" I let out a giggle, finding his unreasonable jealousy adorable.

"I feel like doing so." He grumbled like a stubborn kid, not ready to share his possession at all. I caressed the back of his neck with soft strokes of my fingers.

"Did you eat your lunch properly?" Vaughn asked. His misbehaving hands slid the robe a little to expose one of my shoulders and upper chest, tracing his fingers on the tender skin. Goosebumps appeared on my skin as I felt his lips on my neck and his tracing fingers all over my delicate body.

Snuggly blankets! The man was sinful.

"I had a little. Some scums came to disturb." I was already getting breathless. My pussy was already a wet mess as I felt Vaughn kissing on my cleavage, darting his tongue out to shove in between, licking, and his knuckles stroked my now erected nipple over my flimsy top.

"Jack?" he asked.

I stiffed for a moment and then relaxed again. "How did you know?"

"Guessed."

Right. How could this man not guess?

"Do I need to beat his ass?" His scorching mouth was now covering my nipple over my tank top, making wet patches on the fabric just above my swollen, aching nipples, causing the patches to look even more erotic inside the dark, locked car with only two of us.

"Don't worry. I handled them anyway. Ron didn't even need to say anything."

I was a wet mess, breathing hard.

"That's my girl," he said, right before gripping a handful of my hair and pulling my lips to meet his for a passionate, dominating, deep kiss.

The kiss was rough—dominating every last nerve of my body, showing me who I belonged to. I knew Vaughn missed me just as much as I missed him. Besides, my meeting with Leo was still disturbing the man, but he wouldn't dominate me outside the bedroom matters, as we'd established earlier.

God, I love this man... I crave him. I really do.

Right that very moment, I felt his hand sliding inside my shorts. My breath got hitched, and my movements went still.

"Ah... what are you doing?"

His other hand wrapped around my neck, gripping my jaw from the back, holding me in place for his punishing lips.

"Giving you what you begged for earlier."

Oh, snuggles!

44 | In a Bind

Xena

In the absolute silence of the car, only the sound of heavy breathing echoed.

Vaughn had his hands deep inside my wet core—teasing and playing with my bundle of nerves, bathing his fingers with my juices. All the while, his lips, leaving hot traces over the exposed soft skin of my breasts. His constant caressing made my loose tank top slide down, exposing my ladies for his feast.

His other hand covered my stomach, gripping his fingers on it, imprinting his territorial stamp over my pale, creamy skin. His hot mouth, covering my achy nipples, playing with them with his misbehaving tongue.

"Look at me." His hand moved from my stomach to my tit and groped it—squeezing.

I looked into his eyes, feeling two of his fingers getting buried inside my cunt. With one hand, I clasped his shirt and another wrapped around his neck, trying to find some control over my body.

"Give in to me. Look into my eyes, Sugar. Look."

Oh, snuggles… Those eyes.

Just those eyes and this look could bring me to the point of my sweet release.

His fingers found the rhythm, going wild inside my cunt, making me squirm on his lap. His stiff, hot rod was poking me from under my butt, reminding me of its robust presence.

Even with the air conditioner on, we were sweating, dripping, shaking.

"You are supposed to be mine. Only mine. And you come *only* when *I* let you come." Vaughn's authoritative voice grumbled against my ear. My eyes begged to shut in pleasure, but I couldn't, not under his tormenting fingers and captivating eyes.

"Tell me you understand this."

I sucked in my lower lips, nodding, agreeing with whatever the man asked me.

"See what you are doing. You are so fucking soaked under my fingers. Crying for a goddamn release. Sugar, you are my little pathetic fucktoy who only I can play with. No. One. Else." Like the wolf he was, he growled against my neck.

I was a moaning mess, breathing heavy and hard, clutching him for dear life. My eyes never left him as I stared at the dark pool of his orbs gazing right back at me. His lips, slightly open, devouring my every expression like a hungry wolf in a trance. His fingers never slowed down inside me, his slightly rough palm rubbing against my clit as he went knuckle-deep inside my itching cunt. Touching right where I needed him the most.

"You need to come?" he asked. His voice was so rough I could barely comprehend the words.

"Yes…"

"Say the words I need to hear. And I will let you."

"Please…"

"Whose fingers are you riding? Whose dirty little slut are you?"

"Yours! Master… please. *Please!*"

"And?"

"*Heavens*… Vaughn… I love you," I said what he wanted to hear.

He curled his fingers a little more, creating just the right amount of pressure over my sensitive nubs both inside and out, making me cry out, finally—finally, in my sweet, needy release.

Even after that, his possessive hands never left my throbbing pussy. His palms covered it like he owned it.

He did, didn't he?

When I finally regained my wits, I looked into his eyes once again, snuggling into his chest like a pet.

"Wolf… you will be the death of me."

"And you mine…" he said, kissing my forehead in unbound affection. Then, tightening his hold on me, he growled again. "Mine!"

We stayed like that for a long time, enjoying each other's warmth in utter silence, inhaling each other's scent in pure bliss. His large palm still covered my soaked, sensitive pussy like a possessive wolf, and I didn't mind the feeling. It felt good to be claimed possessively by someone who knew his boundaries.

"My exams start next week." *I won't be able to see you…*

Vaughn sighed with a heavy heart, and then dropping another kiss, he said, "You will pass the tests with flying colors."

"I can't come over next weekend." *I'll miss you…*

"I'll come to you."

I was stunned and moved my head to look into his eyes.

"You will?"

"Why won't I? I know my naughty little Sugar is going to miss me." He pecked on my lips, asking, "How can I let that happen, hmm?" He dropped another kiss on my nose.

"You concentrate on your study. I'll come whenever my little Sugar misses me too much."

"After my session ends, I'm going to visit my parents." *I'll be gone for weeks…*

This time, Vaughn visibly stiffened under me. He pulled out his hand from under my shorts and wrapped his arms tightly around me, pressing my body against his as if taking me in him—hiding me from the world. His face buried in my neck, stubble beard deliciously itching my delicate skin.

"I'll talk to you every night," Vaughn said. His muffled voice vibrated against my neck.

"I'll see you before I go."

Vaughn chuckled in a throaty voice and said, "Of course you will. I'll make sure you do. Before you disappear for weeks, this pussy needs to get fucked enough so that it doesn't forget who the owner is."

I straddled on his lap and wrapped my hands around his neck securely.

"Don't you... need to?" I looked into his dark orbs—moonlight reflecting in his eyes like glass.

He brought his index finger and traced it on my lips, dragging it slowly towards my throat, tingling my skin with delicious tenderness. "I'm dying to fuck this throat. It has to be either that or nothing. I can't bear it if you take me in this bratty little mouth of yours, and I can't fuck the throat. I will wait until your return."

"In that case..." I finished my insinuation by pressing my lips against his.

Vaughn groaned against my lips as his hands gripped my hair and waist in a tight hold.

When his lips took over the domination of our kiss, I didn't refuse. I settled my focus on his scorching, raging, rock-hard cock throbbing right against my pussy. Slowly, I started grinding against his boner as his mouth continued to devour mine. Vaughn groaned against my lips as his kiss went fiercer, grip tightening more and more on my body.

More. More. More.

I needed more. I needed to give him more.

I kept humping my man, grinding my aching pussy against his rampant cock—exactly where it wanted to be all the time.

When I noticed his hazy face as moans and groans of sweet torment came out of his open mouth, it gave me a feeling of being in charge. For a change, I loved that feeling. His chest heaved, nose flared, and cock throbbed when my tingling pussy kept grinding against him. The feeling was addictive, truly making me feel like a queen. His queen.

When it went intense, we pressed each other's heads into our neck, climbing closer to our release. My low whimper and his unrestrained groans went rampant. The moment Vaughn pushed his waist up and hit me right against my clit with his hard-on for a change, I could no more control my release, and sensing my orgasm, the man accompanied me with his.

We stayed just like that until our nerves calmed down. After a while, he swiped the wet hair from my forehead and pecked on my lips, staring right into my eyes.

"You are my naughty little Sugar, aren't you?" There was a hint of amusement sparkling in his eyes.

"Yes, Yes I'm." I grinned like a naughty brat.

Vaughn chuckled out loud.

"I love you, Xena, my little sweet. Study hard. I'll be just a call away. Okay?"

I nodded my head and finally left the car with reluctance.

Before I was out of his sight, I turned back to see him leaning against his car once again. His eyes, both content, yet the longing was there for me. This time, there was a wet patch on the front of his pants, reminding me of the fresh memories we just relished together.

With a subtle smile of contentment, I waved my hand and left his sight.

$$-\heartsuit\heartsuit\heartsuit-$$

A week had passed since I hadn't seen Vaughn. My exams had started already, and I had three more papers left to attend.

It was Friday night. The remaining exams were to take place on Monday. So, as usual, I was in Ron's room, pushing her to finish her study.

"Tell me about what you learned about real estate finance transactions."

"Errrm."

"Ron… Tell me what the different funding types are."

"Equal?"

"Equity Ron, not equal. Tell me about a development process and which type of finance it falls under."

"There was something acquiring something. What was that?" She went deep into thinking.

"Acquiring land, Ron! Land! Now tell me, do you remember which funding type it falls under?"

She looked like she would cry at any moment.

"Well, it's equity, the one you mentioned. Okay, don't push yourself much. Now tell me, what is FSR?"

"For Some Reason? See, I know it!" Her eyes finally sparkled. Smoke was fuming out of my ears.

"Floor Space Ratio Ron! Repeat after me!"

"Now tell me, what is GBA?"

"I know this, isn't it God Bless America?"

"Ron! Why do we need to talk about blessing America now?" I felt like I was on the verge of passing out.

"Aren't we studying about *American* Real Estate Transaction Finance?"

I growled as my hand clutched the book in my hand until my knuckles turned white. "God… Why? Why do I agree to help you study every time? I know each and every time what is about to come! Why do I still do this?"

"Hey, Jay… Jay, please calm down. You know that studies and I aren't best buddies. Go revise your own. I'll finish memorizing my parts. I promise."

"I'm not going anywhere. I'll sit right here, revise the book." I pointed at the book with my finger. "And you, finish the short notes I prepared for you. I'm not moving until or unless you finish memorizing every word."

By the time Ron finished, I was exhausted.

Dragging my legs, I reached my room and lay flat on the bed. The last few hours felt like running a marathon, and I couldn't even read another word for the night. Studying with Ron always sucked out the last bits of my energy.

Besides, I missed Vaughn. It had been over a week since I saw the striking face of my man. The lack of his warmth, his kisses, and his touches was so painful that it was almost excruciating. I missed him way too much than I thought I would.

Without thinking anymore, I picked up my phone and texted him.

Xena: I'm exhausted.

His reply was pretty fast. It wasn't even a minute. As if his cellphone was lying in his hand and he was ready with the text.

Filthy Wolf: Want to release some stress?

Xena: Oh, God... Yes.

Filthy Wolf: Want to use me?

My fingers froze above the cellphone screen, my heart racing faster than before. *Oh, blankets!* Yes, yes, yes, I do! But deciding not to show my over-enthusiasm, I'd rather reply differently.

Xena: How?

Filthy Wolf: I can be your manwhore for the night. Want me to fuck some stress out of your system?

Not to show my over-enthusiasm—my fatty ass! Unveiling my raw need for him and his body, I typed my reply as fast as my trembling fingers allowed me.

Xena: How fast can you arrive?

45 | Secret Little World

Xena

It wasn't even ten minutes when Vaughn texted me he was here. I was already adorned in a loose, flimsy dress with no underwear whatsoever. There was no need for them. Ron was in her room and didn't see me coming out. I rushed downstairs, at the back of our apartment, where Vaughn last time parked his car.

The second I reached there, I finally felt my thirsty soul finding the source of water. Just looking at Vaughn as he stood there in all his tall and handsome glory relieved half of my stress, like a puff of air.

I ran even faster towards my man. There was no way I could wait any longer to be wrapped around him. There was a devilishly handsome smile on his face, and I couldn't wait to slam my lips against his. Every passing moment at such a distance felt like agonizing torture. I had to feel him. I needed to feel him.

Vaughn stood straight to catch me in his arms when I was closer to him. But I had another plan. I opened the backseat door of his car and hoped inside right away. For a second, Vaughn stood in the same place, confused. Then, moving fast, he followed me inside as well.

The moment my man was inside our secret little world, I straddled him as my lips crashed on his in a wild, passionate kiss.

Gosh, I missed him.

The sensation was similar to that of a warm, fuzzy blanket given me on a crispy winter night, enveloping me in its warmth. Vaughn was my warmth.

After a long moment of our heated kiss, when I finally moved my head a little, I found his orbs dark and dilated. Hungry, as they bored into mine. Hungry for me, and I was sure they matched mine.

"You came prepared. My whore is so fucking ready for me."

Only then did I realize where his hands lay. They were digging into the soft, curvy flesh of the bare skin of my ass under my dress.

"I thought you were my whore for the night?" I asked as my hands worked on his belt buckle and zipper. Vaughn hissed out loud, but it didn't halt the movements of my hands.

Soon his hot, ready member was out for me. I waited no more, and then setting it at my entrance, I pushed my hips down.

Heavens...

Vaughn let out a raw growl and clutched onto me tighter. I pushed my hips up and down, fucking just the crown of his cock in my hot, needy pussy for a while. Vaughn squeezed his eyes shut to take in what my dripping core offered him. Then slowly, I started riding his cock, gloving it in my clenching, throbbing, aching pussy.

Vaughn fisted my loose strands of hair with one of his hands and twisted it a few times before he tugged it back. My neck was bare before his eyes, and the man waited no more before claiming the soft, sensitive skin with the sweet torment of his filthy, yet delicious mouth.

His other hand wrapped around my waist as he kissed, nibbled and licked on my neck, showing me a glimpse of the sweet heaven only he could show me.

With our unsteady movement, the sleeve of my loose top slipped from my shoulder. Vaughn tugged them lower to reveal both my full, perky tits for him to devour. My speed went faster with his equal attention to my swollen nipples and aching tits. The wet sound of our intimate flesh slamming against each other as I fucked his cock was a sweet melody to my ears.

Vaughn's cock in my pussy, Vaughn's mouth on my nipple, Vaughn's hand kneading my other tit, Vaughn's hand fisting my hair—Vaughn, Vaughn, Vaughn... I was consumed by him. Floating freely in heaven in Vaughn's secure arms.

My emotions were a mess. I took a handful of his hair, tugging them. Vaughn looked into my eyes for a second before I slammed my lips against his, my hips never pausing its movement.

"You are mine!" I growled in a hoarse voice that I almost couldn't recognize as my own.

Vaughn paused for a second, his body rigid under mine.

"What did you say?" His breathing was heavy and erotic in my ears, and his voice dripped with yearning. "Say that again."

"You. Are. Fucking. Mine!" I didn't care how I sounded the fact that I cursed. The need to claim this man as mine, in every possible way, consumed me entirely.

"I am yours." Vaughn let out a low groan that soaked with pain and longing.

This time both of us moved our hips together as we clutched onto each other's body possessively, tightly—as if our lives were depended on each other.

It was over a week, and we both were overly thirsty for each other's taste. So, it wasn't long before we let it out with a scream. All our frustration, longing, ache, stress, pain—all released together.

I stayed limp over his body for a long time. My head on his shoulder, hands around his chest. His mouth rained kisses and nibbling playfully on my neck. His hands—one was clutching me tightly in his arms and another brushing lightly over my buns. Cock, semi-hard, still buried deep in me.

Finally, I found my wits back when I looked at his clothes. My man was well dressed in a fine suit. He always dressed well, but tonight, I could say at a glance that it was special. I slowly pushed my hand inside his suit jacket, all the while feeling his abs to my heart's content. Inside his suit jacket, just above the inner pocket, there it was. The label of D&G. Undoubtedly, custom made.

"You were busy tonight?"

"Hmm. Meeting." The man didn't take a breather while kissing my neck. As if it was his sole purpose of visiting me.

I yanked his hair again to look into his eyes. His plump, swollen, wet lips looked extra delicious. I ran my thumb over them and asked, "Then why did you come?"

"They can wait. You can't." There wasn't a slight of hesitance in those black orbs.

"I could wait." I lied. No, I couldn't.

Vaughn knew. He knew very well I couldn't. My earlier actions could easily prove me as a liar. But the man didn't point out my blatant lie.

"Let me rephrase the sentence again. They can wait. But when it comes to my Sugar, *I* can't."

I couldn't help when the persistent grin stretched my lips accordingly.

"See, even my baby is happy to see me." Vaughn pecked on my lips, his hand stroking my face and hair like a pet.

"The next time I see you will be before I leave for Virginia. I will stay the night with you." I let out a moan as his mouth did things on my throat, his hand again fisting my hair to have better access to it.

"I can't wait for that, baby."

"I'd probably take Ron with me this time."

"Hmm. Sure."

As he carried on with his sweet torment, I felt his cock getting harder and growing in its full size inside my kitty.

"V-Vaughn… you… you are again growing…"

"Yes, I'm. Why do you think I haven't pulled it out yet?"

Oh, snuggles!

Suddenly, the man pushed me on the back seat with my back against the leather, with him lying on top of me. His cock, still buried deep inside me. One of his hands was flat above my head on the seat, supporting his weight, and the other was behind my thigh, squeezing me in.

"Earlier, I agreed to be your manwhore. This round, you are my filthy little whore. You understand?" Vaughn asked with a sexy growl, making my skin have goosebumps all over.

"Ah!" I screamed out with the first thrust. He was rough and hard, going deep from the beginning.

Vaughn pressed his large palm against my mouth, muffling my moans. I was under him, totally at his mercy.

"Don't make a noise, my dumb slut. Do you want anyone to see us fucking like wild animals? Shut your damned mouth, my pretty little cumdump."

I nodded, already on the verge of coming. Every time the man degraded me, my twisted mind had its own orgasm, but he used the magic word *'my'* to make it sound like words coming straight from heaven.

The man was still in his suit, whereas my dress was crumpled on my stomach, revealing my upper and lower body for him to devour. As he fucked me carelessly, with no mercy, his expensive fabric rubbed against my bare skin, making me feel the most out of the game we played together, in the secrecy of the night, in our secret little world.

Under his rough, careless, yet delicious torture, I came for the second time in the night. But the man went on. Even though I was almost on the edge of passing out, he didn't stop.

When he finally came, I was hanging by a thread from passing out. He dropped over my body and kept chanting my name over and over like an obsessive, possessive man who couldn't get enough.

"Xena... Xena... My baby... You are finally mine... I got you... Real, you are real... I love you. I love you so fucking much, baby. Love you."

Before Vaughn, I never knew an aloof man like him could express his love for someone so deeply. Why did it feel like there was more to the man's unfathomable love I didn't know about? I wrapped my feeble arms around the overly emotional man and hugged him tight in my arms.

"I love you too, Wolf."

—🐺💜💜—

I dropped flat on my bed, heaving a sigh of relief. Exams finally ended. Even though the exhaustion forced me to stay lying on the bed, but when my eyes drifted to the luggage I had yet to pack, I couldn't afford to rest any longer. Besides, Vaughn was waiting for me.

I was in the middle of packing when I got a text. In between running and jogging, I reached for my cellphone to check the sender. But I felt somewhat disappointed when I found it was from Leo. I missed my man like crazy.

Leo: Exams finished?

Xena: Yup. I'm as free as a bird now.

Leo: Dare to answer one more question for the day?

Xena: You and your questions. Ask anyway *unamused emoji*

Leo: Why do women like to have sex with lights off?

Xena: Because they don't prefer to watch shitheads like you?

Leo: Naaaaay... It's just because they can't see men having good times.

For a second, I didn't know what to reply. For some odd reasons, I both laughed out loud and felt offended as a woman at the same time. Then I thought of something and pressed the call button instead.

"Hey, Zippy! I have a question for you."

"Shoot."

"How do you shitheads find such shitty so-called jokes?"

"I collect them to ask you. I'm a great friend, Aren't I?"

"Yeah, yeah... of course, you are. You are an amazing friend! Before you, I never knew there could be a friend who could take his valuable time from days just to look for shitty jokes for me. I'm so thankful to God that I found a Zippy like you. You are so—"

"Hey, hey! Stop, stop, stop! What do you want from me?"

"Want from you? Why do you think I'm so selfish? Can't I just throw a few words of compliments for my dear Zippy?"

"Of course not! You would never! There must be something that you want from me."

"If you say so again and again, then I should ask something from you for real. Shouldn't I?"

"Hey! Who asked you to ask from me? I just know that you want something from me, you evil-minded witch!"

"If you ask, again and again, Xen Xen can't just say no to her Zippy anymore, can she? So, let's ask something from you," I said, muffling my giggle.

Leo sighed on the other side of the line and said in defeat, "Tell me what you want. I will think about it."

"I knew you would agree… My Zippy is so awesome, magnificent, and—"

"Hey, who agreed with you? I just said I'll think about it. What is it?"

"Accompany me to a date."

"Date? With you? Huh! I don't date evil witches."

"Not me, you dumb! I mean, my awesome buddy, my Zippy!"

"Cut the crap."

I could already feel his impatience on the other side. But I also knew he was smiling.

"Accompany me to my date with Vaughn."

"What? Why? I already have a bad feeling about this!"

"I'll see you in an hour. Come and pick me up!"

"Xen—"

Before he could finish, I hung up, but not before saying, "It's time you both meet."

46 | Little Punishment

Xena

Even though Leo sounded quite reluctant on the phone, he arrived on time to pick me up. Ron was also getting ready to receive Bryan. He was supposed to come soon, so Ron was about to go out to buy some groceries for their date night.

When we arrived downstairs, Ron noticed Leo waiting for me. She flashed me a devilish smirk that matched her brother—reminding me of him—and nudged my waist with her elbow.

"Oooh... Mr. Dom is here, huh?"

"Dom?" I scrunched my brows in confusion.

"Hey, don't think I don't see the marks Mr. Dom leaves on your skin. Last time you returned after a weekend with him, have you seen yourself? Your skin turned red and purple all over with his marks."

Oh, snuggles!

It's just... it wasn't Leo. It was your beloved brother Vee, alright?

I sheepishly smiled at her and hid my face with the curtain of my hair in guilt. "I better leave now, Ron. Have fun, okay? And be safe."

"Okay, okay, Mom! You have fun with your *daddy*." She hurried after a wink, sensing that I would hit her.

Well... I would have.

He wasn't my daddy. Rather, Vaughn was my master.

"Prepare your luggage, Ron. We leave early tomorrow."

"Okay!" Ron said, already hopping into her car.

297

I shook my head in a chuckle and walked towards Leo's car. The boy showcased a clear frown on his cute face. "Hey, Zippy!"

"Aren't you feeling good? Using me however you wish?"

"Aw... is my Zippy angry with me?"

"Humph! You are using me for so many purposes. First of all, Ron saw me, believing I'm more than friends with you. And now, you are making me walk into a lion's cave."

Daddy? If anything, this punk could only be a little boy.

"Are you afraid of Vaughn?" I asked, amused to see his reaction.

"Who isn't? Just because the man is smitten by you doesn't mean he hands out roses and candies to every person he sees." Leo visibly shuddered.

"That's my man, isn't he?" I grinned ear-to-ear in pride.

"You!" Leo showed me his pointer finger in anger and then exhaled dramatically. "I don't even want to talk to you anymore! I don't even want to be your friend anymore!"

"Aw, baby. Don't be angry with mamma. Mamma will buy you ice cream." I hugged his arm.

"Leave me, you madwoman!" He shrugged me off, shuddering in feign disgust. "Who is my mamma? You are not qualified. Shoo! Shoo!" He waved me off.

I laughed in a carefree way and leaned in my seat, thinking of Vaughn—the man who was undoubtedly smitten by me and me by him.

When we reached Aphrodisia, Vaughn was busy in a meeting with a couple of Asians. Although the guards were about to let him know my presence, I stopped them. After all, I came early without notifying him.

I asked them about Finn's whereabouts, but apparently, he was also inside the meeting room with Vaughn.

Vaughn might take time, so I went back to Leo, and we hit the bar to wait for the man to be free from his work. Leo seemed more nervous than usual, but he became a lot calmer after a few shots. The

298

only words I could make him admit were that Vaughn intimidated him with his aura.

I almost laughed out loud at his words. But then I remember, he actually *had* this aura Leo talked about.

Suddenly, I heard a familiar voice behind me.

"Boss wants you inside."

I looked behind to see the tall, brawny, handsome man who exuded a dark aura, almost resembling his boss. Finn kept scrutinizing Leo with his penetrating orbs that even I got goosebumps from his stare.

Leo went tense beside me.

Expected, buddy. Who wouldn't?

I glanced at him and said, "Let's go in."

But before I could pull Leo's hand, Finn stopped me.

"Sorry, Ms. Meyers. It's only you who boss wants inside. Leave Mr. Jackson to me."

"What the—? Why would he only want me? Leo is here with me."

"Then you can talk to him first. Leave him to me. I, myself, will escort Mr. Jackson inside when it's time." Finn stood on his words. His straight composure, slightly stretched legs, and folded hands behind his back gave him a dark look that no one would want to mess with.

Gritting my teeth, I marched inside Vaughn's VVIP room. The moment I entered inside, the first glance at the man tugged something in my heart, and my anger wafted like a gust of wind. I was craving for him so much that it hurt.

Soon, Vaughn lessened the distance between us with his large, dominating strides and pulled me by my waist and neck, pressing his punishing lips against mine. Although the kiss felt undoubtedly punishing, my longing for the man pushed me to give in to his embrace.

Vaughn picked me up and carried me to the couch, where he licked and claimed me for the first time we met in this club. Memories kept flooding in my brain, making me go jelly in his arms—shaking and trembling. No matter how angry he was, still, the man had the most secure arms I could ever be in.

When he sat on the couch, Vaughn put me on his knees instead, with my butt in the air.

Moving the hem of my dress, he stroked my butt over my panties and then pulled it off with a rough tug. I gasped at the suddenness of the situation and cried out loud.

"Vaughn! Not now, I have a guest outside."

Slap

I felt Vaughn spank on my ass at my words. Hard.

"You dare to talk about another man when you are in my arms? You dare to bring another man into my territory?"

Slap

"Ah... Vaughn... I brought Leo to introduce him to you. He is a good friend, and I'm sure you'll like him."

Slap

Vaughn pushed my head into the leather couch with his other hand fisting in my hair. Then he leaned down to put his mouth beside my ear.

"The more you talk about how good another man is to you, make my blood boils hotter. You needy brat, you need enough punishment to remember to whom this ass belongs."

"Vaug—"

Slap

"Ah!"

The man sank his teeth into the bare skin of my back, and my body shuddered in reflex. The more his palm went wild, hitting my soft, delicate flesh, the more I felt hotter. I wanted more. I needed more.

"Mmm... Vaughn... L-Leo is outside." I moaned out loud.

"I. Don't. Fucking. Care."

This time, he bit on my scorching, red, aching ass, sinking his teeth deep enough to leave marks. His tongue licked the place after he finished tattooing my fair skin with his sharp teeth. I moaned out once again at the touch of his warm, comforting mouth.

"You are enjoying this, aren't you?" he asked as his fingers went inside my cunt, teasing me in and out.

"Oh… Oh god… Vaughn… out… outside…"

"You still remember who is outside?" Vaughn asked with a sneer, and his fingers started pumping even faster. "Then I must be not doing my job better."

All my wits flew out of the window when I began enjoying his touch. My body writhed under his tormenting fingers as his prominent bulge poked on my sensitive abdomen. One of my hands nailed the couch, and another, his shin. My voice went hoarse with my continuous moans. I was almost there… almost. That was precisely when he stopped.

Slap

His fingers were out of my cunt the moment I was about to release, just to spank on my ass cheek once again.

Tears welled up in my eyes at the rejection of my orgasm.

After stroking my sore ass for a moment, his fingers again went inside cunt. Pumping me. His other hand again fisted my hair erratically, pushing my head further into the couch, holding me in place.

My entire body was on fire. From head to toe, I was in dire need of a release. A release—only Vaughn could give me. My scalp tingled, teeth digging harder on my lips. Tears fell in drops, soaking the leather couch. My stomach clenched, nipples throbbed, and my toes curled. My fingers dug into the man's thigh in a silent plead for a release.

But the man again edged me when I was about to release and went for another round of spank and strokes on my ass—this time, squeezing my ass cheeks in between his strings of spanks.

Then again.

Then again. He repeated the process of spanking and edging until I couldn't take them anymore.

"Have you been a good girl?"

"No… No…"

"Right. You are my bratty little slut. My fucktoy. My dumb doll. Mine to fuck and love. All mine!"

"Yes! Yes, I'm. A-All yours… I'm sorry, Vaughn. Please let me… Please let me come."

The man went softer at this, and this time his hand kept pumping even when I was about to release.

It took me a long while to come back to reality. Did I pass out? I couldn't tell. When I opened my eyes, I was tightly held against Vaughn's chest in an embrace that could crush bones. His lips tirelessly dropped kisses on my ear, neck, and shoulder. His hands brushed on my back, soothing the raw skin.

"Are you done?" I asked in a hoarse voice.

Vaughn came out of his trance and quickly passed me a glass of water.

"I'm sorry, baby. I went irrational. When it comes to you and some other man, I can't think straight, no matter how hard I try."

For some fucked up reason, I understood him. He was Vaughn. He was supposed to be possessive. If he was in my place, could I stay mum? How could I expect it from him?

This was the sole reason I wanted him to meet Leo, so my Vaughn didn't feel threatened anymore. Because Zippy was my goofy, stupid friend, and Vaughn? He was my next breath.

"Can we meet Leo now?"

His jaws tightened again. But this time, he nodded, reluctance clear in his eyes.

I stood up on my wobbly legs, and with my purse, I went inside the attached bathroom to clean myself. My hair and makeup were a mess. I decided to clean my face off makeup and then finger-combed my hair using a bit of conditioner mixed with water.

When done, I came out in confidence and glanced at Vaughn. The man knew he had crossed the border, so without showing any unwillingness, he let me yank his hand and followed me like a little puppy.

When we stepped out of the room, we couldn't find Leo anywhere. The guards said that Finn had taken him somewhere. Suddenly, I was a little panicked. It was me who brought him here today. The boy was already nervous with these men and their powerful aura. Even though Leo was a fine guy, he was more to the cuter side compared to these dominant men.

Yes, I agree with Ron.

"I need to find him!" I started running around people, looking for the familiar face, but found him nowhere. Vaughn, on the other hand, looked expressionless but didn't say anything to rile me up. He knew he had to keep his mouth shut.

Finally, when we went to look into a secluded corridor, what I saw gave me a little heart attack. My hold on Vaughn's hand went tighter at the scene that lay before me.

In the silent corridor, where no people were around, two people had no knowledge about the outside world as they were completely engulfed in each other. As if in the entire world, only they mattered. No one else.

Right there, against the wall, they kissed each other with all they had to offer.

Leo and Finn.

Finn was kissing Leo.

47 | Vaughn, Finn & Leo

Xena

It was Finn who noticed our presence first. He was a high-class trained bodyguard, and even when in ecstasy, his senses seemed to be sharper than an average person. The moment Finn saw us, he shoved Leo's chest and jumped away from him. Leo, who was against the wall, was surprised at this, but he understood his sudden course of action when he followed Finn's line of sight.

I found my wits back, and when I did, a huge grin appeared on my face, stretching my lips from ear to ear. With a screech, I ran towards the men and jumped on their bodies, hugging both of them together.

"OMG! OMG! OMG! I can't believe this! My two favorite people are destined to be together! I'm so happy! Gosh! It's so awesome! Tell me you are already a couple! You are, aren't you? How can you not be? Both of you are so made for each othe—" before I could finish, two strong arms pulled me in a tight grip against the hard, warm wall of his chest, pulling me farther away from the men.

"Behave yourself. The only man you are allowed to hug is me," he said in a threatening tone in my ears.

I stiffened immediately. Who wanted to get spanked again on the same day?

"Vaughn, this is Leo, Leo Jackson, my buddy. Leo, this is Vaughn Wolf, my... my boyfriend." I turned as red as a tomato as I declared him my boyfriend openly for the first time. Vaughn glanced at me and raised a brow in amusement when he noticed the change of color on my face.

Vaughn didn't say anything to me and turned to look at Finn with a changed expression.

"Follow me," he said in his stern tone.

Then he gave Leo the shortest glance and yanked my hand to turn around, proceeding towards his VVIP lounge.

I glanced back and wiggled my brows at the two men whom we caught red-handed just now. Both of them tried their best to hide their eyes from me, clearly startled at the suddenness of the situation.

When I brought Leo here, I never thought things would turn out to be like this. First of all, my jealous wolf spanking me, then finding Leo was a cool gay person, and then finding it was Finn who was trapped in Leo's charms. Besides, who knew Finn was a hot, dominant gay as well? The day turned out to be better than I thought.

With Finn's dominant attitudes and Leo's sweet charms, I could see traces of Vaughn and me in them. They were well suited for each other. Even the thought of them together felt right and brought a smile to my face.

When we entered Vaughn's personal lounge, he took a seat on the couch like a king, bringing me to sit close to him by my waist. His hand never left the possessive grip on me. To be honest, it was comfortable, and I leaned on him a little more to find more comfort.

"Mr. Jackson. Take a seat."

Leo listened to him immediately, but his eyes went to glance at Finn again and again. As if looking for safety from my man. Finn didn't seem to be affected by Leo anymore and stood in a straight composure as always, guarded.

Vaughn, on the other hand, looked at Finn and raised a brow. Finn immediately changed his demeanor and sat on the couch close to Vaughn. His attitude had changed completely. Now he seemed almost like Vaughn, as if they were brothers. This was the first time I watched Finn looking not-so-guarded like a bodyguard. Well, other than he was sucking my Zippy's mouth now, he seemed like he was sitting among a bunch of close buddies, and Vaughn seemed to be his closest.

Soon, some staff entered the place with trays of food. I had no idea when the man asked for them. Without a word, Vaughn served a plate for me, and I found Finn serving for the men. I had no idea how we could eat in this situation.

But until I finished my plate, Vaughn didn't calm down. He glued his dark, penetrating orbs on me as I continued to have my chicken in small bites. When I couldn't eat anymore, the man took my plate and fed me by himself a bit by bit. After I finished, Vaughn ate his portion of food Finn served him earlier and only then did the staff clean our table.

On the other hand, my Zippy was in a pretty miserable condition. Finally, he kind of fell for someone, but my cold, dominant man was scaring him off. How could he eat in this situation?

Poor Zippy.

"So, Mr. Jackson. Tell us about yourself."

"I… I'm a software engineer at MK corporations. Just graduated last year from New York University."

"Very well. Who do you have in the family?"

"I-I… I…" Leo cleared his throat and then said, "I have my parents, both doctors. Also, there is my elder brother, Liam Jackson. He is in the army."

"Admirable. So, Mr. Jackson, if you don't mind me asking, do you happen to kiss every person who you meet for the first time?"

Goosebumps appeared on my skin, and I could sense something flash across Finn's eyes as well. But he seemed calm otherwise.

Vaughn knew about Leo and my kiss. He remembered, and he was going to interrogate Leo now.

"Vaughn…"

"Shh… baby. Let the men talk for a while," Vaughn said, stroking my hair.

"He didn't kiss you," I said in a low whisper in his ear.

Wrong move. The man glared with fire in his eyes.

"Mr. Wolf. I assume you know about my first meeting with Xena. I'm so sorry about what happened. It's just when I kissed her only then did I find out that I was into men."

Vaughn turned to Leo after burning me a little with his flaming glare.

I was suddenly mad. "Hey! What do you mean? Am I so plain? Am I not sexy? Do I make men sway in the other way?" I clutched onto my Vaughn's waist.

Vaughn pinched on my waist and growled. "Behave! Or do you want a repeat?"

I shut my mouth in reluctance.

"No, Xen Xen. You're misunderstanding. It's the opposite, actually. I'm sure Mr. Wolf here will be happy to tell you how sexy you are!" Leo smiled at Vaughn in a feeble attempt to butter him up. From the corner of my eyes, I found Finn smirking as well as he kept staring at the ground.

"It's just you were the sexiest woman in the club that night is exactly why I kissed you. I was pretty frustrated with the confusion in my mind about my sexual orientation, which is why I came here that night, even though it wasn't a weekend. So that I could find the most beautiful woman in my eyes and find out if I felt anything. But when I kissed you and didn't get any reaction from it, I knew immediately that I was into men." Leo carefully looked at Finn. His eyes were as clear as day, filled with unfathomable, shameless longing.

"You used my woman?" Vaughn asked. He seemed to be fuming.

"I-I'm so sorry, Mr. Wolf. I didn't know she was your woman—"

"Hey, Wolf! I didn't know myself back then that I was your woman! Why are you scolding my friend? He clearly was in a life-changing dilemma. If I don't mind, you shouldn't as well. Leave it!" My man needed some scolding because of his attitude.

307

Vaughn seemed to be taken aback by my heated words and slightly nodded. Finn seemed surprised at Vaughn's change of demeanor.

Now, Vaughn was a lot calmer but still observed Leo with a threatening look.

"So, Mr. Jackson—"

I stopped him in the middle.

"Hey, what is this, *Mr. Jackson?* Call him Leo." I scolded him again.

Vaughn nodded again and said, "Leo, nice to meet you. But unfortunately, we don't have much time tonight. My girlfriend is leaving for weeks tomorrow. I hope you don't mind if we end it here?"

"No! No! It's absolutely alright! I will leave right now! Bye-bye, Xen Xen!"

It looked like the faster Leo couldn't escape any faster. Poor Zippy.

"You can stay at the club as long as you want. Hit the bar. It's on me." Then Vaughn looked at Finn and said, "Go see him off."

Before Leo was almost out of sight, Vaughn called him from behind and said, "Leo. I'm good to people as long as they are good to *my* people. Make sure you don't dare to hurt any of them. Goodbye."

Leo showed a helpless, fearful smile and dashed out as fast as he could. Finn silently followed him behind. But before Finn closed the door, he looked at Vaughn and nodded. I didn't understand what it meant, but Vaughn clearly did. It was something like silent brotherly code to them.

"Now, you." Vaughn's deep-set eyes found me. "Come with me. I'm not done with you." He yanked my hand and took me to the lift that led to his penthouse.

48 | The Possessive Alpha

Xena

As soon as I entered his place, I looked at him with accusing eyes.

"You spanked me for nothing!"

Vaughn removed his tie and suit jacket in no rush as he said, "No, you deserved it for kissing just anyone at clubs. Besides, you did it in *my* club."

"But now you can see, he is into men!" I threw my hands in the air.

Vaughn glanced at me from his shoulder and raised his brow. "You didn't know that. Plus, that doesn't make it any better."

"It's in the past! Since you and I are a thing, Leo and I are nothing but friends!"

"It happened today as well. As I said, past or present, it doesn't make it any better."

"Wait… wait, wait, wait. You are jealous of Leo because he likes Finn. Am I sensing it right?" Something clicked in my mind.

"He has eyes for my people," Vaughn grumbled in displeasure. He didn't deny it!

"What? You are possessive and protective of Finn too?" *Wow! This man!*

"I am all of those for the people I care for. He is one of the very few people. I can't risk that boy hurting Finn."

Something tugged in my heart as I found it so cute. How nice was it when someone like Vaughn cared for a friend to that extent?

But I couldn't show him I understood. That would be too easy for the ego of the arrogant, cold man.

"Who dares to hurt Finn? Leo? Have you seen Finn?"

"Xena, heartache can be more agonizing than any physical pain. People can recover from physical damage, but a heart? If it shatters, sometimes it never sticks together again."

I went silent for a moment. The truth was never told so straightforward, yet beautifully. I felt a throb at a tender corner of my heart, knowing how sincere this man was about loving others, how thorough his thoughts were about hurting someone's heart. That was the moment I knew he could never cause heartache to anyone. The dark, cold, and brooding man had a beautiful soul inside.

"Leo would never hurt Finn. I can guarantee you that. But what about Finn? What if he hurt my Zippy?"

"So worried for some other man, I see." Vaughn's accusing eyes penetrated my soul as he walked towards me with his tie in his hand. Somehow, I panicked a little at the possessive, feral look in his eyes.

"Hey… what do you think you are doing?"

"Teaching you a lesson." Vaughn held my shoulders to turn me around.

"W-What lesson? I know a lot already, alright," I asked, my eyes growing wide in shock.

Vaughn discarded my words and yanked my hands back just to tie them up with his necktie.

Oh my god! Oh my god! Oh my god!

"You are yet to learn who this body belongs to." He threw me on his shoulder and carried me to his bedroom just to toss me on his bed once again with my back facing him.

"Tell me a safe word."

What?

"Vaughn…"

"Or I will start without one—"

Before he could finish, I interrupted.

"Pineapple! Pineapple!"

"Pineapple it is."

Within seconds, he ripped off my dress, along with my underwear, and I laid there butt-naked on my knee, like a fucktoy he said I was to him.

My pussy started to leak. By the time Vaughn got rid of his clothes, I was soaking in anticipation. My face pressed against the soft mattress, my body resting on my knee, my butt in the air, and my hands tied behind my back with his red necktie. I was defenseless, lying there like a whore to be used for a man's pleasure. All in one—I was waiting to be fucked.

Fucked by Vaughn.

"Look at you. My greedy whore. My filthy little shameless slut. Tied so helplessly, yet so excited to get fucked by her master. So soaked. So wet for her master. So naughty."

Vaughn gripped my ass cheeks and stretched me all so suddenly. I could feel the cool air blowing to the hidden, wet flesh of my delicate skin, making my kitty contract at the sensation of coldness against the hot skin. Vaughn stared at my spasming, dripping kitty, and then, when I least expected it, he entered me with no warning. I gasped to accommodate his girth in me as his cock dug deeper into my cave. Gosh, he was huge, and I hadn't grown used to this man's girth yet.

He held my waist in a tight grip, pounding my pussy carelessly. My entire body bounced every time he entered me in a long, hard thrust and before I could adjust my shaken sensations, he was out till only the tip of his cock was inside me, just so he could thrust in me once again. His rampant thrust almost took my breath away as I reached on the verge of losing my consciousness already. But Vaughn... the sweet devil, had other plans.

His thrusts were painful, yet I found pleasure in them. I floated in the sensations, wailing under his rampant thrusts. My body felt like a doll with no power to move an inch on its own. I was lying under Vaughn, all exposed, offering the buffet of my body to be used by him

311

in any way he wanted. I used all my power, struggling to grasp anything I could, but all I found was his hands on my hips to hold on.

"Only mine. All mine. All fucking mine."

I yelped in pleasure and pain. Overflowed with the lustful, possessive thrusts that he delivered me, but I didn't want it to stop. The position was perfect for my pussy to press its lips around his hard member, sucking it in the hot, damp cave. I loved it.

Vaughn loved it too.

I knew it from his harder and rougher thrusts. My wailing and moaning echoed in the room as I shook and trembled under my man. I had never felt anything this intense, and it only left me wanting even more and more of it. More of Vaughn.

"Shh... Baby... we just started. A little more. Let me break you a little more. So you remember no one but me."

He took hold of my hair and pulled me back till my body arched at this position, but his grip on my hair didn't loosen.

"Whose little whore are you?"

"Yours..."

"Right... mine!" Vaughn's fingers went from my hair to my throat—choking me.

Vaughn continued to pound me mercilessly, one hand on my wrists that he tied behind me and the other around my throat.

"Hurts... it hurts." I cried out loud.

Then why am I not using the safe word?

"Am I... Hurting you?" he asked. His tone lingered with faux sympathy.

I looked back at him from my shoulders, and I nodded. Vaughn pulled me by my throat, and his hand reached my lower belly from my wrists. My back was against his solid, rock-hard abs. His other hand, still around my throat, his thumb, reaching my chin and lips, rubbing on it roughly, tugging it down—possessively.

"Good."

He didn't slow down from pounding hard and deep. If anything, he went faster than before. Faster than he ever fucked me. One hand slid from my throat to my tits—squeezing them. His other bossy hand slid down from my stomach to my pussy, right on my tender clit. I was aching for some kind of friction against my clit, and when his rough finger pressed on the swollen little bud, I screamed in my heightened pleasure.

Vaughn seemed to be even more turned on by this simple act and chuckled darkly in my ear. His naughty, misbehaving finger began to stroke on my delicate, throbbing clit as his cock continued hammering inside me.

I squirmed under his raging torment. The man had me right on my edge, defenseless, yet I knew deep inside that he had given me the power to stop it any moment I wanted.

I shook, trembled, and cried his torment when I could no longer keep my wits together and came. Vaughn growled like a primitive animal when he felt my orgasmic contractions—my pussy pulsating, clenching around his hot, giant girth.

The man pushed me back on the mattress and continued hammering me in the prone bone position. He leaned on my back as his hands clenched around my throat and my hair, chasing his own release. His mouth was just behind my ear, mumbling filthy words.

"I own you. I own these holes, baby. They are mine to fill. Mine to ruin. Let me ruin them a little more. More. More. More. I want more of you." Vaughn bit on my earlobe, tugging it in between his teeth. "I will mark you with my cock. I will fill all the voids of this body with it. I will fuck you till your body remembers only me."

My toes curled, and tears streamed down my cheeks, soaking the bedsheet. The weight of his body pressed against my lower belly, and his cock knocked against my g-spot over and over again at an unimaginable pace.

That night, the man stopped only when I was unable to even think of any other man other than him. He consumed my entire existence, my consciousness, my subconsciousness. He swallowed me whole.

But no matter how hard he fucked, I couldn't make myself use the safe word.

Maybe that was what I wanted as well?

49 | Missing Him

Xena

I couldn't concentrate on the journey to Virginia, despite Ron's constant chattering. She was too excited about the trip than I thought she would be. If Bryan didn't have to visit his hometown, I was sure I couldn't bring Ron with me. The guy had already smitten my best friend beyond my belief.

But I couldn't concentrate. All I could think of was him. Last night, after tormenting my body and soul for hours, he cleaned my entire body with a warm washcloth when we finally finished. Then, when I was in between my consciousness and subconsciousness, the man forced me to rehydrate my body with a glass of warm milk. Every time I stayed the night with Vaughn, he prepared something for me to drink right after we finished for the night, let it be any juice or a glass of milk. He never ceased to show his simple, yet heartfelt efforts to make me fall a little more in love with him.

My obsessive, possessive, and protective Vaughn had consumed my thoughts completely. I was flying in his thoughts, floating in his memories, dying every second in love again and again.

Did I just say Ron was the one smitten? Then what was I?

When our car was rolling down the valley between the magnificent greeneries of our very familiar vineyard, I sat upright, eager to see the faces of my very own people after so long. As always, my parents somehow sensed my arrival and waited at the roadside with doting grins on their faces. I squealed, almost tripping on my steps as I clumsily opened the car door to reach them. Behind me, I could faintly hear Ron laughing at my clumsiness. My parents were pretty familiar with it, so they hugged me together in their warm embrace. Their eagerness almost matched mine.

"Mom, Dad, I missed you guys so much!"

"My fatty is finally here! See how beautiful and healthy you look today! And here, your mom had been worrying for you," Mom said, hugging me in her tight embrace.

"Let me hug my little fatty too!" Dad said, snatching me from mom's embrace.

Suddenly, strings of laughter came from behind me, and I remember Ron's presence.

"Mom, Dad, this is Ron."

Ron stepped forward and offered her hand for a shake as she said, "Hello, Mr. and Mrs. Meyers. I'm Veronica Wolf, Jay's—I mean Xena's—"

Mom ignored her hand and hugged her tightly, shortening her introductory speech.

"We know you, Veronica. How can we not know you, child?"

Ron looked amused at the warm gesture, and for a second, she looked moved.

I smiled at knowing how Ron was deprived of her parents' love. This was one of the reasons I wanted to bring Ron here in the first place. She should feel what could parents' love felt like. She deserved it.

When dad patted Ron's head, I asked mom, "Where is Aliza? I can't see her."

"She is visiting some friends. Let's go inside. Teensy will be here soon."

Butlers carried our luggage behind as I wordlessly followed my parents, holding Ron's hand.

"Fatty?" Ron asked close to my ear in a whisper in surprise.

"Yeah. I'm fatty, and Aliza is teensy as I'm the curvy one, and Aliza is the petite one in our family," I said matter-of-factly.

Ron didn't say anything in reply, but instead, she slapped my already sore ass and muffled her naughty chuckle with her palm. I just rolled my eyes and didn't say anything to her.

As we walked, Ron excitedly looked around at the stunning sceneries of our vineyard that I only described to her until now.

"Jay, it's beautiful." Her eyes widened, taking it all in.

"It is." I smiled as my eyes looked around. "There is so much to do. I'll take you."

With a beautiful grin, she looked at me and nodded like a little child.

Just as we took a few steps, OJ came running to me like a gust of wind, tripping me on the ground.

"Here, boy! You have become so big and handsome already! I missed you too!" I stroked the huge orange dog as it continued licking my face.

Ron dropped on her knee and tried to approach OJ as well. He didn't reject her, nor did he show any friendliness. I noticed Ron frowning and attempted to soothe her.

"Hey, he will warm up. Don't worry. He's overwhelmed to see me after so long," I said as I stroked the overjoyed orange dog.

Yanking my frowning friend and overjoyed dog, I walked towards my home. My parents were so thrilled that they became restless, not knowing what to feed us first. Ron had never been loved this way at her home. She went emotional when mom fed her with her own hands as she stroked her hair. I could swear I saw her eyes glisten.

"Why are you so thin? Don't you girls have time to cook or eat? Look how thin you are. Veronica... child, eat more. Come, I'll feed you." My mom shoved more of her lasagna into Ron's mouth. For some reason, I felt she was more affectionate to Ron than me. Being a mother, perhaps she noticed the longing for love in Ron's eyes.

After lunch, I showed Ron her room. Just as she finished settling in, Ron couldn't help but say, "Your parents are amazing, Jay." There was that longing in her eyes once again—a little girl's yearning for her parent's love.

I hugged her shoulder from the back and embraced her with all my warmth.

"I'm sure your parents are amazing too."

Ron chuckled in a mocking tone. "I wish I was so sure as well."

"Even if there is any blankness in your life, I'm sure my parents can fill that up. It looked like they are happier to have you than me." I grumbled.

Ron genuinely chuckled this time. "I felt that too. Poor Jay... I guess this time I will be more pampered than the fatty, huh?"

I flickered the side of her head and faked anger. "Hey, Ron, you are such a greedy friend, you know that? Hate you!"

"Hate you too! Now shoo! I need to call Vee. He must be worried for me."

Oh, snuggles!

He must be worried for me too...

"Okay, take some rest. We will visit the vineyards and lavender fields after you are up. They look magical at the time of sunset."

Waving at the ecstatic best friend, I left the room.

Before entering my room, I found OJ waiting in front of my door. He started barking the moment I walked closer. I crouched down before him. "Hey... hey... slow down. I missed you, too. Come inside. We have a lot to catch up on."

OJ jumped on my bed, settling himself like the old times. I laughed at the old orange dog and went for a bath. When I stepped out of the bathroom, I could see a bowl of ice cream mom left for me on the nightstand. I took a spoonful to eat and was just about to call Vaughn when his name appeared on my cellphone screen instead. My heart raced just from a glance. My filthy wolf.

Throwing the spoon in the bowl, I jumped on the comfort of my bed and received the video call immediately. His handsome, sharp features appeared on the screen, and thousands of fireworks sparked

318

above my head, butterflies tickled in my tummy, and heat pooled between my legs. I touched my racing heart with one hand and held the cellphone with another. Words got lost in my mind as I kept staring at the man.

Vaughn flashed me a panty-melting smile. Affection glittering in his dark orbs.

"*There* is my girl."

The care and fondness in his soft purr stretched my lips in an ear-to-ear grin. I bit my lower lip to control the grin and said, "There you are."

"Looks like my girl is missing me already," he said. His voice, cocky and playful, teasing me.

"Who said I'm missing you?" I asked, then moved a little to hug OJ and smirked at the man. "Look, I have got a company."

Vaughn's brows furrowed, clearly frowning to see the dog beside me in the bed. His possessiveness struck when he said, "Looks like I haven't fucked you enough last night to remind you not to mess with me."

I coughed a little at the change of events. "It's a dog, Wolf. How pathetic can you be?"

"It's in bed with you, Xena, and I am not." He was mad, but I could peek a glimpse of the painful longing behind it.

I smiled at the possessive alpha and blew an air kiss to coax him. "It'll be you, Wolf. As soon as I come back to you, you'll land in a bed with me. He is a good boy, see...." I embraced OJ with one arm, and we both faced the screen. "Hey, OJ, say hi to Wolf. He is going to be your daddy in the future."

OJ showed hostility and barked at Vaughn. At the same time, Vaughn barked, "Daddy? Whose daddy?"

"Hey! Guys! Come on... look, OJ... Don't be hostile to this wolf! This wolf won't eat you. He is a good wolf." Then I looked at Vaughn and said, "And you! Don't be hostile to OJ because the only one you will be eating... is me."

319

There was a hint of a smile in his eyes. "I will be needing more if I allow you two to be so close."

I bit my lips with a naughty glint in my eyes. "We will see about that."

Vaughn reclined in his office chair and smirked with a raised brow. "About what?"

"About what this sub will do to serve her master when she comes back." I picked up a spoon full of ice cream and seductively put it into my mouth, licking it with a clear sign of provocation. Then, with the spoon in my mouth, I turned on my bed, on my elbows, giving him a dangerous view of my brimming mounds. Vaughn's eyes darkened at the view, and his teeth sunk into his lower lip. I raised a brow at him meaningfully and slowly took out the spoon from my mouth, teasing the riled-up man a little more.

Suddenly, the man smirked. His eyes, still dark as abyss, hooded in desire. The entire look made him appear utterly sexy, and I had to gulp down to rein control over my hormone.

"I would rather suggest you cut on your sugar intake, my *fatty* Sugar." He deliberately emphasized the word fatty.

The spoon fell from my mouth as I stared at him with my mouth open.

"Even though I don't mind, but I'm sure you don't want that ass to be fatter, do you?" The playful Vaughn kicked in.

"Where did you learn the word?"

He tried to ruffle his laughter with his thumb supporting his lips, which made him appear even hotter.

"I told you I know everything about you." He winked.

I sat on my knee and breathed heavily in rage. A few strands of hair fell on my face. I blew them away from my face and asked, "It's Ron, isn't it?"

"It's not only you. Your entire family is improper at naming, aren't they?" he asked, teasing. He was insinuating how the word fatty

320

was directed to fat asses. But I was sure if my ass was any fatter, Vaughn would be the happiest one.

OJ was impatient by now. He moved and rested on my lap. I looked at him and patted him on his back, brushing on his hair. Before Vaughn could reply, I glared at him and said, "I'm busy right now. OJ and I are meeting after months. We have a lot to catch up and also, I need a nap. You know… in the same bed with him, where you won't be? So, yeah, bye."

Vaughn could no longer control and laughed out loud this time. "Don't be angry, baby. As I said before, your ass is a piece of art. Even if it gets fatter, I will just have a squishier cushion to lie on. And holy hell, do I want a piece of that ass…." He sunk his teeth into his lower lip once again in the end in a raw desire for me.

My embarrassment at him knowing my nickname, intensified at his words. Pink turned red on my fair skin. "I have to get going. Goodbye." I hung up right away.

When I finally lay on the bed, my phone chimed once again with a text.

Filthy Wolf: That ass and that mouth. I'm going to fuck both of them. Soon. They need to learn some lessons from their master to stop being so bratty.

Then another text.

Filthy Wolf: Sleep tight, baby. I love you.

Like I'd be able to sleep now.

50 | Aliza

Xena

In the bonny aroma of the lavender, light and shadow plays of the vineyard alleys, tranquility and peacefulness of the love of family—our time passed like a fluttering butterfly. Ron enjoyed it even more than I did. The poor girl craved parental love, and when my parents showered her with boundless doting, her love-deprived soul floated high in the sky.

One evening, all of us were enjoying the sunset spreading red and gold in the sky, sitting on the picnic bedding in the lavender alleys with some cakes and tea. All of us except Aliza. She had always been like that since our childhood. Even though we were sisters, we had never been close for some unknown reason. Aliza always maintained a distance from me. Hence, we never shared any deep natural sisterly bond. To be honest, Ron was more like a sister to me than my actual sister.

My parents looked amused as they listened to Ron talk about her love of the piano. Ron's enthusiasm tinged in my heart, knowing her parents never had time to learn about her hobbies and passion. I smiled at my best friend and hugged my knees in calmness. Even in the serenity of the fragrant air surrounding the lavender field, a piece of my heart cried in incompleteness. I missed his presence. I missed the man. My man.

With the throbbing pain in my heart, I looked the other way, hoping my family wouldn't notice my brimming eyes. From afar, I glanced at our house and saw Aliza facing us, standing by the window.

I felt a chill in my spine. For some reason, I had a feeling she had been staring at me, to be exact.

I excused myself with a smile and then stood straight to head towards the house. Our house looked like one of the castle types, and it had two wings from the center. All our bedrooms were on the right wing. I walked directly to the room beside mine and knocked on the door.

Aliza opened the door without throwing even a single glance at me and strode back inside. I studied her reluctance to talk to me and felt gloomy inside. After all, she was my sister. I took her slightly ajar door as permission to enter inside, sitting beside her quietly on the edge of the bed.

"Even your disdain towards me feels different this time. Is everything okay, teensy?" I asked with a sidelong glance.

My elder sister had always been hostile and full of distaste towards me when no one was around. In one's presence, however, no one could ever detect her inner emotions for me. It had always been like this, and I was used to it.

In response, she looked away and crossed her hands and legs, all of which were signs of disgust.

"We don't meet frequently. I have come home just for a couple of weeks. To be honest, I was happy to see you are here too. But it looks like you are not. Why, Aliza?"

Aliza snorted in disgust as she looked at me. "Why? Why? You are asking me why?"

She laughed like a maniac. A bad feeling crawled on my back, making me feel cold sweat covering my body as I watched her.

"Because I hate you, dammit! I hate everything you are lucky to have, and I'm not! Why do you have to be so fortunate when I'm stuck here miserable?"

"You hate me? I thought it was just distaste." A gloomy smile appeared on my face.

"Of course I hate you! You have everything that I've ever wanted! You are fortunate to be prettier than me. Since our childhood, boys ever had eyes for only you. I have always been a second option. Then you are fortunate enough to get into NYU, and I was not! Mom and dad are proud of you, and I'm left here as a good for nothing!" she said, screaming like a madwoman.

"Aliza—" I tried to calm her down, but she stopped me on the track.

"Let. Me. Finish. Bitch!" Her eyes emitted fire in abhorrence. "I heard you on the phone. You have a boyfriend who loves a bitch like you! I heard everything last night! You called him both Vaughn and Wolf. Who is he, huh? I searched on the internet. And look what I found! The Vaughn Wolf is none other than the brother of your best friend! He is rich, handsome, and successful, someone you don't deserve!"

"Aliza! It's unethical. This is low even for you to listen to your sister's private conversations!" Her words left me stunned. I was flabbergasted and had no idea what to say to this woman.

Aliza started sobbing. Her eyes were bloodshot, and veins on her forehead popped out. "I hate that you have a man like him by your side, and here I'm, in the process of my divorce! Samuel wants to divorce me! He never doted on me. All he did was physical and mental assault, and even then, I stayed. Because I know I'm not as fortunate as you! I didn't get your looks, your qualifications, a man like you have, and now, left with a divorce!"

I felt a tinge of ache growing in my heart for her. I know how hateful she was, but we share the same blood. Therefore, when I heard the words like divorce, physical and mental assault—my heart cried.

I tried to hug her, but she cut me off. "Just leave, okay? I don't want to see you anymore. I really hope you just died, and I would never have to see you again," she said. Her petite figure turned around and lay on the bed as she cried on the pillow.

324

Tears rolled on my cheeks as I looked at her figure. I knew whatever I said wouldn't help with her confidence at this moment. I could only leave and let her have some time to cool off.

Coming to my room, I took action on impulse. I took my cellphone out and called Samuel. Fortunately, he was nearby and agreed to meet me.

When I walked into the café, Samuel was already there, holding a cup of coffee, his eyes lonely and gloomy. When he noticed me, a low-spirited smile appeared on his face.

With a smile, I sat opposite him and said, "Brother."

"Lil fatty! Long time no see. You have grown up to be a fine woman," he said. His eyes contained brotherly affection.

I smiled politely and felt even gloomier inside. "Why are you not visiting home, brother?"

The depressed man went silent for a while with his head bowing down, looking at the cup with blank eyes. "Liza didn't say anything?"

His sad eyes confused me. They conflicted with Aliza's words from every angle.

"No," I said. Then, after enduring a moment of silence, I looked at him once again and said, "But we just talked. She said you want to... you want to… divorce her?"

Samuel looked at me in a jolt, with surprise clearly written all over his face.

"I want to—what?"

"Uh… she said that you don't love her and assault her. Bro… I have always known you to be a good husband. If there is anything wrong, you can tell me. If Aliza is hesitant to share your problems with family, I could help you guys. It's the least I could do. I can't see you guys falling apart. Let me do something."

Samuel took in my words and started laughing. He laughed so hard that his eyes welled up. The man was handsome. He had average looks and a muscular body. With his brown eyes and dark brown hair, he looked like every other American guy. I had known him for a long time—almost as long as Aliza knew him. Then, eventually, both of them fell in love with each other over time.

"Liza told you that?"

I was perplexed by his demeanor.

"Let me tell you something, little sis. It's up to you if you want to believe me or not. I won't force you to trust my words."

My heart started palpitating.

"It has never been me who intentionally hurt her. Maybe words got heated a few times, but I have always been careful with my words. I love your sister—I really do. But she has insecurity issues. You are a wise young lady, and I'm sure you are aware of your sister's self-esteem issues. She has always been comparing herself with every other woman she sees… and when I'm not capable of giving her what she wants, she gets… Uh… upset."

"I want to give Liza the world. But, if she isn't satisfied with my efforts, it's not in my competencies to make her happy. Anyway, it wasn't me who filed the divorce case. It was her. If you don't believe me, I could show you who the petitioner is in the papers. But that is useless. I don't want to divorce her. Even now, after everything that happened between us, I want to treasure her and make her believe that her husband could turn the world upside down to make her happy. But unfortunately, he has limitations. I… I would even try surpassing that to make my Liza happy if she allows me."

I didn't know what to say. But there was one thing that I was sure of was I believed him.

"What do you plan to do now?" I asked. My voice trembled.

Samuel chuckled. "Now—I'll give her some time and space. Even then, if she wants to be freed from me, I will let her. Because that will make her happy."

"What about you?"

"I'll do anything for her happiness." He looked outside on the road with blank, aloof eyes.

"I really hope Aliza comes to her right mind soon, brother. I really wish for you guys to be together till the end."

"I wish that too," he said in a feeble tone. Lost deep in his forlorn thoughts and memories.

Wordlessly, I left and left him alone in the café with his loneliness. A wave of sadness washed over me as I looked back at the lonely man and then pondered about my sister, who was back at home.

Why would she do it?

When I returned home, everyone was back in their room. I peeked into Ron's room, only to find her talking to Bryan. I waved at her and returned to my room, lost in my own thoughts.

When I entered my room, I sat by the window seat quietly, thinking about how to talk to Aliza about saving her from making this grave decision. Samuel clearly loved her, but Aliza had to feel that. Maybe making her talk to someone might help, but how to do that?

How to save her marriage?

Was it even in her hand?

51 | Zippy

Xena

I took out my cellphone from my pocket and noticed a text from Leo, but nothing from Vaughn. Leo had been grieving for heartbreak since that kiss from Finn. He had been avoiding everyone—even me.

Leo: Why is life like a penis?

I smiled at his text in sadness. He had been hibernating from the outside world for days, and when I finally got a text back from him, it had to be this.

Xena: Because you think with one.

I replied with a chuckle. The three dots under my reply indicated he was writing something back. I could wait no longer and called him instead.

"You are wrong again. The correct answer is—because women make them both hard..." Leo said as he picked up the phone. Then his voice dropped a little as he said, "But they are also wrong. Sometimes men do it, too,"

"If you are ready to talk, you could just call me, you weirdo. Why do you always send lame jokes at first? How many more do you have up your sleeves?"

"That's just me. As long as there is me, you'll be blessed enough to keep enjoying the endless supplies of my lame jokes. Besides, I know you love them anyway."

My Zippy's spirits were down. Even though he joked, he was dejected, and I could feel it.

"Enough of your lame jokes. Now, tell me. What happened that night?"

Leo took a moment to respond. "He had a drink with me and then said sorry for leading me on. That fucker told me he wasn't ready to date. To be specific, too busy to date."

"That *snuggetty*... big bad guy! Let me come back! I'll surely pick a fight with him. What does he think he is? Kissing my Zippy and then having the nerve of saying sorry and rejecting!" I said. My voice rose higher as I heaved in a fury.

"Hey... Xen Xen... come down. He is probably not ready to date yet, but that doesn't make him a bad person. We don't have control over our emotions and insecurities," Leo said.

"You are defending him after the way he treated you?" I asked, astounded. Zippy sounded quite serious to me.

"I'll make him come around. Don't worry, the fucker isn't going to get rid of me anytime soon. I'm going to cling onto him until he gives in and takes me."

His voice was so full of enthusiasm that I couldn't help but believe in him. Besides, no matter how reluctant Finn wanted to be, it was impossible to avoid my Zippy's charms. So with a sad smile, I asked, "What made you fall for Finn?"

"What made you fall for Vaughn?"

"Vaughn is all I could ever want. It can only be him for me, Zippy. No one else."

Leo chuckled and said, "Don't you think they're a little alike? I mean... don't you think Vaughn and Finn have some temperamental similarities?"

I rolled my eyes, thinking of them. "They are practically brothers. As per what Finn said, they have known each other for years and ever since they have been together. Finn has dedicated his loyalty to Vaughn."

"Huh... I'm totally not jealous of your man right now." Leo said. I could practically hear him pout.

329

"Do you have that courage?" My tone had a smirk to it. Their first meet was hilarious, if I was honest.

"Well... he is just scary. But Xen Xen, this scary guy cares for you, no doubt about that. I totally green-signal you! Compared to him, my man is a little less scary and much more gayish. Argh... Why is he so stubborn to take me! I was so ready to sacrifice my hole-virginity to him!"

I coughed at his sudden shameless words.

"Don't be upset, Zippy. I'll pray that you can sacrifice your hole-virginity to him soon enough. That man needs love in his life. You two are the perfect match. Besides, we know he likes you too. Next time I visit Vaughn, I'll take you with me and shove you on him to take care of. Let's see where he goes."

"What about your guy? Won't he mind?"

"Do you think he will have the time to care about any of you? Leave him for me to take care." I smiled mischievously.

I felt a lot better after talking to my Zippy. His confidence and determination filled my heart with indescribable comfort. No matter how difficult Finn might appear, I loved Zippy's confidence to win him over. I wish Aliza were as much determined to uphold such a precious relationship in her life.

I peeked into Ron's room to call her at the time for dinner, but she wasn't there. When I walked downstairs, faint sounds of laughter from the kitchen caught my ears. If I wasn't in there, then who could it be? Aliza wasn't the one to laugh in such a carefree manner.

My brows furrowed in confusion when I walked faster into the kitchen. But to my surprise, I found a very enthusiastic Ron, lending a hand in preparing dinner. She was finished with her phone call with Bryan and came downstairs to help mom instead. My dad was busy preparing the salad, whereas mom and Ron were busy finishing the dishes in a cheerful mood. I stood by the door for a while, watching Ron devouring some family time she never truly had.

330

Suddenly, I felt sad for my Vaughn. Just like Ron, he didn't get parental love as well. An inexplicable feeling to hug my man intensified in my heart. Shrugging off the intense emotion, I looked at his sister and couldn't keep in the urge to tease her.

"Mom, I'm also here. You haven't even doted on me this much since we arrived," I said. Even though my words sounded like a complaint, there was a gleeful smile on my face.

"Be a good girl like Veronica first. The girl has been more around me, even on vacation, and you, being a terrible friend, left her alone to attend to your personal matters."

"Whose mom are you?" I asked, my tongue poking out in a playful manner.

"Both of yours. Veronica says she also has a brother. I was asking her to bring him here sometimes."

My heart skipped. Only if they knew what her brother did to me the night before we arrived here. *Oh, holy snuggly snuggles! I miss him.*

The dinner went smoothly. Ron was the center of attraction at the dinner table, and my parents couldn't help but shower her with boundless doting. I kept staring at them, especially Ron, like her guardian angel.

Aliza was careless of her surroundings and quietly continued with her food. She tried to put food on my plate as a good-girl show a few times, and I didn't reject it. The little sister in me was thirsty to get whatever I could from my elder sister. After I perceived a beautiful siblings' relationship like Vaughn and Ron, the thirst in me only deepened.

After we returned to my room, Ron sat on my bed with a gleam in her eyes. Seeing her so happy decreased the perturbed emotion in my heart significantly. I smiled at her and scooted beside her on the bed.

There wasn't much we did that night. Ron kept blabbering about how wonderful my parents were and about everything she enjoyed throughout her stay. I listened to her with a smile and secretly checked my phone to see if there was anything from Vaughn. There wasn't. My brows furrowed in concern for my man.

Ron thought I was sleepy and left for the night with a reluctant goodbye.

I took my phone in my hand and pondered about calling him. If he were free, he would've called, right?

Instead, I sent a text to Finn.

Xena: Not that I want to talk to a bad man like you, but you promised me something. Now.

Finn: I'm sorry for your inconvenience, Ms. Meyers. Now? He is busy.

Xena: What does that have to do with any of us? Now.

Finn: Fine!

Soon a photo came to my cellphone screen. I heaped on joy and opened the picture as fast as humanly possible. There he was. Looking like a treat as he talked to some business associates. Well, to be honest, he was busy scaring some other business parties, looking intimidating and hot.

Whenever the man was with me, he looked different. He was warm, caring and gave me the impression that he could drop to his knees anytime for me if I told him to. But now—now he looked like a frosty mountain no one could climb on. As if he was so superior that no one could reach him. For other people, he might look as scary as a mafia don. But to my treacherous kitty, he was sex on the legs. My ovaries were already on the verge of bursting from looking at the single picture. I thanked Finn with a short text and went back to ogle at my man's picture.

Those cold, ruthless, aloof eyes, pursed suckable, pink lips, heaps of muscles bulging from every corner of his tall frame, aligned hands on his thigh, and oh, god… his thighs, oh god, oh god, oh god!

He looked scary, intense, and ruthless to the point it brought delicious shivers to my bones. So scary that it looked like he could shred the opponent just any time. Only if I were there, I would run to my man just to ride his thighs by now.

My hands itched to reach inside my pants, but then I remembered how he prohibited me from pleasuring myself. But the photo was so freaking hot that my hand went inside my panties on its own accord.

The moment my fingertip touched my *little baby taco,* I felt like I was electrocuted. It was just like the old-time—jilling myself off from looking at Vaughn's photos. But something was missing. Since my man was busy in a meeting, I got enough time to stroke my bundle of nerves. But to my surprise, no matter how much I tried, I couldn't get off.

At some point, I was so frustrated that I felt my eyes welling up.

Oh god, Vaughn, did you ruin me even for myself?

With my hands and legs scattered on the bed, I was heaving in frustration when finally, my cell phone lit, flashing a call from the devil himself.

Wiping a single tear that escaped my eyes, I connected the cellphone with my ear pods and then picked up the call.

"Meeting adjourned?" I asked.

"Wait." His voice was strict. "What were you doing before picking up the call?" Vaughn asked right when he heard my voice. Oh my, the man knew me more than I knew myself.

And he knew. That was also just from those two innocent words.

52 | The Phone Call

Xena

There was nothing I could hide from this man. He knew me as his own palm. Or maybe better than that. After a moment of silence, I decided to come clean to the man.

"I'm sorry, Vaughn. I tried, but I couldn't—if that makes any difference."

"You tried but couldn't?" He asked, breathing hard with a hint of a surprise.

"Yes," I said, as my voice cracked.

"Hey… Shh… I'm here. I'm here for you, baby."

The care in his tone calmed my nerves by folds. "Where are you?"

"My bedroom. Had a shower thinking of you. Just so you know, I didn't even try."

A wave of guilt washed over me. "I'm sorry."

"You'll get your punishment when you come back. You are not getting off easily after being such a brat, Sugar," he said. His tone changed from concerned to a domineering one. My nipples tingled at the tone of his voice, and I touched them to relieve the itch. I'm sure he could hear my panting.

I could hear some shuffling on the other side of the line, and then with a hoarse, raspy voice, he asked, "What made my girl so worked up, hmm?"

"You," I said in a hoarse whisper.

"Me?" The pain of longing was clear in his voice.

"Yes. Before I came here, I made Finn promise to send me your photo whenever I asked. He agreed for only one–time."

"You naughty brat! Just how crazy do you plan to drive me for you?" he paused to moan low. "Mmm… how did you make it happen?"

"What are you doing?" I could sense my voice shaking.

"Gripping my balls. Hard."

I fell silent for a moment, feeling my heartbeat right in my pussy.

"Uh… It was hard to make it happen. Finn wasn't ready to keep a secret from you. But I knew exactly how to convince him."

"How did you do it?" His voice was full of need and desire. A voice, both hoarse, raspy, and slightly nasal, then again a bit of curiosity lingered there.

"He asked me not to give Leo his number. Since I knew both Finn and Zippy needed time to make up their mind, I agreed I wouldn't give Zippy his number until I was here in Virginia. But the moment I'm back, I'm going to give Zippy Finn's entire biography from you."

"Why do you assume I'll give you that?" he asked. Humor was evident in his voice.

"Because you will. Since I only agreed to the duration of my stay here, Finn also agreed to send me your photo only once. See, what a big sacrifice I made?"

Vaughn laughed out loud on the other side. His laughter vibrated in my ear and shot tingles and throbs right towards my cunt, making me twitch in need.

"Only you have the ability to wrap men like Finn and me around your pinky finger. You know that, Sugar?"

"Just wait and see, my Zippy will have both of you wrapped around his pinky finger too. Very soon."

"Enough talking about other men when we are in bed. Tell me. What are you wearing?"

335

"Your shirt. I secretly stuffed it in my luggage. It still smells like you, Wolf."

"*God. Fucking. Damn. It!* Show me!" he commanded with a growl.

I sent him a photo of me wearing his black shirt with all the buttons open. My nipples weren't showing, but the valley between my heavy tits and my shaved kitty was on display—only for the treat of his eyes.

"Ass. Your ass, Sugar. Show your master your little ass." His commanding voice rang in my ears, throwing me to the edge of a hill, challenging me to jump.

I turned around and took a photo of my ass for him and pressed sent.

"Good god! Such a naughty little slut for me. Baby, you know you are my fucking little whore, don't you?" he asked, panting.

"Yes, master. I'm your slut."

"Hell, yes. Yes, you are. Now, be a good little slut and slap those tits for your master. You have been a bad girl. I need to hear the smacks."

"I'll slap my tits?"

"You will choke yourself, too. Now spank. I'm listening."

"Choke myself?" *Was I whining? Was I moaning?* Even I couldn't tell.

"Do you want me to repeat myself?"

I didn't dare to delay and spanked my tit. The smack electrocuted current in my body, intensifying the need for Vaughn's touch.

"Harder."

I spanked harder. The pussy dripped between my legs, throbbing so hard it was almost unbearable.

"Now slap your cunt."

"My kitty?" I was stunned, yet turned on beyond imagination. My body trembled in need.

"And choke yourself at the same time. Now, you little brat!"

"Yes! Yes." I choked my throat using a hand, and I smacked on my clit with the other. An irrepressible moan escaped past my lips.

"My good little slut... my good whore... my fuck-toy." Vaughn kept moaning, and I was a goner.

"Don't you like spanking yourself, Sugar? I know how you like it when I go rough on you. You get off from pain like a slut. I know you. How I wish I could make you drop to your knees and choke that pretty little mouth on my cock. Hot damn... *Jesus!*"

My heart thrashed so fast I felt like I was dying. "Are... are you touching yourself?"

"Mmm. My cock is in your throat right now. Now put two fingers in your cunt. And two in your mouth. Shove them as far as they can go. Prepare your fucking body for your master's pleasure," he said in a shaky whisper.

"Do you want my cock in your mouth, baby? Do you want it to conquer your throat? Choke on my cum? Tell me, Sugar. Do you want my cock to slide down your throat and fill you with my cum? Hmm?"

My legs trembled, and pussy ached in an unruly manner. I squeezed them tight, as much as I could. I could only imagine how wet his filthy words got me.

"I *really* want to take it down in my throat. But... but you are too thick for my mouth."

Vaughn chuckled in a throaty tone. My inside went through havoc just by his shaky, sarcastic laughter. With a hint of ridicule in his voice, he said, "I'll train you. You will take my full length in *all* your holes. After all, I own them." He dragged the word *all* in a mocking tone and then lowered his tone to a nasal whisper and said, "And you own me."

My breath hitched, and I struggled to catch a breath.

"Will you let me... do it... when I come back this time?" I asked like a pathetic little sex-doll.

"Yes, my good whore. If you be a good little girl, I might take some pity on you. Let you taste my cock and cover you with my cum."

"Please, master, how do I please you?"

"Look at you. My dirty little slut. I bet you are dripping for me right now, aren't you? Isn't it killing you that you couldn't relieve the ache yourself? You need my cock, don't you? You need my cock to fuck your holes to release the fire from your body. I need you too, my slut. The master needs his plaything. So hard, I'm so hard for you. I want my girl to sit on my cock and cum all over it right now. I need my pussy, my ass, my tits, and my mouth to release my ache as well. Fuck, I need my girl. Goddammit, Xena... come back. Come soon. I need you. I need you so bad." Suddenly, something changed in him, and the ache in his voice deepened.

"Come for me, Vaughn. Let's try together."

"Can you?" He sounded like a wounded beast.

"No. You know that. I can't even if I try."

"Then we will come together, baby. Come back soon. I'll wait for you."

"But you—" it was so unexpected. How could he hold for two more days? He was a man, after all.

"How can I pleasure myself when my girl is unsatisfied and aching somewhere so far, where I can't go to ease her pain right now?"

I felt a lump in my throat. But this is Vaughn—the man who remained chaste for five years before getting intimate with me. If it were anyone else, I wouldn't have believed. But this man had an ironclad restraint over his body.

"Tell me. How was your day?" I heard some shuffling from his side.

I took a deep breath as I hugged a pillow in my arms. A smile stretched on my lips.

"We had a picnic in the lavender field. Ron was so happy, you know? She stays around mom most of the time, and the old lady dotes on her more than me." I chuckled. "It feels so good to see Ron so cheerful. Mom was asking her to bring you here sometimes. What do you say, Wolf?"

"I will. But only as your boyfriend. Or else, I'm not meeting them." His voice was determined.

"You are as stubborn as a kid, Wolf," I said, mocking him.

"I just need you to declare me as your man to the world. That's it. I hate to be your secret lover. I'm dying to tell the world that you belong to me. That I own you."

My heart skipped a beat. *Oh, snuggles!*

"Why do I feel there is more, baby? What else happened?" he asked.

"I don't want to talk about negative issues right now. You make me feel so contented, Wolf. I'm sleepy."

"Then sleep. I'm here. I'll hang up once you are asleep."

"Aren't you tired? Have you had your dinner?"

"I had. With the partners, after the meetin—"

I felt myself slowly drifting off to sleep before he could finish the line.

53 | Shortly Afterward

The man stepped out of his bedroom only in his sweatpants. His eyes, still glued on the phone screen that had already turned dark. There was a doting smile on his face that Finn could only see when the man was with his girlfriend. Finn had no confusion about who was on the other line.

After hanging up the phone with his girlfriend, the brooding man looked at him with a glare. The indifferent expression on the man's face didn't allow Finn to detect his actual emotion. Finn's body shook from top to bottom with the sudden chill. He feared such stares from his boss because he knew how ruthless the man could be if he wanted.

"Did you send Xena my photo?" he asked. Just from listening to his voice, fear crawled over Finn's neck.

"I'm sorry, boss. It won't happen again. I'll make sure to say no to Ms. Meyers the next time. No matter how persuasive she ge—" before he could finish, the brooding man standing in front of him stopped him in the track.

"Next time, inform me before you take a picture for her. I'd fix myself," said the man.

Finn's eyes bulged out in shock. He didn't expect such a surprising turn in events.

"I—Uh… okay. Okay, boss."

"I will give you an extra half bonus this month with your salary. You could get a full one, but unfortunately, you didn't notify me before clicking."

The man didn't wait for Finn to say anything. He turned on his heels and left.

Finn stood there with his mouth opened in shock. A thin layer of frost covering his entire body. All the while, only one thought swiveling in his mind.

What just happened?

54 | His Kitten

Xena

Soon it was time for our departure, and no doubt, it was the worst part of my visit. However, this time, my parents were more reluctant to part with Ron than me. I chuckled at how mom kept hugging Ron and stroked her hair, forgetting me, their own daughter. Nevertheless, I was happy for Ron. She deserved parental love like every other girl.

My Vaughn deserved it too. I promised myself I would bring him as soon as things were in order. Deep in my heart, I knew my parents would love him. Even though our age gap was huge, I knew he could make everything alright because he was Vaughn. I trusted his irrepressible charms with people.

On our ride back home, my mind kept drifting to the conversation I had with my sister. I tried my best to make her understand the weight of the situation. But one could only help those who wanted to be helped, and Aliza wasn't one of them.

Before we left, I went to talk to her privately. When I knocked on her door again, she opened it and rolled her eyes.

"You grew such thick skin after moving to New York. Don't you know whatever I said was insulting enough for you to be standing in front of me again? Fuck off, you bitch." She tried to slam the door to my face, but I stopped her in the process.

"Teensy. Please. Just hear me out, okay? No matter what, I care for you; you have to believe me, and even only for that sake, please listen to me—don't make such a grave mistake. Everyone has certain limitations in life, but we try to stay happy with our beloved ones within that boundary. And I know Sam will keep you happy. Just take a step toward him, and I'm sure he will take thousands to reach you. Don't make an impulsive decision and ruin what you have, what you could have."

A light flashed before Aliza's eyes when she asked, "Are you done? Now, fuck off."

She slammed the door in my face. This time, I didn't have it in me to stop her.

"Hey, Jay, what are you thinking so hard?" Ron asked. She had been hugging the food container mom packed in her handbag since we started.

"Nothing much. Hey, do you want some muffins now?" I pointed at the container.

"Yeah." Ron opened the lid, and after offering me one, she picked one for her. "You know, mom never baked anything for us. Vee and I tried a few times, but baking isn't our best talent. But Vee is still better between the two of us. He is best at everything he does, except picking up girlfriends." Ron rolled her eyes.

My heart started beating faster. *Blanketties…* What if she knew I was her Vee's girlfriend?

I took a quick bite of the muffin and asked, "Are you going to see Bryan today?"

"Yup. It's a surprise for him. He doesn't know I'm a day early. This is the best trip I've been on, but I truly missed Bryan and Vee."

"Oh, then I guess I will be going to see Leo." I bit my lips, anticipation building inside me. *Oh, snuggles,* I couldn't wait to meet my man. My eyes went thirsty and sore without him.

"Oooh… I love you two as a couple. So, what is this Leo like, huh? He looks like a soft little bunny, but the faint marks I notice on your body every time you spend the night with him say something different." Ron winked at me with meaningful eyes.

Oh, snuggetty snuggles!

343

No, Ron... I can't talk to you about the kinks I share with your beloved brother!

"Uh-huh. Just how I notice marks on Bryan when he sneaks out?" I asked, smirking at my best friend.

Like brother, like sister.

"What can I say... I prefer dominating in our relationship. You know... Bryan is perfect. How we connect both sexually and emotionally is just too perfect to be real. All my life, I've seen my parents lead the messiest relationship ever. I thought this is how it is for everyone. In my mind, the picture was painted and saved. I thought I'd never get a partner better than that. But see, fate has brought Bryan and me closer, intertwined with our destiny together. How lucky am I?"

I hugged the poor girl and stroked her hair. "I'm so happy for you, Ron. You deserve all the happiness in the world."

"You think so?" Ron hugged my waist.

"Of course. Because every time you'll remember your parents, you'll think about not going through the same path and being a better partner to your man. Your insecurities will turn into your strength. I believe in you," I said, hugging her tighter.

Ron stayed like that for a long time. From time to time, we talked about Bryan, Leo, and my family, and in no time, we reached home. Even the six-hour drive couldn't exhaust us when Ron and I were together.

After coming home, I showered in record time. All I could think about was my man, his love, his safe, comforting embrace, and his touches. My body craved him; I craved him. No matter where I looked at, what I thought, or what I said, the man consumed my mind the entire time. I couldn't do anything without thinking of him.

Oh, snuggles.

I was smitten, wasn't I?

After about an hour, I stood in the lift at Vaughn's penthouse. God, he didn't know I would be so early. I was supposed to be at his place about a couple of hours later, but no, I couldn't wait.

I had to see him. I had to.

Besides, with his men all around the place, I was pretty sure he knew by now that I was here. What was he doing? Was he in his usual black suit? Or gray sweatpants? I craved for the man in both, like a dog in heat. I couldn't help with the Vaughn syndrome.

The moment the elevator opened, I stepped into the place, and my feet paused. My breathing hitched, my throat dried, and my heart knocked against my ribcage. I stared and stared but couldn't move my eyes away from what lay in front of my eyes.

Vaughn was right there, sitting on the couch, looking like a king. As I kept staring at my man in awe, I forgot to breathe. He was in his gray sweatpants, just how I assumed he would be. I felt my mouth watering this time, drooling over the man's handsomeness. His eyes fell on mine, and within a second, it dramatically darkened right before my eyes. Honestly, there was no sight as beautiful as this to me.

"I haven't received the last shipment on time."

He was on a phone call.

I kept staring at the striking man. His hair was tousled, eyes darkened, jaw stiffened, and abs looked as sharp as knives. Eyes on me, holding me captive under his stare, Vaughn moved the laptop from his lap and placed it beside him on the couch. His legs spread a little, and I could clearly see the tent inside his gray sweats.

Okay, once again. There was no better sight in the world than this.

What could be a better sight than your man getting worked up right when his eyes fell on you, no matter how busy he was?

"I need the documents before I set any meeting with your company. Detailed and to the point. No delay this time, or else Aphrodisia will be done with you for good."

Wordlessly, I reached for the sleeves of my pink sundress and shimmied it down my body in a subtle manner, baring my black set of lace underwear. The dress lay in a loop down at my feet. Both of us, still gazing into each other's eyes.

Vaughn's eyes narrowed on me, a dangerous smirk forming on his lips. He curled his finger in a commanding way, telling me to drop to my knees. My hormones went crazy, and I sunk my teeth into my lips to control the tingle in between my legs.

Vaughn curled his index finger, implying I crawled towards him on all fours.

His shoulder muscles bulged deliciously as he rested one hand over the back of the couch and the other holding the cell phone. The thought of those hands touching me almost brought me on the verge of my pent-up climax.

I could wait no more and drop on my all fours. My eyes never left his as I slowly crawled towards him like a kitten. My eyes fixated on the most striking man in the world, my cleavage deep, and exposed for his eyes, my ass up in the air as I moved towards the man. The heat in my body was so high that the floor seemed too cold against my knees and palms, causing shivers to run down my spine.

"Not exactly my business if your employees are out of town, is it? If you want the deal, you have to meet me tomorrow."

The authority in his voice caused my throbbing pussy to drip down. I was so aroused I couldn't think straight. At this moment, I was ready to do anything this man wanted me to do, whatever it was. I could be anything for this man, even if it were an effing kitten.

"After the careless attitude from your company last time, I offered you a second and the last chance, only for the sake of your brother. It's up to you if you want it. Take or leave—it has nothing to do with me."

I was right at his feet, still on my hands and knees. Vaughn's hand, which was previously resting on the back of the couch, reached to pat my head in an untamed manner—stroking, fisting and tugging. As if I was nothing but his furry kitten, his beloved pet.

His hands moved to stroke my cheek, and I rubbed my little face against his large palm like I was a cat, seeking warmth, safety, and love from my master. *Oh, blankets!* He smelled delicious, and I couldn't help when my tongue darted out to give his hand a long lick. Vaughn took a sharp breath and sucked in his lower lip. His eyes exuded fire, showing me how much he was burning for me.

I hugged his leg and rubbed my face against his knee. I missed this man, his comforting warmth, his soft touch, I missed how he loved and worshipped me, and I missed how much I craved being treasured by this man.

God, I missed him.

His hand never halted from caressing my hair and stroking my head—petting me. The tent in his sweatpants was right in the line of my sight. I closed my eyes and gave in to the bliss of our proximity after days. The more I rubbed my cheek against his knees, the more desperate the tingle between my legs went. At some point, I could wait no more and look up.

Our eyes locked, and... I smiled.

Vaughn's jaw tightened even more, and his nose flared. He knew. He knew I had something in my mind.

And yes, master. Yes, I do.

55 | Teach Me

Xena

I held Vaughn's gaze with mine and smiled. A smile that could say a thousand words without even uttering a single letter. He drifted his hand from my head to my lips, touching, circling them with his thumb. The tent in his gray sweatpants only grew more and more, and the smile in my eyes sparkled even further.

Like a naughty little kitten, I climbed up on his thigh—slowly, riding on one of them like a cowgirl. My hands rested on the bulging muscles of his shoulder, eyes boring into his deep-set ones. Vaughn's eyes exuded a fire of intense lust and desire, but his lips had a ridiculing smirk hanging at the corner. By now, I knew he was deliberately still talking on the phone. He could hang it up, but no, he wouldn't because this man had been tormenting me intentionally.

But I'm yours, Wolf. I know how to break through your façade and then play with you.

My hips started grinding on his thick, muscular, strong thigh, and every little grind on his thighs sent thousands of friction right into the bundle of my nerves. I looked deeper into his eyes as my breathing grew heavy. Both our eyes turned dark and dilated in desperate and undeniable need of each other.

"I need the documents by tonight," Vaughn said. He was so aroused that his desire could be taken as his wrath.

I closed my eyes in the bliss of his powerful tone and the delicious friction of my clit rubbing against his rough, firm thighs. A stubborn moan escaped past my lips. Vaughn was quick to press his

348

palm against my lips to muffle my moan, but my clouded mind rather bit into his palm. Vaughn didn't move his hand; instead, he kept his palm over my mouth and heaved like a patient beast preparing to pounce on his prey.

I bit my lips, moved my hands to my breasts, squeezing them over my soft lacy bra. Vaughn's eyes darkened even farther, looking at my jiggling, squishy, grownup melons.

"Tomorrow. Aphrodisia. 6 pm. Last chance," Vaughn said. He hung up the call and threw the cellphone somewhere on the couch with no care whatsoever.

Within seconds, his hands reached my throat, and his fingers tightened around it, choking me.

"So fucking aroused, huh? My slut is so aroused she is grinding on her master's thighs even when she isn't permitted yet?" he asked, ridicule clear in his eyes.

"M-Master—" I said, whining in need.

"Shut up. Fucking grind on my thigh as I'm choking you. Go ahead. Show me what you can do. How much do you want your master's thigh? Show me."

My hands rested on his chest, feeling the bends and curbs of his firm and sexy abs as I continued grinding on his thighs. His tightened fingers around my throat aroused me even more, leaving my mouth open as I tried to breathe. Vaughn's other hand reached my hips, and his fingers dug into my soft flesh, imprinting his marks on me.

"You are so fucking desperate for me, huh? So fucking desperate for me, you are rubbing that wet little pussy all over my thigh. It gets you off, huh? Such a filthy little slut you are, Sugar," Vaughn said, desperate in his need.

"Your... your slut, master. I missed you."

"Yes. Yes, you missed me. I can feel your desperate little needy cunt—fuck! It's... so wet, it's drenching my sweatpants with your juice. Oh, god... Look at you shaking, drooling, and moaning for my thigh. You are such a fucking whore for your master, aren't you, Sugar?" Vaughn groaned in pleasure when my moans intensified.

"Faster. Move your hips faster, my dirty little whore, my pretty little slut. That's what you are, yes, look at you. That's exactly what you are," then his voice dropped to a low whisper, *"for me."*

"Yes... master, yes I'm."

"Yes... yes, you are. I bet your pussy is aching down there. So wet, Jesus, you are so fucking wet. Show me, my slut, show me how desperate you are for me. Push your clit over my thigh, drench it more with your juice." Vaughn said in a needy, strangled, breathless voice.

God, I would grind over that voice, too, if I could.

I rode him faster, sucking on my lower lips hard. My eyes were still boring into his while strings of stubborn moans kept escaping past my lips, no matter how much I tried to keep them in.

"Fucking ride my thigh. *Fucking. Ride. It.* Yeah, harder. Circle your hips. God, those hips... so fucking hot. Circle them on your master's thigh. Fucking do it." A tight slap dropped on one of my ass cheeks, and my body jerked, reaching even closer to my release. One could say he despised me from his voice, but I knew better. I knew just how much this man craved my release. Perhaps even more than me.

I felt my orgasm nearing. My body shook and trembled as I rode my man's thigh like a cowgirl. His dominating hand wrapped around my throat was a turn-on, and I couldn't help but listen to everything the man said.

"You've been wanting this. Haven't you? You've been wanting to ride my fucking thighs as I dominate you with this hand around your throat. I know you've been wanting this, my dirty little whore. You've been fantasizing about this. Tell me. Didn't you?"

"Yes, master... yes. A hundred times and over."

Vaughn let out a chuckle at my confession and said, "Yeah? Such a fucking slut for me. I can feel you soaking my sweats. God... just how desperate are you?"

"So... so desperate, master. I want to come."

350

"You couldn't come yourself, and now you can come on my fucking thigh? That's how much you want your master, my dripping whore? Then do it. Rub your clit all over my goddamn thigh. Come. Come all over your master's thigh, my needy little plaything."

I couldn't come up with a word as I reached the edge of my release. My hips were grinding even harder and faster on Vaughn's thigh. His grip on my hips and throat was painful, but that only pushed me more and more towards my sweet, pent-up release.

"Come. Yes. Fuck... yes, baby, come for your master. Fuck yes..." Vaughn continued to throw strings of curses, and filthy words as my orgasm rippled through me, my body quivering and shaking from top to bottom.

It had been days since I couldn't come, no matter how much I tried, and here I was, coming right over his thighs. Vaughn was right. I was a dirty little whore for him, and that only made me feel happier, fulfilled.

I could be anything for this man.

Vaughn pulled me by my neck and slammed his lips over me. Kissing me. I moaned into the kiss, still recovering from the orgasm that washed over me in waves and waves of pleasure. His hands brushed my hair in a possessive manner, holding me close to his body. His lips showed me how much he missed me, asking for everything all at once.

In between the kiss, I slowly moved from his thighs to settle in between them, gradually dropping to my knees once again. My hands looked for the elastic of his sweatpants, inching it a little to get a grip on what I had been craving for all these days, finally. *Oh, blanketties.* I missed his cock.

"Let me... let me try. Teach me, master. Teach me to take you all down my throat until your heavy balls reach my chin."

Vaughn paused for a second, astonished at my desperation, but Vaughn was Vaughn. He found his composure soon. "Oh, fuck... So needy to suck my cock. God, just how dirty, how shameless are you? Asking for your master's cock with no shame?"

"Please, teach me to take you," I said with my hand wrapped around his cock and another under his balls.

Vaughn leaned down to touch his forehead with mine and whispered in a concerned, nasal tone. "Are you sure, Sugar? It's going to be painful."

"I want you in every way."

"Fuck yes—" Vaughn let out a primal growl, "—yes, I fucking want you in all ways, too. I want to fill up every little hole of my slut with my goddamn cock, claim them."

I kissed the tip of his cock, slowly dragging my lips over it. "Teach me your way."

"Jesus Christ…" Vaughn groaned as I took the tip in my mouth, swirling my tongue around it. His glistening cock was as hard as a rock, purple in pain, and the veins looked like they were almost on the verge of popping out. It was the most beautiful cock I had ever seen in my life, and it was mine.

"See how further you can take it. Before I decide how much you can." He said in a low tone.

I pushed his cock further into my mouth, back and forth, easing up my throat for him as much as I could. Vaughn was struggling there to keep it in, I could say. The man didn't release in my absence, for god's sake. It must be hard for him.

I tried taking him further, but my gag reflex kicked in. It wasn't strong, but it was still there. I looked at my man in desperate eyes as they bored into mine—silently pleading with him to teach me.

56 | Take Me

Vaughn

My girl was trying.

I could see her desperate tries to slide my cock all the way in her tight, clenching throat. The thought that no one had ever been in there tightened my heart with immense joy and pride. Mine, she was all mine, and she was trying to take me all in. Gosh… her gags were beautiful and left me wanting for more. Holy fucking hell—so hot.

I knew what she needed. I knew what I needed.

I clutched the back of her neck and pushed my cock into her eager little mouth. My little girl was suddenly so scared, gasping and struggling for air. I chuckled at her faint attempt to break free because I knew it wasn't her limit. I would know when it was.

"Holy hell… look at you, drooling over my cock. Your drool is dripping from your chin to your tits—fuck… I love it. I love to take away the air from your lungs, replacing it with my cock right down your throat."

She moaned on my cock. Fuck. So eager, so willing, so desperate—trying harder to take more of me as I bobbed her head up and down with my possessive hands. My girthy cock stretched her cute little mouth to its highest limit. A centimeter more, and she couldn't have taken it.

She was miserable with the need for air, but her need to take me all the way in won over and over again. For a second, I wanted her to stop, but then again, her eagerness to take me all in was so hot, and I could only see how far my little Sugar could go.

This goddamn lucky cock.

"Open your throat for me, my little fucktoy. Loosen it. Breath through your nose and take my fucking cock." My voice was a strangled, breathless mess as I watched her choking on my cock, drooling all over both of us. Hell, we both were a mess from my precum and her saliva, and I fucking loved it.

Her tongue swirled around the crown of the head of my cock, flicking on my frenulum at an insane pace. The sensation brought jolts of electricity rushing throughout my body, and I let out a loud primal groan. Fucking dammit! From where the fuck did she learn to do it? Who taught her to do that?

No. I couldn't come yet. I couldn't come yet.

I kept chanting in my head. My chest heaved as I panted in need, my mouth dried, and my eyes squeezed shut again and again under the torture of the cutest little tongue, no pun intended.

She used one hand to cup my balls, squeezing them now and then, feeling them at her heart's desire—driving me crazy over here. Her other hand gripped my leftover shaft, trying to fit it in her throat.

I chuckled again and said, "You know you are going to struggle to talk tomorrow, right? You are. And every time you'll open your mouth, it'll remind you of me, of my cock. It will remind you, my Sugar, that you are mine—" I gripped her hair, pushing her more on my cock, "—*Fucking. Mine!*"

"Ah!" she moaned and gagged, choking on my girthy shaft.

Goddammit! Her moan not only created a sweet, delicious vibration on my cock, but it also opened her throat a little more for me. A little more space opened up for me to conquer it.

Hot hell.

"Today or tomorrow, I'm going to have those lips pressed against my stomach as I'm balls deep in your throat. It will fucking happen. I'll make it happen!" I let out a strangled growl as I held her head down on my cock for a long while as she kept struggling and

354

making choking noises. More threads of the mixture of my precum and saliva drenched her large melons and dropped down on the ground.

"Fucking hell. Yes, yes, yes, swallow my cock. Moan on my cock. Fucking moan on my cock. Moan, my little slut!"

When I let her up, her eyes were tearing up, her face was a flushed, dirty mess, and holy Christ, did she look even more beautiful than ever. I was transfixed to her beauty, sucking my lower lip in, so much entranced by her sensuality, I forgot everything else.

She took a moment to gag even more on my cock.

I growled like a shackled, strangled animal. My voice turned nasal yet rugged, with all the moans of satisfaction escaping past my lips. "Yeah… gag on my cock. Fucking gag on my cock. You like it, don't you?" I heaved, panting, "You're fucking desperate slut for my cock. You hot damn thing."

I took out my cock from her mouth. No matter how desperate she was, no matter how strong she thought she was, still, my girl needed to breathe. Even though she forgot while pleasing me, I had to remember.

"Breathe. Breathe before you take me in your little throat once again." I slapped my cock against her cheek. "You like being slapped with my cock, don't you.?"

"Yes, master… yes."

My thumb caressed her swollen pink lips—rubbing on them, pinching them, tugging them. My naughty little girl darted her tongue out and took my entire thumb in her mouth to suck on it as well.

Hot damn thing.

I pulled out my thumb and pinched her chin.

"God, you are a dirty little slut… my little slut… mine. Take me in again. Take my cock in your mouth again."

She willingly took more than half of my cock in her mouth, and I hissed out.

"Oh, my god… god… yes, yes, yes. Your mouth is made for sin, you goddamn little fuckthing. It'll be the death of me. Oh god, oh yes... fuck!" I screamed in euphoria. The more I moaned, groaned, and growled, the more sounds she made over my cock. My sounds of pleasure turned my girl on, huh?

"Come on... oh, fuck... deepthroat me. Fucking deepthroat me. Gag on my cock, my dirty little whore. It feels so good. It feels so fucking good inside your little mouth. Hot damn... It feels so good... so good... suck my cock. Suck me... fucking suck me."

She started to bob her on my cock even faster. I held her head with both my hands as she tried her best to take me in, her other hand still squeezing my balls.

I could hear the faint sound of a cellphone ringing, but we were on no right mind to think about attending the call then. We were too deep into the carnal pleasure to think about anything or anyone other than the two of us.

"You are so fucking dirty... my dirty little fucktoy... Holy Christ... What do I do with you?" I asked.

She put more pressure on my cock with both her hands and took my balls in her mouth, sucking them raw. With her eyes locked on mine, she said, "Master... Am I doing it right?" her words muffled with my balls in her mouth.

God... fucking... dammit!

With shudder after shudder, I spurted my loads in white threads. For a while, I saw white lights appear before my eyes as I stared at the goddess kneeling down at my feet.

"You are so fucking dirty, you can't even keep calm with my goddamn balls in your mouth," I said, heaving. The naughty girl was nowhere listening to what I said since she was busy licking my cum from all over my cock, cleaning it. I looked down and noticed a few drops of my cum on her tits. I pointed at it and said, "Lick it. Lick every drop of my cum that exists only for you."

She smiled like a little vixen, and then holding my stare, she cupped her bra-cradled tits and brought them near her mouth. Darting her tongue out, she licked on them with a hint of a smile consistent at the corner of her lips.

I gripped my cock and kept staring at her. Those naughty, sinful eyes. She held the hell of fire in them to burn me alive, and good god, I didn't want to die in any other way.

My cellphone rang again, but I paid no heed. Not when my girl was on her knees in front of me.

"Next time, I'm going to take it all in, Wolf."

I pulled her by the neck and kissed her messy, dirty lips. God, I had to kiss those lips.

The sound of a cellphone once again invaded our senses. This time, it was her phone.

"Let me check who it is."

I pulled her into my lap just as she picked up her phone from her bag. Her eyes narrowed, and she asked, "Ron? Was she the one calling you earlier?"

I looked for my phone and noticed it was indeed Ron trying to reach us.

"Ron... I'm sorry I couldn't pick earl—" she paused, and suddenly, her breath hitched. "Come down... come down... I'm coming."

She looked at me in terrified eyes and said, "We have to see her right now."

57 | Wretched Ron

Xena

Ron needed us. Vaughn and I were both out of our wits and quick to reach Ron. I knew what Ron meant for Vaughn, and here he was, freaking out, losing his composure. It was so unlike Vaughn because he never lost his temper, but it was Ron, and anything regarding his little sister shook the world under his feet.

Honestly, I was worried, too. Ron was too important to me. She was not only my best friend, but she was also my sworn sister, and now, she was also the most important person in Vaughn's life, which pushed her significance to me even higher than before. There was no way I could take it if she were going through a time like this.

The moment we reached the address she was in, I jumped out of the car even before Vaughn stopped the engine. The man was scared at my approach and screamed from behind, "Careful!"

I was impatient to reach Ron. My heart was right in my throat, threatening to come out at any moment. I had no time dilly-dallying with him at that moment. My best friend needed me.

I ran towards the silent alley and found Ron sitting on the dirty ground, hugging her knees. She had no care to the world, shaking and trembling as tears kept rolling on her cheeks.

I ran to my best friend, dropping beside her as I took her frail body in my arms.

"Jay…"

Ron let out a sob, crying and crying. Her tears soaked into my fabric as I cried with her. Both of us stayed like that until I felt her

358

body calming down. Only then did I look up and notice Vaughn staring at us with concerned eyes.

Ron glanced at the line of my sight and noticed Vaughn. Immediately, she let out a sob again and dashed out to jump into his arms.

"Shh… Shh… Ronnie, don't cry. I'm here. Tell me, tell your Vee who hurt you. I'll take care of it, I promise."

"Why are you so late? I called you again and again."

"I'm sorry I couldn't pick up your call. Look at me... I'm here now. Let me take you home, and then we can talk."

When we got to the car, Ron jumped into the passenger seat, and I went for the back door. Vaughn stared at me through the rearview mirror once and then sped up the car. The man was exuding fire. His eyes were completely dark, forehead scrunched, and jaw set in a hardline. He looked too dangerous, too ready to kill. Someone hurt his sister, and he was in no way acceptable to such behavior. For a second, I pitied the person who would be on the other end of his wrath.

Ron was still crying, but silently. Her eyes were blank as they stared out of the window. My mind kept coming to the same conclusion every time I wondered about what might happen. If what I was thinking was right, it had been killing my Ron.

God, don't let my suspicion be correct for once in my life.

When we reached home, I tried to talk to Ron, but my voice was coming out rough. Every time I attempted to speak, I ended up coughing because of my throat ache. Vaughn noticed the situation, and silently, the man walked into the kitchen to heat some water in the microwave.

"Ron," I paused to cough, "tell me… W-What happened?"

Vaughn walked in with two glasses of water and handed them over to us. As we sipped in the water, Ron said, "I-I walked into Bryan with someone else. They were fucking in his bed, where we…" Ron trailed off before she ended up sobbing once again.

She hugged her brother and said, "I'm sorry, Vee… you said, again and again, not to trust people so easily. I'm sorry I didn't doubt him. He played me so well… I started trusting him. Vee… is every relationship like this? Like our parents? No love? No respect? Does everyone cheat and betray, Vee?"

My tearful eyes gazed at Vaughn and found his dark orbs right on me, his eyes glistening as well.

Vaughn's arms tightened around his little sister. "No, not every relationship is not like that, Ronnie. There are some wonderful relationships in the world where two people love and respect each other. They can close their eyes and sleep beside the same person all their life, knowing they're safe. Those who want nothing more than their partner's smile in the entire fucking world. Just a smile from the person is enough to make their day. There are still people like them, Ronnie. He wasn't the one, and that doesn't mean there isn't one for you," Vaughn said. The man uttered every word, looking directly into my eyes with firm resolution.

I stroked Ron's hair and said, "I've seen you, Ron. You are the strongest girl out there. Even if someone plucks the flower out of your life, you know how to grow and bloom once again. You are that amazing. With your brother by your side and me, you're never going to feel alone. We won't let you. We are here for you."

Ron freed herself from Vaughn's arms and looked at me. "You know why he played with my feelings? Not just because he wanted to date and dump me. He is the nephew of one of the old employees at dad's business, and he knew today to tomorrow I'd take over our family business. That bastard played because he wanted to marry me just for the wealth that comes with me," Ron sobbed. "He never liked or loved me, Jay. No one ever loves me."

I gripped her hand with tearful eyes. "No, Ron, look at us—we love you. We love you selflessly, and we'll be here for you whenever you need support. A person like Bryan is gone from your life, and that's nothing but a blessing. Now you can give a good person a chance to be with you. Thank god everything happened early."

"Is it early? I almost fell in love with the cheater." Ron sobbed again.

"Ronnie, I promise you I'll take care of the motherfucker. I can't wait to see how he escapes from my hands."

Vaughn helped his sister to her room and tucked her into the bed. I followed him to the main door, and when he was about to leave, the man took me in his arms and pressed his lips against mine.

He kissed me. But the kiss felt different. Something about the kiss told me that for the first time, the kiss was more for him than for me. He was trying to calm himself through the kiss. When I realized it, I gave even more into the kiss. My fingers buried in his hair, and I rubbed my fingers on his neck, behind and under his ears, calming him down in every way I could.

"Take care of Ronnie." He dropped another kiss. "Also, drink plenty of warm water. Your throat is going to hurt tomorrow. I should've used lube with you. Next time I got to be more careful with my girl. I can't hurt you. I can't afford to."

"It's alright. I'm okay. Are you?" I brushed my fingers at his warrior cheekbone.

"I'll be once I teach the motherfucker some lesson. He can't mess with people who matter to me. I should remind him of that, for good."

"Don't go overboard, okay?" I stood on my toes to peck on his forehead.

"I can't promise anything, Xena. It's about Ronnie. He hurt her and made her cry."

"Okay, but take care of my man."

"Mmm. I'll come to see you both when I get the time." Vaughn pressed a soft kiss on my temple and left.

When I went back inside our apartment, I chose to stay the night with Ron. As I went entered her room, I found her crying again. With an aching heart for the girl, I got into the bed beside my best friend and hugged her tight, comforting her with my presence so she could sleep in peace.

I didn't see or hear from Vaughn the next day. Besides, I was too occupied with Ron. After she woke up in the morning, the girl appeared to be completely fine. But there was no fooling she had been faking it.

"Ron, you know, you can cry and lighten your heart, right? I'm here for you," I asked when I found her looking for food with loud music on.

"I'm past the grievance. There is no point crying over spilled milk, right? Remember what you said last night? I am strong, and I can bloom again? I believe in those words. Now drag your ass over here. We need to binge-watch some Ryan Reynolds. I need to remind myself such men exist."

All I could do was to be with her and support her. See where it went.

My throat hurt all day. I was on hot water therapy as Ron continued with her ice cream and pizza. It was so painful for me I couldn't eat much.

Later at night, Ron convinced me it was okay for us to sleep in our own room. I didn't argue with her, but I checked on her all night after she fell asleep from time to time.

It was about three in the morning when I couldn't help much and texted Vaughn with a simple *'I miss you.'*

Within seconds, the cellphone vibrated in my hands.

Vaughn was calling me.

58 | Impatience

Xena

"Baby, I thought you were sleeping by now," he asked in his usual heavy, husky tone.

I entered my bedroom, closing the door behind. "Uh—I was. I got up to check on Ron. She convinced me to sleep in my room tonight."

Vaughn stayed silent for a long moment. Then, in a gentle tone, he said, "Thank you, Xena. For being there for her, even when I can't."

"Thanking me for taking care of my best friend, Wolf?"

A sexy chuckle escaped from Vaughn's throat, and then in a low, raspy voice, he said, "We are lucky to have you, baby."

"Uh-huh." I disagreed. "It's me. I'm lucky to have you. So, where were you all day, huh?"

"Taking care of something. How is your throat, baby? Still hurting?"

I took a sharp breath. The man had a voice to mess with my hormones, no matter how far he was. I leaned against my door and put my hand on my chest, feeling the erratic heartbeats. The throbbing in my pussy grew unbearable with every second.

"Every time I talk, it reminds me of..." I trailed off.

"Of what, baby?" he asked.

"Ah-I... Uh... your..."

"My what?"

"Oh, blanketti! Your... cock. I missed you all day, Wolf. I..." I was at a loss for words. How to ask how much I wanted sex from the man in a dignified way? It had been long, and I was addicted to him.

"And you wanted me to pump in between your legs with my cock, didn't you?"

I stayed silent, my breathing short and heavy. He knew me like the palm of his hand.

"Sugar... I wanted it too, baby. It had been long. If things didn't take turns, I would've ruined your pussy last night. I wanted to fill you up with my thick seeds. As my good little slut, you'd have taken it, wouldn't you? I'd have filled you to the point where it flowed down your inner thighs. Your mouth... drooling, and you'd be whining as I would've carried on pounding my tight little needy pussy—recklessly. *Argh!"* he growled and then said, "I miss you, baby."

My mouth was slightly opened, breathing coming in heavy. Eyes were closed in the euphoria of his voice and all the dirty words coming right off his filthy mouth. My hand was in my shorts, my fingers still over my clit, too eager to play. But all my pleasure belonged to him. I can't. Not without his permission.

"Wolf. Are... you touching yourself?"

"I'm holding my cock, Sugar. Too tempted to pump, but it belongs to you. I won't. Just the memory of my cock halfway down your throat and your eyes locked into mine... is enough torture for me, baby. You are the only fucking reason I want to touch myself at three in the morning," Vaughn said. His was a shaky mess in a breathless whisper.

"You have my panties, don't you?" I asked—my heart racing in my chest.

"Uh—Yes... I have a couple of them." He seemed skeptical about the question, but too aroused not to answer.

"Jack off to my panties, video it, and send it to me. I want to see you jacking off to something that belongs to me." Goosebumps appeared on my skin at the thought.

364

"You want a video of me jacking off to your panties?" he asked, a genuine surprise was clear in his tone.

"Yes."

"Wait for me," he said and hung up the call.

After about ten minutes, I received a text message, followed by another one.

Vaughn: Can't seem to record me. Give me a hand or two, maybe?

Vaughn: I'm downstairs. Waiting. Come, baby.

I was as fast as humanly possible. My man was here. Right here. For me.

The moment I saw the car, I ran faster. This time, he wasn't leaning against the door like the other times. Instead, the man was sitting right in his driver's seat.

I opened the front passenger door to have a peek inside.

Snuggly blankets!

Vaughn was sitting there, looking as intimidating as ever in his black shirt and black sweatpants. My breath hitched the moment my eyes fell on his lap. Oh god.

His raging, hissing hard-on was right in his hand, looking purple, swollen, and angry as ever. His long fingers were tight around the shaft. My mouth watered in a matter of seconds.

Oh, Vaughn.

Slowly, his head turned, and his dark eyes fell on me. A smirk stretched his seductive lips, and my heart threatened to come out from the vigorous pounding.

"Get inside."

There it was. His authoritative tone.

I got in, and Vaughn started the engine, wasting no more time. We went near a secluded area where there were no people in our line of sight. All the while, his cock was right before my eyes, in his grip. My nipples hardened over my soft silk tank top, and my throbbing pussy dripped, soaking the fabric of my shorts. Vaughn stopped the car and turned on the dimmed lights of the car.

"Record me." He pushed his seat back a little, spreading his legs for comfort.

My eyes were transfixed on the man. His eyes were fixed on mine as his sexy hand bobbed on his enormous girthy length up and down.

Oh god! Oh god! Oh god!

"Give me your shorts," he said in his dominant tone. A slight hint of impatience lingered in it. "Your panty doesn't smell like your soaked, dripping pussy anymore. I want to smell your addictive nectar."

I was so turned on that my mind stopped working. With no further word, I hooked my fingers in the elastic of my shorts and pulled them down. Even before I could hand it over to Vaughn, he snatched it from my grip, pressing it against his nose, inhaling the scent of my arousal audibly as if he was thirsty for it, as if he had been starving and deprived of it.

He found the wet patches of my shorts and gave them a lick. His eyes, still on me, hands busy pumping his enormous length.

"Record. Me." The order came again.

I turned on the video recorder of my phone and pointed at the sexiest man alive. His hooded, lustful eyes looked into my soul as he treasured my shorts with his mouth and nose. All the while, his strokes went faster, harder, and erratic on his meaty cock. The way his chest heaved, I felt breathless.

Oh, snuggles! He was so turned on, and the fact alone aroused me beyond belief.

My other hand went to my kitty on its own. Vaughn's eyes dropped to my kitty in an instant and darkened even further. His throat bobbed, making mine feel dry.

"Touch it. Play with my pussy for me."

I touched my clit, rubbed it, teased it, stroked it. Two of my fingers went inside to stroke the inner walls of my pussy. The man looked like he was in a trance. His hand slowed down as he kept staring at my dripping cunt.

It didn't take me long when my orgasm hit me in waves. My body shuddered in ripples of pleasure as I creamed all over my fingers, even ruining the expensive leather of his car seat.

When my eyes opened, and I came down from my ecstasy, I found Vaughn still before me. His eyes were occupied, taking me in as much as he could. As if a blink of his eyes will take me away from his line of sight.

I offered him my soaked fingers, knowing how much he would love to taste me, and proving my assumption right, Vaughn licked on my fingers earnestly, one by one, leaving not even a little space deprived of the stroke of his tongue. He was in a predicament whether to lick my nectar or sniff my scent from my fingers.

His hand went faster and faster. A string of uncontrollable groans and growls escaped from the deepest corners of his chest, vibrating in the small space of his lavish car.

I felt the vibration. I felt it right in my throbbing kitty.

The moment I felt him getting off, I leaned in and took his pulsating cock into my mouth. Vaughn was startled at my approach and let out a hiss that implied both his pleasure and sweet torment. This time, surprisingly, the cock went further than last night. Inside my throat, I could feel his hot seeds spurting in waves. The salty taste of his cum was an aphrodisiac, and I wanted more of it.

I didn't let him go, even when he finished his load down my throat. I kept my mouth on work, swirling my tongue, kissing the slit, licking him, until I knew there was no more load left inside his balls for now.

Vaughn pulled me on his lap, making me sit sideways, holding me like a baby. I had no pants on, and his sweats were down with his cock hanging out, not to mention still semi-hard.

"That was amazing, baby. You are so perfect. My perfect little slut that I love. God... Xena, I love you."

"I love you too, Wolf." I pressed my lips against his soft ones for a long kiss.

After the kiss, Vaughn held my head against his chest, stroking my hair, and another hand rubbed my back with boundless affection, as if coddling a child.

"How was your day, Wolf? What did you do to Bryan?" I asked. My hand wrapped tighter around him, rubbing my face against the hard surface of his chest like a bunny.

"What he deserved. I had a talk with Ronnie the moment I had a hunch she was serious about that fucker, but she asked me not to meddle in this time. I respect Ronnie's decision, so I obliged. But today, I had no obligation to do what needed to be done."

"And what is it that needed to be done?" I looked up, peering into his eyes.

"Ran a background check for his crimes. Found some faults in his and his uncle's record. I just had to intensify the color of their crime and use some threads to put them behind the bar. I wouldn't have let him wandering out in the daylight even for a day more." His lips brushed against the edge of my ear.

"Are you sure it's a good decision? I mean, they can apply for bail. If somehow he tries to take revenge and something happens to any of you—" Vaughn pressed his lips on mine with a kiss.

"If I'm the person to send him behind the bar, it's hard for them to come out. You're underestimating your Wolf, mate." Vaughn pressed a gentle kiss on my forehead.

A smile stretched on my lips. I brushed my palm on his delicious stubble beard and asked, "Aren't you tired, Wolf? You've been busy all day. It's four in the morning."

"I wouldn't trade this moment with any goddamn thing in the world." He tightened his hold on me, as if treasuring his most valuable, and another hand pushed into my hair, bringing my neck closer to his lips to worship.

"As much as I love being here with you, Wolf, I need to check on my best friend."

Vaughn stroked my hair in affection. "How is Ronnie doing?"

I sighed. "She is either in denial or suppressing her pain. It was a heavy blow for the poor girl. Don't worry... I'm there for her. Under my hawk-like eyes, she can't do anything stupid."

"God... baby. I can only remain calm knowing you are there for Ronnie." Vaughn kissed my forehead again. His thumb brushed over my lips as his eyes bored into mine.

"Expect to see me at lunch tomorrow."

59 | At Lunch

Xena

The next day, at lunch, Ron and I prepared some grilled beef, barbeque chicken salad, and some mashed potato after Vaughn informed Ron about his arrival in the morning.

He arrived a little earlier. As usual, the all-black formal clothes on the man got me weak in my knee the moment I saw him walk into our apartment. Our small apartment looked so tiny in his powerful presence, as if just standing there, he ate up most of the space. His dark eyes swiped over me, and naturally, I missed a few beats.

Ron took him to the living room, and the siblings settled there, emerged in their conversation. No matter how involved I was in both their lives, I decided to give them their privacy and stayed in the kitchen, playing with my phone, stealing secret glances at my man from afar, and preparing the table—just the normal, usual stuff.

From the corner of my eyes, I noticed Vaughn saying something to Ron with a stern expression, and Ron, on the other hand, looked perfectly normal. She was listening to everything Vaughn said and replied in nods. I couldn't hear what they were saying, but I had an idea from yesterday's talk in the car.

After a long talk, when I found the siblings laughing at something, I decided it was time for me to call them for food. I decided to be playful and said, "Lunch is ready, in case anyone is hungry over here."

"Coming," Ron said. The siblings stood up and approached the table. I looked up and found the pair of dark eyes looking at me mischievously from Ron's back. There was a twinkle on his lips that turned me into a puddle in a matter of seconds. I sat down on a chair in an instant since the man had me giddy.

The man walked closer and stood right in front of me with his slack-covered cock at the line of my sight. My heart nearly tumbled out on the floor, and my mouth watered at the delectable sight.

He pulled the chair to my left, and Ron sat on my right. In any way we sat, I would be sitting beside Vaughn. After all, it was the only way among three people to sit together at a round table.

I could feel the heat radiating from his body. My senses perked up, and my pussy tingled at the proximity. I badly wanted to forget everything happening around and sit on his lap like I did when we were alone. My teeth sunk on my lips at the thought, and my breathing grew heavy. *Snuggety,* this man could really play with my hormones in any way he wanted, couldn't he? And he wasn't even trying hard.

"Where is the actual salt, Jay?"

"This is actual salt. If you need extra salt for your food, use pink salt instead. It's good for your health."

Ron rolled her eyes and went to bring the white salt that I asked her not to consume uncooked.

The moment Ron got up, Vaughn leaned close to my ears. "I really want to kiss you right now, Sugar. Been thinking about you a lot, and it's not at all innocent."

My wine went to the wrong pipe, and I started coughing. His uncultured words grew my eyes wide in surprise, and my heart started drumming against my chest.

Oh, Vaughn.

Before Ron reached me to pour a glass of water, Vaughn handed me over one and patted on my back a little. Ron was too shocked to see me that she overlooked Vaughn's touch of concern.

We started eating again once I overcame my scattered hormones. The air around us felt hotter and hotter even though the window was opened. I was once again a hormonal mess, resembling our second

371

date. My hands shook on the date when Vaughn fed me the food with his hands. Only this time, he couldn't—not before Ron.

Suddenly, I felt something brush against my feet, teasing me, and I jumped in my seat.

Oh, snuggles!

Both the siblings looked at me at my strange behavior, but I had nothing to explain to them. I was already unable to coherent words when I felt his leg brushing against mine in a slow, seductive motion.

Snuggety snuggles!

"Hmm... That's juicy." Vaughn muttered after his eyes brushed over me in a quick glance.

Ron agreed with her brother and said, "Yup, Vee is right! Jay, the chicken is indeed very juicy. Soft, and the spices just come along—" Ron kept going, but I didn't catch up with her words anymore. My ears burned, knowing her brother wasn't talking about the chicken at all.

I gulped down but failed. Then I tried once more, but to no avail. Anything—I just had to say anything to acknowledge their compliments.

"Thank you."

"You shouldn't talk with your mouth full," Vaughn said.

I grabbed the glass of water once again and tried to swallow the food with water.

No, once again, the man's words weren't contemplating *anything* innocent.

"Vee, be nice to Jay. She cooked the chicken you find juicy."

"Oh, yeah. I find it juicy, alright."

Every brush and stroke of his leg sent thousands of sparks right to my kitty. I didn't know which throbbed more, my heart or my pussy. The man messed with my body with his mere presence, with no apparent effort whatsoever.

Summoning all my courage, I looked into his eyes and asked, "Then why don't you *dig in?*"

No, I didn't mean to dig in the chicken at all, and the way his eyes grew even darker, I knew he understood my insulation pretty well. How could he not? After all, this man was none other than the mighty Vaughn.

"I would love to." A smile—a wicked smile with thousand promises appeared on his striking face, and I looked down. If I continued to stare at the man for a second more, I would've yanked him by the collar and claimed his smirking lips.

The thumb of his toe brushed and circled on the sensitive skin of my feet, and goosebumps erupted all over my skin, causing me to heave for breath in secret. My head was low as I stole a glance at my man. At once, his mesmerizing set of eyes caught mine, and my breath got hitched.

Why so handsome?

The look in his eyes pushed the level of my confidence higher. I lifted my left hand to place it gently on his thigh under the table. Vaughn went stiff for a moment and took in a sharp breath.

Yes, my touch affected him just as much.

I smirked as I felt the confidence grow and climb like ivy inside me. Slowly, I began to tease his thighs with my fingers. But I was careful enough only to move my wrists, so Ron didn't know what I was doing to her brother.

Suddenly, Vaughn pushed the plate and picked up the wine.

"You done?" Ron asked her brother.

Before Vaughn could open his mouth, I said, "I wasn't expecting you to be done so quick."

The mischievous sparkle in my eyes didn't slip from his stare. Vaughn's eyes brushed over me, and then he smiled.

He smiled, and I knew something was going to be wrong. Very, utterly, and absolutely wrong.

As I continued with a conversation with Ron, I tried to devour my mashed potato with one hand and caress the firm, thick thigh of her brother with another. Suddenly, I understood why he smiled when I

373

felt his left hand gripping my wandering hand over his thigh and pressed it right on his brimming bulge. The moment my soft palm touched his rigid rod, I felt it throb uncontrollably.

Oh, blanketties…

I stayed unmoved for a long time when I felt Vaughn rubbing my dainty palm over his rock-hard cock with his much larger hand.

"It tastes delectable with whipped cream."

I almost jumped in my seat. *What did he just say?*

"I like it better with custard filling. Besides, Jay doesn't like whipped cream much."

Vaughn looked at me with curious eyes and asked, "How do you know you don't like whipped cream over it if you haven't tried yet?"

No, the filthy man was not at all talking about some *snuggetti* dessert with whipped cream, and he was undoubtedly not recommending me to try any *Snuggety* dessert. No. He was too filthy for an innocent talk.

But his gleaming eyes, his smirking lips, his comfortable warmth, and his throbbing hard-on—once again, I was a goner.

In an instant, I pooled in my panties. My mind was nowhere near grasping whatever Ron had been saying. My world turned out to be only what was happening under the table, and my throat dried. My heart raced like a factory machine, and my pussy was threatening me an orgasm with violent contractions.

I excused myself and ran for the washroom. I needed to breathe; the man got on the end of my every single nerve, pushing me more and more to the edge. Time after time, I splashed water over my face, but no use.

Vaughn. I needed Vaughn.

When I opened the door after a good ten minutes, I let out a shriek when I noticed Vaughn leaning against the wall opposite the washroom door. His suit coat was out of the picture, and his sleeves were rolled up to his elbows.

And those gleaming eyes and smirking lips I was talking about—yeah—they were on me.

60 | Quickie

Xena

"You? Wh-Where is Ron?" My voice was shaky, no doubt.

Vaughn shrugged with a mischievous smirk on his lips. "Didn't you hear? She wanted to buy some dessert—I didn't say no."

"Why? Where is Finn?" I was breathless.

"Finn is not... available." He flashed a filthy smirk. "Besides, didn't you say Ron should go out for a breather?"

"N-Not when we are alone here!" My heart knocked in my ears. "Why?"

Vaughn straightened up, his smirk stretching even more on his handsome face as he passed me, entering the bathroom. "Don't you already know, Sugar?"

Before I could comprehend the meaning of his words, he pulled me inside and locked the door behind us. The worked up man gave me no time when I felt his hands turn me around and push my face against the cold tiles of the wall. *Oh god. Oh god. Oh god.*

The man pushed his chest against my back, his hands curling on my chest and stomach as his lips found their way to my neck—kissing me, teasing me, savoring me. Next, his right hand went up to my throat, curling his fingers around me, tightening them. I choked a little, gasping for air, when he pulled me by my throat, causing my back to arch against him. My hands laid flat on the tiles as Vaughn arched my back holding my throat with one hand and hair by another.

"So naughty. So dirty. So teasing. You like being playful with your master, don't you, my little girl?"

His seductive lips moved so effortlessly, and I just watched him like a bitch in heat—thirsty, heaving, panting. There was a certain pleading in my eyes. Vaughn's breathing was loud to my ears as he stared at every inch of my face, memorizing them. The man was hit to the limit when he could waste no more seconds and slammed his lips against mine. My back was still towards his front, arched. His possessive hand tightened over my throat and chin as his mouth claimed every inch of mine.

He made satisfying sounds against my lips, humming and breathing hard, showing me how much he craved for me, how much it meant to him to get his hands on me finally.

His tongue darted out to feel mine, invading every inch of my mouth. His audible moans were too much for a feeble girl like me to take in. Every time my dream man, my Vaughn, made a sound like *'Mmm'* or *'Hmm'* in the kiss, slurping against my mouth, I felt a little more and more energy in me evaporating from my body.

"Come on, little Sugar. Pull your dress up for your master. Hold them up for me. For me, so I can fuck you. So I can fuck this pussy. My pussy." His hand reached in between my thighs with a possessive grip.

I did what he said. I pulled my dress up with one hand and supported my body against the wall with another. Vaughn pushed my panties down, pulling them off.

The sound of his belt unbuckling was a satisfying crackling of a fire in my ears. God, I couldn't wait anymore. I need need need this man in me.

This time, he didn't torment me for long. Within a second, the man was in me with a forceful shove. The air in my lungs puffed out with the force of his plunge, but I wasn't in mind to care.

His thrusts in me were impatient. They were angry, vengeful, demanding. I was so wet for my man and his needy pumps that it aided him to rail me effortlessly.

The sound of us fucking—I loved it.

"You hot damn thing, my little slut. Why are you smiling? Hmm? What is causing you to smile when I'm railing you?"

"Ah—I... love the sound of you railing me."

He paused for a second. Even the sound of his breathing halted for a second.

I looked back at him from my shoulder and found his entranced eyes staring at me in an expression that could only be called fascination.

As soon as the man got his wits back, he pulled me by my throat and slammed his lips against mine, kissing me, sucking my soul out of my body. The forceful plunging went harder and rougher inside my pussy.

"You are not going to fucking walk tomorrow, my little fuckdoll."

I just nodded enthusiastically as I moaned out loud.

God, I didn't want to moan. All I wanted was to listen to this man breathing uncontrollably, moaning, and grunting in ecstasy as he fucked me. The wet sounds of our sexes slamming against each other—I wanted to hear that. The smooth, closed surface of the bathroom caused the sound to reach louder to our ears than usual. God, I loved it.

Vaughn noticed my struggle to keep it in, and he chuckled in a low growl, ridiculing my attempts to keep my moans low. As if to threaten me, his hands went to my clit to show me who was in power—teasing me, stroking me.

It wasn't long when I let out a muffled scream of release against my palm, creaming all over Vaughn's massive cock. My legs shook uncontrollably, and my pussy squeezed the man, contracting all around his thickness. It wasn't long when he let it go, too, with a primal growl in the crook of my neck since we didn't have much time. There was no time for edging, as Ron would be here anytime.

I was shaking in his arms after we finished. It was the shortest yet the most powerful fuck I ever had. Vaughn turned me around and pulled me in his arms. He sat on the closed toilet lid with me in his arms. He held me by my waist and my neck for a deep, passionate kiss. The soft, gentle kiss was assuring, doting, loving—contrasting with our previous reckless time together.

Snuggetties... I loved them both.

"Get clean. I'll be going out first, okay?"

"Uh—Don't you need to... clean yourself?"

"Nah. I love the feel of your nectar all over my cock. I'll treasure it as long as I can. Since I can't bring you to my place right now, I'll take what I get," Vaughn said as he buckled up his pants with a breathtaking smirk. My heart raced once again as I watched the hanging smirk at the corner of his lips.

I was still stunned when Vaughn pressed a gentle kiss on my forehead and left the bathroom.

Ron had been a handful for the last couple of days since her breakup. She had never been an easy roommate, but this time, it was different. The girl was trying her best to conceal her heartache and pretended to look happy, which I knew she wasn't. So, it was only natural that I chose to be with her rather than spending time with her brother.

Vaughn wasn't sitting idle either. For some reason, he was so busy and in a strange mood for the past few days. I tried talking to him on the phone, but he didn't intend to share. Even our late-night car rendezvous was also on hold because of the reason.

Ron needed her brother too, but she couldn't reach him much, just like me. At some point, it started to bother me so much that I started looking for a night to spend at his place. Vaughn never shared his problems and issues with me. What if he needed support, too? All the man did was support others. What if he needed a shoulder to lean on as well? It was only natural.

What if he needed me?

Thinking no further, I decided to talk to Ron.

Ron was not as enthusiastic about me spending a night at Leo's place as she was at other times. I understood her situation, but I had to reach my man. Even after her reluctance, I left to look for Vaughn.

The moment the lift opened at his penthouse, I looked for him. There was some shuffling coming from his bedroom. I walked in the direction when Vaughn came out. His eyes widened, seeing me standing in the middle of his place.

"Xena? You didn't tell me you are coming."

"I missed you, Wolf. Can't I come if I miss my man?"

"Of course, you can, baby." He dashed towards me in large strides and hugged me tightly in his arms. My leg hung a foot higher than the ground as he crushed me in his strong arms.

Snuggles! It felt like home!

"Jesus... I missed you too, baby. I missed you too." He smelled my hair, and then pressed kisses on my cheeks, shoulders, and neck. His brawny arms tightened around me more and more every second.

"Are you going somewhere?" I asked. He looked ready to go out in his usual black suits.

"Yes. I've something to take care of, which is why I was surprised here to see you, Sugar. Gosh... you're here, and I've to head somewhere, baby." He pushed his head into the crook of my neck, inhaling my presence.

"Don't worry about me. I'll stay the night. Besides, I've some cases to do. Can I use your laptop?"

"Yes, baby. Feel free to use anything." He cupped my face and pressed a kiss on my lips, still relishing my presence.

"The password is Vaughn's one naughty Xena. Our initials in Caps, one in number, and the A in your name as at sign. No space."

My mouth was agape. "Are you kidding me, Wolf?"

Vaughn's brow furrowed in confusion—and my, oh my, my man looked adorable and sexy.

Adorablexy!

I giggled at the new nickname.

"Where are you giggling? Hmm? Aren't you my naughty Sugar?" He asked with brimming affection in his eyes. Eyes—that had a hint of dark circles under them if I looked closely.

"If I'm naughty, you, my man, are *adorablexy*." I grinned at him.

Vaughn laughed out loud this time. With eyes full of love, he looked at me and said, "Two hours, baby. I'll be back in two hours, and when I do—" His voice lowered to a husky tone. "—I want you on your hands and knees. All ready for me."

"And, if I'm not?"

He brought his lips close to my ears and whispered in a low growl.

"Then wait for my punishment, instead."

Oh, blankets!

61 | Sit

Xena

I glanced at the clock and gasped out loud.

Snuggetties!

I was out of my given time, yet I wasn't done with my case. It was longer and more complicated than I thought it would be. A part in me was terrified of the fact that Vaughn would be here any moment by now, and I wasn't finished, but another part was somewhat gleeful, anticipating the punishment.

What the—?

I typed faster. The more I concentrated, the more my mind drifted back to thinking about the slight dark circles under my man's deep-set eyes. My heart wrenched every time, thinking of what could be the reason for his fatigue and sleepless nights.

The lift opened with ting, and my heart thumped, thumped, thumped.

He was here, and I wasn't finished.

Holy snuggles!

I turned my head around and found him standing behind me with a stoic expression. His eyes were glued to me. If he was angry, annoyed, or exhausted, I couldn't tell.

"I'll be finished in ten minutes, I promise!" I said, flashing him a guilty yet innocent grin, which felt more like pleading.

The man stared at me for a bit longer, holding my gaze as if in a conflict with himself. Then he turned around and went to the bathroom in silence.

I turned my head, hurrying to pack things up. Vaughn didn't look like he was in the best mood, and I could finish my half an hour's worth of work later. I was about to shut down the laptop when I heard him speak behind.

"Finish it."

I turned my head again, and standing right behind me was his large body frame, resembling rocks and mountains—sexy rocks and mountains—only in his gray sweatpants.

"It's okay. I can finish it later."

Vaughn brushed over the side of my cheek with his large palm, swiping away my hair, and his ever-so-light touch sent an electric spark to my skin, awakening my sleeping senses. My eyes closed in their own accord as I leaned into his touch, taking in as much as I could.

"Stand up."

I stood up on my shaky legs. His eyes looked so intimidating that I couldn't look into them, feeling they would swallow me whole if I glanced even once.

"Take off your clothes." His voice carried the hypnotizing dominance that I never managed to get past, and honestly, I never wanted to.

I yanked the hem of my dress, pulling it off over my head. Since the day Vaughn asked me to, I've always been in sundresses before him, and my, oh my. I didn't regret it.

There I was, standing before the man in my pink sets of underwear and nothing else.

"These need to go, too." He pointed at my bra and panties.

My chest heaved with anticipation. I loved when Vaughn dominated me. He knew just what to say or what to do to send me to my peak. But at the same time, I knew I had the power to turn the table anytime, and he would give it to me.

I unhooked my bra, taking it off all the way, and from my peripheral vision, I noticed his chest heaving a little at the bounce of my girls in front of his eyes. My nipples were erected and pointing in his direction, as if provoking, challenging the wolf to have his claim on them.

Yes. My girls were as naughty as me.

"Panties, too," he said. This time, his voice was even more rugged and hoarse in need.

I hooked my fingers inside the elastic of my panties and slowly rolled them over my thighs, down my ankles, crouching in front of him. The anticipation and desire whirl winding in my body as I looked at his feet. My eyes, glazing his body with my lust, coating every inch of him bit by bit. My gaze was drawn to a prominent tent on his sweatpants for more than a few seconds. My throat bobbed as I looked at his abs, wanting to touch the solid curves—lick over them.

The moment my eyes reached his, I gasped a little for air. I could swear they could swallow me whole.

His large palm reached my cheek once again, stroking it, pinching my chin, and brushing over his thumb over my lips, showing me how he possessed me.

Yes, he did.

"My little girl… so needy."

My gaze locked on his deep, fixed eyes. My pussy pulsated just from the hungry stare of the man. And the moment he stroked his cock right over his sweats, my mouth opened in O—salivating—and I died a little in need of it in my mouth.

Then Vaughn surprised me, pushing my face to the side so he could make his way to sit on the chair I had been sitting on earlier. I was crouching down on the ground, looking at the man from my shoulder in furrowed eyes.

Vaughn looked at the laptop that had my project open on the screen and made himself comfortable on the chair. He spread his legs a little and took his cock out as it stood erect in ovation. My eyes took in the engorged purple monster, sketching it over and over in my mind when I heard him talk.

"Sit."

Sit where?

My eyes jumped to his face just to find it devoid of any expression.

"If I were you, I'd be faster."

My heart jumped, and so did I. In a matter of seconds, I was right on my feet. He yanked my hand and made me pull my hips on his cock with my back facing him.

Slowly, I sat down on his cock, sliding the giant monster deep inside me. A gasp escaped my lips as I supported myself, holding the desk in front of me. Vaughn wrapped his hands around my waist to make me find a comfortable spot, and by the time he was satisfied, I was completely sitting on his lap with his cock buried deep in my pussy.

"Now, finish your case."

What?

"What?"

"Your punishment, Sugar," Vaughn said, squeezing the flesh of my soft belly, digging his fingers in.

"H-How can I work like this?" I asked, already out of breath.

"Finish it fast, and until you do, don't even dare to move."

"You're cruel, Wolf." I cried out in frustration. My pussy clenched and unclenched, dripped and soaked around his cock.

Vaughn growled and wrapped his fingers around my neck, pulling my head on his shoulder.

"It's Master. And if you can't do it, then don't provoke me to punish you." His other hand reached for my nipples and pinched on them, tugging them.

He slapped my tits, and his fingers tightened around my neck. "I know you like me punishing you. Don't you?"

I bit my lips and arched my back, shoving my tits more into his palms. Vaughn noticed my slight movements and chuckled, ridiculing me.

"Finish your work and don't move, my cockwarming slut." He left my neck with a shove.

I felt full. Full of Vaughn. His cock was raging and pulsating inside my pussy, filling me completely, stretching the walls inside. As always, the feel of his cock gave me a sense of completeness.

But I needed him to move.

My body trembled in need as I reached for his laptop. My breathing, uneven as his warmth sipped into my skin. His hot breath tickled my skin, sending currents and shivers down my bare back.

"Read as you type it."

Oh, my lord!

"Master…" I moved a little on his cock. Needless to say, unknowingly.

"Stop fucking moving!" He snapped, slapping on my clit, and I jumped with a gasp. "You are nothing but my fuckdoll. Do as I say."

In my breathless, hoarse voice, I started to read as I worked on my case. I was almost done when Vaughn arrived. But the ten minutes' worth of work felt like a sack full of sand over my head.

He continued to feel everywhere as his hands reached over my body—teasing me, making it harder for me to keep my focus. Every time I stuttered or mistakenly moved for a bit of friction, the man either roughly pinched my nipple, or bit on my neck, sinking his teeth in.

Possessive. Territorial. Feral.

By the time I finished my work, a good half an hour had passed, and I was already a mess. I sent the project to me via email and closed the laptop.

I closed my eyes and took a deep breath. Before my filthy wolf could say anything to me, I turned around on his lap, once again shoving the thick meat inside me. My hands wrapped around his neck as I looked deep into his eyes.

"I've gone through all your punishment, Wolf. Now I need what I need."

"What is it you need?" he asked. His eyes carried surprise at my action.

"Your goddamn cock."

I began to slide up and down on his cock at a slow pace. We groaned in our heightened pleasure from finally getting the friction we both needed. For a few moments, my eyes squeezed shut. Then I opened them once again to look into his eyes.

When I opened them, his eyes were already on me. I had no idea who started it, but within a second, our lips collided, sucking in, and our tongues were in a battle, fighting for dominance over each other.

My pace picked up as I began to bounce on his cock. My heavy tits bounced as I rode my man, inevitably drawing his line of sight at them. Vaughn stared at them in cloudy eyes before his hands reached for them, tugging them to take my pink, erected buds in his mouth.

My hands reached for his hair as Vaughn continued to devour my tits with his cock inside me. One of his hands reached in between my legs and stroked my clit. Sweat trickled down our skin, my senses perking up until I couldn't think of anything else other than the man I was straddling and riding like the finest stallion.

My orgasm took over my entire body as I felt them from my scalp to my toes. White lights were blinking and taking over the back of my sight as I dropped my head on his shoulder. Vaughn's hands wrapped around me as he continued with the thrusts while I creamed all over his throbbing cock.

I shook as I rested over his body. My hands wrapped tightly around his neck. Vaughn picked me up by my thighs and stood up, walking somewhere.

"Where are you going?"

"To bed." He slapped my butt. "To finish what we started."

This time, the man had no mercy. He pounded me over and over—rampantly, roughly, needily. By the time he was finished, I was a breathless, sweaty puddle under his body. Vaughn took his time to come down and stroked my wet hair from my forehead.

"Stay here. Let me bring something for you to drink. Okay?" he asked, kissing over my sweaty forehead.

I nodded with a grin.

Oh, snuggles!

I missed him so much. I missed my man.

With Vaughn in the kitchen, I lay on the bed thinking about all we had done for the last two hours, and a smile found my lips again. My pussy felt empty after feeling him inside me for long hours. His cock completed me, giving me a feeling that my body was missing a puzzle piece, and it was the one I had been missing. I craved him. Again.

Suddenly, something caught my eyes outside.

A white flash in the sky.

I jumped on my bed in fear—sweating, trembling, as the hairs of my body stood up with a crawling feeling.

I hopped out of bed with the bedsheet wrapped around me, running towards the kitchen with a scream as I heard a loud sound of thunder booming outside.

Vaughn was scared to see me. His eyes widened in fear when he saw my state. As I reached my man, I jumped over his body, holding him for dear life.

"Baby, what's wrong?"

I began to cry.

"Xena... baby, what happened?" he asked again. "Are you... Are you scared of thunders?"

Strings of thunder crackled outside, and I screamed once again. Tears rolled down my eyes, and soon I knew nothing more or heard whatever Vaughn had been asking me as I fell into a dark abyss.

62 | Opening Up

Xena

My eyes opened slowly, trying to take in the surroundings. The light was dimmed, helping me see where I was. But the moment my eyes opened, I heard a concerned voice rumble beside me.

"Baby! Oh, thank god you are awake!" Vaughn pulled my head into his chest. I looked at the man from the tight embrace. He had been sitting on the floor beside me, whereas I was lying on the ottoman.

"Where am I?" I asked.

"In the closet. Sounds come least inside this room."

Yes. Now I could see I was in Vaughn's luxurious, huge walk-in closet with no window.

"Are you okay now, baby?" His concern for me tugged the deepest core of my heart.

"Yes. Has it stopped?" I brushed over his cheek, feeling the stubble of beard scratching over my palm.

"Yes. You stay here. I'll bring something for you to drink."

"I'll come with you."

"Are you sure you want to come out?" He asked, with dark eyes full of concern.

I nodded. "It has stopped. It's okay now."

Vaughn nodded once and picked me up. Only then did I notice he had put on his shirt on me while I was unconscious. How long was I passed out?

He carried me to the kitchen and placed me on the counter before bringing me the watermelon juice he had prepared earlier. I took the glass from my man and stared at him. I could swear sometimes he felt too good to be true.

He urged me to drink, and I took a sip, looking out of the window. The storm and thunder had subsided, and the sky had a gloomy look after the heavy rainfall.

"Let's head to the roof."

"Are you sure?" Vaughn asked, worry and reluctance clear in his tone.

I nodded in enthusiasm as I jumped on my legs. Opening the fridge, I picked two bottles of Samuel Adams and walked to the roof as Vaughn followed me closely behind.

The icy wind blew my hair as I put my bare feet on the grass. I looked at the bed and found a safety cover on it.

Vaughn walked to the bed and removed the cover as he laid down on it, offering his hands to lie in his arms. I grinned and followed him. He took the bottle from my hand, and we continued to drink in silence for a while. My head rested on his shoulder with his arm holding me secure.

"I was little when one day I had been playing hide and seek in the park with my friends after school. Suddenly, the sky turned dark out of the blue, but I didn't realize the upcoming storm since I was hiding. All of us were so little, they ran and left, leaving me alone, hiding in the concrete pipe."

Vaughn's hand around me tightened, but he stayed silent, listening to me.

"When I heard the rumble of the first thunder and the pattering of rain above my head on the pipe, I missed mom. It scared me." I paused to exhale, reminiscing the darkest moment in my life that passed me the trauma.

"I ran. I ran as the rain drenched me. Strings of thunder boomed in the sky, and every time I heard it strike, my heart jumped, almost threatening to come out of my mouth." I dry chuckled at the memory.

Vaughn stroked over my head as he pulled me closer in his arms. I snuggled into the safety the man offered to me, and I continued. "I almost passed the park—the field was almost out of my line of sight when I looked back after hearing a scream." I felt my body shudder. "In the middle of the park stood Lara—the most innocent kid among my friends. Aside from me, she was also left behind."

My grip on the beer bottle went tighter as I hugged it against my chest. "Before I could run to Lara or ask her to follow me, a thunder struck right on Lara." My voice broke, and my vision blurred at the memory. I could hear Vaughn taking in a sharp breath, feeling my pain.

"I passed out at that moment, and when my eyes opened the next time, I found I couldn't hear anything. My hearing was damaged because of the thunder, and it took me a whole year to recover from that. But you know what? The TV was on at the hospital, and I read the news." I wept at the memory.

"Lara died on the spot. I was right there, but I couldn't save her, Vaughn."

Vaughn took the bottle from my hand and placed it beside me before taking me into his arms, hiding me from the world. His warmth seeped into my skin, making me feel the safety in his arms.

Just like that, I knew Vaughn was my protector, and I had nothing to worry about anymore.

"You were small, and you suffered too."

"I suffered for a year, Vaughn. But Lara died," I said, clutching his waist, weeping like the small girl that still lived in me.

"It was not your fault, Xena. Look at me." He held my chin and made me look into his eyes, and said, "Sometimes bad things happen in our lives when we have no control over them. My little girl is so strong to survive it." Then he pressed his cold lips on my forehead, lingering there longer than usual.

"I never told it to anyone. I never talked about it other than with my therapist. Not even with Ron. It feels too good to share with you."

Vaughn pulled my head against his fast-beating chest.

"My parents are getting a divorce."

The suddenness of Vaughn's words shocked me. I looked at him, but he avoided my eyes. Then he pulled me into his chest once again, and this time his grip was even tighter than before.

"When I was little, one day, I was supposed to stay at a friend's house next door for a sleepover. But suddenly, he had a temperature, and I had to return home."

I could hear his heartbeat pacing up—drumming in his chest.

"When I returned home, I found my mom in the living room. Right on the couch with five men—all naked." He said the last two words in a whisper, but I understood each of them and the hidden meaning anyway, and goosebumps appeared on my skin instantly.

"My dad was right there, sitting with a glass of whiskey on the single couch—watching them go all the way with mom." My hands clutched around his waist harder.

Good god, just what has this man survived through when he was so little? Nobody deserved it.

"It wasn't forceful. Apparently, it had been happening all their lives. It helped dad's business to trade his wife with a group of men at the same time, and mom was cunning enough with her sound knowledge on business law and knew just how to trap people or come out of it."

"Vaughn…"

My eyes burned once again, feeling his pain. Vaughn clutched my head and stroked my hair so that I couldn't look at him. I was sure he was shedding tears as well and didn't want me to see them.

"They were never in love with each other—just using one another for themselves. Ronnie and I are just their covers to have a good image in the society to run their nasty business behind the door, which is why I was never into my family business and worked hard to build mine."

I rubbed on his chest—a feeble attempt to soothe his pain, calming his thudding, aching heart.

"No one knows. Not even Ronnie. They sent Ronnie to boarding school and then manipulated her to move out and live with you so she couldn't find out about it. I also thought it was right for her. She only thinks our parents have disputes sometimes, and still, she faces panic attacks over it. Now that mom is no longer planning to use her—" Vaughn paused to let out a helpless breath, and then said, "—you know, she wants out. No matter how bad it can damage Ronnie, they don't care. They never did."

"I have money, Xena. A lot of it. I wish money could solve this situation because… love can't. I tried both. Mainly for Ronnie. It'll break her."

"When did you get to know about it?" I asked.

"Last day when I had lunch at your place. I've been trying to convince them to keep up the façade of a marriage for a little longer— at least for Ronnie. I don't know how to break this news to her. She just got betrayed in the first serious relationship she ever had."

I understood Vaughn's concern. Didn't all of us betray her? Her parents? Her so-called boyfriend? From her best friend and her brother?

Suddenly, I felt a knot in the pit of my stomach.

What had we been doing?

I should've told her already. What if Ron took me as a betrayer, too? What if she had a dispute with her brother because of me?

Oh god.

"I don't care about my parents getting a divorce. They can go to hell, not that I care. But I care about my sister. No matter what, I don't want to see her break again like last week."

"I could sacrifice the last drop of my happiness, my blood, my soul for my little sister. All my life, I only had one goal every morning I woke up—well, till I met you," he kissed my hair. "That I have to keep my little sister happy, no matter what. No matter how much I

393

have to sacrifice. My happiness, my priorities are nothing when it comes to a hint of a smile or a drop of tear in Ronnie's eyes."

I understood him.

"This is where I'm lucky. That you feel exactly like how I do. Every time I watched you take care of Ronnie, I knew what a lucky bastard I was to find you. With you and me by her side, we will be happy. Won't we, Xena?"

I clutched him tighter and nodded against his chest. "We will, Vaughn."

"Ronnie is the only blood-related family that matters to me. Since the day she was born, I knew I was all she had. I had been taking care of her since then. Not only as a brother, but also as her father, her mother, her only guardian. She had no one other than me, and I... her."

"Later, Finn came into my fucked up life, and you came into hers. You are like an angel coming into our imperfect life, Xena... completing us." Vaughn chuckled in pain.

"And now you and I are all Ronnie has," Vaughn whispered in my ear.

I broke free from his hold and shifted my head to look into his eyes. Just how I assumed—his eyes were red with tears streaming down.

My Vaughn was crying.

Wordlessly, I leaned in to kiss his tears. Vaughn was startled at my action and stared at me with widened eyes. I had never imagined seeing Vaughn—my Vaughn—to see this vulnerable. Inching a little, I pressed my lips on his—a try to drink his pain, releasing him from his agony.

That night we stayed up, kissing each other, relishing each other's presence for a long time, until the weather turned even colder. Only then did Vaughn pick me up, and we lay down on his bed—cuddling to sleep.

As I stepped out of Vaughn's car the following day, I felt reluctant to leave him. Since last night, I felt even more connected to this man, and there was no way I wanted to be parted from him. When leaving Vaughn, I felt like I was leaving a part of me to him.

I only took three steps towards the next block where I lived with his sister when Vaughn called me from behind. I looked back and found him reaching for me in large strides. Within seconds, I was above the ground in the tight embrace of his strong arms. His lips covered mine in a dominating, possessive kiss—swallowing my entire existence.

"Xena... I love you to the point of insanity. Love me back, okay?"

"I do, Wolf. I always will."

63 | The Weekend Trip

Xena

When I reached home, Ron was already sleeping in her room. I peeked from her door to find her resting under her blanket. She had hidden herself so well that I could only see her raven hair spreading in every direction.

My heart swelled up, aching for the girl. An unbound need to hug her overpowered my emotion, and I tiptoed just to climb onto her bed. I wrapped Ron in a tight hug with my hands and legs over her body.

"Hey! What's with you this morning?" Ron snapped as I suffocated her.

"I can't hug my best friend?"

"I need more sleep...."

"Okay." I fell silent but didn't move. "Ron, I need to tell you something."

"Now?"

"Uh-Okay... What about we go on a little weekend trip? You and me?" I pulled the blanket from over her head and looked at her face.

"You don't want to take Leo?" she asked, narrowing her eyes at me.

"No, Ron. I have something to tell you."

"We can go after we submit our final case next month. I haven't been working much recently."

A month more? Probably that would be better since we would be done with our studies.

"Let me help you with your case. I'm almost done with mine."

"Don't you always tell me to do my own work?"

"Okay," I said, letting out a sigh. There was no way I wanted to hide it from her anymore.

"Now leave. I need my sleep." She snuggled more into the pillow, hiding even her raven hair under the blanket this time.

"Okay. I'm making lunch!"

She showed me her thumb as I left her room.

The Bryan situation changed something in Ron. She hadn't been the cheerful Ron anymore. The girl had no interest in movies, songs, nightclubs, or even teasing me. She didn't talk much, let alone go anywhere. All-day long, she worked on her last case of our graduation life. I tried several times, but she refused to take any help, saying she had to grow self-respect and stop depending on anyone else.

Honestly, I admired her thoughts. But deep inside, my heart cried for the girl.

I talked to Vaughn, refusing to meet him until I came clean to Ron. Not to mention he despised the thought of not meeting me, but the man respected my decisions. He could have come to our place in the name of meeting Ron, but he didn't. He met Ron outside—not that I kept track.

The man had been suffering—missing me, and I had been suffering too. But I couldn't keep up with the guilt any longer, and it was only a matter of days now.

I believed Ron would understand. At first, she would be irritated because we had kept it a secret from her for so long, but then, Ron had to give in. Who could love her more than her brother and me? And who could love her brother more than me?

At the time of our final Independent Research Project presentation, I was astounded to see Ron acing it. She was thoroughly prepared and did a fantastic job putting even me awestruck by her presentation skill. I knew Ron had it in her, but this time, I understood the depth of her hidden potential, and I was never any more proud.

When we returned home, Ron and I packed our luggage for the two-day tour to New Hope, Pennsylvania. All the while, my thoughts drifted to my man again and again. He left for California for his business expansion. Besides, his parents were there at that moment. Vaughn was trying his final luck to save the marriage-façade for some time for Ron.

I opened our last texts before he left this morning.

Filthy Wolf: Best wishes to you, baby. When I return, we'll celebrate your graduation.

Xena: I hope this time we can celebrate the day with Ron.

Filthy Wolf: Are you sure about telling her?

Xena: Yes. What do you think this trip is for?

Filthy Wolf: Honestly, I'm happy. When I return, I can kiss you, embrace you, and look at you with no secrecy at all. We can stay over at each other's place any time with no issues. I love the thought. I'm sure Ronny will love the idea sooner or later. Don't panic.

Xena: Hope so. I can't wait for that moment to arrive, Wolf. I love you.

Filthy Wolf: I love you too, Sugar. Can't wait to claim you before the entire world. Miss me. Love me back, okay?

Xena: There is no other option. Miss you already, Wolf. Bye.

Filthy Wolf: Wait for me. Bye.

"Jay, are you done?" Ron yelled from outside of my door.

"Yes, coming!" I shut the screen off and picked up my luggage to leave for the trip.

I settled into the passenger seat as Ron slid behind the wheel. For the first time in my life, I wasn't one hundred percent into the trip. A knot formed in the pit of my stomach, thinking of every possible reaction Ron could have.

The last thing I wanted to do was hurt any of the siblings.

"Why are you not excited about the trip, Jay? You planned it in the first place, but now it looks like I'm forcing you."

"It's not like that. It's just..." I trailed off.

"It's just what?"

"Let's get there first." I glanced at Ron, flashing a forced smile.

"Do you want to have a nap or something?"

"Uh—No... it's just an hour or so left before we reach New Hope, anyway."

"Chocolate?" Ron offered me a king-size peanut butter cup from Reese's. A grin appeared instantly as I grabbed it from her hand. This girl knew me better than anyone else.

Well... except Vaughn. That man read me word by word.

Antioxidants from the chocolates helped me to soothe my anxiousness. Soon, I felt my nerves relax as I sang along with Ron, with her favorite Ariana Grande playing in the car.

"Jay, you look tired. Already missing Leo?" she asked.

"I... Uh—kinda."

"Just close your eyes for a while, okay? I'll wake you up once we get there."

I listened to Ron and closed my eyes.

The next time I opened my eyes, I couldn't see anything. I blinked my eyes—squeezing them open and close, but even then, I saw nothing. A stinking smell of latrine and drainage hit my nose, causing bile to rise to my throat.

Where was I?

I tried to move my hands, only to realize they were tied together at my back. The coldness from the dampish floor gave me chills as fear crawled at the back of my neck.

Dark, damp place, and my tied hands were clear signs of what might've happened to me. When did it happen? How did I get myself into this? Why didn't I wake up?

Where was Ron?

Oh god oh god oh god...

I knew I was unharmed. There was no pain anywhere in my body. But what about Ron? Was she okay? Even if something happened to me, I couldn't let Ron get hurt. How would I explain it to Vaughn? Anyhow, I had to save her.

I tried to break free. My legs felt wobbly, but I tried my best to stand on them to look for a way out. My head felt dizzy, and my body felt hot.

Since my hands were tied, it was difficult for me to move and see if I could get out of the room. My body trembled in panic as I knocked into something, and it dropped, making a loud noise.

The clattering noise caused the door to open, and I noticed a silhouette of a woman standing right there. The sudden flow of light coming from behind the woman caused my vision to go blurry for a minute. I closed my eyes and opened them to adjust to the sudden invasion of light.

But when I opened my eyes, my blood ran cold at the sight of the woman.

"You are up, finally. Had a good rest?"

"Why?" My voice was foreign to my ears. I was in shock.

"Why? Why you ask?" She feigned a surprise, as if my question was ridiculous. "Because I can't let go of a single chance of making your life miserable."

"What have I ever done to you? I've always wanted the best for you. You know that," I said, my voice breaking in the end, tears streaming down my eyes.

"Argh. Don't cry. You make me sick!" Her loud voice echoed in the room. "This is where you belong. In a dirty, filthy place. Vulnerable and helpless. I hate how you have proud parents, a rich boyfriend, living in a city in an apartment... And a perfect *best friend*," She began to laugh hysterically as I kept staring at her face in surprise.

A face that had been beautiful in my eyes forever. Since my childhood, I had always thought she was the most beautiful girl in the world. But right now, there was no face I could remember that looked as ugly as her.

A perfect best friend? Ron?

Oh god. Where was she?

"Aliza! Where is Ron? Tell me you didn't do anything to her! She has nothing to do with your wrath."

Aliza kept laughing, clutching her stomach. As if it was the most ridiculous joke she had heard for a while.

"Best friend?" Aliza asked with a smirk. "Who do you think has brought you here? I'm only helping her, little sis. As I said, I couldn't let go of the chance to see you miserable."

As if I could hear thunder striking right above me. With the support of the wall behind me, I stood there like a statue.

Ron?

No. That couldn't be.

"You are lying," I said, looking into her eyes.

"Am I?" Aliza asked with a challenge in her eyes.

When I thought back to what had happened before I fell asleep, sickness intensified at the pit of my stomach.

Ron pushed me to fall asleep after having the chocolate she gave me. Now that I thought of it, the chocolate even made me feel dizzy— dizzy enough to pass out for hours.

Suddenly, I was in denial. Why would Ron do this to me? It was simply a ridiculous thought. It's my Ron. My best friend. My sister— more than my blood sister herself.

"Where is Ron? Aliza! You are out of your mind! If you hate me so much, let's deal with each other! Don't say just anything about Ron! She is not a betrayer like you—" before I could finish, someone else entered the room and interrupted me.

"You mean to say a betrayer like *you*?"

Ron.

401

64 | Darkroom

Xena

I thought roars of outrageous thunders were the only thing I was scared of. But no, I was wrong. Looking at Ron's bloodcurdling face under the dimmed light was even scarier than anything that ever terrified me.

"Ron... Ron, are you okay?"

"Stop with this drama!" she screamed.

"Ron..." I was so shocked I didn't know what to say.

"Stop fucking calling me Ron!" Ron marched towards me in large strides and stood right in front of me. My eyes had adjusted to the dimmed light, and I could see her nose flaring as her eyes flashed fire. Hatred was all I saw in them.

"You have no sympathy for me. You only used me. You only fucking used me for my brother, you whore!"

I gasped at the suddenness of the situation, "Ron... I was about to—" before I could finish, my head jerked sideways at the sudden force and my cheek sting.

My chest heaved as I kept looking down at the floor in disbelieving eyes.

Did Ron just hit me? What was happening?

"You whore! You used me to get to my brother, didn't you?" Ron broke into tears.

"No... Ron... Never! Let me explain, please!" I begged her, pleading with her as tears after tears rolled down my cheeks.

Slap!

Another tight slap landed on my other cheek. The sound of her palm hitting my cheek echoed in the room; even then, Aliza's laughter didn't fail to reach me. I disregarded her to look at my best friend.

"Ron… It was never planned. It's only been a few months. I promise! The first time we met was when we stayed in your parents' place—" Another slap dropped on my face, and I had to take a pause. My ears, ringing because of the force, but I had to say these to her. Now or never.

I was late, anyway.

"—We both had a secret crush on each other… And when we met, things took a turn so fast. Ron…" I hiccupped, "Ron, I know how protective you are of your brother… I never wanted to hurt any of you—"

Another slap.

"—Ron, just because I never wanted to hurt any of you, I made a stupid mistake. I should've told you earlier… Ron… Ron, I'm sorry!"

"You were together when you were at my parents' place! You were together at Hudson Valley, right under my nose! Huh, you enjoyed it, didn't you? You enjoyed making fun of me! You thought stupid Veronica would never know. Countless nights you spent at my brother's place, but you lied to me. You fucking whore! Fucking my brother in broad daylight and stupid me… I never realized!" Ron screamed as she gripped her raven hair as if she was in pain.

"Ron, I'm sorry. Your brother has no fault in this. It's me who was afraid to tell you." Ron was about to hit me again when I desperately said, "Didn't you once say if a man keeps me happy, I can be with him? That nothing in the world could shake our relationship?"

"And it has to be my brother?"

"Ron, it's just that the man is your brother… nothing else changes! I promise!"

"Nothing changes? Xena? Really?" Ron looked at me with unbelief in her eyes. But those eyes—those very familiar eyes looked so different, so blank, and so vulnerable when she looked at me.

"My Brother has always loved me most in his life. I had always been his priority! Now he doesn't give me time like before. Why? Huh? Because of you!" her voice cracked as she accused me.

"Ron… it would be the same with any other girl. Even if it weren't me, there would be someone else."

"But it's you! When I called him after catching Bryan red-handed, he didn't pick up! My heart broke when he wasn't there for me, even after my several calls. But then…" Ron let out a dry chuckle of ridicule, "then both of you turned up to me at the same time with a lame excuse of running into each other! How funny!"

Ron clenched her jaw and leaned forward to grip my hair. "You! Because of you, my brother wasn't there when I needed him! Because of you… he spends most of the weekend with you now! He doesn't spend time with me anymore! Lonely… he left me lonely."

"Ron… he cares for you. I'm sorry you feel like this but… but I was there for you, Ron. Vaughn was there for you too!"

Slap!

My body fell to the ground as I sobbed and sobbed.

"Don't you dare say my Vee's name with your greedy, whorish mouth! You leeched off me! To get to my brother!"

Leeched off her? Did I leech off her? The shock from her words silenced me.

Suddenly Aliza came forward to kick me in my stomach.

"She is just like that. The bitch steals people from others' lives. Because of her, I was never the one my parents loved the most. Because she is the brainy one, my parents let her come to New York, and I could never find a man as successful as she did."

Then, like a madwoman, contrasting her previous words, Aliza said, "The bitch found a friend like you, yet she betrayed you because of a rich, handsome, successful man? Sleeping with your brother… Jeez… Did she ever have any respect for you, Veronica?"

A silent sob clogged my throat.

Ron snorted. "If I didn't catch Vee dropping you that morning about a month ago, would you've ever told me?"

"Ron, your brother knows... I planned this trip to tell you about us."

Ron screeched out in disgust, scaring me.

"Whore! No—witch! You are a witch! There are so many men in the world! You could target anyone... I only had Vee. No one else loves me... not mom, not dad, not Bryan.... only Vee...." Ron's vulnerable body leaned back on a damp wall.

"Ron... I love you. Vaughn loves you too! We will *always* love you, Ro—"

"You witchcraft him! You are his priority now and not me!" she showed me my cellphone. "See... two texts to you and none to me!"

"Ron... I *love* him. We love each other."

Ron broke into laughter, laughing like a maniac. The look on her face was so different—it was nothing like the cheerful and full-of-life Ron I used to know. My heart cried for the girl.

"Love? A girl loved Vee. She loved him all her life. The only girl around my Vee I have ever seen. The girl even managed to seduce him enough to sleep with him several times, but never in his life had Vee ever prioritized her. He only slept with her and still loved and cared for me the most."

"But then... when it's you... it's not how it was six years back when he was with Lisa. This time, it's different. This time, he prioritizes you more than me. You know, Xena? I'd have loved it if it was Lisa, not you!"

"I only had Vee. No one loves me other than Vee. Everyone leaves me, hates me. They hate I exist. The only person to whom I mattered, on whom I could rely on... you had to snatch him from me... I hate you! I hate you! I hate you!"

Ron dropped to the floor, hugging her knees. Her posture reminded me of the night I saw her having a panic attack for the first time at her parents' place. Suddenly a scary feeling crawled on my

405

neck. No one can save her from the attack other than Vaughn. How to help her?

Ron kept screaming, "You took away my Vee. Vee! Vee, why did you forget your sister? How could you love a woman more than your sister? Vee... Vee! Vee, I have no one except you. No one loves me, Vee... Everyone betrays me... why did you betray me too? Vee, where are you... Vee!"

Ron's body trembled as she swayed back and forth, bringing back the memories of her last panic attack. I tried to free my hands, but no matter how much I tried, I couldn't break free. I looked around when my eyes fell on my only hope—Aliza.

"Aliza, please free me. Ron needs me right now. Let me help her!"

Even though Aliza looked terrified to see Ron, she still sneered at me. "Are you kidding me? I'm not untying you!"

"Aliza! You don't understand! Ron is having a panic attack, and only Vaughn can help her. I need to—"

"Then I'm calling Mr. Wolf," Aliza said as she pulled out Ron's phone from her pocket.

"No! Don't call him! He'll ask for me. What will you say to him if he can't reach me?"

Aliza stiffed at my words, realization hitting her.

"Free me, Aliza. Ron needs me. I promise I won't run away... not when Ron needs me." I stared at my best friend, still sobbing and hysteric.

"I can't free you at any cost. You deserve to rot in here." Aliza said, determined.

I took a sharp breath in and almost had a panic attack myself.

"Then at least hug her. Tell her that her Vee loves her, and he'll be there for her once she returns home." I pleaded with her. "Can you do it?" I asked.

Aliza listened to me this time and did what I said. Ron was reluctant to listen to anything Aliza told, but at some point, she gave in and fell asleep in Aliza's embrace.

I lay helpless on the damp ground of the stinky room with my hands still tied. My body itched to run to Ron and hug her. I knew her insecurities, and I understood why she was upset. Yes, I never expected her to go to this extent, but it was my fault that I was scared enough to hide things from her.

What was the most she could've done?

Suddenly a thunder boomed somewhere far from where we were. But it was still loud enough for me to jump in fear. The sound caused Ron to stir and wake up from sleep.

She opened her eyes and stared right at me with blank eyes. Her eyes looked so void and empty that they gave a feeling there was no life left in them.

The thunderbolt struck again, and I let out an involuntary screech. This time, I was the one having a panic attack. The heavy downfall of the rain intensified the damp, stinky smell even more. I trembled on the ground as the thunderbolt continued to crackle outside.

Ron stared at me for a long time and stood up to leave.

Panic raised inside me even more.

"Ron... Ron, I know you are angry with me... but please don't leave me alone." By the time I finished the sentence, Ron had already left. "Teensy! Ron! You both know I'm scared of thunder... Don't leave me alone! Please!" I wailed in fear—tied and helpless in the dark, damp room.

Just as Ron left, Aliza turned back, walked to the old window, and opened it. The moment the shutters were moved, the sound of thunder intensified in the room, and cold air gushed through the window, sending chills down my bone.

I cried and cried, calling out Vaughn's name—the only person I could think of who would've taken me right into his safe embrace. What if he saw me like this? What would he do?

Wouldn't he be angry with Ron? No, I couldn't let that happen.

But I needed him. I needed to see him. I needed the safety of his arms. Who else would ever save me? Love me?

"Vaughn…" I let out a helpless sob, and a lone tear rolled down my eyes.

Aliza smirked and left me just like that.

65 | Soon After

Xena's phone rang in Aliza's hand.

Filthy Wolf.

That's the name that appeared on the screen. She smiled, wishing she could know just how filthy the man was.

When she didn't receive the call, a text appeared.

Filthy Wolf: Baby, I heard there is a storm near New Hope. You alright?

Aliza sneered. Samuel was like this, too. Caring and shits. But he wasn't as handsome and as rich as this Vaughn Wolf. Since she couldn't raise doubt in Vaughn's mind, Aliza decided to do something. She walked to where Xena was, already passed out from the trauma. Her limp body lay like a cocoon on the floor. Aliza reached near her to use Xena's finger to unlock the cellphone. So she could respond to the man's texts.

Xena: Yes, I'm hugging Ron to sleep. Will talk tomorrow.

Filthy Wolf: Don't be afraid. I won't let anything bad happen to you. I love you.

Aliza broke into laughter at the text. Not let anything bad happen to her?

Did he even know in what condition his 'love' was lying unconscious on the stinky floor right now?

66 | Decision

Xena

My head hurt. My eyes felt weighing tons when I tried to open it. The moment shutters of my heavy eyes opened in a slit, the blinding sunlight made it hellish for me to clear my vision. The throbbing in my head intensified when I forced myself to open my eyes.

Hurt. It hurt so bad.

The damp, filthy floor of the empty old room welcomed my vision. I tried to stir, but the ache in my entire body was too much to move, even for an inch. My hands were still tied behind my back, restraining me from making any movement. A lone tear rolled down my eyes when the memories of last night flashed back.

Ron said I used her. My best friend, my sister—my very own person. I wanted to give her the love of a sister, a best friend, and not only that, I attempted to shower her with the love of a real family—my family. When did I ever use her?

Just because Vaughn and I fell in love with each other?

But yesterday, it felt like she was not in her real self, as if her life had been sucked out of her body. The usual Ron I knew, I couldn't see her when I looked at her last night. I was scared of this. Previously, I thought she would react badly, which is why I didn't want to give in to Vaughn. But I never knew she would react this severely.

How do I make her believe I will never steal Vaughn from her?

The sharp pain in my body intensified, and I trembled at the coldness of the air. Last night I lay on the damp floor all night as the rainwater fell on me through the open windows.

I think I had a temperature.

Suddenly, I heard footsteps in the room, and then, summoning all my energy, I looked up to meet the same blank eyes of Ron.

"Ron..." my voice sounded harsh and dry. "I think I've fever. Let's go home and talk about it?"

"Do you think you can call the same house where I live your *home*?" Ron chuckled, as if it was the most ridiculous thing she had heard. "The only place I have as my home can't be shared with a betrayer like you, Xena."

I kept staring at her.

Ron walked closer and stood beside the window, looking outside for a few long seconds.

"Break up with my brother." Her voice was stern. There was no place for discussion.

My heart dropped from a cliff, shattering into pieces. A pain arose at the pit of my stomach, spreading throughout my body, and bile rose in my throat even though my stomach was empty. Vaughn's face flashed before my eyes when he said to me, *"I love you to the point of insanity, Xena. Love me back, okay?"*

Fat tears rolled down my eyes, and I gulped down the bile that threatened to come up.

"I love him, Ron. And he loves me."

"He doesn't need your love, and he definitely doesn't need to love you."

"It will break him, Ron. We are too far to even think of leaving one another."

"He doesn't need you."

"It will break both of us if we separate, Ron. Don't ask for this, please. Let's go home, okay? I'll make some of your favorite spaghetti, and then we can talk over some wine."

"Leave. Our. Life!" Ron screamed out in frustration.

"Ron, look at me. I'm Jay... your best friend, and I never want you to be unhappy. I know you love me too, and you'll regret what

411

you are doing. But I promise you I won't hold any grudge—even...
I'll never let Vaughn know about any of this. Please, Ron, I'm sorry
for my mistake that I kept it a secret... Let's—"

"Shut the fuck up!"

I sobbed in helplessness. "Do you want to see your brother
unhappy? Broken? Ron, he loves you, but he loves me, too. We both
have different places in his heart. We can never steal one another's
places. Don't you think I can understand you better than any other girl
who will be by his side? You will always be our first priority, Ron."

"I don't fucking need your priority! I need you out! Vee has
never prioritized anyone more than me in his life. But now, look at
what you have done! The only boy I ever loved betrayed me, the only
friend I ever had betrayed me, my parents are separating, and Vee is so
much consumed by you, he forgets his sister, who only has him to rely
on!"

"You... you know about your parents?"

Ron looked at me in disbelieving eyes. "Don't fucking tell me
you know about them, too! Vee shared it with you and not me! God! I
hate you, Xena! How could I ever trust someone like you!"

"Ron... Ron, don't get it wrong! Vaughn didn't tell you because
he was still trying to save you from all the pain. He was still trying to
beg them to stay together so that you get enough time to get it together
after your breakup. Your brother cares for you a lot, Ron. No one can
replace your place in Vaughn's life!"

"Yet you are the one who knows about it first!"

"Ron..."

"Shut up, Xena! Don't make me hit you again!"

I kept looking at my best friend in helpless eyes.

Ron looked outside from the window once again, deep in her
thoughts. After a long time, she finally broke the silence.

"From my childhood, I craved my parents' love like every other
child. For some reason, I knew I wouldn't be as loved as my other
friends in school, but even then, I craved a little... something...

412

anything. Was it too much to ask? They were never there, never truly cared for me."

"I hardened myself with time, hiding the vulnerable lovesick girl behind the mask. The only time I couldn't keep myself in place was when I saw them fighting. But then again, Vee was always there for me. He was the only one I had." Her voice cracked in the end, and my heart throbbed at her pain.

"Vee had always been there for me—protecting me, loving me, supporting me. Every time I lose my mind, he holds me. He is not only my brother... My Vee is my father, my mother, my guardian, my savior, and my angel. If I lose him over someone, I won't have a single thread to hold on to in life. I will be long dead."

"Ron..."

"If Vee ever decides to leave me, I'll lose the last hope to live."

"Ron... he won't. I won't. I love you too, Ron."

Ron glanced at me with her blank eyes. "If you truly love us, why don't you leave?"

"Ron... how can I leave? I love you both." I felt my heart tearing apart.

How do I make her understand?

"If you love us, then why are you trying to ruin the only blood relationship that matters to Vee and me? Why are you stepping between us siblings?"

"I'm not... I—"

"I lost everything, Xena. Now that you want Vaughn, I'll lose everything to want to live anymore."

"Ron... don't say this, please. I'll never let anything happen to you!"

"Then leave. Vee and I will be happy ourselves. And if you stay and something happens to me, what do you think will happen to Vee?"

My eyes widened at her clear threat. Was it really my Ron?

413

"You have got an hour. Think. If you agree, I'll set you free, and if you disagree with leaving us, you'll be free as well, but then, you'll have to take my corpse from here."

"Ron…"

"You can't change my mind. Think and decide."

She left the room.

No water, no food, no warmth—yet all I could think about was the man I loved—my Vaughn. How could I leave him?

Even if I did… would any of us survive?

I remember the last time I met Vaughn—our last night together on the rooftop he redecorated only for me, how he opened up to me and shared every bit of darkness in his life that he shared with no one else. Only me. Because we were a team and I was supposed to stay.

Then again, I remember what he said. His every word imprinted deep inside me, echoing through my mind. The night, his words, his heartbeats, and every drop of his tears—I could never forget any of it.

Ron's happiness was his only goal in life every morning he woke up for since she was born. How beautiful was an elder brother's love when there was no one else to love you or take care of you? My heart cried for Ron and my Vaughn. How hard he had been forced to grow up. Where was the childhood of my man—if I could still call him that?

He said he could sacrifice every last drop of his happiness, blood, and soul for Ron. If he could sacrifice the last drop of his existence for his little sister, who was I to stand between them? If Ron keeps up with her words and really harms herself, what would I tell Vaughn? How would I ever face him? If his priorities were truly nothing before a hint of a tear in Ron's eyes, then what if Ron…

I couldn't even imagine. The thought alone brought such terror to my body that I lost my control over it. I never felt so helpless in my life when I knew what I had done. I hadn't been allowed to use the washroom since I woke up in this room, anyway.

414

I wept. My heart shredded like ribbons, promising to spatter my soul until I had nothing left. Vaughn… my Vaughn… how could I leave him? How could I let Ron get hurt?

What do I do?

No matter how much he sacrificed, Vaughn vowed not to make Ron cry again. Just cry. And here she was adamant on…

No matter what he sacrificed…

No matter what…

I screamed and cried. With no food, no water, my throat clogged so painfully that every sob bled past me. My body ached, but my heart ached even more. What if she killed me? What if Aliza killed me right in this room? Would I have hurt the same?

Not really. No.

Vaughn… all he had in life was Ron and me. How in the name of God could I ever decide only one of us for him?

If anything happened to Ron, Vaughn would be either nothing but a living dead—or dead.

But if I wouldn't be around… wasn't it how they were before I came into their life? They will have each other, like how it always had been. They shared blood, and I—at the end of the day, if the choice was no more optional, I was nothing but an outsider.

No one in the entire world could replace Ron in Vaughn's life. But my place? Maybe.

I was lying in the pool of rainwater, dirt, moss, and my own urine like a breathing dead when Aliza appeared with a bun in her hand—eating.

"Wow, smells so uptown." She scrunched her nose and threw away the rest of the bun at a dirty corner. "You have never looked so beautiful, little sis. I wonder what your high-class, sophisticated boyfriend would've said if he saw you here like this." She laughed like a madwoman.

"Ron is a fool. She should just make him see you. It would've made her job easy to separate you both. One look at you right now, and no sane man would ever want to be in the same room with you," she tsked.

My Vaughn would want me. I knew it by my heart.

An hour was up, and I knew it when Ron appeared beside Aliza. Her eyes were still void of every emotion.

"So? Should you clean up and carry on your vacation? Or are you ready to travel with my corpse?"

When I go out into the world again, I would never let Vaughn know about any of it. It would kill him.

"Ron… you have been in love, haven't you? What if Bryan was innocent, and you had to decide something like this?"

"So you won't break up?" her eyes blazed fire. "So you want to be responsible for my corpse? Because Aliza is ready to testify on my behalf. The world will know you kidnapped me because you were jealous and didn't want any obstacles to get my brother."

"Will you be happy without me, Ron? Will you make sure Vaughn is… alright?"

"I would kill for you to leave us."

"Will you hold him if he breaks?" A strangled sob left my clogged throat.

"Vee never breaks. He mends."

"Promise me… Ron." Sob after sob made it too hard for me to talk. "Promise me you'll hold him if he breaks. Promise me you'll be there for him. Promise me you'll tell none of this to him."

Ron snorted. "You don't tell me if I need to take care of my brother. I don't want drama. I want a clear-cut answer."

"Fucking. Promise. Me." A curse growled out of my throat— something I never did.

"If it makes you leave us for good, then yes."

It took a long moment for me to say the following words.

"Then I'll… leave."

67 | Caging Herself

Xena

I stood at the door of the room I booked for Ron and me. The bright, lively exterior did a little to lift my dead soul. I knew how the walls were made of glass with a spectacular view of the beautiful Delaware River, but I had not a piece in my heart to look anywhere. My heart was long dead on the ground of the rotten, filthy room I passed through the night.

My eyes swept over the room—the same room I intended to stay together with Ron, to open myself and share everything about her brother and me. About Vaughn and me.

Vaughn.

My heart sobbed at the slightest thought of my man.

Would I never be able to hug him? Smile at him? Kiss him?

Would he ever forgive me for leaving him? Would he hate me?

"Enjoy your vacation… or not. Not that I care. All I care about is the scars on your body from last night to fade. I'll be staying in the next room with Aliza."

Ron almost left after the words, but I called her from the back.

"Ron…"

She halted in her step.

"When did it happen? You and Aliza?"

Ron looked back with her hands crossed against her chest. Her black hair was open, contrasting against her pale face without a trace of makeup. I stared at her, watching the same set of blank eyes I was unfamiliar with. Even when Bryan cheated on her, she had bits of emotion left in her, but this Ron… she looks like a living dead person with no feelings at all.

I couldn't even look at her. My heart ached and bled the seconds my eyes were on her blank face. I wanted to hate her… I wanted to hate her so badly, but I couldn't.

"So eager to know?"

"I will leave anyway."

Ron smirked. "Right. You will." She leaned against the door frame and continued to say, "She warned me about you in Virginia. She told me you are dating my brother."

"But you didn't believe her."

"No. I didn't. I should've, though. She is more of my well-wisher than you ever were, Xena Meyers."

"When did you believe, then?"

"When he dropped you that morning and k-kissed you. I went back to my room before you returned. You came to see me and told me about this magnificent trip for the first time. Remember?"

"Why didn't you ask me anything? I didn't even meet him since then… at least until I shared everything with you."

"Why would I ask you anything? I don't want you in any of our life. And about not meeting him since then…" Ron let out a chuckle of ridicule. "That didn't keep you from fucking him all these months. I remember the marks on your body, about how active your sex life has been, Xena. And all this time, I thought it was with Leo. Now… knowing it was… it makes me sick. *You* make me sick!"

"Aliza is the last person you should rely on, Ron."

Ron broke into laughter. "Goodbye, Xena."

"I never used you, Ron. You are the sister I never had." I said to her back as she halted in her steps again. My gaze landed on the floor and stayed there. Then, in a low, broken tone, I said, "I have always loved you and always will."

I didn't even have to look up to know she left. The loud thud of the door closing was enough.

Earlier, Ron handed me a dress, and I washed and donned it on for the journey to this inn. But that wasn't enough.

My frail body soaked in the cold water, and I didn't care enough about the temperature. I wanted the icy coldness of the water to numb both the visible and invisible pain in my body. Nothing, I wish I felt nothing.

The cold water washed away the temperature of my feverish body. My body shook, and finally, I felt nothing. My mind was not in the closed space caged in the walls. It was far, far away to the man my heart was bleeding for, aching for, longing for.

A whiff of all that happened would damage the siblings' relationship, and I couldn't let that happen, no matter what. But then again, how could I find the courage to tell him that I would… leave him?

Vaughn wouldn't let me go. He wouldn't unless I had a reason. What reason could I give so he would let me leave? So he would rather hate me than be hurt?

The mere thought of Vaughn hating me caused pain to shoot all over my body, starting right from my heart. I clenched my hands as I wrapped them around my knees and let out a scream. Whatever emotion was left in me flowed through my eyes, turning my inside void and dark.

I screamed and screamed until I couldn't anymore.

"He has been calling you continuously and is now on his way to return home earlier than intended. Talk to him. Stop him for now. Until you are back to the city to face him."

I took my cellphone from Ron's grip and glanced at the pool of missed calls and text messages. Just looking at them, I could tell how worried he had been for me. But, surprisingly, my heart was so void that I felt next to nothing.

"Okay."

"Dial. Put him on speaker. I'll listen to everything you say to him."

419

She shouldn't ask this. I shouldn't agree with it.

But I did.

Vaughn picked up the call at the first ring.

"Thank goodness... baby. Where are you? I have been calling you."

After a moment of silence, I said, "I needed space."

"Space from?" Vaughn sounded alert.

"From everything."

"What's wrong? Are you alright? I'm coming back on the next flight. I'll meet you, okay? Tell me what's wrong, I'll solve it—I promise."

"Don't. Don't look for me for now. I need space."

"You need space even from me?"

"Yes." I was surprised to see just how emotionless my voice was.

"I haven't seen you for a month, Xena. For a month, I haven't laid my eyes on you, held you, kissed you. How much more space can I give you? I... *need* to see you, baby. Right fucking now."

"I need space."

Vaughn took a long moment, and I could practically feel the wheels in his mind spin.

"Did you talk to Ronnie? How did it go?"

"I didn't get to have any talk. Lately, I've been busy with my thesis and presentations and didn't get to think through things that have been happening in my life. This trip... I need this space, far away from everything and everyone. If I feel, I'll share with her."

"What has been happening in your life? I'll back you to solve every single issue, Xena."

"I need space."

"Xena... baby, let me come. Let me hold you for a while. *Please...* baby, allow me." The man sounded desperate.

"Do you remember once you mentioned to me, you'll never hamper my absolute privacy? That you'll never force on me.

Vaughn… give me some time to sort things out." I took a deep breath. "I'll see you when I return."

"Xena…" Vaughn was at a loss for words—something I'd never thought I'd see someday. "I'm returning home right now. So you have me whenever you are ready. I'll be right where you want me." A moment of silence and his whisper pierced right in the middle of my heart. "Take very good care of my girl. Okay?"

"Hmm." My free hand clutched the bedsheet.

"I love you to the point of insanity, Xena… I love you."

He didn't ask for me to love him back this time. He just said he loved me. My now-stone-cold heart trembled at the vulnerability of his words.

"Bye," I said. Ron snatched the cellphone before I could make myself cancel the call.

"Good job." With that, Ron left the room, leaving me in utter loneliness that I needed.

I skipped eating anything that day, too. No one died without food for two days. Besides, whatever I felt, dying didn't feel like a less appealing option. Even if I managed to gulp down something, I didn't think I would be able to keep it in for much longer.

I spent hours under the duvet. My voice didn't allow me to make a sound without scratching my throat, but tears after tears rolled down my eyes. I cried and cried until I fell asleep. Even when I woke up, my cheeks were still wet. I cried even in sleep.

Vaughn… my Vaughn.

How could I make myself face him when I return to the city?

The next day, Ron came to see me once again. She opened the door without a knock and walked in. I was sitting on my bed by the massive window, looking outside blankly, but the beauty of the Delaware River failed to attract my attention. My hands wrapped around my knees, hugging close to my chest as if it was the only way I could protect myself.

Protect myself from Ron. My Ron.

421

"See… Vee. I am with Xena. Why do you think I'm wandering around by myself? You know Jay and I never leave each other alone!"

Vaughn said something in response, but since Ron had her Airpods on, I couldn't hear anything he said.

"No… why would she look upset?" Ron and my eyes met, and we paused for a second. "Jay… Say hi to Vee. He thinks we had a fight or something. I wonder why."

No no no… I couldn't let Vaughn doubt his sister. Not Ron… god, no. It would kill him.

I forced myself to smile at the back camera of her phone. Ron wouldn't let me see him, and I knew it. I could wave, but he would see the traces of the rope marks that were yet to fade from my pale skin. I kept them tucked securely under the duvet that covered me.

"See? Xena and I are fine. She's just relaxing after the thesis and finals sapped all our energy."

"You want another view of the river? It is nothing compared to what you see when you travel around the world."

Vaughn didn't want to see the river… no, not at all. It was me he wanted to see. I was right in the frame.

"Fine." Ron gritted her teeth after she aimed the camera at me again. This time, I didn't look in her direction. I couldn't make myself do so. I kept staring outside, hiding my puffy eyes as much as possible.

After a couple of beats, Ron didn't give Vaughn any time to ask for something else, including me, and left the room in a rush.

I cried again for the rest of the day. And then for the night. Whenever the thought that I would meet Vaughn the next day crossed my mind, I couldn't keep my tears in. I knew how much I would hurt him, but I had no other choice.

If the choice was between Ron and me, it had to be Ron. It would always be Ron. Till I was breathing, I would never let Vaughn face a situation like this. If I could take all his pain, I would have, but it was the next best option I could think of.

I cried that night. I let myself cry.

Until I couldn't anymore.

68 | Reminding Her

Vaughn

She was here.

I knew the moment she entered Aphrodisia. My eyes remained glued to the elevator that opened right into my penthouse as I kept my ass placed on that fucking couch. My elbows rested on my knees as my shaky wrist did a great job to support my chin. As I watched my fingers tremble violently, my brain kept telling me to stay, wait for her to reach me, but my body almost gave into running to my girl, crawling to her—begging for whatever mistake I had made that she *needed* space from me.

My girl—I hadn't laid my eyes on her for over a month.

Blood pumped through my vein, and every part of my goddamned body felt almost as anxious as my mind.

I needed to see my girl, hold her, kiss her, make her smile. She hadn't smiled the last time I talked to her over the phone. Even though she tried to hide her face, I managed to have a peek at how puffy her face looked, how frail her usually glowing body looked through the video call I had with Ron.

God… I needed to hold my girl right against my heart. I needed to feel her in my hold to calm these unnerved emotions I had been facing over the past few days.

A fear, an eerie feeling, the unrest—it will only be gone when my girl would be in my arms. Right where she belonged. And once again, I would be able to comfort her, protect her… love her.

Only then my unrelenting heart would get its rest.

The moment the elevator opened, I could no more keep seated and sprang right on my heels. My heart pounded against my chest, threatening to come out at any moment. She was upset; she was sad, and I couldn't be there for her. She didn't let me.

She needed fucking space from me.

The elevator opened, and there she was... looking right back at me.

Those eyes—I didn't know them. The girl I could read like my own palm, I couldn't read her. But I could say, whatever it was, it wasn't something I should be happy about. That look alone could bring nothing but devastation.

She stared at me as if she didn't know me. As if I meant nothing to her. As if... as if she didn't love me.

With only a few big strides, I reached her and pulled her right into my embrace. Holding her as close to my heart as humanly possible, inhaling her scent, knowing she was right there in my arms. My girl... My Xena.

But she didn't hold me back. Her arms remained limp at her sides.

Havoc hit my heart. I was falling and falling and didn't know what to hold on to, how to survive. My girl, who always made sure to hold me as tight as her delicate arms allowed, showed me she needed me just as much as *I* needed her. She felt like nothing but a dead shell.

What was happening? How could I stop it?

I kept thinking and thinking. My chest heaved, pondering over a thousand possibilities, but none of them encouraged me to take another breath.

Could she sense the slight trembling of my body?

My hands reached her face as I slammed my lips on hers before she could say something. I didn't know what was on her mind.

But whatever it was, I knew I didn't want to hear them.

Every time I kissed my girl, it was always to show her how much I loved her, how much she meant to me, how far I'd go to protect her.

But this time, I wanted to tell her I needed her to live. To breathe. To survive.

I kissed her lips, not caring if she kissed me back or not. I wanted nothing from her. If she allowed, I could live all my life simply giving and giving and giving her.

"Vaughn…"

"Shh… Baby. Let me kiss you first. So long… So fucking long…." I sucked on her lips, stopping her from saying another word.

Afraid. I was too afraid to listen to anything she had to say.

"I…" I stopped her again with kisses on her neck, behind her ear, wherever her weak spots were. I couldn't stand the blank face any longer. Not a fucking second longer. It killed me to see her like this. My heart bled to see my girl in pain when I had no idea what it was about. It was a living fucking hell.

I needed to remind her of me, my love for her, about what she meant to me, and how fucking much I needed her. I need to remind her I worshipped the ground she walked on, to remind her I was celibate only for her for five goddamned years, and I could do that again and again and again if she asked me. She needed to know she was my entire world, my treasure, my precious, and without her, I was nothing, and I had nothing to live for.

"I need to talk to you…."

"Whatever you want to say… let me love you first. I beg you, Xena. *Please.*"

"Vaughn… But…"

"Please…" My forehead touched hers, baring my vulnerability. If that required me kneeling or crawling before her, I would do that any day—just to remind her that there would be no Vaughn without Xena.

Hesitation, internal struggle, and a tinge of pain flickered in her eyes, but then again, she didn't say a word. She didn't say no.

I lifted her in my arms and walked on my unsteady legs towards the bedroom. The exact moment I knew sex was the last thing on my mind, I realized intimacy was the only way I could remind her of me. With my body.

Every time I looked into her eyes, I felt like drowning, and I needed to hold on to something… anything to keep her right in my arms—contented, satiated, and protected.

I laid her on the bed, glancing at her blank eyes one more time. I almost let out a gasp at how void they looked, piercing right through my heart.

No. I couldn't look into her eyes. Not again. Not until they had some life back into those blue abyss.

I crawled over her body and looked at her face, searching if I was allowed to touch her.

God. Fucking. Dammit!

I never imagined I'd see a day when I wouldn't know if my girl wanted me when I'd be needing to ask for her permission.

My body was a raging, tormenting volcano, ready to erupt and die.

What happened to my girl?

I would make it alright… I'd have to make it alright…

I kissed her. I kissed her lips—fiercely—pouring my heart through the connection, showing her how much I needed her to breathe. Relentlessly, I kissed her void, lifeless eyes that held no emotion, no spirit, like they always did. Through my warm, loving touch, I tried to bring back life in the blue orbs.

I kissed her nose, her cheeks, her forehead, chin, and then her eyes again.

Kiss after kiss… but they didn't sparkle like fireworks like they *always* did when they saw me.

She laid there. Just like an inanimate toy.

No no no.

I kissed again. Her ears, the nape of her neck... her throat. I unbuttoned her shirt, one after another, and she didn't stop me—she didn't do anything—*any fucking thing.*

Where was my Xena? My sweet girl?

My lips traveled to her breasts, kissing the swells—worshipping her body. I threw the shirt away, kissing her arms, her fingers, her palm.

Her palm drenched from something... something from me. I rubbed my face in her palm again and found it soaking from my... tears? The tears I had no idea when they rolled down my eyes.

My nose rubbed over the inside of her wrists, right on her pulse point. I wanted to tickle something that could bring any emotion to her beautiful face that suddenly lost all her spark.

I went back to her breasts. Kissed them, sucked on them—but she didn't bury her fingers in my hair like she always did.

My heart was in my throat as I slid down to her stomach, her beautiful, deep navel... caressing them with my lips and teeth. My girl wore jeans—something she never did when she was with me. She always made sure to wear beautiful sundresses whenever she was around me, since the day I asked her to before going to Hudson Valley. Long time... it has been so long since then...

I unbuttoned her jeans and slid them down until I took them off of her. She didn't say no, nor did she look at me.

I kissed her feet, toes, her shin, her knees, behind her knees... kisses after kisses after kisses... but I couldn't stop. I couldn't stop cherishing her, worshipping her, showing her I *needed* her.

I kissed her wet folds and right between the center of it—the part that drives her crazy with the slightest bit of friction from me... only me. Caressed it with my lips, tongue, and teeth. Finding her hole, teasing and teasing her until her back arched a little, and she gripped the bedsheet. Only then, I paced up, faster and faster, working more to bring out more emotion from within her. More, so my girl would scream my name, as usual, so my girl would show me… show that she needed me, too, as usual.

But she didn't make a sound. Not a single one.

Her body shuddered as she came, but there was only the sound of her deep breath at the peak of her release.

Right after I got rid of my black vest and sweatpants, I went back to her mouth. I kissed her as my hand reached her cunt again. A silent pleading for permission. My lone tear dropped on her milky-smooth cheek.

Her hand reached my face as she looked into my eyes. "Do it."

I stared at her.

"Fuck me, Vaughn. Fuck me with all you have."

There was no emotion in her eyes—maybe… maybe a drop of warmth I could see somewhere along with a tinge of pain. But even then, I couldn't stand it.

I struggled in my head. I struggled to determine what I should do. But then, she brought me to her lips, the first touch from her.

And I gave her all. All I had. All I could have given her.

All the while, I kept chanting, breathing, sobbing only three words—I love you—like a mantra. As if, other than these three words, nothing in the world mattered. I didn't pause, not even for a second.

Even at the point when we both released together, her eyes squeezed shut—not letting me see if I could fill the void in her eyes with my love, with all I had.

I dropped my forehead on hers, breathing hard… waiting for my girl to open her eyes.

When they did, they looked nothing but… dead.

I gasped as I rolled down from her body.

She slowly got off the bed, collected her clothes, and went inside the bathroom.

Leaving me right on the bed as my entire world shook under me.

69 | Frozen

Vaughn

Bile raised to my throat as I waited for my little girl to emerge from the bathroom door. I felt sick. Sick as hell, to my gut. A bad vibe poked into the pit of my stomach. My breathing went erratic, and everything felt wrong… so wrong.

The door opened silently. As if the inanimate thing grew a brain to know better than making a sound. I looked up to see my girl… my Xena, standing right there at the door. Her shoulders sagged as she looked downwards. Her face was crestfallen, guilty, and… I couldn't read anything else. For the first time, I couldn't read her, and it killed me.

Stabbing, twisting, and stabbing again right into my heart.

My sweet girl didn't meet my eyes.

Crack.

I felt my heart crumble—just from assuming what would come to me at any moment.

How do I stop it? I kept asking, no idea to whom.

As she took a few steps towards me, I took the rest of it. I needed to touch her, to feel her warmth seeping right in my palm.

"Baby…" I cupped her angelic face, making her eyes meet mine. She tried to step back. But I didn't let her.

"Baby…" My voice dropped to no more than a mere whisper. "I love you."

I could see her swallowing the lump in her throat. And mine hurt.

"Xena… my little Sugar… Love, let's go for a drive, okay?" I stroked the back of her head, showing her the deepest affection from my heart that existed only for her. "How about Hudson Valley? How about this time only the two of us spend some time there?"

She hid her eyes from me.

"How about we go out to some park? We can walk barefoot. You love it, don't you? I'll hold your hand and walk by your side."

Not a word in response.

"How about we go to the roof, then? Let's watch stars and talk, okay? I'll make you some watermelon juice. Or would you like some pasta from your favorite place?"

Silence.

"Baby... Tell me, baby. What do I give you? Anything... *any fucking thing,* and I'll bring it to your feet, baby." I was desperate. So fucking desperate. Despair and helplessness spread inside me, wanting to erupt like a volcano.

"I'm sorry, Vaughn." Her voice was so grim and determined. "I can't."

Time seemed slammed against the wall, and my world began to crumble—mocking me.

"Can't what, Xena? *Can't what?*" I couldn't keep my voice down anymore.

"I can't... be with you anymore."

No sorrow, no pain, not a sign of tear appeared in her eyes. A hint of guilt maybe—but that's it.

God, I've never wanted to read her more than I wanted right that very moment.

And this was the first time when I couldn't.

"Baby... Have I made a mistake? Did I unknowingly hurt my girl? Are you angry with me?" I asked, searching for answers in her face. "Because whatever it is—I promise I'll make it alright. I'll solve it. If I have to kneel, I'll kneel. If I need to crawl, I'll crawl. If I need to grovel—tell me, and I'll do that too. Just say it. But don't say anything like that, I beg you, baby. Please!" My throat felt tight, and every word came out raw.

"I-I don't want to be with you."

My body sagged, bones melted, and I was a thread away from dropping to my knees.

"Bullshit. I don't believe it. You love me, Xena. I have felt it—not once, but every fucking second we spent together. I have felt it in every pore of my body. You love me! I *know* you love me."

"Love means nothing in our case. I can't be a part of a... a family like that."

My hands dropped to my sides. Everything clouded before my eyes, and I could no longer focus. In a feeble voice, too hard to catch, I said, "You are lying."

"It..." she swallowed again, "it disgusts me."

My body finally gave up, and I dropped to my knees. I dug to seek an explanation to protect us from breaking, but there wasn't one that I could think of.

"How... How do I make it right, Xena? I'll do every fucking thing to make it right. Please... tell me."

"You can't. It's not your fault. But after knowing everything, I can't look past any of it."

Tears blurred my vision as I looked up at her. "How do I stop you from leaving me?"

"You can't."

"What if... What if I sever my connection to my parents? What if I create our own little world, Xena? You and me... Ronnie... and our kids?" I wrapped my hands around her knees, embracing her for dear life. My head pressed right against her thighs, my tears soaking her jeans, creating wet patches.

"I have thought about how they would look countless of times. Every time it's you who I saw whenever I imagined them. Exactly like you. How will it be possible if you leave me? Our future?"

Silence, but I could feel her knees tremble in my embrace.

"How do I live without you, Xena? How do I breathe without you?"

"I can't look at you the same way. The thought of you are their flesh and blood disgusts me. You are talking about kids... the thought of my kids having parts of your parents disgusts me. I want out." She moved from my embrace.

Empty. That was exactly what I felt without her comforting warmth.

I placed my hand against my chest. The pain was becoming unbearable with every passing second. It ached so bad I thought I would pass out any moment. Too happy... I had been immeasurably happy with her. Was it my price for such happiness?

No, hell no. This can't be happening.

"You said you love me back. You said you'll always love me back... That I can be the only one for you. Xena, you said we'll be happy together. You promised." My throat felt like sandpaper as I managed to say the words.

"Priorities change. People change. I didn't know or thought enough about it when I made such promises." She almost reached the elevator. "I had time to think in New Hope, and I'd rather leave you both than stay in your life."

Pain clouded my vision, and her every word was a punch in the gut.

"You don't mean it—any of it."

"You say you love me. If you ever cared at all about me, you won't stop me, Vaughn. At least not after knowing I can't stand any of you."

"You can't stand me, Xena? Not even Ronnie?" My voice was strangled in pain.

"No." her tone implied I should know that better.

"Xena... don't end this, Xena. Don't end us." I dragged my hands down my face. "Anything... Ask anything from me. I'll sweat my last drop of blood for you. I fucking love you, Xena. You know how much I love you. You know I could kill for you. You know I never kneel before anyone, and I could kneel for you all my life, Xena. I'll give you everything—every happiness in the world. Don't go...."

"I hope you find love again, Vaughn—because it can't be me. I can't live with such disgust all my life. Don't make me."

"It will ruin me. You are asking me not to take another breath."

"I hope you find peace."

My hands gave up as well as they dropped to the floor. I felt cells after cells in my body collapse. I was failing, breaking, shattering only at the thought of her leaving me. And she wasn't even out of my sight yet.

"Xena..."

It was nothing but a beseeching for survival.

The elevator door opened, and she entered, sparing me not a glance. I was on my hands and knees, looking up, and tears rolled down my eyes—watching her leaving.

Never. I had never cried in my life after my early childhood when I watched my mother fuck a group of men. But for her, I couldn't stop it. I hated that tears clouded my vision, and I couldn't see the last glimpses of her before she left my place. Then again, I had not an ounce of energy left in me to wipe my tears off.

"Xena," I called her. My voice was earnest enough for her as she stopped the elevator door from closing.

"You and me, it's bound to happen." I looked at her as I straightened my back, still on my knees. "Mark my words."

She finally stared at me.

I flashed a mocking sneer through my tears. Fire fuming in every vein of my body—so fierce that it burned. She was leaving, and the realization surged through me like unstoppable ripples—tearing me apart.

"But remember... Xena." For the first time, her name sounded foreign as it rolled off my tongue. "Once the door is closed, I won't make it easy for you to come back to me."

Slowly, her hand slipped from the button, and we stared into each other's eyes until the door closed between us, and the tears iced in my eyes.

(To be continued in Book 2 - "Xena's Vaughn")

Thank you for reading my book. If you enjoyed the love story of Vaughn and Xena, kindly **leave a review.**

The next book—**Xena's Vaughn**—is already ongoing on the Radish Fiction app. It will be out on Amazon as soon as it's completed on the platform.

Sign up for my newsletter to get an instant update — http://eepurl.com/hlp6iL

More steamy stories by M.I. Rosegold:

- *The Innocent Beast*
- *The Evil Beast*
- *The Unconventional Ritual*
- *The Wife He Never Noticed (Currently available only on Radish Fiction)*